Rachael Stewart adores con... heartwarmingly romantic to... been writing since she could put pen to paper, as the stacks of scrawled-on pages in her loft will attest to. A Welsh lass at heart, she now lives in Yorkshire, with her very own hero and three awesome kids—and if she's not tapping out a story she's wrapped up in one or enjoying the great outdoors. Reach her on Facebook, on X @rach_b52, or at rachaelstewartauthor.com.

Nina Singh lives just outside Boston, USA, with her husband, children, and a very rumbustious Yorkie. After several years in the corporate world she finally followed the advice of family and friends to 'give the writing a go, already'. She's oh-so-happy she did. When not at her keyboard she likes to spend time on the tennis court or golf course. Or immersed in a good read.

FAKE FLING WITH THE BILLIONAIRE

RACHAEL STEWART

With love,

Rachael

MILLS & BOON

To all the Dreamers and those that go the extra-special mile with the sleepwalking, like those closest to my heart, my hubby, this one is for you.

xxx

CHAPTER ONE

Cassie's favourite time to venture out in recent years. Though she was no witch. No matter how much her ex and his family would like to paint her as such.

She sipped her vodka martini, finding peace in those precious minutes between two and three in the morning while most around her slept.

In the distance, the Eiffel Tower had emitted its final sparkle long enough ago to see the last of the tourists in bed. Its structure a dark silhouette in the inky sky. The avenue of the Champs-élysées and impressive Arc de Triomphe below flaunted their own muted glow. Equally beautiful in their subtlety, just as reassuring in their solitude too.

'Would you like another, Your Highness?'

Her fingers tightened around the crystal stem of her glass. 'Just Cassie, please, Beni.'

The young waiter bowed his head, his dipped gaze polite. Every night for the past month Beni had opened the rooftop bar for her after hours and every night he had addressed her like so.

Tomorrow, she would still be a princess. And the day after. And the day after that...well, who knew.

Public opinion was a fickle thing, especially when it was fed by the lions—her ex, the Prince of Sérignone. His royal family, the Duponts. Their loyal staff. The world's press.

They'd all crowned her long before her marriage to the Prince...would they go on crowning her long after she was done?

It had been a month. A month divorced. Two years separated. Four years married. Five by his side. A sixth of her life. A sixth she would sooner forget...if only the world would let her.

There was only so long one could bear the title that reminded her of the fool that she had been. The fool that she had let him take her for. And if she was honest, the fool that she had been long before then, courtesy of her parents and their skilled puppeteering from birth.

But she was done dancing to the tunes of others...it was time to choose her own tune. Her own path. And she couldn't afford for it to be derailed by the vitriol now coming out of Sérignone.

She picked at some invisible lint on her black shift dress as she mentally picked at the remnants of her life. At thirty-three, she'd gone from cherished British social-ite to prized princess of a tiny Mediterranean kingdom a thousand kilometres south of where she sat now, as a woman trying to find herself while the world at large tried to keep her pigeonholed.

Though pigeonholed as a beloved princess beat being painted as the scandalous woman the Duponts and their team of spin doctors were trying to turn her into. Spin-ning the tale of the woman who had *driven* her husband into the arms of his many lovers. By being emotionally unavailable and 'overfamiliar' with the household staff. Fuelling rumours that she had taken more than one to her bed, because there could be no smoke without fire… not when it worked in their favour. As it did now. Because, in the Duponts' minds, the Prince could not come out of their divorce smelling of roses while she still did.

One of them had to suffer. And so, it had to be her. Someone had to be blamed for the shocking behaviour of the Prince, and it made most sense—most royal and socioeconomic sense—for that someone to be her.

Didn't matter that she had already suffered enough. *Witnessed* enough. That the behaviour they laid at her door, belonged solely at the Prince's own.

She didn't know what was more galling—to learn that Georges had married her purely for the money, what with the royal reserves in dire need of a cash injection that her father had been all too willing to provide.

Or that she had been naive enough to have believed that she was enough for Georges. That her appeal— her beauty and intelligence, her charity endeavours and European connections, her ability to converse in several languages and win over the people—had been all Georges could have wanted in a princess. That he had wanted her. That he had, as he had told her and she had so desperately wanted to believe, loved her.

But no, it had been a lie and she had been a joke. A laughingstock to all who were in the know. The *real* know.

Behind closed doors. The palace doors. They'd been laughing at her.

Had her parents been cruel enough to laugh too?

They certainly hadn't been laughing when she'd

turned up on their doorstep almost two years ago. Desperate for a place to stay. A place to escape to. A place to feel safe from the speculation and the censure and the pain.

They'd only delivered more of the same and tried to force her to return, because heaven forbid, she'd walk out on the Prince and bring shame to their door...

A frenzied stream of reporters too.

'Your Highness?'

She blinked through the painful haze to find Beni still stood over her, waiting expectantly.

'Apologies, Beni. *Ça va, merci.*'

'You are sure?'

No, she wasn't sure. She wouldn't be sure of much for a long time—how she felt, who she could trust, what was real, what was fake, but as far as her need for a drink went, she was done for the night.

'I think I'll head on down, Beni.' She smothered a yawn—at last, sleep beckoned—and rose from her cushioned haven, the scent of the night lifting with her. Far from natural, the fragrance drifted from the inside out... the hotel's signature scent. Bold and woody, a touch of citrus too. Expensive but heavenly.

She gave him a smile filled with her gratitude. 'Thank you again for this evening.'

'So long as you need the rooftop—' he gave a nod of respect, his brown eyes soft '—it will be here for you.'

If only her own parents had been so generous. She swallowed the tears that she refused to let fall. She'd cried enough over them, and she was done grieving for what she'd never had in the first place. A family. A place to call home. A real one.

'*Bonne nuit*, Beni.'

She tugged the lapels of her jacket around her throat to ward off the chilly autumn breeze now that she wasn't protected by the decorative trees that bordered the roof terrace and stepped away.

How crazy it was to think that once upon a time, she had thought herself in love with a handsome young prince. A real-life prince with a horse and a carriage and a castle to boot.

She gave a choked laugh, mocking herself like all the others, and pressed her fingers to her lips, steadying herself as she checked Beni hadn't noticed.

If he had, he made no show of it as he cleared the table she had used. Her mini sanctum. She didn't have a lot of spaces to hide away in, and whether Beni knew it or not, it really was quite precious. As was the suite she was staying in one floor down. Louis's suite. One of her oldest and dearest friends. One of her *only* friends, if she was honest. Because as she'd swiftly learnt, fame brought out the worst in the best of people; private stories sold in exchange for a price or a royal favour or two.

The crown had cost Cassie her friends, her family, her identity, her financial independence and her freedom, but she was on a mission to take it all back...save for the family and friends. Those that hadn't stuck by her were not worth keeping. But the rest...she'd get there. She would.

She weaved her way through the empty tables and headed for the lift. Too tired to take the stairs. Another good sign that sleep would come easily tonight.

The ornate brass doors welcomed her in, and she stepped inside, stretched out her tired limbs as they closed around her. Breathed in the soothing hotel scent and let it calm her as the lift slid to a gentle stop on her floor and the doors opened.

She walked out, head down as she searched her bag for the key, when something made her still. A sixth sense, a prickle along her spine—she was used to having her space invaded when she was out and about, the odd stalker or excitable fan getting too close and then security having to intervene. But the hotel was locked down. No one got to this floor without a pass, and at this time of night, there should be no one else around but...

Her lashes lifted, head slow to follow as her mouth fell open, because there, straight ahead, was a man. A very tall, very broad, very *naked* man.

The first thing Hugo became aware of was the cold. The second was a soft ping. The third was a gasp. A very horrified, very feminine gasp!

His eyes flared wide. Every sense now alert as he registered his reflection in the French windows ahead; his nude silhouette against the dimmed lights of the Champs-élysées far below. And that's when he realised, the ping was an arriving elevator car and the gasp—

Oh, Mon Dieu!

He spun to face the woman who'd stepped out of the lift. Dressed in tailored black to her knees, nude tights, classic heels, she stood as regal as a queen...of the haunting, screaming kind!

Her handbag hit the deck as he watched, her belongings spilling free as she pressed her hands to her ghost-like cheeks and the elevator doors slid closed.

'*Oh, Mon Dieu!*' he repeated aloud, clamping his hands over his front. '*Je suis désolé!*'

Perfectly arched brows disappeared into a sweeping dark fringe, and unthinking, he stepped forward. Her eyes darted down and she stumbled back, one hand blindly reaching for the elevator button. 'Don't come any closer!'

'*Pardonnez-moi!*' He scanned the hallway, wishing that for all it was opulent and timeless, it had something he could readily use as a shield. He discounted the bronze bust on the console table—too weird. The baroque lamp. It was plugged into the wall. The bin. Just, no. And grabbed an ample-sized vase complete with high-rising white foliage, thrusting it before him as he turned to face her again.

'Please.' He spoke English with her, blowing a stray white frond out of his face. His allergies were *not* going to appreciate this up-close encounter. But they had nothing on her and his nakedness. 'I didn't mean to scare you. I live here.'

Cascading brown waves shimmied with her panicked head shake as she batted the button, which seemed to be having no effect whatsoever. Was she even hitting it? He'd be taking *that* up with hotel maintenance come morning...

'I *do*,' he stressed, focusing on more pressing concerns—panicked hotel guest versus his indecent exposure. 'Just here!'

He nudged his head in the direction of his very closed, very *locked* penthouse door.

He swallowed a curse. 'And it appears, I am now locked out.'

She eyed the door, her hand ceasing its attack on the elevator button as she lifted it to the pearls around her neck. Did she think he was going to rob her? A naked robber? Was that a thing?

He shuddered and hurried to explain. 'I know this looks bad. And I'm not making this up. I sleepwalk. And just now, as far as I knew it, I was stepping into a cab, going who knows where with who knows who, when the elevator went ping and you gasped and I came to. I *swear* it.'

The fear in her big round eyes eased a fraction. He couldn't make out their colour in the low light favoured by his hotels at night, only that her perfectly applied makeup accentuated their alluring shape and size…the kind a man could readily lose his mind in.

And yes, he had to be half asleep if *that's* the thought he was entertaining while the chilling draft from the ancient glass continued to assault his very exposed ass.

'Then why haven't I seen you before?' She gifted him the side eye with a hint of fire. *Hallelujah*.

'I've been away on business for the past month. I got back a few hours ago. You can call Vincent on the front desk. He'll confirm it. In fact, *do* call Vincent because I don't have a key on my naked person and I really don't want to terrorise the rest of the building by going down there like this. Terrorising one hotel guest is enough, and as I own the place, it really won't look good for business.'

Her mouth twitched. The pink glossy shape pulling back into one dimpled cheek, a hint of colour creeping in—*Dieu merci!*

'You own the place?'

'This and many others. *Oui*.'

'You are Chevalier of Chevalier Clubs?'

'I know, yes. It's very original. I've heard it all before. '

She laughed softly and *damn* if the sound didn't warm him all the more. He needed more of that.

'I'm just relieved I can trust you to be well behaved while I call in the cavalry, Mr Chevalier.'

'You can call me Hugo. I think we're long past the need for surnames here...'

She didn't comment as she dipped to the floor, not once taking her eyes from his as the elevator doors eased open behind her. He half expected her to scurry back inside and get the hell away while awaiting said cavalry. But she didn't. She swept up her belongings, dropping all but her phone back inside her bag.

He was right about her regal air. Every movement was so carefully poised, the way her knees stayed pressed together, her head remained high, her shoulders held back. There was something about her too. Something familiar...achingly so...

Or was it just the late hour, the hazy remnants of his dream messing with his head? His memories? The warped world between reality and make-believe...because if he'd met her before, surely, he'd have remembered her name at least.

And what was a woman like her doing wandering the halls of the hotel at such a late hour, or early, depending on how one looked at it. Alone too?

She looked like she'd been to dinner, or the theatre, a function perhaps. Her appearance *too* pristine to be doing the walk of shame. Too composed to—

And what are you even doing debating her presence when you're the one stood in the public corridor? Butt! Naked!

He watched as she dialled the front desk, her elegant long fingers making light work of the task before her eyes returned to his. Her gaze thankfully more bemused now as she lifted the phone to her ear and Hugo rocked on his feet. Wondered where to look. As first meetings went, this had to be up there with the most embarrassing, most memorable…

And still, the question remained. There were only two penthouse suites on this floor. His and Louis Cousteau's. And she wasn't Louis's type. Wrong sex for a start.

'Vincent, c'est Cassie…'

Cassie. The name softened her somewhat. Made her more…accessible. He listened as she spoke to his night porter. Her French seeming to come easy, though there was an awkward stumble when she got to the state of his…he cleared his throat…undress.

Hugo pulled his shoulders back as a shiver threatened to roll through him. He couldn't do much about the head-to-toe goose-bumps, though, or the rapidly shrivelling… *Oh, dear.* Throat clearing could be quite habit forming—who knew?

'He's on his way.'

She slotted the phone into her bag and Hugo gave an abrupt nod, which in turn sent the floral fronds right up his nose. He scrunched his face up, battling a sneeze, battling it…battling it—

'A-Achoo!'

She flinched. 'Bless you.'

'I'm sorry!' He turned his head to the side, swallowed another. 'Allergies.'

'Oh, dear, perhaps flowers weren't the best choice of a shield.'

'Short of pulling the lamp out of the wall, I didn't have much choice.'

She looked around too and then stepped forward, shrugging out of her jacket as she went. 'Here.'

Now he was the one taking a back step. 'I couldn't possibly.'

There was no way on earth he was going to put her clothing anywhere near his—

'It's fine.'

She was a stride away, jacket held out, decorative vase the only thing keeping her from getting another eyeful. This time, up close and personal.

Maybe he should install coat stands complete with coats throughout his hotels for such random eventualities in future...hell, he'd settle for an umbrella!

'I promise not to look...' she said, her eyes meeting his as her delicate little throat gave a delicate little bob '...not again anyway.'

What on earth was she doing?

The only man she'd ever seen naked in all her adult years was her ex, the Prince. But if anyone deserved to wear the title visually, it was this man.

He was a solid wall of muscle. Tall. Broad. Fierce. And she would have said Eastern European, but his accent was all French. Thick and seductive and...and she really should have stopped at one martini.

She turned her head away, eyes averted as her skin

prickled and warmed. Every millimetre aware of him being so very close. So very close and so very naked.

'Are you sure?'

She nodded, not trusting her voice.

And as he moved, the air shifted between them. Her senses strained. The soft clink of the vase against the marble ridiculously loud as he returned it to the side. The heat of his fingers sweeping like fire against hers as he took her jacket from her outstretched hands. His scent invaded her nostrils. He'd showered recently. He smelled clean, masculine, and her head...her head was busy visualising far too much. The reflection in the gold elevator doors, distorted, but revealing enough. Especially when her memory was all too willing to fill in the blanks.

'Thank you, Cassie.'

Her lips parted with her breath. To have a stranger address her by name...it had been too long. Louis still called her Cassie. Always had. Always would. They'd been friends long before the crown. But this man...this Hugo Chevalier. She wanted to kiss him. *Not* a good idea.

She opted for a much safer smile, turning back to him as she secured her arms around her middle. 'You're welcome.'

'But now you're cold...'

He gestured with one shoulder as he tied her jacket around his waist, his brow furrowed in concern as he took in her bare arms and tight grip. Her clenched jaw likely too.

'I'm fine.'

She tried to keep her eyes level with his, but this close

she could see every exquisite detail of his face…and the man was, well, he was bewitching. Maybe there was something mystical to this whole witching hour after all, because she was losing her ability to think straight.

From his dark cropped hair with the slightest peak that gave him a heart-shaped brow…a kind brow. To his dark eyebrows that arched over eyes that spoke of a strength, a steeliness, but also a sweetness…and how was that even possible? They could be grey or blue. It was hard to tell in the low light of the hall.

He had a kind nose too—straight and smooth. And a mouth that softened into a smile that made her stomach turn to goo. The dark stubble that bracketed his mouth and followed the sharp cut of jaw seemed suave and deliberate. The man *liked* to look good. *Knew* he looked good. Just like Georges. Which should put her on edge.

But how could she be on edge when he was the one naked and locked out, her tiny jacket his only protection…

'I think it looks better on you,' she murmured, a teasing quirk to her lips.

He chuckled, his pecs giving a delightful ripple that had her palms tingling against her arms.

'Once again, I do apologise. I'm sure this is the last thing you wanted to come home to.'

'You're just lucky it's me and not Louis. I don't think he would have been so kind as to offer out any form of a shield.'

'Louis is a friend of yours?'

'*Oui*. He's kindly gifted me his place until I…' Her gaze drifted to the Champs-élysées beyond the glass as her thoughts drifted to her unpleasant reality and she beat them back. 'Until I can find myself a more permanent home.'

With a career that she had yet to get off the ground…

'Are you looking to stay in Paris?'

She frowned at him. Did he really not recognise her?

At first, she'd been too stunned by his nakedness to think about him recognising her. Then she'd been too caught up in getting him covered up. But with him calling her 'Cassie' and the continued ease? An ease that shouldn't really exist. He was still very much naked, and her jacket wasn't covering all that much. And seriously, those abs and those legs…they looked like they could crack a—

'Cassie?'

Gulp. She tugged her gaze back to his. *'Pardonnez-moi.'* She really wasn't used to such a fine specimen of a man this close and this naked. 'What were you saying?'

His eyes lit with something—something she wasn't all too sure she should be identifying with. 'I was asking if you're looking to stay in Paris?'

'I'm looking to stay in…' she repeated dumbly, wondering if she could stay a whole lot longer if these were the kind of encounters she might experience with the owner of her current abode…which was a wholly inappropriate thought to be having. Once again, she blamed Beni's excellent martinis.

And thank heaven for the ping of the elevator at that precise moment.

She sprang back. 'Vincent!'

Hugo's mouth, a rather deliciously full mouth for a man, quirked to the left and flashed a dimple. 'Funny place that…?'

'I should let you get back to your bed.' She backed up, all the way to Louis's door, scrambling for the key in her handbag. 'I hope your sleep is much more restful from here on out, Mr Chevalier.'

'Wait! Your jacket...'

She waved him away—*oh, God no*—eyes anywhere but on him as she fumbled over the lock. Telling Vincent the situation over the phone was one thing, having Vincent *witness* the ex-Princess of Sérignone in a deserted hallway with the naked hotelier, aka his boss, was something else.

Especially with the flush of colour she was now sporting from the chest up.

The door finally sprang open and she sprang in.

'Goodnight, Mr Chevalier. Sweet dreams!'

Because she was sure to have plenty.

Though perhaps *sweet* was the wrong descriptor for the hot and tangled mess of Cassie's sheets that night...

CHAPTER TWO

THE NEXT MORNING Hugo knocked on Louis's door, rolled his shoulders back and waited.

He was sure she was in. The floorboards in the old building gave enough groans away to indicate that someone was home...and that was without him being extra sensitive to her presence following their impromptu encounter.

He eyed the flowers in one hand, her dry-cleaned jacket in his other. The former, an apology he'd had sourced from his favoured florist early that morning. The latter, hers to return.

He didn't want to leave them on her doorstep like some coward. He didn't want her to think him too embarrassed to say hello. Even if the smallest wriggle in his gut told him there might be some of that going on.

He'd never been so quick to escape Vincent's presence as the night before. Though his concierge had handled his state of undress remarkably well, he wasn't ready to be reminded of it just yet. And though he was sure his concierge hadn't shared the news around his staff, Hugo hadn't done his morning rounds as was his usual way upon his return. He'd simply requested that the bouquet be sent up and left it at that.

Besides, he had more pressing matters to attend to. Like a personal apology to deliver now that he was in full possession of his faculties and his clothing.

The elevator pinged and his cheeks heated as he re-lived Cassie's arrival... Okay, so the embarrassment was still there. But, *Dieu*, it was hardly ideal meeting anyone for the first time in one's birthday suit. Only your parents should get that privilege, and even then...

The elevator opened and the cleaning trolley emerged with two members of staff. One he recognised, one he didn't. Must be new. He sent a polite smile in their general direction and went back to his business while they went about theirs. Clearing his throat, he knocked again.

This time he heard footsteps on the other side. Slow but coming closer. They paused and his senses came alive, awareness prickling as she eyed him through the peephole. An eternity seemed to pass. Was he going to have to explain his presence through a...*closed door*?

Click. The lock turned. The door eased open a crack and one eye peeked out. Vibrant and green. *Sans* makeup today too.

'Mr Chevalier?' She seemed to breathe his name, the delicate sound doing something weird to his chest and that ring of familiarity upped a notch. 'What are you doing here?'

'Good morning.' He tried for a smile, feeling oddly unnerved. Was it the familiarity or the fact that she wasn't exactly welcoming?

Well, would you be after seeing you naked?

'I come bearing a gift as an apology and one freshly laundered jacket.'

He lifted both items into view and a delightful flush filled her cheek. He caught the hint of a smile too.

'You really didn't need to do that.'

'I must confess, *I* didn't. I had my staff do it for me.'

'But you would've missed housekeeping for this morning...'

'There have to be some perks to owning a hotel.'

The door eased a little wider, as did her smile, and his shoulders eased from their surprising position around his ears.

'That is most kind.' She reached out for the jacket and her oversized cream sweater slid down her bare shoulder. She hurried to tug it back up, her blush deepening. 'You really needn't have troubled yourself further.'

She was looking at the flowers as she tucked the jacket to her chin. Eyeing him beneath her lashes as though she was shy. *Was* she shy? Hell, he'd been the naked one, but then maybe she was still *seeing* him naked. *Mon Dieu.*

Until he could bury that image, she would likely keep seeing him so.

'Here, please.' He offered the bouquet of classic cream buds, which she took, her green eyes lighting up as she brought them to her nose.

'Hydrangeas?'

'I put in a special request for a hypoallergenic variety.' He gave her a lopsided grin and cocked his head towards the floral display that had been his protection a few hours ago. 'And I'm now considering that for the health of all my guests, I should have these evil varieties replaced throughout.'

Her eyes danced. 'Hydrangeas certainly would have hidden a lot more.'

She was warming up. And her teasing had him warming from the inside out too, which encouraged him enough to say, 'Can I tempt you to a coffee? There's a barista down the road that the tourists have yet to discover, and I'd love to...'

His invitation trailed off as the colour drained from her face. Had he dropped his pants unawares again, because now she was back to being aghast? Not quite the screaming, Hail Mary affair of the night before, but pale, nonetheless.

'What's wrong?'

And truth was he hadn't *meant* to invite her for coffee. It hadn't been his intention at all when he'd come here. But he didn't feel in any hurry to leave her orbit. Not after the week he'd just endured with his parents in LA. His father had refused to stick to his retirement plan and keep his nose out of the global security business he'd set up forty years ago...a business that would take his dying breath if he let it.

Only, Hugo hadn't thought of his father and his firm since Cassie had stunned him awake.

And today was Saturday, the weekend for most. Not that he had treated it as such in a long time. Especially since he'd rolled his father's business into his ever-expanding list of responsibilities.

But now he was taking a moment to think about it, it was the perfect excuse for a leisurely coffee with a companion who certainly looked like she was enjoying her own chilled-out weekend. Her jumper having resumed its slouched position off one shoulder, her soft grey leggings and fluffy white socks designed for lounging, her hair hanging free and tousled to her waist...

He could feel another throat clearing coming on, and what was that about?

You really need to ask?

'Nothing. I'm—' She licked her lips. 'I'm not dressed to go out.'

'I'm talking coffee, not cocktails at the Ritz.' He was hoping to reassure her, to tease a little too. Surely she had to know how good she looked? Sweet and cute, in a sexy girl-next-door kind of a way. But her smile remained weak.

'I should get these in some water.'

'Of course.'

She eased away from the door and a chill washed over his front. Disappointment wrapped up in that same sense of familiarity—ringing stronger, resonating deeper. But then, he'd walked many a hotel corridor, attended many a black tie affair, met many, many people over the years. Though it was more than how she looked. It was the way she was. The regal air. The shyness. The sweetness and light.

'I'll leave you to get on with your day.'

He turned on his heel and moved off, cursing the disappointed burr to his voice. It wasn't in his nature to guilt trip people. Problem was, he *was* disappointed, and it had taken him by surprise.

'Mr Chevalier...'

He paused, angled his head just enough to say, 'Hugo, please.'

'Would you like to come in for coffee?'

His brows drew together—was she just being kind, polite...?

'I was about to have one myself,' she added as though sensing his hesitation.

'So long as I'm not keeping you from whatever you had planned for today?'

'Not at all. To be honest, it would be nice to have some company.'

His frown lifted. 'You're sure?'

She stepped back to make room for him to enter. 'Though I don't know how well you know Louis or if you've been in here since he took ownership of the apartment, but...'

Her voice trailed away as she let the space speak for itself, which it did, a thousand times over as he crossed the threshold and chuckled. 'I believe one's home should always be a reflection of the occupant's personality, and since this is Louis's and Louis Cousteau is a flamboyant fashion designer, I think it is perfection.'

The twinkle in her eye was worth every eye-watering item adorning the large entrance hall. 'That's one word for it.'

He and Louis's penthouse suites were of a similar size and layout, but there the similarity ended. Statement pieces, whether it be in colour or shape, personality or origin, filled every wall, every space. And if Hugo was honest, it gave him the twinge of a headache, but who was he to judge? He was a minimalist through and through. Everything in his life had been about pleasing others, or at the very least, avoiding offence.

The same could not be said for the great Louis Cousteau.

'You do get used to it after a while.'

She was at the glitter-bedazzled sink, in the equally bedazzled kitchen, filling a vase with water.

'I'm saying nothing.'

She smiled. 'You didn't need to.' Sparkling green eyes went back to the vase as she arranged the flowers within it. 'Louis was never one for toeing a line of any sort.'

'A trait I can admire.'

And he did. That was no lie.

Hugo had grown up in a household at war...whenever his father was at home at any rate. He'd been trying to find the line to toe forever, and then beseeching everyone else to toe it too. He'd been the doting son, the people-pleaser, the peace facilitator in his parents' marriage, where there had always been three according to his mother—her, his father, and the company.

Not any more, though... *Retired*, remember.

If only his father would get the message and leave well alone.

'Is filter coffee, okay?' The hesitation in her voice already had him giving a smile in reassurance—*see*, people-pleaser. Even though he'd long ago left that boy behind, some habits were harder to shift. 'Or I can try and master the machine?'

He looked at the contraption against one wall, too shiny and new to have ever been used. 'A filter is perfect.'

And if he was honest, he liked his coffee by the vat. He might be French—well, Polish if one wanted to go a generation back, but he'd take a giant mug over a measly espresso cup any day of the week.

He entered the living space, leaving her to get the coffee going. He got the impression she didn't entertain often. Which again was strange, considering how she'd appeared the night before. How sophisticated, elegant, and dressed for entertaining.

Or was it that he'd been the complete opposite, so unprepared for company?

No. He didn't think it was that. More that she was used to being waited on. And unaccustomed to entertaining anybody when dressed so casually. But if he was honest, he liked her like this.

Even if she did stand out against the backdrop, her hesitation and muted presence against the garish backdrop a bit like setting a skittish kitten down in a neon nightclub. Maybe he should have invited her round to his place...she'd have fit right in with all the monochrome and he could have taken care of the coffee. Though he'd need to put a few coffees between them and his nakedness before that could happen!

He followed the criss-crossed panels of sun coming through the many French windows and doors to the low-slung coffee table that was scattered with drawing paraphernalia. Pencils, pens, sketches of clothing and accessories...

'Please excuse the mess.'

He turned to find her behind him.

'Louis left it like this?'

The man didn't strike him as the kind to leave stuff just lying around. Chaotic but not messy. Especially when such designs were obviously in their early stages and likely to be considered top secret. His cleaning staff could be trusted but...

She coloured, swept her hair behind her ear. 'No, they're mine.'

'*Yours?* Wow, they're really—' He was about to say *impressive*, but she was already hurrying forward, gathering the sheets into a pile. Did she not want him to see? Was she self-conscious? Or was it as he thought...

'Top secret?'

'What?' She straightened with a laugh, clutching the drawings to her chest. 'Hardly. Not really. They're—they're just some designs I've been working on.'

'Do you work with Louis? Is that how you two know each another?'

'Not officially, no. We've known each other for a long time. We went to school together in London.'

She stacked the papers on a side table shaped like a palm tree and gestured for him to take a seat on the velvet sofa, the colour of which made him wince but the fabric was soft enough. He swung an arm across its back, was about to ask her which school when his gaze landed on the pile of magazines her cleared-away sketches had unveiled.

Or rather, landed on the cover model of the top magazine...

The cover model who then took a seat beside him in the flesh.

'Yes,' she said, and he started. 'That's me.'

No, he couldn't have been so unaware, so sucker-punched by their first encounter that he'd missed... missed...

He blinked and turned to face her, eyes widening and seeing every detail anew. The green eyes. The dark hair. The petite frame. He thought of the recognition that had been nagging at him. The familiarity. The poised elegance with the touch of shyness—something thousands if not millions adored, and others questioned.

Cassie was Cassandra, Princess of Sérignone. *Ex* Princess.

English socialite. A woman of the people. A woman whose recent divorce was the talk of the world's media, and there he'd been…naked…unawares…how stupid she must think him!

'Mr Chevalier?'

Though he hadn't been in his right mind. And it had been dark in the outer hall. And even this morning, he'd been too concerned with making right what he had made wrong. And then she'd been all shy and sweet and…

Princess *Freaking* Cassandra?

He dragged a hand down his face.

'I'm sorry. I didn't realise.'

He contemplated standing. *Dieu*, he contemplated bowing, but it all felt a little late for that.

She gave him a coy smile. *That* smile.

'I know. And I wasn't quite sure how to tell you.'

'I would bow but…'

Her eyes danced, her thoughts travelling all the way to his naked backside and beyond, he was sure…

'So, you're the reason for the extra footfall outside when I arrived home yesterday? I'd assumed we were having an out-of-season flurry of tourists.'

She grimaced. 'Mostly press I'm afraid. I'm sorry.'

'Why are you sorry?'

'For bringing the madness to your door, to your hotel.'

'Considering I brought you my nakedness, I think we can call it even, don't you?'

She gave him a full-on smile. The beam of which

made him lose his breath. *Breathtaking*. It was a word he'd heard of, knew of, never once had he deemed it fit for another person. A hard run, a spell in the boxing ring, a blast round the Nürburgring. But never about a woman.

And that's when it hit him. The nagging recognition, the stirring in his gut—it wasn't because she was Cassandra, Princess of Sérignone. It was that she reminded him of another woman. Another dark-haired, shy yet teasing woman. She reminded him of Sara. Of his past and his one big mistake.

Ice rushed his veins, goose-bumps prickling against the sleeves of his shirt.

'Your hotel security have been amazing, Mr Chevalier, but I am sorry for the extra work I'm putting them through.'

He swallowed the chilling boulder that had lodged itself in his chest. 'We're an exclusive hotel, we deal with clients that require extra security all the time. It's their job to handle it.'

'Still...'

She looked hesitant, and he knew his tension had seeped into his words. He cursed the memories for rearing their ugly head. It was ancient history. Over a decade old. He'd not thought of Sara in so long. She had cost him dearly in so many ways. She wasn't just the woman he'd thought himself in love with, she was the woman who'd lost him his father's respect, his first career, almost his life as well as hers...back when he'd been a rookie bodyguard.

A bodyguard who should have known better than to fall in love with his principal.

It's why he kept a tight hold on his emotions now. Especially when it came to people. He didn't depend on them to give him a rush of any kind.

Now he was thirty-six, a billionaire hotelier with a finger in the pie that was his father's global security firm. The biggest lesson he'd learnt was that you couldn't control what others thought or did or felt. They would go the way they wanted. And it was best to disassociate your own happiness, your own feelings, from those of others.

Which left him all the more disturbed now, because he cared about this woman. This woman who was no more than a stranger to him personally, but he'd seen enough in the press to know her life had to be some kind of living hell of late. Her divorce as loud and as messy as a catastrophic world event. He wasn't one for reading the gossip columns, but she often featured in the mainstream headlines. People picking and probing into her personal life like they had every right.

'I'm sorry you're under such attack, but if my hotel and my staff are helping you to feel safe from their prying presence, then that's as good as any five-star review for me.'

Her eyes warmed with his words. 'Are you going to ask if any of it is true?'

'If any of what is true?'

'I don't know—take your pick. People usually have their favourite headline...corrupting the son of my ex-husband's driver seems to be the latest story.'

'You're confusing me with someone who cares, Cassie.'

To anyone else, his remark may have caused offence.

Instead she positively bloomed and, in her warmth, the chill within him eased.

'It really is none of my business, unless of course you would appreciate a friendly ear.'

Her lashes flickered, her green eyes signalling something that he couldn't read but it had the unease returning—the familiarity, the need to protect, the urge to run and stay at the same time.

'Anyway...' He shifted back in his seat, creating an extra inch between them like it would somehow release the weird hold she had over him. 'The extra income from the reporters staying and dining here will be good for business, but if one crosses the line, you only have to say the word and they're out. Though to give them their due, they all seemed rather well-behaved upon my arrival.'

'That's because it was you in their orbit.'

And not her.

She didn't need to say it for him to know that's what she meant. And there was so much in that one statement. So much vehemence, so much power that she had bestowed on them—the press—and so much fear. Just like Sara.

He opened his mouth to reassure, to tell her she was safe in his building, to tell her he'd evict them all, if need be, when she stood. 'I'll get the coffee.'

He doubted the pot would be ready but he got the impression she wanted a breather more than the drink, and so he let her go. It could wait.

And if he was honest, he could do with a breather too.

It wasn't so much that she was royalty—*ex*-royalty. He'd protected royalty. He'd housed royalty. Hell, he'd *dated* the equivalent of royalty. And there came Sara again.

'You know what your problem is, son? You've got a thing for a damsel in distress, and until you can keep a lid on it, you're no use to me...'

His father's decade-old words were in his ear, his disappointed gaze in his head too...didn't matter that it didn't apply now. That his father's grave dismissal had no place in the now.

His career was his own. His money was his own. His life was his own.

But the damsel in distress, was that what this was...? Sara. Cassie. Both damsels of a sort?

He shook off the thought, dismissed it even as it tried to come back at him...history on repeat just in another form.

But if it was a case of history repeating itself, didn't that mean he had a chance to rewrite the ending and come out the hero this time? Could he help Cassie get through this turbulent time in her life and not play himself for a lovesick fool, because this time he wouldn't *be* a lovesick fool.

Cassie brought the tray back into the lounge. She couldn't tell if Hugo Chevalier had a sweet tooth. Her gut told her not. Or rather, his well-toned physique did, but she brought the brass pineapple sugar pot anyway. More because it made her smile.

He started to rise. 'Let me help you with that.'

'No need.' She set the tray down, careful not to spill a drop from the two steaming mugs filled with coffee or the jug of milk. 'Despite the rumours, a princess can manage to serve her own coffee...'

And brush her hair, cleanse her face, clothe herself... *how novel*!

He settled back into his seat. 'Do you have to do that a lot? Justify what you can and can't do, fend off the would-be waiting staff?'

She didn't meet his eye. She already felt like he'd leapt inside her head, read her every thought as she'd had it. Not that there were any staff waiting in the wings here. Not any more.

It didn't stop the learned response though—the slight tension in her spine, an attuned ear, and the tight lip, which she swiftly loosened into a smile for his benefit.

'Once upon a time, in a castle far, far away...' She handed him his mug and he thanked her, his gaze flitting to the exposed skin of her shoulder, and she fought the urge to cover it as her cheeks heated. She was dressed for comfort, not for company. A fact she'd tried to point out when he'd made the joke about the Ritz. But there was being dressed for the Ritz and being dressed like she was. Braless and in her comfiest clothes. Her go-to outfit after a morning's workout, when all she'd planned to do was to block the noise of the world out and let her creative juices take over.

'But not any more?'

'No.' She sank back into the sofa, curled her legs up under her. 'Now I get to make my own coffee. When I want, how I want, and drink it with who I want.'

'And this is a good thing, right? Because from where I'm sitting, there seems to be some unresolved tension about the whole situation.'

Her eyes shot to his. Had he really just gone there? Outed her and her 'situation' again without a moment's hesitation? She gave a grimace. 'Did it really come across like that?'

'A little.'

'Sorry. I'm not very good at this.'

'Good at what exactly? The coffee. The talking. Or...'

'The company.'

'Am I that hard to be around?' But his eyes danced with the question, the soft curve to his lips telling her he hadn't taken offence, and he didn't mean any.

She laughed, the tension between her shoulder blades easing with every ripple. What was it about this man that made her feel almost normal. 'Not at all. Just... different.'

'Different?'

'To be honest, a coffee date of any kind is a new one on me. Even with Louis it's usually a glitzy affair that revolves around fashion and dogs.'

He cocked a brow. 'Dogs?'

'Oh, yes, he *loves* dogs.'

'I can *try* and talk fashion and dogs if that'll make you feel more comfortable, but I can't make any promises about how riveting it'll be. Or accurate. I can do colour, size, maybe the odd name drop, but that's my lot.'

'I take it you have people who pick out your clothing then, because for one who claims to have little knowledge of fashion, you clearly have an eye for it?'

'Is that a roundabout way of complimenting me on how I dress, Cassie?'

Her cheeks warmed and his eyes dipped, taking in the flush that must have risen up her chest, too. Oh, dear.

She was so out of practice and very bad at this. 'It was merely an observation, Mr Chevalier.'

'Now that we're enjoying coffee together, do you think you could drop the Mr? Especially since technically if anyone should be giving anyone a rank, it's me to you.'

Her coffee threatened to escape her mug as she thrust her hand out. 'Please don't!'

He raised that same arrogant brow.

'I've been called *princess* enough to last one lifetime, and I know that probably sounds ungrateful when it's many a young girl's dream but...'

She shuddered. She hadn't meant to, but the chilling memories creeping along her spine were impossible to suppress.

'Let me guess, the reality isn't all it's cracked up to be?'

'No.'

He captured her gaze in his. The warmth, the understanding in his crystal-clear blue eyes choked up her chest and had the words spilling forth before she could stop them, 'It's more prisoner than princess.'

She bit her lip. Shocked at what she'd said. Because she knew full well how that line would be printed in the press. How it would look to the world when shown in black and white and worse still, it would be the truth. Because she *had* said it.

And she didn't know Hugo from Adam. How could she trust him not to spill all when he left here? To sell her story like so many others had before. Her nearest and dearest, people she'd once thought of as friends. 'I shouldn't have said that.'

She clamped her teeth down again so hard she thought she might draw blood, because the truth was, she wanted to talk to him. The urge like an ever-swelling tide within her. She couldn't explain it. She'd had no one for so long. Not even Louis would sit quietly, calmly, and listen like this. Oh, he was a good friend, so long as it was surface level talk. The practical or financial. Designs and creative fun. But this…the deep, emotional, real.

There was just something about Hugo. Something that told her he understood. That he got it.

'It's okay, Cassie. You can trust me.'

He lowered his mug to the table, rested his elbows on his knees as he interlaced his fingers and gave her his full attention.

'I don't make a habit of gossiping, and I certainly don't talk to reporters, and in all honesty, the idea that *you* could go outside and tell the world that you found me wandering one of my hotels in my birthday suit fills *me* with dread.'

A streak of pink marred his cheeks and she found it endearing. Both the blush and the honesty.

'That aside, it would hardly look good for business if I were to go about selling stories on my guests. And in case you need it spelled out, I really don't need the cash or the press attention.'

There was no arrogance, just fact.

'So, if you keep my secrets, I'll keep yours. How does that sound?'

'*Très bien*, Hugo,' she said, and with all her heart, she meant it too. 'I agree.'

CHAPTER THREE

'SO, A PRISONER, you say? How so?'

Though he could take a wild guess. Not so wild if he was to think of Sara and her life as the daughter of a head of state. Her father may have been the figurehead, but the rules and expectations very much applied to her. Governing what she could and couldn't do. Where she could and couldn't go. Who she could and couldn't see. Who she could and couldn't *date*. Him.

'Where do I even start?'

He settled back into the sofa, making clear he had all the time in the world to listen. 'Why not start at the beginning, it's as good a place as any...'

She sipped at her coffee, her mouth twisting around the mug. 'You might regret saying that, Hugo.'

He waved a hand through the air. 'Feel free to remind me later.'

She gave a soft huff, the returning shadows in her green eyes chasing away the amusement and making him want to close the gap between them. But he also sensed the persistent skittishness about her, the wary kitten-like quality he'd spied earlier.

'If I'm honest, I never had freedom like other kids growing up, so it wasn't like I could miss it. My parents had my life mapped out from birth. Every step was strategic and they played me to their best advantage.'

He gave a slow nod. 'That sounds…'

'Militant?'

'Exhausting.'

She blew out a breath. 'That too. But the palace was different. Every day had a schedule. Breakfast, lunch, dinner. You name it. There was a time for it and someone would produce it. And if you were especially lucky, there'd be a different outfit for each.'

'Where my family comes from in Poland, such abundance would be severely frowned upon.'

'You're from Poland—I thought so.' Her smile made a return. Bright, genuine. 'And I would agree with them all. And I said as much to the King. Who was of course horrified, as was his mother. I was quickly shushed and escorted from the room by Georges and told never to give my opinion in public, or private, again.'

'How lovely.'

'Quite.'

'What are they like? Really?'

'His family?' Her eyes flashed and her nose flared. 'The King is a brute. His wife is a spendthrift. And while the Queen Mother despairs at their behaviour, his son runs amok. If I was to be kind, I would say the King is angry at the world for daring to mock his virility. His wife spends to make up for the abundance of children she so desperately wanted. His mother despairs at her lack of power, and as for Georges, well, the apple doesn't fall far from the tree…after five years of marriage I failed to provide even one heir.'

His gut clenched. 'So, he divorced *you*?'

'God, no. I divorced him. When I realised I was the only one who took our wedding vows seriously.'

His shoulders eased as he released a breath he hadn't noticed he was holding.

'I'd had enough of the real Georges and everyone laughing at me behind closed doors. I think he shares the worst qualities of both his mother and his father, and now he can share those qualities with whomever he chooses, as I no longer need to care because I'm no longer there to witness it.'

Hugo shook his head, unable to understand how she'd been able to bear it for so long and still hold her head as high as she did. All that poise and elegance, she had it in spades. She hadn't lost it. Georges hadn't stolen it. No matter how the palace had tried.

'And so, they sow seeds of twisted dealings and affairs on your part, suggesting it was *your* unfaithful behaviour that led to the breakdown of your marriage? Despite all the stories that have been in the media over the years about him?'

She gave a sad smile. 'I know.'

'But how do you stand it? All the slander being thrown at you.'

'I ignore it as best I can. I made my bed. I knew who he was when I agreed to marry him. I knew of his reputation, but I thought I'd done the unthinkable and reformed the playboy prince. Though even I hadn't known just how much there was to reform when my parents presented our engagement as a fait accompli.'

'But surely you had a choice, you could have said no?'

She gave a tight laugh. 'One does not say no to my parents.'

'Why?'

'I'd lived a life doing what was expected of me and so I did it.' She tilted her head at him. Green eyes probing as they scanned him from top to toe. 'Call it fear, impotence, apathy… I can't imagine someone like you knowing what it means to live like that.'

He shifted under that gaze because he'd felt it all. Once. Feared for his life. Watched the woman he'd believed in walk away, powerless to stop her. And when his father had stripped him of his role in the company, he hadn't cared. He'd only vowed never to feel any of those things again.

'Did you ever rebel, even when you were younger? There must have been times…?'

She caught her lip in her teeth as her eyes drifted to the coffee table. 'When I was seven, my mother bought me a dress to wear to a summer function. I hated it. It itched like crazy, making my skin red raw, and I refused to wear it. She locked me in the basement and left me there in the dark. Told me I could come out when I had the dress on. The party was two days later…'

He waited for the punch line and when nothing came, he realised that was it.

'She came and got you…'

She nodded. 'Yes. Two days later. The staff fed me scraps but she saw to it that my hair was scraped up, my blotchy cheeks were well covered, and I smiled until my face ached.'

He felt the bite of his nails in his palm and flexed his fist. 'Some parenting technique.'

'Mind games were always my mother's way.'

'Dare I ask about your father's?'

'My father was all about the purse strings and the silent treatment. It could have been worse.'

And he'd been thinking worse. Now he felt bad to be relieved!

'I often wondered if it would have been easier if I had had a sister or a brother to love and to share the load a little, but I think that would have made it worse. I would have worried about them too.'

He could believe it.

'And the truth is, I *was* the one who said yes to the marriage. I met the Prince and he—he charmed me. Georges was good at making you believe what he said. He had these dreamy blue eyes and this compelling smile. And I'd been so caught up in his flattery, his attention, his *kindness*. He gave me everything I'd been starved of as a child. While my friends were all craving sweets, chocolate, the kind of treats Mum would never permit, all I'd wanted was love, a kind word, cuddles...' She gave a shaky laugh, her cheeks blooming with colour that killed him now. 'God, I sound pathetic.'

'No. No, you don't. *They* do. Your parents. Georges. His family. The whole lot of them.'

Hell, he wanted to storm the castle and hold them all to account.

'He made me feel special, and I—I was swept up in it all. I thought we were falling in love and so I married him. I believed our own love story. *The English Socialite who had snagged the Playboy Prince.*'

Her green eyes misted over, her thoughts travelling back in time as she relived those early days. 'I didn't realise I was being played for a fool until it was too late. My father had saved the royal reserves with Fairfax money and I was Princess of Sérignone. There was no going back…until I couldn't take it any more.'

He studied her quietly, admiring the strength it must have taken to walk away, to *stay* away. 'And what about your parents now? Where are they?'

'At home in England, last I checked.'

'Have you…'

'Have I spoken to them? Oh, yes, they were my first port of call when I ran from the palace. I'm not sure why I thought they would shelter me, but what choice did I have? A princess doesn't really have many friends they can trust, and I figured they wouldn't want me roaming the streets stirring up ever more trouble…'

'But?'

'My mother tried to talk me into returning—like I said, mind games are her speciality—while my father physically escorted me to his private jet back to Sérignone.'

'Your own father?'

'*Oui*. So you see, I am done with them, Hugo. Since then, the few friends I have left have helped me by giving me places to stay while I build up my portfolio, in the hope that soon, I'll have enough to launch a career in fashion and become financially independent once more. Then I can pay back all those people like Louis who have helped me get here and I can also get back to my charity work that I have missed so much.'

He shook his head. 'I can't believe that you're here, fighting to take your life back and already thinking about giving back to others.'

She gave him a lopsided smile. 'I'm sickening, I know.'

'Is that what Georges would tell you?' Because he wasn't seeing the funny side.

Her eyes widened. 'How did you...?'

'Something tells me that that man and his family tried to stamp out every good thing about you so that it may make him shine that little bit brighter.'

'Funny you say that.'

'How so?'

'Because after our marriage it often occurred to me that it wasn't just the Fairfax money the Duponts were after, but my 'clean' image too. I was a way to mop up the mess that Georges was making with his wild and hedonistic parties. *Now*, if I'd known about *those* at the time of our engagement then I might have been more reluctant to trot down that aisle...'

Hugo didn't think he could take much of the Georges revelation train, or rather, his teeth couldn't. 'Seems to me the Duponts got plenty out of the marriage, and I can see how you were duped, but what I don't understand is what your parents got in return?'

'Status. Royal connections. Another boost for the family tree? I don't know and I don't want to know. Unpacking that only leads to me understanding my true worth to them, and I'm not sure I want to know that. Whereas I do know that I want a fresh start and a clean slate so that I can focus on my future free of them all.'

She gave a smile and, cupping her mug in both hands, she retreated further into the sofa. He knew the mug was giving her the warmth her body lacked. The sofa, the comfort. And he had the deep-rooted urge to provide both.

'And heaven knows there are people in this world who are starving, who don't have a roof over their head, live under threat each day with zero hope of change. People who I want to get my life in order for, so that I can get out there and help.' She shook her head, her knuckles flashing white. 'People who are truly powerless on their own, and I have no right to say such things about my own experiences.'

'You have every right.'

Because she'd clearly been punishing herself with those same words for heaven knew how long. Since she'd married into royalty or long before then too.

'Now you're just humouring me to be kind.' She gave him another of her shy smiles. A hundred times genuine. He'd bet his life on it.

'I've been called many things in my life, but *kind* isn't one that springs to mind.'

Fierce or *fun*. Depending on the circumstance. *Stubborn* or *obstinate* to use his father's most recent favourite when his retirement had been forced upon him. But, *kind*?

'I don't believe you.' She rested her head against the back of the sofa, not so shy now as her gaze narrowed on him. 'Your eyes are kind.'

'Regardless of what you think of my eyes...' Though her words did warm his voice, his smile '... I always say what I mean, Cassie. As for what you are going through as a person, not as an ex-princess or as a lady of the English aristocracy, but as a person with real feelings, it's a lot under any normal circumstances. Divorce is one of the hardest, most stressful challenges anyone can face...'

'You sound like you're talking from experience.'

'No, not me personally. Though there were times as a kid that I thought maybe my parents would have been better off apart. And even then, the arguments were mainly about Dad not being home enough, so maybe not.' He gave a smile that was so caught up in her present hurt he wasn't sure if it came across as more of a grimace. 'But what I'm trying to say is, at least most of us get to go about our business without the whole world breathing down our necks through a camera lens and forming an ill-informed opinion on it. It stands to reason you're going to have your moments.'

She gave a soft huff. 'I've not been permitted such moments for a long time.'

'And how do you cope with that?'

'I'm not sure I am coping all that well.'

'I don't know, from where I'm sitting you seem to have done remarkably well.'

'What?' She gave a brittle laugh, and he missed the woman of seconds before—the one that thought him kind and looked increasingly relaxed in his presence. 'By spilling my heart out to a total stranger who I met only yesterday?'

'You carry yourself with such grace and poise, I never would have known that the woman who stood before me last night and thought to offer out her jacket was the same woman being hounded by the press, vilified by a royal family, and as you've now explained, ostracised by her own. You are a wonder, Cassie. And if you don't know it, allow me to tell you it is so.'

Her mouth twitched, the warmth once again blooming in her cheeks and her chest and, *Dieu*, was he glad to see it. 'Ah, well, last night you had me distracted.'

He fought the reciprocal warmth in his chest, the cheeky twitch to his own mouth. 'And when you're out in public, I assume you have a team with you to help keep the masses at bay?'

She gave another laugh, this time it sounded more delirious than brittle and it had him worried. Not that he could say why.

'I don't go out.'

'What do you mean, you don't go out?'

'Just what I said.'

'Cassie, everyone goes out at some point.'

'Not me.'

She couldn't be serious. Something inside his chest shrivelled.

'So last night…before you came upon me?'

'I'd been to the rooftop bar for a drink.'

'Alone?'

She nodded.

'Beni is a sweetheart and is kind enough to open it after everyone else has gone to bed.'

'Because that way you don't have to see anyone?'

Again, she nodded, and again he felt this weird shrivelling sensation inside his chest. If he wasn't so traumatised by the whole conversation, he'd be touched that she had taken the time to learn the name of his bar staff.

'Don't get me wrong, sometimes there's the odd person, but in the main, it's just me.'

She smiled. Actually *smiled*. And he wanted to cry. Which was as ridiculous as this whole situation. Ridiculously unfair.

'When you've lived enough days and nights being chased down, Hugo, with no regard for your personal space, you begin to crave those quiet hours while the city sleeps. And the witching hour has kind of become my time to dine. Though I don't really eat as such, more get some fresh air while everyone else is asleep.'

He took up his coffee, needing something to do that wasn't taking her hand and walking her out of here right now...

'How long have you been here for, Cassie?'

'What? Staying at Louis's?'

'Oui.'

'A month.'

'And for that entire time, you haven't left this apartment?'

She gave a subtle shake of her head, as though she could sense the storm brewing within him as he stifled a curse with a sip of his coffee. 'Have you seen the sights, walked the river, been to the Louvre, the parks?'

She was shaking her head at everything, and he was—he was losing his mind at the very idea that she could have been in the city for a whole month and seen nothing. Nothing at all!

'But I am lucky because your hotel is well positioned. I have a view of the Eiffel Tower, Arc de Triomphe and Champs-élysées depending on where I stand. The balcony is vast, the private plunge pool a delight, and the room service is all-encompassing.'

'But, Cassie!' Her eyes flared and he immediately softened his posture and his words—remembering that for all she was fierce in some ways, she was still that skittish kitten in others, and he couldn't blame her. Living a life being papped 24-7. A life like Sara had led. 'Living inside these four walls day in, day out, is not living.'

'People regularly survive on a whole lot less.'

'Survive, sure. One's sanity, however...?'

'And as we have established, I cannot move for reporters...some days I only have to turn my head in the wrong direction in the presence of the wrong person and someone will make something of it, and that could be as catastrophic as a natural disaster on the world's stage.'

As he had seen for himself. But to know that she had escaped one form of prison only to land herself in another—his Parisian paradise of all places—when she had the City of Love on her doorstep.

To live in it like a prisoner, when her only crime had been marriage to a prince.

A prince whose own reputation was scandalous at best, who'd managed to make her feel ridiculed and laughed at in her own home. *Mon Dieu*, if he ever met the man...

'Do you care what the world thinks that much?'

'It's not a question of care as it is being impossible to ignore. They're like pack animals and I'm their prey. I can't go about my day without being set upon. Though that's probably being unfair to pack animals...'

'But now you're divorced, surely, things will start to ease?'

'When the Duponts stop stirring the pot, perhaps they will. Right now, they need me to lose face so that he may save his. It is far safer for me to keep a low profile while our divorce is so fresh. He needs to find a new bride, someone willing to look past his reputation like I once did, and they will paint the picture they need in order to make the future look how they wish.'

'No matter what damage it does to you?'

'The picture is not yet tainted enough.'

He cursed. The heartless nature of it all too much to take.

'Precisely. And I have my own dreams to consider

and protect.' Eyes likes emeralds, glittering and bright, drifted to the drawings she'd set aside. 'While all those girls dreamt of being a princess, I dreamt of one day having my own fashion label.'

He'd warrant she'd dreamt of a lot more than that... before her prince had shattered those dreams, had she wanted mini princes and mini princesses to fill her fairy-tale castle?

And why on earth had his head gone there? Maybe because he could see her as a mother? With the good heart she wore on her sleeve...it must have driven the Prince crazy that she bore that trait so effortlessly, that people flocked to it, trusted it.

'I even had a name...'

He lifted his chin, focused on what she was saying and not the wild assumptions he was making about the man he really would like to put in a ring and go ten rounds with.

'Care to share?'

'Cassie Couture.' She laughed softly. 'I know. I know. It's probably a little cheesy.'

'Only as cheesy as Chevalier Clubs, perhaps.'

They shared a laugh. 'How true.'

'And if it's good enough for Coco Chanel...'

'Ah, life goals!' Her gaze lifted to his. 'As for the dream itself, it still feels out of reach, like the foolish dreams of a foolish child. But maybe, one day...'

'And the drawings?'

'Louis thinks he could test some out on the catwalk next February.'

'Louis? Why not you? Surely with your name, you could secure funding, put yourself out there?'

She nibbled on her lip. 'For now, I'm content hiding out up here, sketching.'

'And letting someone else take the credit?'

'All big names have a team behind them, and we all have to start somewhere. I'm lucky I have someone like Louis willing to take a chance on me.' She was saying the right things, even if they sounded hollow to him. 'Hopefully, soon enough, the press furore will calm, and I'll be able to step outside once more, live my life again.'

'How I wish you were talking metaphorically, but you're not.'

'No.'

'But that's not healthy, can't you see? What about fresh air? What about everyday things like taking a walk, fetching some groceries, seeing a film, eating out?'

Mon Dieu, the list was endless. His father's firm— *his* now—provided protection for people like her day in, day out for this precise reason. To make sure they lived as normal a life as possible. To make life about saying 'yes' again, within reason. So long as situations were assessed, prepared for, managed.

She smiled. 'You know what I miss most?'

'No.' But he knew it was going to kill him, whatever it was.

'Aside from the charity work, which I truly am desperate to get back to, but I don't want it tainted by all this noise.'

'I think you put too much stock in what the Duponts are throwing about. Your charities will still benefit from your presence regardless.'

'I want the attention to be *on* the charity work. While it's on my personal life, it defeats that.'

He nodded. 'I take your point...so you were saying?'

'You'll think I'm odd.'

'Try me.'

She beamed. 'Running.'

'Running?' He choked over his coffee. Not what he'd expected her to say. Enjoying a drink in a bar uninterrupted. Taking her art to the park. Sketching in a museum or a fashion house where she could feel inspired. Even dress shopping. But *running*?

'Yes. See. I told you.'

'Of all the things...'

She raised her brows, eyes sparking. 'You thought I was going to say clothes shopping, didn't you?'

'In my defence, you'd already said charity work, so...'

He shifted against the fabric of the sofa, willing it to open up and swallow him whole. He'd never considered himself sexist before.

'I apologise.' And swiftly, he went back to the reason he'd landed himself in this mess, 'So, you like to run?'

'I do. And I used to like to run outdoors, even back in Sérignone. The palace grounds were vast enough that I could fit in a five-k run without ever having to venture outside the gates...that was until the rumours became too much for the palace.'

'The rumours?'

'Oh, yes.' She gave a wry smile. 'At which point the King put a stop to my exercise outdoors.'

Hugo clenched his jaw to stifle a curse.

'Apparently a princess in running gear, exerting herself no less, is unacceptable. I was seen as flaunting myself in front of the grounds staff, courting trouble.'

'Meanwhile his son could carry on how he liked?'

'He knew I would listen.'

He clenched his jaw once more and there went a tooth, Hugo was sure of it.

She didn't wait for him to respond, which was lucky, because there were no words Hugo could give that he would deem fit for her ears as her gaze drifted to the French windows. The balcony with its abundance of flowers hanging on to the end of the season, just a sample of what she'd see if she was to hit the vast and varied parks Paris had to offer, not to mention the incredible views along the river Seine.

So much beauty on her doorstep, it was a crime she didn't get to see it. Had she *ever* seen the Seine up close? He didn't dare ask. She'd probably tell him another horror story. And he didn't think his teeth could take any more grinding.

Whether it was the similarity to Sara, the knowledge of what Cassie had been through, what she was *still* going through at the hands of the Duponts and the press...

'But yes, I love to run. I love to feel the wind against my face, in my hair...it didn't matter what troubles I faced, there was something about the way I could lose myself in the rhythmic rush of it that just worked. Some women choose yoga—' she shrugged '—I choose to run.'

'Then do it.'

Because in that moment, he was one hundred percent determined to see her do it. And as soon as humanly possible.

Her head snapped around, her eyes flaring wide as she looked at him like he was crazy to suggest it. And maybe he was.

'Just like that…get into my kit, my trainers and poof, out the door?'

'It's what millions do every day.'

'Have you been listening to me? I'd barely make it into the hotel lobby without a wall of people forming a human assault course. I'd do myself an injury, if not someone else.'

'What about your witching hour?'

Her eyes flared further, which he wouldn't have believed possible. But then, she really did have the biggest, greenest, most alluring…

'Because that's going to be so safe?'

'You'd be safe with me.'

She gawped at him, a solitary strand of glossy brown hair sticking to her luscious pink lips. 'You can't be serious?'

'Absolutely. And if you don't want to use your security detail, I will bring in—' She pulled a face that gave him pause. 'What's that look about?'

She hesitated.

'Cassie?'

'I don't have a detail.'

'You don't…'

'Do you see any guards hovering, Mr Chevalier?'

No, he hadn't noticed any extra security people hanging about, but then the best always managed to blend into the background. And as she had already said, she didn't venture outside of her room, so it wasn't like she went anywhere to require one. But someone of Cassie's status would have at least one Certified Protection Officer on a permanent basis.

'Obviously, not right now, while we're here, but if we were to venture out…'

'If we were to venture out, I wouldn't suddenly have the funds to pay for one. And yes, before you say it, I am aware of the risks. My continued love-hate relationship with the world, the would-be stalkers and so on. However, I took nothing from Georges in the divorce. We have no children to provide for and so it didn't feel right. And yes, I am more than aware of how foolish many consider that to be, my lawyer was very open on the matter, but I just wanted to be free of the Duponts and any hold they had over me. Yes, that has kind of backfired in the aftermath, but in the long term karma will hopefully be my payback.

'As for my parents, they have to all intents and purposes disowned me, and until I can sell my designs, I am beholden to my friends and your hotel's excellent hospitality and exceptional security. So, I will make do. Can we consider this conversation done?'

Why did Hugo feel like this conversation had been done many times before him? With her lawyer, like she had already said, and Louis too, perhaps.

'We absolutely can.'

'*Bon.*' And then she smiled as she considered him with a tilt of her head. 'You would really take me running?'

'Are you saying I don't look like the type to run?' He feigned insult over his physical ability rather than accept she was questioning the generosity of the offer. Because then he'd have to question it himself. And that would mean examining his own good conscience and whether he was in his right mind to suggest it too. After everything that had happened with Sara—gone *wrong* with Sara— But this was about getting things right this time… With access to his father's firm—*his* firm now, he could make sure they were well protected, and he could give her the freedom she so desperately deserved and needed.

'Because I can assure you, Cassie, I'm quite capable of a five-k run at a decent pace. And further if you really wanted to push it out, but any longer and you'll be hitting the early-morning commuters and I believe that defeats the point.'

'It's not your ability to go the distance that I'm questioning, it's the fact you're offering to run at that ungodly hour.'

He shrugged. 'If we stick to the Seine, it's lit and, aside from the odd stretch of cobbles, perfectly safe.'

'You really are serious…'

'You're awake anyway, so why not?'

'But you're not! Unless you're planning another…'

She coloured, clearly thinking of his naked night-time misadventures.

'I don't plan them. They happen when they happen.'

'Of course, I shouldn't have teased. Forgive me.'

'There's nothing to forgive.' And this time he softened his tone, stripping it of the defensive note she'd clearly picked up on, because it wasn't directed at her. She wasn't the reason he'd been wandering the corridors in such a state.

'They must be quite unsettling for you…to go to sleep in one place and wake up in another.'

'Thankfully they don't happen all that often. It's usually when I'm not sleeping very well to begin with.'

Her brows twitched but she didn't press. Was it a learned response to life in the royal family, her time before with her parents or was she leaving it up to him? Whichever the case, he found himself starting to explain…

'I've only just returned from LA which means I'm still on their time.'

'LA? Business or pleasure?'

He gave a tight laugh. 'Family. Which sort of makes it a hashed attempt at both with a side order of stress.'

'Ah…' She placed her mug down on the coffee table, pulled the sleeves of her jumper over her hands and curled back into the sofa. 'Goes without saying that you have a friendly ear willing to listen if you want to offload some of that?'

He choked on another laugh, because in that moment he realised two things: one, he'd never spoken to anyone about the pressure he was now under, running his hotel empire alongside his father's global security company. Made worse by his father's inability to let the latter go.

And two, he was about to spill it all to Cassie. Not the caricature the press liked to flaunt. Poised, shy, scandalous or otherwise. But the very real, very warm, very attractive brunette, curled up on the sofa beside him. Patiently waiting for him to speak as though she had all the time in the world for it. For him.

And it felt like bliss.

A sensation he'd never quite experienced before… The world and his wife could wait…or rather, the global companies on his shoulders could. And as though summoned, his phone began to ring, and he checked the screen.

It was Eduardo. CEO of Dad's—*his*—security firm.

Eduardo was capable. He'd been his father's number two for twenty years. He could cope for a day. A *Sat-ur*day. He should just ignore it, follow her lead and hide out from the noise.

'Do you need to get that?' she asked.

Did he? He was a few months into his reign. Would it do for Eduardo to report back to Dad—which he would do at some point—that he was deflecting calls?

But you're the boss.

Still, he needed Dad to back off, which he wasn't going to do if he thought Hugo wasn't getting the job done. 'Give me two minutes.'

'So, LA?' Cassie said as he returned to her, his phone tucked away, his smile enigmatic.

'Yes.'

She imagined him, the broad-shouldered man before her with his kind blue eyes and chiselled features, as a son. With a doting mother and a proud father. She could see it so readily. The warm and happy picture painting itself. Could see them all walking down the palm-lined strip of Sunset Boulevard or Rodeo Drive, places she too had been. But she believed her experience to have been so very different.

'My parents—or rather, my mother has decided they should retire out there.'

'Sounds lovely.'

'My mother thinks so.'

'You don't?'

'Oh, I do.'

She frowned. 'So, it's your father who doesn't?'

'My father thinks any home that's not on the same continent as the company headquarters he has been forced to leave behind is anything but lovely.'

'I take it the company headquarters are here?'

'*Oui.*'

'And he likes to keep a toe in?'

'A toe?' He chuckled, the sound deep and throaty as it rippled through his burly frame and did something unidentifiable to her own. Something that felt awfully close to excitement. 'He likes to keep his whole body in.'

'Was he not ready to retire?'

He eased back into the sofa, one arm along its back, one leg hooked over the other by the ankle, everything about him relaxed, though she sensed that, like a panther, he was never far from pouncing should the need arise. She knew he had the physique for it, beneath the crisp dark shirt, the carefully pressed chinos too.

'If I'm brutally honest, I think my mother feared we'd be carrying him out of his company in a box. At first it was getting him out of the field, then it was getting him to simply stop.'

She frowned. 'The field? You make the hospitality industry sound like the military.'

He gave another chuckle. 'Oh, we're not in the same business. Well, we weren't. We are now. Or at least I am.' He paused. Took a breath. 'I'm not making much sense, am I?'

She smiled. 'Perhaps it's your turn to start at the beginning.'

'You're right, I should.' He returned her smile, though it lacked the warmth that had existed moments ago, and she wondered at its cause. Was it his father? The business? Businesses, if they weren't one and the same. And the recent stress he'd eluded too? 'My father's company, now mine since he retired, is in the business of protection—money, data, people—if there's a risk, we protect it.'

'So, you're in leisure *and* protection… How come you ventured into one when your father was in the other?'

'I guess you could say, I carved out my own path.'

There was something about the way he said it. Something that made her want to delve deeper, like a child wanting to ask 'why?' on repeat. And perhaps she would have if he hadn't said, 'but he always intended for me to take on his firm one day, when he felt I was ready.'

'And how old is your father?'

'He celebrated his seventy-fifth birthday while I was in LA.'

'Seventy-fifth!'

'Quite. And I say *celebrated* in the loosest sense of the term. The man does not take kindly to growing old.'

'But growing old is a privilege.'

'Of that he would agree, he just doesn't appreciate the ailments that come with it.'

'Or the retirement?' Because to wait until one was seventy-five to hand over the reins…?

'Or the son who has filled his shoes.'

She stilled, caught off guard by the unexpected bitterness in the man who, up until now, had been the biggest, strongest, cuddliest, and sexiest of teddy bears if such a thing were to exist. 'I'm sure that's not true.'

He fell silent, his gaze shifting to the outdoors as she lost him to his thoughts. Maybe she'd been too quick to paint Hugo's family as picture-perfect. But it was a habit she'd formed long ago. Imagining what everyone else's life was like to avoid having to think about her own.

'I don't know, it's complicated for him.' He gave an awkward shrug. 'To see his son grow stronger as he gets weaker. Especially when things were so much harder for him. Hell, at my age he was fleeing Poland with nothing more than the clothes on his back...' His mouth twisted to the side as he stroked the stubble of his chin, admiration flashing in his eyes. 'And that's another secret I probably shouldn't share, especially when it isn't mine to give...'

'I think we've already established that secrets are safe here.'

She tucked a hand around her legs as his gaze returned to her. Gave him a smile that she hoped would encourage him because she had shared so much of herself, and she hoped he felt secure enough to share a little of himself too. He returned her smile and for a moment, they shared nothing but that look, though she felt it—the connection, the warmth of it. It caught at the air, at her breath, at her pulse...

'My father was part of the Służba Bezpieczeństwa—the SB, Poland's secret police,' he added at her raised brow. 'He didn't agree with Soviet rule, wanted out and he came to Paris. Went into security. It suited his natural talents. He met Mum. Fell in love. They got married. He took her name. And the rest as they say, is history. He built a home and a global security firm that protects everything from data to individuals. He left Poland with nothing. No family, no support. And I guess, I grew up with all of that...'

She frowned. 'But why would that make it hard for

him to hand the business over to you now? Surely he can't begrudge what he gave you.'

It didn't make any sense to her. The man should surely be proud that he had provided for his family and their future. Escaped a life that he hadn't wanted for himself or for his future family. And to see his son take on the mantle of his firm...

'I think it's more that his life made him hard, whereas he perceives me as the opposite.'

'I still don't follow.'

A shadow chased over his face. A shadow she wanted to catch and probe and soothe away. But before she could press, he shifted forward. Gave an awkward laugh. Changing the mood up so entirely she didn't feel she could.

'I'm not sure I do either. I'm rambling.'

'I don't think you are. I'm just trying to piece it together.'

'How did we get to this point again?'

He gave her a lopsided grin that made her stomach flip over. Almost making her forget the sombre mood of seconds before.

'I think you were telling me how you ended up responsible for two global companies in two very different industries.'

'Ah, yes. And I went off on a tangent telling you all about how my father doesn't want to give up what he built, despite building me to give it to...'

'That's quite the conundrum.'

'It is, and so when I went to LA last week, I gifted him a digi-detox for his birthday in the hope that it would gift me some temporary quiet in return.'

She laughed. 'You did *what*?'

'It's one of my most exclusive resorts—a Caribbean haven, cut off from the outside world. No comms, only paradise. A true digital detox for a month. No expense spared. They should have checked in yesterday.'

'And your father was happy to receive such a gift?'

'I'm not sure *happy* was the word I would use, but desperate times call for desperate measures. He needs to find a new way of living, and I'm hoping a month on the island with a life coach and other specialists in their fields will help retrain his brain. And my mother will get a holiday.'

'Is he really that bad?'

'Put it this way, in the three months my father has been retired, he has called me almost daily for an update. Between him and his number two—now my number two, Eduardo, the man who just called—I'm on speed dial. I figured at least this way he's forced to try a new way of living and Mum gets to relax.'

'And you get some peace.'

'One can hope.'

'And no more sleepwalking.'

'That's the dream,' he teased.

'What about Eduardo? What does he make of your father's constant check-ins?'

'Eduardo could run the company with his eyes closed. He knows what he's doing, my father just never left him alone enough.'

'And yet, he is the one ringing you on a Saturday?'

'More out of habit than necessity.'

'I see. And is that a habit you intend to break.'

He paused. 'Perhaps. Right now, my priority is exerting my authority. For forty years my father was the boss. Now I am, and it's important that they know that. My father included.'

She heard the vehemence in that one statement. The fierce sense of ownership. Whether he was trying to prove it to himself or his non-present father or employees, it spoke volumes.

'And you will. And you will do him proud too.'

He gave a grunt.

'But you need to be your own man in the process. Don't lose yourself in trying to become him. You need to do it your own way.'

She didn't know where the words came from, or why it felt so important that she said them. Perhaps it was the sense that he was battling a vision of the man his father wanted him to be, rather than simply being the man he was...and she knew how that felt. How it felt to be caged by someone else's ideal.

His clear blue eyes narrowed on her. 'You know, for a morning coffee, this got deep pretty quickly.'

'And there was I, thinking we couldn't get much closer than last night's escapade.'

'You're not going to let me forget that, are you?'

She gave him a smile full of the warmth she felt inside. 'It will be nice to get to know you well enough to let you forget, Hugo.' Because she wanted to get to know him better. She wanted to make a friend. A true friend. Not one that was looking for a way into Princess Cassandra's inner circle. But one that she could confide in and who could talk to her in return. 'If you will come for coffee again?'

'I'd like that, Cassie. Very much.'

CHAPTER FOUR

THE NEXT MORNING Hugo was eating his breakfast while reviewing the financial headlines when his phone started to ring. He checked the ID. Mickie. On a Sunday. This early?

His friend rarely saw 8:00 a.m. on a weekday, let alone on a Sunday.

What kind of mischief had his friend got into now?

He swiped the call to answer and prepared himself for the worst. Of course, there was nothing to say Mickie wasn't on the other side of the globe in which case it would be late rather than early for him. And that probably made the potential trouble worse...

'Hugo, my friend, you got something you want to tell me?'

'I don't know that I do, since you're the one calling me?'

Mickie's laugh rumbled down the phone. 'So that's how you're going to play it?'

'Play what?' Hugo put down the toast he was about to bite into. 'It's too early for riddles, Mickie.'

'Come on, don't be coy! Fancy my surprise this morning when I wake up to see you plastered all over the celebrity gossip channels.'

'The *what*?'

'Funny, you sound about as shocked as I was.'

'Is this some joke?' Hugo pressed his forehead into his palm and took a breath. It really was too early for this.

'Skylar, chuck us that remote...' his friend said.

'Skylar?' Hugo repeated. 'Who's...?'

'My date from last night. You didn't think I was the one catching up with the celeb goss, did you?'

Hugo didn't know what to think. Didn't *want* to think for fear of what was happening outside his four walls if Mickie knew all about it and thought it was worthy of this kind of a call.

'Thank you, darl.'

'For what?' Hugo said.

'I wasn't talking to you.'

Clearly, but...

'Get yourself onto Celeb 101, Hugo. Your mug's right there, right now.'

'Celeb 101?'

'Use the TV guide...you'll have it there somewhere. Right next to those 24-7 reality TV channels...'

Like Hugo would know where any of those were either...but on autopilot, he switched on the TV embedded in the wall above his sleek black countertop. Searched the guide with rising trepidation. Especially as his phone started to chime with another incoming call, then another. He eyed the screen. One was Eduardo, another was his PA.

This wasn't good. His skin started to crawl, the hairs on his neck rising. There was only one reason he could have made that kind of news...one reason only...

'You found it yet?'

Just. He clicked on the channel and the screen filled with a pimped-up news studio starring living, breathing Ken and Barbie lookalikes seated behind a desk. A fuchsia-pink ticker tape ran along the bottom spewing out 'news'. And there, in the top right corner of the screen were photos. Photos of *them*. Cassie and Hugo. Him on her doorstep with the flowers. Her with her naked shoulder, all flushed and—*for the love of...*

'In the two years since her separation from Prince Georges,' the Barbie lookalike was saying, 'speculation has mounted over the breakdown of what was once considered the marriage of the decade if not the century. A real life fairy tale has become a tale of tragedy. People were quick to blame it on the Playboy Prince, his reputation making him an easy target, but with stories surrounding the Princess, friends and ex-lovers selling stories to the tabloids, and now this latest scandal, it really does beg the question, do we truly know who this woman is? We were so quick to adore her, yet here she is jumping from the bed of one man to another, the seal on her divorce barely dry. And who is this man? Our very own Suzie is out in the field to tell us more...'

'Got to hand it to you, man, I didn't know you had it in you.'

He'd forgotten Mickie was on the line. He'd forgotten the world existed. He'd forgotten everything but the woman next door and the impact such a report was going to have on her.

Such a ridiculous report, but a report out in the world all the same. And one with a picture to back it up. A picture he might as well as have handed to the greedy mob pounding the pavement outside...

Taken inside *his* hotel, on *his* watch, on *his* floor. *'Merde!'*

Cassie hadn't slept. Not properly. She kept tossing and turning, feeling the after-effects of Hugo's presence well into the night. The apartment had never felt so vast and so empty...even with Louis's abundance of ornamental delights.

She'd become accustomed to her own company long ago. Being in her own company amongst others most of all. Loneliness was something she'd learnt to live with rather than bemoan. And normally she would throw her restlessness into her designs or lose herself in the pages of a good book. Always something creative if she could choose.

But she'd been left with this frenetic energy that she just couldn't shift, so here she was on the treadmill, trying her second run of the morning because all else had failed. She increased her speed because a jog wasn't working. Turned the volume on her music up too.

A sprint to Taylor Swift full blast—this *had* to work, surely?

She snatched up her towel from the rail on the treadmill to swipe away the layer of perspiration already thick across her skin. Adjusted her earbuds. Slugged her water. And felt Swift's lyrics to her core as she pounded the rolling road beneath her feet.

For years she'd worked hard to be the woman her family had wanted her to be, eager to please them, eager for a kind word too. Then it had been all about the Prince and *his* family. Trading one impossible mission for another.

She hadn't stopped to think about her own happiness in any of it. She'd been too focused on their happiness equating to her own. Now she'd finally broken free. Finally realised the only person she could truly depend on for her own happiness was herself. And to achieve it, she needed to find herself. Who she was without the noise of the outside world and the constraints she'd lived her life bound by thus far. And she was getting there. Kind of.

So why did she feel all at sea again?

She had no clue and she wasn't hopping off this treadmill until the noise in her brain resembled something more like the quiet she had found of late. The quiet of—

The ring of the apartment's ancient doorbell broke through Swift's triumphant chorus, and she checked the time. Frowned. It was still early. Not that the time made any difference to her surprise. She wasn't expecting anyone.

Room service had already been and gone with her breakfast plates. That day's housekeeping too. It came again, more insistent. She hadn't imagined it.

She hit the pause button and grabbed her towel, headed to the door.

It couldn't be Hugo. It had been a day. Twenty-four hours since their impromptu coffee date. Her eyes caught on the flowers he had brought her, the classic white bouquet blooming bright and beautiful in the hallway. He had no reason to call again so soon. Unless— she smiled helplessly into her towel—he too had found himself in some curious state of limbo since he'd vacated her orbit. How weird that would be.

Weird and kind of wonderful if she was being totally honest with herself.

Careful, Cassie, don't be getting carried away.

Especially over a man like Hugo, who would be so easy to get carried away by…

She was supposed to be focusing on herself and what she wanted from life.

But what if that something was a six-foot-four hunk of male charm?

And that was precisely the kind of want that would land her in trouble. The kind of trouble her ex and the rest of the royal family would use to their advantage and she would do well to avoid. Though who was to say he was interested in her in the same way? She hardly had the best track record when it came to reading others. Case in point!

Love, affection, desire…what did she truly know of it? A bit fat zero.

Hugo had been kind and understanding, that was all, and now she was likely projecting her own feelings onto him. Just as she had done with Georges in those early days.

She caught her reflection in the free-standing gilt-edged mirror at the end of the hall and grimaced. Both at her thoughts and at her flushed state of disarray. Hardly presentable. Unless one was trying out for a sports advertisement, and even then she'd leave a lot to be desired. She lacked the glow of sun exposure for a start.

And here she was, debating her appearance like it was him on the other side of the door, projecting her hopes, when it was probably—

The doorbell rang again, and this time Hugo's urgent cry came with it, 'Cassie!'

Okay, so it *was* him, but his voice…

With a sharp frown, she swiftly unbolted the door and yanked it wide. 'Hugo, what's wrong?'

'Cassie, Dieu merci!'

He grabbed her arms and she stiffened, heat surging to her already scorched core. Tiny, frenzied currents, the likes of which she'd never felt before and barely understood now, zipping through her and spreading fast.

She gawped up at him and he cursed, his hands falling away as he stepped back to give her space.

'Désolé. I shouldn't have.'

She closed her mouth, swallowed. What was going on within her? Desire? Is that what this was? The heat, the fire, the need…because Georges had never done this to her. Not with a simple grasp of his hands.

'You *are* okay?' His desperate gaze raked over her. 'Aren't you?'

Answer him…

She nodded, her unease building by the second. Because the words coming out of his mouth suggested something was wrong. Very wrong. And it was pressing back the heat his contact had stirred up, common sense overriding her body as she forced the words through her teeth, 'What's wrong?'

'You don't know?' He dragged a hand down his face. 'You haven't seen the news? How can you—can I come in?'

'So many questions, Hugo.' She gave a shaky laugh, clutched her towel beneath her chin as goose-bumps prickled across her skin. Aware more than ever that she was wearing nothing more than an exercise bra and cropped shorts.

'And I'm not the only one with questions, believe me.'

A trickle ran down her spine, the chill on the rise as she dabbed at her cheeks, which felt fuzzy and faint. 'You're scaring me.'

'I know and I'm sorry, Cassie. But it's best we talk inside.'

She backed up, making enough space for him to enter as he swung the door closed on them both. Though she didn't move from the vestibule. Her stomach rolling too much to put one foot in front of the other.

'What is it?' she said to his back as he made his way into the living area, scanning the room like one would for danger, checking every nook, every cranny.

'Hugo?'

'I thought you would have seen. I thought you weren't answering because you *had* seen, and you were—I don't know. Despairing. Panicking. Packing!'

He rubbed the back of his head, up and down, eyes chasing over the objects in the room, anywhere but her, and slowly she joined him.

'How could you not have heard the commotion out there?'

He threw a hand towards the balcony and the muted sounds beyond. Granted, there was more noise coming from the street than usual. But she'd long ago stopped listening to what happened outside the four walls she was in. Beyond the conversation she was involved in too. The whispered words of judgement, the gossip, and the snide remarks.

'Hugo,' she said softly, wishing to steady him, because she sensed that whatever this was, it had more to do with her than it did him. And she was used to her own baggage, he didn't need to carry it for her. 'Whatever it is, I am sure it can't be as bad as—'

'Someone saw me come to your room yesterday morning,' he said as he paced up and down. 'They took a photograph and it's everywhere. *We're* everywhere.'

Cassie's heart did a weird little dance, rising part-way up her throat. 'What do you mean, *we're* everywhere?'

Though she knew, of course she knew. She'd been the subject of enough tittle-tattle over the years to know exactly what he meant. But she was stalling. Biding her time while she processed it.

'I'm sorry, Cassie.'

He stilled, his eyes finding hers. She saw the guilt weighing heavy in his crystal-clear blue eyes. Saw the guilt as she also imagined the glee in her ex-husband's face.

'The world thinks we're together. That you and I—' He shook his head. 'I'm sorry. I don't know how this could have happened, and had I known the trouble I would cause you by coming to your room with flowers and—and the kind of headlines it would stir up...'

Slowly she brought her hand back to her chest, steadied herself against the onslaught of what was to come—what was already happening out there. The Duponts wouldn't hang around. They'd be straight on this salacious piece of ammo, using it to elevate Georges's reputation and sully hers.

And all because she'd had the gall to get up and walk away.

'I don't understand how you didn't know.'

Hugo snapped her back into the present, his face blazing with concern and obliterating Georges from her mind.

'My phone is always on Do Not Disturb,' she said, her voice devoid of emotion. Because this wasn't Hugo's fault. This wasn't hers. And this *would* blow over. It was the nature of the beast. She just had to keep it in perspective. 'I don't watch live TV. I don't listen to the radio. Only the people that I care about and want to hear from get through, the rest I mute.'

'But out there, the noise...' He gestured towards the balcony once more...at the commotion outside that suggested there were more vehicles. More press. More people. The hotel would be cursing her name. *He* would be cursing her name. 'I'm sorry, I will sort myself somewhere else to stay as soon as possible. This is the last thing you and your guests need.'

'Oh, no, you won't. You're fine to stay here.'

'But Hugo...'

'I mean it, Cassie. Louis gifted you his home, and I stand by that offer.'

The stubborn set to his jaw, the flash of steel in his blue eyes told her he meant it. 'I'm sorry.'

'You don't need to apologise to me.'

'Oh, I do. Because if they're making something out of this, I'm sure you're not coming off too lightly either. If not in today's news reports, then tomorrow's. Georges and his ego will see to it.'

'I couldn't care less about myself in all of this. It's you I'm worried about. You must have a PR team, a spokesperson you can liaise with to issue a formal response?'

She gave a soft huff. 'A PR team? Because they don't cost the earth.'

'Right. Of course you don't. We can use mine.'

'No, Hugo. There's no point. They'll print what they want to print. You deny it and they'll think there's more to it. And what are you going to say? Tell them the truth of how we met and tackle *that* tale, too? No. It will blow over. They'll tire of it eventually.'

'And in the meantime, what? You sit back and let them rip apart your character?'

He was so fierce. So ready to fight for her honour. And there was something magical and wonderful and surreal about it. No one had ever looked ready to do battle for her. Not ever.

'Sticks and stones, Hugo.'

'No, Cassie.' He shook his head, legs wide, fists on hips. Fighting stance. 'This happened on my watch, in my hotel. I besmirched your character and I need to fix it.'

'This wasn't your fault.'

He raised his hand. 'It doesn't matter that it wasn't my intent. What's done is done and I will not stand by and have them twist the person you are into someone you are not. You don't deserve it.'

Her heart swooned. *Positively* swooned. 'Then what do you suggest?'

'For starters, I'll be speaking to the head of security. It must have been one of the cleaners from the lift. You can't access this floor without the right pass and there was only me, you, and the staff that morning.'

She shook her head. 'I don't want to cause any more trouble, Hugo. My presence has already caused enough.

All the extra security, the extra checks, the chaos outside the doors… I'm a headache for everyone concerned.'

'But what they did was wrong—it needs to be investigated and the person responsible held accountable.'

'I'd rather just let it blow over.'

'That out there isn't blowing over any time soon, and in the meantime, what? You're going to hide away even more?'

'If I have to.'

'No, Cassie. You've lived your entire life on hold for others. It's time you started living it for you, and you have the city of Paris on your doorstep to get outside and enjoy.'

She gave a shaky laugh. 'No one could enjoy Paris hounded by that lot.'

'I think it's high time you tried another strategy.'

Her chin lifted, ears and heart pricking with something akin to hope. 'Like what?'

'I think you should give them more not less.'

'What on earth are you talking about?'

'They think you and I are together so let them think that. Let them think that rather than a fling, a brazen hop from one man's bed to another, that this is more than that. Deeper than that. A romantic tryst in the world's most romantic of cities. And while we give them more, I can give you what you deserve. I can give you Paris. I can show you the delights of the city, get you out of these four walls and out into the real world. Let me make up for my part in what has happened and give you something you're long overdue in return.'

'I told you…' She gave a laugh that sounded as deranged as she suddenly felt, because his idea was making her feel all manner of things. Some crazy. Some fabulous. Some wonderfully thrilling. 'It isn't possible. I can't step foot out of this building without a gaggle of reporters and photographers dogging my every step, without drawing the attention of every innocent passer-by too and causing chaos. It isn't pleasant for anyone.'

'And so you've hidden yourself away. But by hiding your face, you've made it a rarity. Don't you see?'

'What choice do I have?'

'You can choose to give them more not less. And soon your face will be a novelty no more. And that rare photo opportunity will be as common as the next among a million of snaps. Granted, they won't all be of your best side, but if you can learn to live with the odd stray bit of snot or lucky bird poo drop...?'

'Hugo...' She shook her head, laughing at the ridiculousness of it all. Because it was ridiculous—*wasn't* it?

'Think about it, Cassie. It's all about supply and demand, give them more and they will demand less. And in the meantime, you get out of these four walls and live in the real world.'

'And the stories they are spreading, what about those?'

'By hiding away you've allowed the rumours to build, fed the gossip and the whispers, let them draw their own conclusions. Why not paint the tale you'd rather have spread? A love story, however short-lived, is far better than the harlot they seem determined to label you as.'

'Not them,' she said through her teeth.

'What was that?'

'I said, not them. Georges and his family. They're the ones who want to paint me as such. I told you—it suits them to make me look bad. He needs a new wife and quickly, with his father...'

She bit her lip. She'd said too much. She may not have any affection for the Duponts, but there were things she was not permitted to divulge. The King's health and her ex-husband's imminent succession to the throne being two of them.

'He will need to find someone to replace me as his wife. Someone willing to look past his behaviour and provide him with an heir too.'

Something she'd been unable to give him and something at the time she'd seen as another of her many failings. Now, of course, she saw it as a blessing, because to have a child caught up in all of this... She shivered and wrapped her arms around her middle, and Hugo's eyes dipped, a crease forming between his brows as his hands flexed at his sides.

'Do you want to change, and we can talk? I can wait here.'

'No, it's fine.'

He nodded, though his frown didn't ease. 'So, you think the Prince might have had a hand in this—this photograph?'

'I don't know. Maybe. Perhaps.'

'I assume he knows you're staying here.'

'There's not a lot the Prince doesn't know about me. He has his *spies* everywhere.'

'Then he will also know this is nonsense.'

'So long as it works in his favour, he doesn't care about whether it is true or not.'

'In which case, we'll make it work in our favour too.'

'I really don't see how we can spin this into a positive for us.'

'Everyone loves a good love story, Cassie.' And then he grinned, and it lit her up from within. 'You of all people should know this.'

And he was right.

Her marriage to the Playboy Prince had been one such adored tale once upon a time.

Which was why their breakup carried such media weight now.

Were ex-princesses permitted a second chance at love?

Even if the first had never been a love story at all...

'But, Hugo, you have two global companies to run. You don't have the time to spend ferrying me around Paris.'

'I will make the time. I will give Eduardo the autonomy to run the company he has been running for long enough anyway. And I will take a long overdue holiday from the hotel group, let Zara, my number two step in. Besides, it will do wonders for business...just think of the headlines... *Cassie Couture and Chevalier Clubs, a match made in heaven*—you couldn't write it better!'

She laughed wholeheartedly now. 'Hugo! I'm not even out there as a designer yet.'

'Not yet you're not. But you will be if I have my way.'

She shook her head, her chill forgotten. In fact, she felt positively balmy. All thanks to him.

'But I am serious, Cassie. Being seen on your arm can only do great things for Chevalier Clubs, so you have nothing to fear for me on a personal or professional level. And, dare I say it, we enjoy each other's company, and it has been a long time since I have taken any kind of holiday, as my latest night-time misadventures prove, so I am long overdue a break too. You will be doing me a favour as much as I you.'

How could she turn down such an offer?

He was handing her the perfect solution to her current nightmare.

A chance to come out with her reputation intact, protect her dream, and get back out into the land of the living…but was it right to bury one falsehood with another?

And what choice do you have? The Prince threw you to the wolves the second you dared to leave. It's time to push back. Play them at their own game.

'What's that look about?'

'I've never been…*bad* before.'

He gave a low chuckle. 'It's not all that bad, Cassie. You're divorced. Very much single. I'm single in case you need that clarified. There's nothing wrong with us dating. Nothing to say we didn't meet here in this very building—which we did by the way—then hit it off and chose to date. Like millions of people do every day.'

'And you're okay pretending be in a relationship with me?'

A curious spark came alive behind his eyes. 'It would be an honour to escort you around Paris as your friend, and if the world wants to read more into that, then so be it. But if, on the other hand, you wanted to present us as more than that or even go as far as to make a formal statement about us dating, I will do that too. Your wish is my command.'

And now she laughed. Because this truly was crazy.

And fun. And no matter what he said, it still felt bad. Very, *very* bad.

'But if it makes you laugh like that...' He took her hand in his and squeezed, the look in his eyes stealing her breath away. 'I refuse to believe there can be any bad in it.'

And maybe Hugo was right.

One thing was for sure, it was time she got back out in the world. As her. The *real* her.

Not Cassandra, Princess of Sérignone.

But as Cassie. Fighting for the life *she* wanted.

Nobody else.

And with a little help from Hugo, her very hot, very capable next-door neighbour and new-found friend, that feat didn't feel so impossible any more.

CHAPTER FIVE

'YOU READY?'

Hugo hadn't known it was possible to nod and shake your head at the same time, but Cassie had just perfected the move. And the sight amplified his guilt.

The similarity to Sara had been disconcerting before... with their public-facing roles, controlling families, lack of freedom. Poised yet shy. Quiet yet teasing. Kind too.

And to find himself in this position again.

With Sara it had been his fault. He'd thought their love worth outing, worth fighting for, and then he'd almost got her killed.

With Cassie, he had taken her already troubled situation and piled on a whole heap more. And Cassie was right, it wasn't his fault, but it didn't make the situation any better.

And he was determined to make it better.

He was determined that this time, he would get it right.

He would see to it that she was okay. That she would come out of this situation better for knowing him. Not worse.

'It's going to be okay.' He took hold of her hand. 'We have the best security detail looking out for us. A path has been cleared and all you have to do is smile and wave.'

'All?' She gave a tremulous smile, touched her free hand to the braid that fell over one shoulder. It looked simple but he'd warrant she'd spent hours making sure she'd perfected the casual look this morning. The pale pink sweater complemented her English rose complexion. The skinny jeans, knee-high boots, tailored coat and beret gave off every bit the Princess on tour vibe, whether she wanted to or not. Because she had a regal air about her that was all natural. Something her family and the Duponts would have bled dry.

'Or you could do the classic?' he said, pushing away the thoughts that would have seen his fingers crushing hers.

'And what's that?'

'Pretend they're all naked.'

She laughed. 'I thought that was a presentation technique.'

He shrugged. 'Whatever works, right? And once we arrive at the Louvre you will only have eyes for the museum and the architecture anyway.'

Vincent stepped forward. 'The car is ready, Monsieur Chevalier, Princess.'

Cassie's hand tensed around his. He knew she hated the title. But he also knew it was going to take time for the world to drop it. She was their beloved princess, whether she wanted to be referred to as such or not. If she could only see that it came from a place of affection rather than being a cold-hearted stereotype.

No matter the names being thrown about, the slander coming out of the palace, and the trouble Prince Georges was determined to stir up following *that* photograph. It would take more to ruin the woman most of the world at large adored.

And Hugo would do his best to see to it that they continued to adore her.

By fulfilling this role for as long as she required it.

He'd done some extra digging into the Prince of Sérignone, and the more he'd learnt, the more his protective instincts had kicked in. The idea that the Prince had once had any claim over her riled him enough. The fact he now dared to ruin her from afar to save his own face...

Hugo fought the tension coiling through him anew. But the deceit it took to behave like so, the duplicity and the cowardice too. The nerve of the man to transfer his own crimes onto her.

'Hugo?' Her soft prompt brought him back to his senses.

'Shall we?' He released her hand to offer out his elbow, and she gave him the coy smile the cameras knew well. The smile he knew to be as genuine as she was because she *was* nervous, but she wasn't backing down. The nod she gave him now devoid of its contradictory shake.

'Let's go.'

They stepped through the revolving door together and the wall of noise instantly upped, threatening to press them back. He'd anticipated it, of course he had, though nothing could have prepared him for the reality. And though he had worked in the field many years ago, this felt different. But then it was different. This was personal.

And for a split second, he was in another country, another place, another time. And there was another woman beside him. A cold sweat broke out across his skin, the world closed in. Cameras were going off. Blending with the shouts.

A gun. A man.

He turned.

Left. Right. Ahead. *Bang!*

'Boss.' It was the driver in his earpiece, grounding him in the present. 'Are you good?'

Focus. Focus.

His people were doing their job; they were keeping the crowd back. The car was straight ahead. Everything was good. They were waiting for Cassie and him to deliver the agreed smile, a wave, and then he ushered her into the car.

'Are you okay?' He didn't waste a second to ask.

'Are you?' She blinked up at him. Concern glittering in a sea of green. The black interior all around and the smell of leather, a reassuring cocoon.

'You think to ask me that?'

'I'm used to this, but you...'

He checked her seat belt was secure before fastening his own. 'I know this scene well enough.'

'They were calling your name as much as mine.'

They were also 'name-calling,' but he didn't feel the need to point that out. Not when she could hear it for herself. And though those names were only few and far between, they were the ones that would've landed the loudest and the hardest.

'Drive on,' he urged their driver, his chest too tight for comfort.

'It wasn't as bad as I feared.'

His eyes snapped to hers. 'No?'

Was she mad? Delirious or on something?

She smiled up at him. 'No. Though you're making me question myself now.'

Yes! He mentally cursed. *Get a hold of yourself. You were the one taking a trip down memory lane. Not her. Dieu Merci.*

'You were exceptional.' He righted his jacket, gave a brusque nod and a smile. 'As calm and as regal as a—'

'Don't say it, please.'

'*Désolé.* You took it in your stride, Cassie. No one will have known that inside you were feeling any different... I'm glad you found it okay.'

'That's because you were there.'

She met his eyes, her own big and wide, her vulnerability genuine and tugging on his heartstrings. Strings he never left exposed. Not since Sara—

And that's why you're freaking out now. And you're supposed to be making her feel better. Not worse.

'You and your team.'

He took her hand in his once more and gave it a squeeze.

'Good, because you're stuck with us for the foreseeable.'

He held her gaze as the vehicle pulled away from the hotel, the camera flashes hammering against the blackout glass and the noise of the reporters muffled by the whirring in his ears. She truly was stunning. Her smile, her eyes, her trust in him...

He had this...didn't he?

He could keep her safe and give her a glimpse of the life she deserved.

And what about you? And your heart? And those strings you never leave exposed?

It was a short drive to the Louvre. Nowhere near long enough to ease the tension that had built throughout his body with the flashback that had come from nowhere. But he forced himself to appear at ease for her sake.

Now he just had to hope all went smoothly, because he sensed that his skittish kitten was only one pit bull away from scurrying back to Louis's and he was determined to see this day through. The first of many outings he had planned if all went well...

As for his own tension, he'd deal with that later. If he had to go ten rounds in the ring with Mickie, he'd do whatever it took to exorcise that demon once again.

And be there for Cassie now.

Cassie had felt the impenetrable shield form around her the moment they had left the hotel.

And for someone who had spent years behind a security detail, indeed being directed by one, this felt different. And she knew that was down to Hugo. Something about this great big bear of a man, with warm eyes and a strong sense of honour, made her feel like nothing could hurt her.

No camera flash or threat from afar. No snide remark or snarky look.

Never had her family or the Prince made her feel quite so invincible.

With her head held high, she walked the grounds and the halls of the Louvre, in awe of its beauty and its art. Its history and its majesty. And it was wonderful.

To breathe in the air and the space and be amongst the people too.

They'd even paused and conversed with a few groups. Taken an extended break when Cassie hadn't been able to resist a group of children who had likened Hugo to a real-life superhero. And he'd spent at least twenty minutes 'flexing' his muscles to whatever feat they had devised. Something their teacher had indulged since they were on their lunch break. Though Cassie got the impression it had more to do with Maîtresse's pleasure than the children.

'I think she liked you...'

'Huh?'

'The teacher...are you *blushing* Hugo?'

'Non.'

She paused, forcing him and his team to pause too as she peered up at him. 'Yes, you are.'

'I do not blush.'

She pursed her lips. 'Whatever you say, but for the record, I'm more than happy to share the limelight.'

And he chortled at that, clearly pleased to have her so at ease.

Because she was at ease. Surprisingly so.

She couldn't care that the headlines that morning had been less than kind. That they had smacked of the Prince's skilled spin doctors. She was living in the moment, thanks to him. And the more she thought about his whole idea, the rules of supply and demand, it really did make sense.

'This really is wonderful, Hugo. Truly. Thank you.'

'You're welcome. Now, are you hungry?'

Was she? She hadn't thought about food at all. Her

senses were too busy being overloaded by the sights, sounds, and scents of Paris, having spent the last month cooped up in Louis's apartment. But she must be.

It had been many hours since breakfast—a coffee and the smallest dollop of yogurt on fruit had been all she could manage with the nervous churn, courtesy of the headlines.

'I reckon I could eat.'

'That's lucky.'

'Lucky?'

To their left, a grand doorway had been roped off and a liveried footman bowed his head to them both.

She frowned. 'Hugo, what's this?'

'I believe it is the location for dinner.'

'In the Louvre? But the restaurant is back...'

'I thought you might enjoy some privacy for our meal.'

'But I thought the whole point was to give them more and they will demand less?'

'But I'm also a firm believer in balance. There will be a gazillion photos from this morning, Cassie. Now *this* is for you.'

He placed his hand in the small of her back, and she caught the sudden gasp that wanted to escape. It wasn't like his hand was hot. Or that she could feel his palm's heat through her coat, the cashmere of her sweater or the silk of her camisole but she *felt* it.

'This?' The question was more breath than spoken word.

'You'll see...'

He led her through the door that was now being held open to them. A classical tune played softly through some invisible sound system, and inside, the rich red walls created an intimate backdrop for the table that had been lavishly laid out for two with a gold candelabra adorned with white roses at its heart. And to the side, glass cabinets had been rolled in on wheels, each displaying pieces of art.

She sent him a questioning look, unable to form a word.

'When you've worked in the hospitality industry for as long as I have, you build up an extensive contact list... and the odd favour or two.'

'*This* was a favour?'

He didn't reply, only smiled as she made her way over to one of the cabinets. Hand to her throat because she couldn't believe any of this was real. That Hugo had organised this. It was too much. Too sweet. Too thoughtful.

'I arranged for them to be brought from the Prints and Drawings Study Room. They can only be viewed by appointment anyway, and I thought...well, enjoy.'

She looked down and gave a soft chuckle. 'The Gallery of Fashion by Heideloff... You brought these here.'

He came up behind her. 'Not me *personally...*'

She gave him the elbow. 'Funny.'

'Like I already told you, I don't know much about fashion, but a quick search of the Louvre brought up this collection, and I thought since we're here, it might inspire you with your work and...'

He leaned over her shoulder to take a closer look, his warmth, his masculine woody scent enveloping her as he did so. She felt her eyes threaten to close, the desire to savour the moment as ludicrous as it was real.

'Though looking at them now, I can see how foolish *that* was.'

She forced her eyes to widen at his sarcasm, forced herself to take in the beauty of the drawings that were over two hundred years old. 'Hugo! They're of their time, but no less exquisite!'

'Of their time? How you women managed to sit down let alone put one foot in front of the other in all those skirts is beyond me.'

'But look how delicate they are, and who doesn't love a good fan?'

He gave a soft chuckle.

'You laugh, but back then a fan could convey a multitude of secret messages.'

'Right,' he drawled.

'I'm serious! They weren't just a beautiful accessory but a way of communicating with a lover or a would-be suitor…it could be as innocent as declaring your wish to stay friends or as ardent as "I love you".'

She could feel her cheeks warm under his gaze, though she kept her own fixed on the images beneath the glass. They truly were beautiful.

'Seems dangerously open to interpretation to me. I'm a literal man. You've got to tell me how it is.'

She laughed. 'I'll remember that—*not that we're…*'

She let her words trail away with the background music as her blush deepened further. The effect of his body so close behind her, enough to make her feel like he was a furnace in full flame.

'Monsieur. Madam. Dinner is ready if you are?'

An older gentleman entered the room and she sidestepped away, feeling oddly caught in the act. The act of what she wasn't sure. Only that her blush made her look as guilty as she felt. But to have someone other than Hugo address her as something other than princess... to know that Hugo must have had a word...that he had done all of this for her too. She was walking on air and her smile filled her face.

'Favours go a long way,' Hugo whispered in her ear, his hot breath rushing through her veins as his thoughtfulness continued to warm her heart. 'Henri, it is so good to see you again.' Hugo swung away from her to greet him. His handshake and arm clutch the kind one would give an old friend, not an acquaintance delivering on a favour.

'And you, sir. I trust everything is as you wanted.'

'Impeccable, merci.'

She felt the older man's curious gaze drift to her and she kept her gaze lowered. She was giving too much away. For a woman used to locking her true feelings and thoughts inside, this was definitely too much. But then she wasn't used to someone doing such things for her. Such deep and meaningful things. And she felt overwhelmed. Tearful even.

'And you're sure you want us to leave the food to the side?'

'Absolutely, Henri, we will serve ourselves. We have everything we need.'

And they did, because as the two men talked, another two delivered trolleys laden with food and drink. More than she and Hugo could ever hope to consume in their time here.

'All we require now is privacy.'

'And for that you have come to the right place.'

'Thank you, Henri.'

Henri clipped his heels together and bowed. *'Bon appetit, monsieur...madame.'*

'Merci,' she managed to say with a shaky smile.

'Do you want to help yourself while I pour us a drink?' Hugo said, checking the labels on the bottles. 'Would you like some wine or some champagne perhaps?'

'Champagne would be lovely.'

Because it truly would. And, *oh, my*, she simpered on over to the exquisitely arranged trolley. What on earth was wrong with her? She was used to people going overboard to make her feel welcome when she visited establishments. To serve and to lavish her with the best they had to offer, but this was so different to all of that.

Just as Hugo's protection felt different to all that had come before.

'Are you okay?'

She sensed his frown rather than saw it, because for the life of her she couldn't look at him. Not with the tears in her eyes, and the chaotic race of her thoughts and her feelings.

'Of course. This is incredible, Hugo.' She focused on filling her plate with all manner of delicacies, not that she saw a single one. 'I'm just a little overcome, if I'm honest.'

'But you must be used to such attention? I know you're not used to serving yourself dinner but for the rest...'

She spun to face him. 'No, Hugo!' She placed the plate down before she dropped it, her entire body trembling as she shook her head. 'I'm not used to any of this!'

He paled as he straightened from the table—champagne forgotten. 'Cassie?'

'I'm sorry! It's just too sweet. Too thoughtful. Too—just too much! *All* of it. Georges knew my passion for fashion. And that rhymed and it wasn't meant to rhyme.' She gave a laugh that sounded as silly and as stupid and as ungracious as she suddenly felt. 'But never would he have thought to arrange such a private viewing. So intimate and thoughtful and caring. Yet here you are, knowing me what—a few days? Whisking me up in this…all of this?' She lifted an unsteady hand to gesture around her at the beauty of it all, her eyes misting over. 'It is too much and yet it is wonderful, and I am so grateful and I am so sorry because I am not behaving like one who is grateful should.'

He was across the room in a heartbeat. His hands wrapped around hers. His body—tall, strong, and warm—before her. 'Breathe, Cassie. Just breathe.'

She did as he commanded. Took a breath and another. Looked up into his eyes that were calm and steady and sure.

'It's okay. You are okay. Nothing can hurt you here. No one can hurt you here.'

She shook her head. 'I don't know how I can repay you for this—this kindness you have shown me.'

'You insult me by suggesting that such an act requires payment. This has been a pleasure shared, Cassie. To see you leave that hotel room has been all the payment I need.'

'But it is too much, all of this. You know I have no money of my own. Not yet.'

'I care not for your money but your happiness.'

And there was such strength to those words, such warmth to his touch, his hands caressing her own, his body pressed so close to hers that she felt like she could combust on the spot and would still be the most deliriously happy person alive.

'Apologies, Cassie, yet again I overstep.' He broke away from her, so quickly she staggered back. 'Please excuse me.'

She snatched his hand back, eager to reassure. Eager all the more to make him see that this was more on her than it was on him. It was her own insecurity, her own uncertainty about where her head was at, her life and her heart, to know what was and wasn't okay.

Hell, her friends, those people that she could really trust, were few and far between, and he was so new and so dizzying in the way he made her feel, too.

Feelings that, if she was truly honest, she had no experience in understanding or trusting, let alone managing.

Especially when she feared that she was projecting those feelings onto him too.

'There's nothing to excuse...' And leaning up on her tiptoes, she pressed a kiss to his cheek. It was fleeting and barely there and very much driven on impulse. 'Thank you, Hugo. For getting me out of the apartment and for all of this. Georges may bear the title, but as far as fairy tales go, you most definitely befit the role.'

And then she turned away before she said anything more revealing, *did* anything more revealing, and focused on the delicious spread of food to devour rather than the man.

Though, if she were given the freedom of choice, she knew in a heartbeat which would win.

CHAPTER SIX

A FEW DAYS LATER, Hugo knocked on Cassie's door.

He'd called ahead to make sure she was up for a day out. Told her to layer up in outdoor exercise gear and left it at that.

She'd been in the public eye a lot over the past week. Following the success of the Louvre, they'd crammed in plenty—the Palace of Versailles, the Musée d'Orsay, Sacré-Coeur—the list went on and the press were spoilt for choice when it came to pictures and stories. Last night's trip to the opera had been particularly romantic and snap-worthy.

Though today was once again about striking a balance, gifting her Paris and some anonymity in one, and it was either going to be a brilliant surprise or an epic disaster. He couldn't wait to find out which.

The security detail could though. Their faces when he'd told them what they'd be doing…he should have recorded it for his father. That would have made the old man laugh.

Not that his parents knew about Cassie yet, because if they'd heard, *he* would have heard. And right now, digi-detox land was gifting him more than just a quiet life workwise, it was protecting him from the third degree on a personal level. Because his mother would be all over this, her excitement unbearable.

Almost as unbearable as his father and his work interference.

He was going to have to get ahead of it and tell them the truth *before* his mother got wedding planning. Though he had a few weeks before they were out of digi-prison—his father's choice of name—and that should buy him some time. He could cross that bridge then.

And he'd just tell them the truth. It was a fake relationship to protect a good woman's reputation. Hell, his father might even be proud of him. They were well protected by the firm. And ultimately, Cassie wasn't Sara, so he wasn't about to make a public fool of himself. They would manage the breakup, when it came to it, with dignity on both sides. No harm, no foul. Simple.

Her door opened and she smiled up at him, all tentative and unsure as she finished tying her hair back into a ponytail. 'Will I do?'

He took a second to steady his heart, another to reply...and even then, he paused to look at her, truly look at her. Taking far too much pleasure in drinking her in, but knowing she wanted his honest opinion.

Was there anything this woman couldn't pull off? She was wearing trainers, socks slouched at the ankles, black leggings, and a sports jacket zipped high to her chin—nothing sexy about it but...

Just tell them the truth, he quoted himself back. *But which truth? That this is a fake relationship or that you find her sexy?*

'Are you windproof?' he said, ignoring the inner taunt as he mentally waved the platonic flag...though he might as well have waved a red rag to a bull. 'We're not due any rain but without any cloud cover the wind has a bite to it.'

'I'll be good.' She pursed her lips. Green eyes sparkling. 'Thanks, Mum. And that's a compliment by the way, because my mum was all about how we looked and *not* whether we caught our death.'

His cheeks warmed while his heart chilled over the woman he'd now been able to put a face to thanks to one of his late night googling sessions while catching up on some work. Yes, he'd taken some overdue holiday, but there were some things he couldn't just drop last minute, not at his level.

'Of course she was. But just in case, do you have a buff?'

'A what?'

'A neck warmer? Something you can pull up over your face?'

Which would also have the added benefit of concealing her lips from view...lips which seemed to get more alluring and distracting by the day. And how was that even possible?

She unzipped her pocket and pulled out a tube of fleece from her pocket, her smile proud as punch. 'You mean one of these.'

A brusque nod. 'That'll do. Let's go.'

'Wait.' She grabbed his arm as he started to race away, and he had to resist the urge to snatch it back as the connection thrummed through his veins, leaving him craving more of the same. 'Do I need my purse, a drinks bottle, snacks, anything else?'

'Everything else is taken care of.'

She gave him a peculiar look. 'You going to tell me what we're doing?'

'You'll find out soon enough.'

She let him go and closed her door. 'Are you always so mysterious?'

He didn't reply and she hooked her fingers in his as they headed for the elevator. A connection they had come to do so often when in company of late that she obviously did it now, and ordinarily it would be fine. But they weren't in company yet, and there was no one around to put a damper on what she had sent licking along his veins...

'What's that frown for?'

'Huh?'

She was pressing the button for the lift, but her green eyes were very much on him.

'Nothing.'

'Liar. I've not known you very long, Hugo, but I know when you're pensive about something.'

The elevator pinged, launching him back to the discomfort of *that* night and the present moment in one, and he propelled himself inside as soon as the doors slid open, taking her with him.

'Hugo?'

His eyes slid to hers.

Nom de Dieu, she's had enough dishonesty in her life...just give her something.

'If you really must know, I was thinking that I'll have to come clean to my parents about our relationship and the reasons behind it at some point.'

'Oh, goodness, of course.' Her eyes flared up at him.

'I'm sorry I hadn't even considered it. How thought-less of me!'

'Hey.' He squeezed her hand. 'These are my parents, my concern, and we don't need to worry about them just yet. They're still enjoying my birthday gift, remember? We have a few weeks' grace.'

'You reckon news isn't going to slip through the re-sort's net?' She gave a dubious laugh. 'I can't imagine any place on this earth being *that* secure.'

'Depends on how desperate you are to get a fix, I guess.'

'Your father strikes me as the kind to get his hands on a phone at the very least.'

'If he does, the last thing my father will be checking is the celebrity news.'

She gave another laugh. 'True. Though are you sure one of your staff isn't going to let something slip about the boss of the hotel chain? Especially when the father of said boss is a guest...'

'I think that makes them all the more likely to be dis-creet, don't you?'

'You put a lot of faith in your staff.'

'I do.'

She eyed him from beneath her lashes.

'What's that look about?'

She chewed the corner of her mouth.

'Cassie?'

'Did you find out who took the photo?'

He clenched his jaw. He hadn't wanted her to ask because he hadn't wanted to tell her, but he wouldn't lie. 'Yes.'

'And?'

'It's been dealt with.'

'Hugo, please...?'

'She was a young, single mum. Desperate for the money. She passed all the checks, there was no reason for my team to be concerned. Though we can assure you changes are being made to avoid the same thing happening again.'

'I see.' She fell silent for a moment then, 'Did you report her to the police?'

She sounded sad, forlorn, and his mouth twisted to the side as he thought of the young woman's face, the evidence of drug addiction too obvious to ignore.

'No, Cassie. I did not. Vincent has put her in touch with a women's support group that his wife is involved in. Hopefully getting help that way will set her on a path to a better future.'

She looked up at him, the golden light of the lift sparkling in her emerald depths.

'What's that look about?'

'I'm not sure you want to know.'

'No?'

She shook her head. Her ponytail sashaying down her back and taunting him further.

'Cassie...' It was a low growl and she nipped her lip, eyes still sparkling.

'You really don't, Hugo.'

He reached out and hit the emergency stop button. 'I'll be the judge of that.'

Her eyes flared. 'Hugo! You can't stop the lift.'

'It's my lift, I can do what I like. Now, I gave you the truth, so out with it.'

She lifted her chin, the defiant angle triggering a rush

of heat south. 'If you really must know, you give off this Mr Suave Sophisticated Hotelier Tough Guy vibe, but you're as soft as they come, Mr Chevalier. An absolute teddy bear! And you should be out in the suburbs setting up a home with some lovely woman and popping out glorious mini-Chevaliers with hearts as good as their papa's.'

Her finger was pressed into his chest by the time she had finished her little speech. Her cheeks were streaked with the passion of her words and her mouth was parted on her last breath and her eyes held his, fierce and determined.

'Is that so?'

And hell, she could have said anything, done anything and he would have taken it, because in that moment she was glorious, impassioned, and so far removed from the wallflower who had been hiding out in her room that first morning.

'It is so.'

'*Monsieur, madame, quel est le problème avec l'ascenseur?*'

Hugo looked up at the camera above his head, to where Vincent was likely eyeing them in confusion and gave an apologetic wave.

'*Tout va bien*, Vincent.'

He sent the lift back on its journey to the basement, where his team were waiting to kit them out with their mode of transport for the day. And counted his lucky stars for the camera keeping watch and his team that would continue to keep watch. All holding him to account that day and every other day, because what he'd been about to do no one should have witnessed.

And his good conscience should not have permitted. He was supposed to be helping Cassie on a journey to a better life, not complicating it.

As for what she'd said, it was so close to what his mother had been begging him for since he'd turned thirty. But as he'd made clear, he had no interest in going there. His relationship with Sara had left him scarred not just physically but emotionally. And whilst the former had healed, the latter not so much. And his mother knew it.

Knew it and still she pressed, wanting him to move on. To find love, to trust and have a family of his own. But you couldn't simply stitch the heart back together. It didn't just heal.

A strange warmth crept along his arm and he looked down to find Cassie's thumb caressing the back of his hand. A mindless caress that had him clearing his throat. Did she even know she was doing it?

The lift came to a gentle stop at the basement level, and he pulled his hand free, raked it over his hair.

'I hope you had a hearty breakfast,' he said, more for something grounding to say as the elevator doors opened and they stepped out.

'You know exactly what I had—you sent it.'

'But did you eat it?'

'I ate— Oh, my God, Hugo! You're kidding!' She came to a standstill, her hands pressed to her cheeks as she took in the van ahead with the bikes, the bags, all the equipment and his team...

'It's not quite running but you said you missed the wind in your hair, the freedom. I figured this was the next best thing. And with the helmets and the clothing, no one will even know it's us sneaking out of here on the bikes.'

'They'll work it out at some point.'

'Let them. I think we rock the exercise gear, don't you?'

She laughed, her cheeks warming under his gaze that was likely ablaze with far too much appreciation and not enough jest.

'And your team are up for this?'

'They're all up for it, aren't you, guys?'

There were a few grunts, a few smiles, even some boisterous lunges from the back. 'We have an inconspicuous mix of runners, cyclists, and a car. We're good. We'll get to see some sights and so long as the weather holds, we'll have a late picnic in the Bois de Boulogne. Maybe even spot a red squirrel or two.'

Before he could say anything else, her arms were around his neck, and she was squeezing the very air out of him. 'Thank you!'

'Well, we haven't left yet. This could be my craziest idea so far, cycling and picnicking at this time of year in Paris, but I figured it gave you the best chance of beating the foot traffic.'

She dropped back just enough to look into his eyes. 'See! Teddy bear!'

And then she was racing off to get her bike, and his team were all easy smiles and eager to please because nothing was too much trouble when Cassie was in the room. Nothing whatsoever.

The spell she cast over all around her was as effortless as it was unintentional.

No wonder the Prince was behaving like a man still half mad, a man still half possessed by her…

Hugo had breathed the same air for a week and it might as well have been a year for all he felt overrun by her.

She mounted her white-framed bike and tested out its bell, her laugh lighting up his world, and he accepted that he didn't mind being overrun at all. Not if it meant he was going to get it right this time and she was going to walk away happier for having met him.

And what about you? Are you going to walk away happier? Whole?

But this wasn't about him. This was about her.

Cassie not Sara.

And he had this, he reminded himself firmly. This time, he had it, because he wasn't a man being led by his heart but his head. He was in control. And he would do this to make up for the past and fix the future for a woman who had no one else to fight in her corner for her.

Though if he was honest, he could see her fighting for herself very soon.

Cycling around Paris with Hugo made Cassie wonder why she hadn't thought of getting a bike sooner. With the helmets and all the layers, no one recognised them to begin with. The varying modes of transport meant the team as a whole blended in with the general population, and at their core, they just looked like a group of friends taking a ride out.

And it was amazing. To act the tourist, to *be* a tourist. To be able to stop and take photos, rather than be the subject of them. To have a drink and sample the street food, rather than dine at prearranged times and prebooked establishments.

To see and experience the real Pah-ree!

They weaved their way to the Bois de Vincennes—a sprawling expanse of woodland to the east of the city—and from there he told her they would take the Rive Gauche, the left bank of the Seine all the way along to the Bois de Boulogne, another stretch of woodland to the west. Though if she was honest, as she took in the boats floating on the picturesque Lac Daumesnil, she felt the smallest pang of envy.

'Would you like to do that another day?'

She found him looking over his shoulder at her. Was there anything this guy didn't detect? He seemed as skilled as any one of the bodyguards. The way he scanned a fresh room. The way his body somehow managed to be ahead and behind her all at once. The way he seemed to spy a potential problem before the team could fully express it.

There was the feeling of being safe and protected because of Hugo, and then there was the feeling of being all warm and fuzzy and cherished because of Hugo.

And that's where things got tricky...

'I wasn't expecting so much hesitation after such a smile of longing.'

She gave an abrupt laugh. 'Don't you have a job you need to get back to? You've already taken a week out to show me the city.'

And now she just sounded ungrateful.

She bit her cheek and winced.

'Eduardo is thriving now he's off the Chevalier leash.

And Zara, once she picked herself up off the floor, is very grateful to have been entrusted to run things in the hotel group for a while. Your appearance in my life couldn't have come at a better time it would appear.'

'To be considered a blessing when I've been something of a distraction...' She shook her head. 'I never thought I'd hear that one.'

He slowed his bike so that he was alongside her, his piercing blue eyes seeking out hers, which she purposefully kept averted. 'That wasn't what you were thinking about though, so stop trying to distract me and spill.'

'You need to keep your eyes ahead Mr Chevalier, else you'll end up in the lake *today*.'

'Are we back to titles, Princess?'

She winced. He was right. And she knew why she'd done it. She was hiding behind the respectful form of address, using it to create distance between them, which wasn't fair. Not when he had done nothing wrong, and everything right. Not when she was purely protecting herself by pushing him away, inflicting hurt in the process, and that wasn't on.

'Sorry, Hugo. Consider me told.'

'I don't need you told. I just need you to stop it.' He smiled. 'And you don't need to tell me where your head has gone, not if you don't want to. Your private thoughts are your own and I'll respect that.'

She shook her head. 'It's just... Why are you doing this, Hugo?'

'Because I want to.'

He sent her a guarded look that she so desperately wanted to rip apart and understand. Regardless of the privacy he had just granted her. Which she knew was about as unfair as her pushing him away, and still she pressed. 'But why?'

'Because I couldn't bear the thought of you trapped another day inside that apartment with all of this on your doorstep.'

'I would have got out eventually.'

'And that's the problem—*eventually*! Life's too short to live your life like that. Trapped by what you can't control.'

'So, you thought to lure me out?'

'I figured it was high time you had yourself an ally, someone to fight in your corner with you... Is that so bad?'

'No.'

'And I'm afraid it's in my nature. You speak to my mother and I was always one for bringing home the stray and injured when I was a kid. Not that I'm comparing you to the stray and injured,' he hurried to add when she gave a choked laugh. 'But I'm serious...if you ever meet her, she'll likely tell you the tale of the water boatman I tried to save from drowning, not that I knew what he was at the time.'

She frowned. 'Water boatmen. But don't they...?'

'Swim. Yes. I soon learnt as much. Once she got over her fit of the giggles.'

'Oh, Hugo, you really are a—'

'No more teddy bear, please. It's bad enough that my father always accused me of being too soft. And I was four.'

'Yes, and now you're a full-grown man...'

One sexy specimen of a man who she had all these feelings for, and she didn't know what to do with them or whether he felt them too. And that was scaring the hell out of her. Not that she was about to tell him that.

'And you have a company to run and friends you must want to spend time with. A family too. You shouldn't be out here, spending all your spare time with me.'

'I told you, my parents are on their retreat, and yes, I have friends of which you are now one. As for work, a perk of being the boss is that I get to choose when I do it, which is something I've forgotten in recent years. Besides, this is kind of working, getting to see this side of the business that I've not been a part of in so long.'

'But I'm not paying you.'

And what did he mean—*a part of in so long*? Had he worked for his father? And when?

'See it as extra training on their part.'

'And do they need it? The extra training?'

He grinned.

'Hugo?'

'We only employ the best, Cassie.'

And there was her answer...he wasn't boasting, he was simply stating a fact. And she admired him for it. Her gaze swept over every chiselled feature in his stocky frame, which somehow managed to look lithe and athletic as he pedalled beside her.

'I'm sure you do.'

'But the best always leave room for improvement.'

She snorted. 'My father would see that as some kind of ridiculous riddle never to be solved.'

'Impossibly high standards?'

'You could say that.'

'And your mother?'

'You know the saying, if you can't say anything nice, don't say anything at all?'

'*Oui.*'

'I think she makes it her mission in life to live by the opposite.'

'Oh.'

'She's a delight.'

They fell silent as the path narrowed into single file for a stretch before widening once more and he was back alongside her.

'I was thinking about how safe you make me feel, Hugo. Just now,' she blurted before she could chicken out a second time. 'When you asked. It's not just about your team, the security detail, but it's you, how thoughtful you are, how your presence is like this shield that's several times your physical size, and it...it feels good.'

Heat bloomed in her cheeks and she hoped he'd attribute it to the exertion and not the extra kick to her pulse that her confession had triggered. Though maybe it was as simple as what Hugo himself had said. That he *was* her ally. Her champion. That for the first time in her life, she had someone to encourage her to go after what she wanted for a change. And it felt good.

It didn't have to mean she was starting to have *feelings* for him. Messy. Complicated. Feelings. That ran deeper than friendship.

'*Bien.* That makes me happy.'

'You said something just now, something about seeing this side of the business after all this time...does that mean you used to work for your father?' she found herself asking, needing the focus off her, but also wanting to understand what he'd meant. Whether he'd tried it out and walked away at some point. Whether, like her, he'd chosen to break away from the expectations of others.

'I did,' he said after a long pause. 'Many years ago.'

He didn't look at her now, the tension in his jaw telling her he wasn't happy with the change in topic. She wanted to press, but she also wanted the man at ease back.

Ahead, the art deco masterpiece that was the Palais de la Porte Dorée came into view—something she'd only previously glimpsed from the speed of a passing vehicle. She wanted to stop and take a closer look. The National Museum of Immigration History was something that truly interested her, but she also knew that as soon as their helmets came off, the anonymity they were enjoying would swiftly be gone.

The noise of the traffic built as they came to the edge of the park and they slowed to a stop in silence. Took a drink.

'My father is a hard man to please,' he surprised her by saying. 'I had to do more than prove myself before I joined his company. I had to prove myself above and beyond those that he employed, because heaven forbid it looked like he'd given his son a free ride.'

'Would you have had it any other way though? Truthfully'

He gave a soft huff, took another slug from his bottle. 'I would have taken a kind word occasionally, some encouragement… I guess I resented it at the time.'

She frowned. 'The fact that he made you work for it?'

'No, not that. But the fact that he made me feel like nothing I ever did was good enough. Until one day something changed, and he saw me. Congratulated me. Welcomed me in.'

'And let me guess.' She smiled as she thought about how much that must have meant to him, meant to them both. 'By that time, you were better than all the rest?'

He gave a tight chuckle. 'Are you going to break out into song for me?'

'God, no. You never want to hear me sing.'

'I'll be the judge of that.'

'So, what happened?'

His eyes wavered as they stayed connected with hers, shadows chasing behind his eyes that she couldn't read.

'You ready to go again?'

No, she wanted answers. But she could wait until he was ready. He'd gifted her so much of his precious free time, after all.

She nodded, and they eased off. Falling into single file as they hit the busier streets of the city and though the traffic made conversation impossible, she was no less happy. No less grateful too, because she was out in the fresh air, seeing Paris the best way possible thanks to him.

Her teddy bear made of steel…

CHAPTER SEVEN

'ARE YOU WARM ENOUGH?'

The late-afternoon sun hung low in the sky. Its orange glow more visual than effective at keeping off the chill now that they'd swapped the bikes for the picnic rug. And though their spot beside the lake was sheltered from the wind by the trees and the general public by his team, he was starting to question his choice to dine outdoors.

The autumn chill did mean less of an audience though, which also meant less chance of an unwarranted intrusion and therefore more pleasure for her. Or so he would have thought. But she'd fallen unusually quiet through their meal. Her gaze on the lake turning distant. And, yes, Lac Inférieure, with its pretty little island and its rounded monument dedicated to Napoleon III, deserved to be looked at, but he got the impression she wasn't seeing any of it.

'I'm fine.' She snuggled deeper into the blanket he'd wrapped around her, the curve to her cheeks giving him a hint of the smile beneath. 'I'm more than fine. This has been the most perfect of days. Right up there with the Louvre.'

He cocked a brow. 'A day of cycling...many would see that as some kind of torture.'

'You knew I wouldn't though.'

'That's true enough. And yet you seem a little distant now that we're off the bikes...was it too much food? I warned Lucile you ate like a bird.'

Now she was the one cocking a brow as she eased out of the blanket cocoon to give him the full weight of her unimpressed stare. 'A bird?'

'A bird with very discerning taste.'

That earned him a laugh. 'Sorry, old habits and all that. I'm getting better. Moderation is your friend. Mum was all about the slippery slope growing up.'

'Hence the no sweets and chocolate.'

'You remember me saying that?'

'Of course I remember. Hearing someone say they were forbidden treats as a child isn't something you forget in a hurry.'

'So that's why Lucile provided them in abundance.'

'No, Lucile just likes to do her own thing. Just like you're getting to do these days.'

'Well, you can tell her it was delicious, all of it. And I am pleasantly full and very much looking forward to the cycle back so that I can work it all off again.'

'Oh, no, there's no more cycling today. We have a van returning all of this and we're taking a car back so we're free to enjoy this.' He turned to pull a bottle of champagne from the cool box. 'If you're not too cold for it?'

'One can never be too cold for champagne, surely? Especially in Paris, the city of...' She bit her lip, her cheeks flooding with colour.

'You can say it, Cassie.' He eyed her, wondering why she wouldn't. Was it for his benefit? Was she worried he would get the wrong idea? 'It's what we're here for after all.'

'Only we're not.'

And what did he say to that?

She wasn't wrong. But she wasn't right either. Because the whole point of this pretence was to show the world they were in love. But no one was eavesdropping this second, he'd muted the comms. And visually, *he* was right. They were out in the open. On a picnic rug. Sharing champagne. Any passer-by could snap the classic 'love shot'. So why had she felt the need to say it?

'I'm sorry.' She touched a hand to his arm. Gave an apologetic smile. 'You're right. This looks good. Sets the perfect scene. I was just…overthinking.'

He returned her smile. *Overthinking*. That sounded about right. Because he felt like he'd been treading those murky waters too of late. Questioning things too much. The way he felt, too much. The desire, too much.

He popped the cork, the explosive action too in tune with his thoughts, and she gave a small squeal as it overflowed. 'Was it a stubborn one?'

'A little,' he hurried out, clinging to the excuse she had gifted him as he plucked two flutes from the hamper and offered one out to her.

'Thank you.' She wet her lips. 'You're very good at this, you know.'

'Which bit? The cycling or the opening bottles of wine?'

She gave a soft laugh. 'I was thinking more the romancing.'

He filled her glass before seeing to his own—at least she seemed comfortable mentioning the *R* word.

'We have to make it look believable remember…'

'I think you're doing that very well…it's only been a week and the press are lapping it up—lapping *you* up.'

He grinned. 'Sorry. You can't blame a man for wanting to look good in the process, and if my hotels are taking a boost, all the better.'

'Not blaming you at all, though I apologise now if they start interrogating your exes.' The bottle hit the bottom of the hamper slightly harder than he'd intended, but he didn't make a show of it. 'That's something they can't seem to help themselves with.'

'There isn't much of substance to report on I'm afraid.'

She leaned closer, trying to get a better look at him. 'Explain?'

He shrugged. 'There isn't much to explain, I'm your classic bachelor. I date for fun, nothing more.'

Because the really interesting titbit—the bit the press would love to get their hands on—had been well and truly buried by the people with the power and the influence to make it so.

Much like the remnants of his heart.

'And besides…' He forced a smile, refusing to let Sara out of the darkest recesses of his mind and into the moment that up until now had been warm and quite enjoyable. 'They'll be too busy reporting on us. Like I said, they love a good love story as much as they love a bad one.'

She gave a tiny shiver and eased her legs up to her chin as she gestured to the path ahead. 'Well, something tells me one of these walkers will have a snap of this out in the world tomorrow.'

'Tomorrow? Don't you mean in the next thirty seconds.'

'Probably.'

'And so long as we're controlling the narrative, it's all good, right?'

She met his gaze. 'Right.'

'And that feels worthy of a toast, don't you think?'

She smiled, green eyes twinkling with gold much like the Eiffel Tower in the distance. 'To us.'

'To us.'

She clinked her glass to his, and he opened up his blanket to her, offering to share his warmth as well as the perfect camera opportunity.

Sure enough, he could sense a snap in the distance as she snuggled into his side, and he suppressed the twinge of annoyance—he was courting it after all—as much as he suppressed the warmth her body provoked. And focused on what mattered, her and the little bit of her past she had divulged. Because talking about her past sure beat thinking about his...

'So, tell me, was it just your mother's controlling influence or society's in general?'

'Hmm?'

'The eating habits...'

'I don't know. I guess it's easy to blame others when really, the true person to blame is yourself. I should have been stronger. If I wanted the cake, I should have eaten the bloody cake.' She gave a tight laugh, shook her head. 'Yes, my mother watched over me, made sure I was always careful, always knew how many calories were in what. I knew from a very young age that every delicacy came with a price, and hell, the press never let you have a day off. But maybe I shouldn't have cared so much about what they thought in the first place. And then maybe it wouldn't have hurt so much when they turned their back on me.'

'Your parents never deserved to have you as a daughter.'

'On that, I think they will now agree. After the shame I brought on them...'

He squeezed her into his side, his jaw pulsing. 'They did that to themselves when they backed you into a very public marriage with a man who no more deserved you than they did.'

'Not how they see it.'

'That's their problem, not yours.'

'I guess it is. I guess it's also the difference between you and me. Railroading me into the future they wanted for me is a move they will live to regret, whereas for your father, I can't imagine he will ever regret choosing you to take on his firm.'

Oh, there was a time...

'Do you really want to talk about families when we're in this amazing parkland, red squirrels playing at your feet?'

'Red squirrels. Where?'

He dipped his head to a spot in the distance. Nothing but fallen oak leaves now lay at the base of the trees but there had been a red squirrel not so long ago...it wasn't a complete lie. But she knew.

She nudged him with her elbow, the contact as provocative as the truth tightly packed inside his chest. Just not in the same way. 'Hugo!'

'I made him regret it.' He ground out. 'Once.'

It came out as raw as it still felt. Because *he* regretted it. The pain. The foolish act. The stupidity. He stared at where their glasses almost touched, watched the bubbles rising in the glass, but his head had travelled back. Reliving the past as she searched his face and likely saw it all.

'When?'

'When I worked for him all those years ago… Carving out my own path and going into the leisure industry wasn't entirely by choice, Cassie.'

'No?'

'No.'

She shivered and he pulled her closer. Kissed her hair on autopilot. 'In my defence, I was young. Twenty-four. It was my fifth close protection detail. But even then, I should have known better.'

'What happened?'

'I made a mistake. One I would never be so stupid as to make again, but my father wasn't a man you ever got to disappoint twice. Though when you're in the business of close protection, such a hard rule saves lives.'

'Did someone get hurt? Did you…?'

She looked up and he tucked her back under his chin, unable to look her in the eye as he admitted, 'I got involved with the principal.'

He sensed her tense, her soft gasp barely audible as he eased back on the rug and she came with him.

'Her father was a head of state in a country where culture and custom would prohibit any sort of a relationship between us, and that was before you put my job into the equation…'

He was so grateful that he'd killed the comms with

his team before they'd sat down, grateful all the more for the twenty-foot safety perimeter that meant no one could overhear his shameful tale.

He'd thought he was over it. He'd endured the therapy. Relished the recovery.

Yet here he was, retelling the tale over a decade later, and it felt as raw as if it was yesterday. The heartbreak. His father's disappointment. It didn't matter that he was a billionaire hotelier now, his father's firm under his wing too. He felt transported back to that moment. The twenty-four-year-old son who had broken his father's trust and his own heart in the process. Lost. Susceptible. Weak.

'What was her name?'

Her soft request pulled him back to the present. So typical that Cassie would want to put a name to the face that she didn't know because it mattered to his past.

'Sara.'

'I take it her family weren't very happy when they found out?'

His mouth twisted into a derisive smile, because of course that's where her head would go based on her own experience.

'They had every right to be angry. Cultural and family expectations aside, I was supposed to be protecting her. Love shouldn't have come into it.'

'And did you love her?' she said quietly.

He threw back his drink, but it tasted bitter, unpalatable, or was that just the memory?

'Hugo?'

Answer her.

'I thought I did, at the time.'

'And did she love you?'

'She said she did.'

He took another swig and realised his glass was empty. Reached for the bottle and topped himself up. Went to do the same for her only hers was still full. Not a good sign. He tried to relax. Took a breath. This was ancient history. Dealt with. Though, as he had discovered in the last week alone, it wasn't as buried as he wanted it to be.

His heart too was beating far too close to the surface.

'Then what happened?'

He ground his teeth. He didn't want to go there. But refusing to give it airtime was as bad as admitting it still hurt...

'Her family forced her hand. She made her choice and it wasn't me.'

Whatever she heard in his voice had her hand reaching up to cup his cheek, her palm soft, her green eyes softer still. 'I'm so sorry, Hugo.'

But that wasn't everything, was it? She wouldn't be so sorry when she knew how he had failed Sara. How he had let his heart get in the way of his head.

He was back on that street, Sara's car waiting, door open. The heat suffocating. The look in Sara's eyes all the more so as he caught at her wrist. Desperate. Helpless. Weak. *Don't go.*

'Hugo?' Cassie took the glass from his limp fingers, returned to cup his cheeks, her thumbs gently stroking. Her face so close he could see the ring of fire around her pupils. Could see his pain being reflected back at him in the swirling sea of green—and *this* is what love did. *This* is why he never wanted to go back there.

And Cassie was giving him all this compassion when he deserved none.

'It's okay, Hugo.'

He grabbed her wrists, almost threw them down before realising how it would look to a passer-by. How it would feel to her too. An outward sign of rejection that *she* didn't deserve.

'No. It is not.'

'It wasn't your fault.'

'What I did, that was my fault.'

She searched his gaze, unflinching from the pain she could see there. It was the first time she'd witnessed it within him. Such hurt. So raw and unguarded. He had loved. Hugo had loved. More than she ever had.

And he hadn't denied it either. *'I thought I did, at the time.'*

Though Sara had crushed it. Walked away. Chosen her family over him.

Cassie couldn't imagine it. No matter how hard she tried. Cassie couldn't imagine having the heart of the man before her and choosing anything but that. Though he wouldn't have been the same man…at twenty-four he would have been young, untainted by the world and all the work that would have hardened his shell since. The heartbreak that would have toughened him too.

And she needed that reminder. She needed it now because every day in his company, every day they played out this charade that was their epic love story, she could feel herself getting as lured in as the press. Lured in by him and his kind gestures, his kind smile, his kind heart.

Because it couldn't be so easy as this, could it? After

a life of living for others, an adulthood of having her men chosen for her, she couldn't be so lucky as to have landed her own perfect love story right next door. To believe that would truly be naive, wouldn't it?

And she'd almost given herself away too.

It's why she'd blurted out. *'Only we're not.'*

Hugo hadn't needed the reminder. Cassie had.

Her *heart* had.

'By falling in love? I can't see how that's your fault, Hugo.'

He stiffened. 'No,' he ground out. 'But leaving her exposed was.'

The chill ran from him into her and she lowered her palms from his face, rubbed them together. 'I see.'

'No. You don't.'

'Then make me see. Tell me what happened.'

He kept his gaze fixed ahead, but she could see his self-loathing, the sickness in his pallor, and she tucked her hands between her legs, forbade them from moving. He didn't want her touch right now, no matter how much she wanted to give it to him.

'You don't need to tell me, not if you don't want to, but…'

His throat bobbed as he swallowed, his dark lashes flickering over his eyes that were so haunted she prayed that talking about it would in some way release the ghosts from his soul. Ghosts he must have had buried deep for so long.

'I lowered my guard. I was focusing so much on her, fighting with her to see a different future for us that I didn't see the threat until he was upon us. I had my hand around her wrist, I wasn't prepared and when he drew his gun, she was completely exposed. The only thing I could do was throw myself into it.'

She failed to suppress a shiver as it played out in her mind's eye. 'You threw yourself into the path of the bullet?'

'He never should have got that close.'

'But you did what you were trained for,' she whispered.

'Far too late.'

He raised his hand to his shoulder, scratched at the skin beneath, the scar that must exist and Cassie tracked the move. 'If he'd been any further to the left, or if I'd been any slower…'

She felt the tremor that ran through him with his breath. 'But you weren't.'

He shook his head, stressed, 'He *never* should have been able to get that close.'

'But you were there. And you saved her.'

'I took the bullet but—' he choked on thin air '—it was not my finest moment.'

'We all make mistakes, do things we're not proud of, but you were in love—'

'I was a fool.'

He sounded so angry, so hurt, so bitter, and Cassie's heart ached for him. She could think of nothing else to do but to fold into him, moulding her body into every hard ridge of his until the tension gradually seeped from his limbs. So grateful to have him here now. That he hadn't lost his life in the line of duty to the woman who hadn't loved him enough to keep him.

'I'm so sorry, Hugo.'

'I'm not. Like I said, the only time I let my father

down was when I was distracted and infatuated. I learned from that mistake, and I've been committed ever since. Proved myself to my father. Made myself into the man I am today. As for the press, you needn't worry about them digging this story up. Sara's family made sure there was nothing to discover. Nothing to ruin their reputation and her marriage potential back then, and I've told no one of it…my family certainly don't speak of it, and those at the firm are under NDAs.'

She lifted her head a little. 'You think I'm worrying about any of that?'

He gave a stilted shrug.

'I'm more concerned that your relationship with Sara has seen you walk away from the possibility of love in your future, Hugo. This is why you don't have a home in the country with those mini-Chevaliers I mentioned, isn't it?'

He stroked the hair away from her face. 'You make that sound so tragic, Cassie.'

'Because it is tragic.'

He gave a choked laugh. 'Love isn't for everyone. *Mon Dieu*, if you saw my parents…it's a miracle they've got to where they have. My mother has the patience of a saint, I'll say that for her. And I'm a better man without it. I don't need someone else to make me feel fulfilled. I don't want to rely on someone else to make me feel whole and happy again, because when you lose that someone, it's like—it's like having your soul ripped out, and you struggle to see the path for the pain of it.'

'I understand why you don't want to rely on love to make you happy again,' she whispered eventually. 'It's not all that different to me spending my life tying my happiness to that of others. My parents, Georges, things you can't control. But... I don't know. To swear oneself off it because you fear losing it again... I'm not sure that's all that healthy either.'

'I never said it was healthy, Cassie. Just that I don't intend to suffer it again.'

And that was her told.

So why did she get the distinct impression her heart wasn't listening...?

CHAPTER EIGHT

HUGO KNEW PARIS like the back of his hand. He'd grown up in the city. Lived and worked in the good and the bad. Spent time as a driver and on the doors of its clubs until his father had deemed him good enough for the family firm. And then, of course, he'd been launched on the path that had led to his independence.

But he'd never seen it like this…like he did through Cassie's eyes.

And for the next two weeks, while balancing his return to work with his mission to show Cassie off to the world and vice versa, he lost himself in her pleasure, her joy as he took her to his favourite spots, some well-known, some less so.

'I can't believe I'm eating ice cream outdoors when it's almost November.'

Her green eyes sparkled up at him as she touched a finger to the corner of her mouth—*always* smiling—and scooped away some imaginary stray dribble of the sweet delight he had coaxed her into buying.

If he was honest, he couldn't believe he was doing it either. On a Monday too, when he should be at work, but he'd taken one look at the blue sky that morning, the amber leaves on the trees lining the Champs-élysées creating a stunning walkway all the way down to the River Seine, and he'd known where he'd rather be.

And who he'd rather be with.

And he hadn't questioned it. He'd just gone and got her.

Which in itself was a bad sign to add to the ever-growing list of bad signs…

'I can't believe you've never had one of Pierre's ice creams before.'

'If someone had told me croissant infused ice cream existed down the road, I think I would've sneaked out of my room sooner.'

He had to force his jaw to relax. The memory of her hiding away still too recent to ignore. The gossip head-lines that morning, or rather a flippant one-liner from the palace spin doctors, even more so. Not that he was about to ruin the moment by giving it any airtime now.

'It's pretty good, isn't it?' He filled his mouth with the creamy goodness and focused on the tasty delight instead.

'Oh, yes,' she murmured, her pleasure obvious as she licked at her own, her eyes rolling back. The red of her jacket working with the flush in her cheeks and the gloss to her lips as she swept up the remnants with her tongue…

Don't look at her tongue.

'And the nutty chocolate sauce,' she was saying, 'it really takes it to another level, don't you—'

'Princess! Hugo!'

Her eyes widened as he stiffened.

'Give us a smile!'

The shout came from across the street, and like an

echo more shouts followed in quick succession. Other voices, different people.

'Sourire à la caméra!'

It was inevitable. There wasn't an outing where they flew under the radar for its entirety, but his plan was working. The interruptions *were* less frequent. Less intense. Less intrusive. And less insulting with it, too.

Or was that just wishful thinking on his part?

He searched her face, looking for any sign that the unbridled joy of seconds before was dimming. 'What do you say?'

'Do I have food on my face?'

He cupped her cheek, swiped his thumb along her lower lip, felt her subtle tremor beneath his touch— or was that purely within him? The act driven by the thrill of it, rather than to remove any trace of chocolate or cream.

It was the kind of act they'd been indulging in, playing up to the cameras, fulfilling the role of the loved-up couple with ease. Driving the Prince crazy, if the reports were to be believed, and sweeping the public up in their love story. Winning them over to Cassie's side. As it should be.

The only problem was training his body to calm down, reminding it that this wasn't the real deal—because A, he wasn't in love. And B, he never would be.

Which meant *this*—the sexual attraction—it needed to be caged.

'All gone.'

He wondered if she noticed the husky edge to his voice. Noticed it and knew its cause, like he did. That this pretence, the desire, was no act at all.

But her grin widened, and she leapt up, her eyes flashing with mischief as she caught the tip of his thumb in her mouth. *Mon Dieu*. Never mind the cameras going wild, his entire body surged—heart, mind, and soul— urging him to tug her body to his and kiss her deeply. An act they hadn't been so bold as to share, and it was that deep-rooted desire that had him slipping his arm around her waist and urging her into walking instead.

Because if they were moving, they couldn't be doing all the other things his brain was fervently entertaining...

'You okay?' She leaned into him as she asked, her body readily moulding into his as they fell into an easy step together.

'Better than okay. It's a glorious day. Even the river looks more blue than brown today...which feels like something of a miracle.'

'*Everything* looks and feels a little better when the sun comes out to play.'

He glanced down at her, his brow creasing. 'And are you needing the sun today, Cassie?' Because the wistful note in her voice told him that she did.

Had she seen the same headlines, was she too pondering what her no-good ex would say next. Did he raise it, or did he let it go?

'Are you enjoying your bit of rough, Princess?'

The voice came out of the trees up ahead, but no one stepped forward and he nodded to his team to check it out as he slowed their pace.

'Do you want to comment on the suggestion that Prince Georges was always a little too refined for you, Princess?'

Hugo saw red. His emotions a sprint ahead of where they should ever be, and not in defence of himself. He couldn't care what the guy said about him. He was lowering Cassie to Hugo's level. And hell, he could say what he liked about Hugo but Cassie...

She tugged on his arm. Her steady hand holding him back when he would have launched forward as the smug-faced journo peered out from between the trees.

'I beg your pardon?' Cassie stepped forward, her hand still on Hugo's arm urging him to hold his ground. Was his skittish kitten finding her claws?

His team in the wings looked to him and he silently gestured for them to hold their position. They were close enough to move if she needed them, but she wanted to handle this, and he wanted to give her that opportunity.

The man came out of the trees. Dark, shaggy hair. Leathers. A motorbike just behind for a quick exit should he need it. Phone ready to snap a pic. 'I said...'

'Oh, I heard you.' She gave her classic coy smile, a lick of her ice cream as she eyed him up and down. 'I just needed a better visual to do this...'

And then she stuck her cone, ice cream and all, right on the end of his nose.

So swift the man had no time to dodge it.

So surprising all the man could do was gawp back at her like some frozen human snowman.

'What can I say? Georges was probably right. I always did have a more playful side to me, and now I'm all about having fun with my man. Life is for living, after all. Don't you agree, Hugo?'

She turned and beamed at him.

'I think I need to go and buy you another ice cream, *mon petit chaton*.'

She wrinkled her nose. 'Did you just call me...?'

'My little kitten, *oui*.'

She hooked her arm back in his. 'Care to explain?'

'Later.'

She gave him a sparkling smile before turning to throw over her shoulder, 'Oh, and, Mr Reporter Sir, I hate having to waste anything, so please be a good soul and lick as much of that up as you can. It truly is delicious.'

And then she practically skipped Hugo back to Pierre's.

'Are you going to explain the kitten reference?' she asked as he handed her a replacement ice cream.

He chuckled. 'To be clear, to call one *mon petit chaton* is a common endearment in France so you shouldn't take offence.'

'I wasn't.'

He cleared his throat as he thought back to that first morning in Louis's apartment, when he hadn't known who she was...

'And...?'

'It was something that sprang to mind when I saw you standing in the middle of Louis's apartment that first morning.'

'The morning of the photograph?'

He nodded. The story that had triggered all the rest. 'You were wearing that oversized cream sweater, grey leggings, soft and muted against the garish backdrop. Sweet, but skittish too. Wary of me, I guess. Why I was there? Could I be trusted?'

'I suppose I was.'

'And all around you was this chaos and colour and it made me think of a kitten being set down in a noisy neon nightclub. And then you talked about how you were hiding out, and it reinforced that view.' He swept her hair behind her ear, scanned her face as he saw how far she had come to be the woman before him now. '*Mon petit chaton*, hiding from the world, but not any more. My little kitten has found her claws.'

'Hugo…' She wet her lips, her eyes glistening up at him. 'I don't know what to say.'

'Well don't cry.'

'I'm not. I think that's possibly one of the nicest things anyone has ever said to me.'

'And yet, you're crying.'

She shook her head, blinked the tears away. 'I'm not. I'm—I am angry though.'

'I told you, it's a compliment.'

'Not at you! At the reporter for insinuating what he did.'

'Which bit?'

'That you were unrefined.'

'You took that from what he said?'

'Well, the suggestion was there.'

He gave a low chuckle. 'I really couldn't care less what he said about me.'

'Tomorrow's headlines might make you think otherwise.'

'Something tells me that reporter got what was coming to him, I think the reports will swing very much in your favour.'

'You reckon?'

He grinned, his admiration for her swelling out of his control as he caught another stray hair before it found its way into her mouth with her ice cream. 'Hell yeah, you were incredible.'

She stepped closer, so close her chest brushed his front. 'You truly think so?'

He hooked his hands into the rear pockets of her jeans. She felt good. So very good.

'Cassie, I have seen some fierce take-downs in my career, but that is up there with one of my all-time favourites.'

She laughed, though it sounded strained to his ears, strained with the same kind of heat that was working its way through him. 'Now I know you're exaggerating.'

'I swear on my mother's life. Just remind me never to get on your bad side. Like I said, *mon petit chaton* has found her claws.'

She placed said claw over his shoulder. 'I still can't believe that's how you saw me—*see* me, even.' She bared her teeth and gave a playful little *'raa'* that made him laugh...made him feel more than just the flutter of amusement too. 'But have no fear, I don't plan on wasting Pierre's amazing ice cream a second time around, even if it's on your delightful nose... I will share it though.'

Then she licked her ice cream right beneath his nose before lifting it over his shoulder and kissing him. Whether it was for the benefit of more hovering reporters or for her or for him, he had no clue. And he had no good sense left to question it, or prevent it, because he was lost to it. The touch of her lips against his, the taste of the ice cream and her, a delight like no other. And it was heaven and hell in one.

Heaven because it was sheer bliss, and hell because it wasn't enough. And he wasn't sure it could ever be enough. And he shouldn't be doing it. Taking what she was offering, but he was.

Whether it was fake or not. He was rolling with it. Rolling with it and revelling in it. His hands forking into her hair, deep and hungry. The growl low in his throat, fierce and unrestrained. Because he was finally giving it free rein, the desire that he'd been suppressing for so long. It was vibrating through him. Taking over every part of him, until he realised it wasn't just within him, it was against him, in his pocket between them—his phone!

Bzzzz...bzzzz...bzzzz...

He squeezed his eyes closed, swore he heard her whimper, felt her claws along with the drip of her ice cream down his neck.

Bzzzz...bzzzz...bzzzz...

He cursed and she fell back with what sounded like a sob come laugh. 'Maybe you should get it.'

She pressed her fingers to her lips, her other hand outstretched with the dripping ice cream as she kept her gaze low. *Mon Dieu*, she looked thoroughly kissed. Hair mussed, lips swollen, cheeks pink. He wanted to toss the ice cream, drag her back to the apartment, forget the world and why this wasn't real. Why this couldn't *be* real.

He tugged the phone from his pocket as it cut off, cursing the unknown caller for the unwelcome interruption.

Unwelcome? You should be grateful for the reality check!

He raked an unsteady hand over his hair. Took a breath. And another as he stared at the screen and anchored himself in the present. Who she was. What this was. Why he couldn't pick up where they'd left off.

'Do you need to call them back?' she asked, and he could hear the hesitation in her voice, the uncertainty that their kiss had put there. That *he* had put there. Though she had kissed him, that much was certain. But he hadn't had to kiss her back.

'Unknown number. I'm sure they'll leave a message if it's important.'

She nodded but they remained at some weird kind of impasse. Neither knowing how to press Play again... how to resume...not back in each other's arms though, that was for sure.

Maybe he needed to get back into a steady routine. There was something to be said for the reassuring monotony of the daily grind. Less emotion, less hormonal churn, and more making money and decisions with clear thought and logic.

None of which he had when she was around, not any more. And that was a problem. A big Sara-style problem.

Bigger even. Because he was supposed to be older, wiser, and better than the mistakes of old. His phone gave the solitary buzz of an answerphone message, and like a lifeline now he pulled it out. Nodded to one of his team to step in.

'I'll just check what this is,' he said to Cassie.

'Sure.'

He walked a few strides away and dialled his answerphone, surprised when his father's gruff voice came down the line.

'Call me back, Hugo.'

Ice ran down his spine. Was it Mum? Was she sick? Had something happened?

He immediately dialled the number and his father picked up in one.

A stream of Polish flew at him, so rapid even Hugo struggled to piece it together, but he'd caught enough. Princess. Cassandra. Sara. *Imbecyl*—much like the French *imbécile*. So much for his parents being blissfully unaware in digi-detox land.

'Father, stop.'

'Don't you tell me to stop. I knew we shouldn't have left. I *knew* I couldn't trust you to manage things with me so far away.'

Hugo's chest grew tight with every word. 'It is not what you think.'

'How? How can it not be how I think? When your mother learns of this—'

'She doesn't know?'

That was something at least...

'No. Thanks to this *ridiculous* place she's in cloud cuckoo land.'

'Which is where you should be—not the cuckoo—' Hugo broke off with a curse. This was coming out all wrong. Why did his father always get to him like this?

'Did you honestly think I wouldn't find out?'

'And how did you? You're not supposed to have any contact with the outside world.'

'I abide by my own rules, son. You of all people should know that.'

Hugo raked a hand over his hair, gripped the back of his neck. He'd suspected as much. Hell, even Cassie had warned him his father might do as much. But again, he'd been too distracted by the same to do something about it before now.

'Eduardo says you have a team on her 24-7.'

He huffed. 'Eduardo needs to remember who he works for now.'

'Don't change the subject.'

'I'm not. My CEO should be more concerned with running the company than telling tales to my father, who should no longer be getting involved.'

'When those tales pertain to mistakes my son is making in his personal life which could affect his work life, it's my business to know. I thought you'd learnt your lesson with that disastrous affair. Sara and your silly infatuation almost got you both killed. Or has time made you forget?'

'No, Father. And I don't need the reminder now. This is not the same.'

'Then you best enlighten me because from where I'm sitting, it is precisely the same. She is a client and you are—'

'That is *not* how this is.'

'In what way is it any different?'

Hugo blew out a breath. 'Because we are friends and what you're seeing is all for show, Father. I'm helping her out of a difficult situation.' And then he added because he couldn't help himself. 'But even if we were in a relationship, this is nothing like what happened with Sara. I *run* the company now. I'm not in the field. I'm not running the protection detail. I'm being protected right alongside her. And I trust my team. Just as you trusted them. And now, I need you to trust me.'

The line fell silent. Nothing but the sounds of Paris on Hugo's side of the world and the early-morning wildlife in the Caribbean.

'Please, Father, I promise you, I have it all under control.'

Only you don't...

'For the first time in your life, can you just trust me?'

His father grunted. And then he was gone. And Hugo had no idea whether that was a yes or a no. Much like his entire life.

But he knew one thing for sure, he needed to get it under control. His feelings for Cassie and the entire situation and prove to his father once again that he had this.

And prove it to himself while he was at it.

'Everything okay?'

Because Cassie knew it wasn't.

The moment they had kissed, her world had tilted and failed to right itself again.

Cassie now knew how it felt to be wanted by Hugo. Not the kind of want that was make-believe. Projected or otherwise. The kind that she could confuse because he had been so kind and understanding towards her. Because he cared for her.

No. He'd *wanted* her. She'd seen it in his eyes when he'd called her his *mon petit chaton*. She'd heard it in his growl as he'd kissed her. Felt it in his hands as he'd forked them through her hair. Felt it in his body as he'd pressed against her. And she'd wanted him too.

But she'd also sensed the fight in him. The way he'd pulled away and withdrawn.

The phone call gifting him a get out that she had permitted him to take.

And now the wall was well and truly up and he wasn't meeting her eye.

'Hugo?'

'*Oui.*' He pocketed his phone, then his hands. 'But something's come up and I need to get back and pack. I have to fly out to New York for a few days.'

'Oh.'

And she really didn't like the way her heart sank at the thought.

'I have some business to take care of out there.'

Of course he did, he had a life with responsibilities. Just because he'd *chosen* to spend most of his free time with her of late didn't change that. But now it felt like he was running. From the kiss. From her.

'When will you be back?'

'I'm not sure. Friday maybe? It depends how it goes.'

She nodded. Tugged the collar of her jacket high around her neck, wishing they hadn't bought the replacement ice cream as her stomach threatened to throw it back up. 'I'll miss you.'

And why on earth had she said that?

His eyes caught on hers. For the briefest second their gazes locked, and then he turned away but took her hand as though softening the move. Gave her fingers a squeeze. 'I'm sure your designs will benefit from the extra attention you'll be able to give them without me around to distract you.'

She interlocked her fingers in his. Cherished the connection as she focused on the conversation rather than the weird dance of her heart that was telling her plenty if she dared to listen.

'You're right. If Louis is to unveil them on the catwalk next February, I need to have them ready soon.'

'Still not up for going it alone then?'

She laughed. 'Not yet I'm not. Our little love story may have worked wonders, but I don't think it's worked that kind of magic yet.'

'Our love story has nothing to do with it, Cassie. I'm talking about you and your designs. I've seen them, remember—they're incredible and the world will think so too.'

'And as you so rightly pointed out, you know nothing of fashion so…'

'But Louis does, and he wants them *so*…'

She gave a small smile as she considered what he was saying…while also acknowledging that he was probably saying it to distract her from whatever else was going on inside his head, and between them too.

Was she reading too much into it? She'd kissed him… had he just been going along with it for her sake, for the cameras, for the role?

Or had she gone too far? Crossed a line in kissing him so brazenly? Maybe she should just ask him outright? Or maybe she was overthinking the whole lot, and it really was work taking him away and she was just being paranoid?

Because the real problem came down to what was going on within her. Her own feelings that she was struggling to contain.

So maybe his work emergency was actually a blessing in disguise.

Some space after all the time they'd spent together. A chance to be herself, the new and energised and fierce her. On her own two feet. Alone. And she'd be perfectly fine and perfectly happy without him.

Because she didn't *need* Hugo. She wasn't *in love* with Hugo.

She cared for him. He was a wonderful human being who'd given her so much joy. Saved her from herself and her self-imposed little prison.

She was indebted to him—that was all.

Nothing more.

Absolutely not.

And she'd prove it.

CHAPTER NINE

CASSIE WAS HUNCHED over the coffee table in Louis's living room, a frenetic energy flowing through her fingers and onto the page. The scratch of pencil on paper as soothing as the classical tune she had playing in the background. The tune similar to what had been playing at the Louvre the first time they'd dined together. When he'd had those cute fashion plates brought in for her eyes only.

Had that really only been five weeks ago?

She felt like so much had changed since then. She had changed. Life had changed.

It was half two in the morning. Her witching hour. A time she hadn't needed. Not since Hugo. But in the past week, she'd found herself getting up again...

He'd said he'd be away for a few days, but it had been almost two weeks since she'd seen him. They'd exchanged messages. Mainly him making sure she was okay and that his team were looking after her. Safe topics.

And what exactly is safe *supposed to mean?*

She nipped her lip and went back to her drawing. More focused. More frenzied. Even though her hand and back protested. She lost herself in the beauty of what she could create and control. And her creativity was soaring, her designs were taking shape. She was almost ready to share them with Louis, who'd been messaging daily for an update. Which made her think of Hugo again and his parting words, to think about going it alone. That Louis's eagerness meant the world would be eager too.

But it was still early days. Even with the great strides she'd made to stand apart from her royal identity, standing beside another man was hardly standing alone…but the idea of standing up there without Hugo?

The pencil fell from her grasp and she shivered as she pulled the sleeves of her robe into her hands and curled back into the sofa. She wasn't cold because she feared going it alone.

She was cold because she didn't want to think of life without Hugo in it.

And *that* scared her.

The problem was, she knew it was an act for him. The fake dating, the playing up to the camera. She knew he cared for her as a friend, but the rest—the loving touches, caresses, gestures—they were all part of the act. Though that kiss… Her fingers fluttered to her mouth that burned with the memory of it…her heart fluttering too.

Because her heart had been fooled.

And her heart wanted to carry on being fooled because it had fallen for the man who had cared enough to coax her out. Who had cared enough to save her from herself.

And when he touched her, when he looked at her, when he made her smile and laugh and feel special in all the ways he did, planning days out that meant so much to her…activities that not even her husband or her parents would have thought to do, would have understood her *well enough* to do…it felt like more. She *felt* so much more.

And she missed him. *God.* She *missed* him.

Waking up each morning knowing he was so far away, that he wouldn't be calling by that day, or the next… She blew out a breath and stood. Walked to the window and gazed out over the darkened city.

How different it now felt having walked it many times with Hugo. Hugo and his team. But that couldn't be her life forever. At some point she was going to have to move out, take her own path on her own two feet.

That was the deal. That was what she'd wanted more than anything when she'd first fled the palace. Louis had come to her aid with the apartment, and then Hugo had come to her aid in ways she'd never have had the means or the gumption to pursue. Not in the short term when everything had been so fresh and raw.

She had so much to be grateful for, so why did it feel like something was now missing in her goal for the future?

A gentle knock—knuckles against wood—made her jump. She turned from the glass to squint down the darkened hallway. It came again, slightly louder, but very definite. Someone was at her door. At this time of night?

But who would call now unless it was an emergency, and even then, they'd use the bell or pound a lot harder…? She padded towards it, tightening her robe.

A loud whisper came next. 'Cassie?'

Hugo!

She raced the final few steps, unbolted the door, and threw it open. Would have thrown herself into his arms too if she hadn't had the last-minute foresight to realise that would be unwise. Unless she wanted him to know *exactly* how she felt about him.

'What are you doing here? I thought you were still in New York.'

'I was. I just got back.'

'Like—' she waved a loose finger and swore her heart was about to soar right up out of her chest '—*just* this minute got back.'

'*Oui.*'

'And you're knocking on my door *because*…?'

He raised his arms out like it was obvious and she eyed him up and down. He was a sight for sore eyes. Even in joggers and a training top.

'Because in the last month we have done many things, apart from the one thing I told you I would do that first morning we had coffee.'

She frowned. 'Remind me…'

Maybe she was losing her mind. Maybe she'd fallen asleep sketching, and this was some weird, Hugo-starved dream.

'A run! It's your witching hour. And I could hear you moving about in there, so I figured, why not?'

Her face broke into a grin. 'You're serious?'

'I've dressed for the occasion, haven't I? You, how-ever…' His eyes dipped, dipped and heated, and heaven help her, she felt the flush creeping up her chest as he cleared his throat and clapped his hands together. 'Right! I'll give you five minutes to get changed because that gown isn't conducive to any form of exercise.'

'Are you—'

'Shoo-shoo!' He took her by the shoulders and turned her around. 'I'll be right here when you're ready.'

And then he closed the door on her, and she was alone once more. Only this time he was on the other side of it, and she was laughing and shaking and completely abuzz with him.

Hugo was here and he was taking her running.

At two-thirty in the morning!

Was there anything this man wouldn't do for her?

He won't love you, so don't be getting any funny ideas!

She dismissed the sarcastic retort—*hell*, what did she care? Her parents hadn't loved her. Georges certainly hadn't loved her. What was another man to add to the list?

But Hugo was different and therein lay the problem.

He was worth loving.

And, breathe.

Watching Cassie run was extraordinary.

Or was it the act of running with her that was extraordinary? Because Hugo didn't feel tired. He felt fired up. Exhilarated.

He hadn't slept since the previous night in New York and, granted, it was only nine in the evening stateside. *She* was the one who should be tired.

But then he'd barely slept the last two weeks away. His sleep was disturbed, and he'd found himself back on the sleepwalk train. Troubled by his own unease. The past and the present colliding. Worry over how he'd left things. Worry over the future. Over what he wanted. What he didn't want. Worry that her ex would cross the line. That another hack of a journalist would. There was the slightest niggle that one would uncover his past too, and the idea that his tainted past could ruin her…he couldn't bear that.

It didn't matter that she'd shown how strong she was either, he'd still worried.

So, the second he'd heard her footfall on the other side of the wall, he'd been racking his brain for an excuse to see her. To see for himself that she was okay because the reports from his team simply wouldn't do.

Running and her witching hour had been a spark of desperate inspiration.

But now they were out in the cool night air, he was loving every second.

All the more so, because she was.

Her entire body encased in black Lycra, she was a powerhouse. A petite, lithe powerhouse. Her hair was tied back in a ponytail, her face half hidden by a cap, but her eyes shone out, glittering into the night as she turned to him and grinned.

'This is immense!'

They were crossing the Pont Neuf, the Seine flowing black beneath them, the starry sky above, and if he had to choose a perfect moment in his life, he might have chosen this one. 'I'm not going to lie. It is surprisingly awesome.'

She laughed. The sound giddy and light and nowhere near as breathless as it should be. 'Epic!'

'But you know we do need to turn back if you want to avoid the early-morning risers?'

'I know.' She gave him what could only be described as a cheeky look. 'You want to race?'

'Back to the hotel? It's almost five kilometres!'

'*And?*' She broke stride to give him a light elbow. 'You chicken?'

'Am *I* chicken?'

She nodded, eyes goading him beneath the rim of her cap.

'You're on!'

And like that, they were off. Any thought of gifting her a head start forgotten as he realised this woman didn't need it. What was she powered by? Moonlight? The reflective details on her kit taunting him further as they flashed him all the way.

By the time they reached their hotel, he swore he'd got a PB along with a rather unpleasant stitch. He cursed as he came to a halt in the outer courtyard, clutched his side as he struggled to suck in a breath. 'You're dangerous!'

'You can't come to an abrupt stop, it's not good for your heart.' She pulled on his arm, her eyes dazzling in the warm glow of the hotel's lighting. 'We'll take the stairs up. You can jog it off.'

He stared up at her. 'Jog it off?'

She nodded. 'Yup.'

'Did you just "*yup*" me?'

'I guess I did.'

He shook his head, hands on knees. 'Who are you and what have you done with my Cassie?'

'I've got claws now, remember?'

She perfected her cat pose, claws and all, before spinning on her heel and jogging inside, ponytail swinging.

'I've created a monster,' he murmured, pushing up to standing with a laugh. 'Never mind a cat.'

Not that he was complaining. Not in the slightest. He followed her on through to the lobby and to the stairwell. There was one thing to be said for jogging up the stairs behind her, he had the most amazing view of her in Lycra. And, *Dieu*, that did not help. Not one bit. It stopped him thinking about his stitch though.

Probably because his blood was rushing elsewhere.

Two weeks apart was supposed to have dulled this.

Made it go away.

Made it containable.

All it had done was made it explosive.

And if he didn't get out of her orbit like now, he was going to do something profoundly stupid, the kind of stupid his father had cautioned him against, the kind of stupid that had made him run two weeks ago...

'Drink?'

'Huh?'

She had her hand on the door to Louis's apartment. 'I make a mean post-workout smoothie?'

The last thing you need is a smoothie...

Though he found himself saying, 'Sure.'

He followed her in and she stripped off her jacket. Underneath she wore nothing but an exercise bra with her leggings. *Gulp.* She pulled her cap off and tossed it aside, her ponytail swinging free down her back as she set about mixing stuff together in a blender. 'Water?'

'Please.'

At least it was supposed to have been a please. Instead, it sounded like someone was strangling a cat and the look she sent him as she pulled open the fridge said she thought so too.

She tossed him a bottle, which by some miracle he managed to catch, and he twisted off the cap, took a long slug. Wiped his mouth. 'Cheers.'

She set the blender going and the noise was about as loud as his pulse in his ears. She set two tumblers on the side with straws and drummed her nails while she waited for the blender to finish.

Was she as edgy as him? She wasn't looking at him and the way those nails were working against Louis's psychedelic marble, the way every exposed muscle of her torso looked clenched... *Dieu*, he wanted her.

Wanted her more than he could ever remember wanting anything in his life. More than he'd wanted the family firm in his twenties. More than he'd wanted to make his first million. More than he wanted to taste the ice cream on her lips a fortnight ago. And that kiss...

The blender finished its incessant thrum, and she let out a sudden breath, her head snapping up. She'd been lost in her thoughts, too. Had she gone to the same place? Unlikely, but the slash of heat still in her cheeks, across her collarbone...

She reached for the jug and poured the luminescent liquid into the awaiting glasses.

'It tastes better than it looks, I promise.'

She stepped up to him, glasses in hand and as her eyes lifted to his, the world stilled.

Because he knew in that moment that nothing could taste better than her.

That he wanted to *taste* nothing but her.

And that he needed to get the hell away from her. Now.

'I'm sorry, Cassie, this was a bad idea.'

'The drink?'

But he was already turning away and walking, and she was right on his tail. Drinks forgotten on the side as she grabbed his arm to pull him back. 'Did I do something wrong?'

'No, no, of course not. You could never do anything wrong. I'm sorry, I just...' He turned to face her and she was so close, her body virtually pressed up against him, and they were so hot and sweaty from their run. Everything was in some heightened overdrive. Now wasn't the time to make any crazy decisions or cross any rational lines when there was no press corps to excuse it.

'Then what is it?'

She reached up. Her palm soft against his cheek. Her brow furrowed with concern. But there was something else in her green eyes. Something so akin to the fire in his gut, and *hell*, he wanted to act on it.

He cursed under his breath, and her luscious mouth quirked to one side. 'You do have a filthy mouth at times, Hugo.'

'If you could read my mind, you'd say I had a filthy one of those too.'

Her eyes flared, the fire he had glimpsed turning into a full-on blaze. 'What are you saying?'

'What do you think I'm saying?'

Her delicate throat bobbed, her eyes raking over his face as her fingers trembled against his cheek. 'Don't tease me.'

'*Me?* Tease *you*? When you're the one standing before me in nothing more than a bra and skintight pants?' His voice was raw—raw with a need that had been building for weeks! And *Dieu*, he wasn't a monk!

Two weeks without sight of her in the flesh! Oh, he'd seen plenty in the press. Plenty enough to tease him and drive him half mad. Plenty of dated coy shots with the Prince too. And he wasn't a jealous man. He *wasn't*.

'Then why aren't you kissing me?'

'Because I don't believe in taking what I want without express permission.'

'I am granting you permission, Hugo. Right here...' She pressed her body up against him, hooked her hands around his neck. 'Right now.'

And then she kissed him, and this time, he quit thinking. He quit every sense that wasn't all about her and took all that she was offering because consequences were tomorrow's concern.

Or today's, depending on how one looked at it.

Only he wasn't looking, he was living in the moment and loving every second.

Cassie was no virgin.

The Prince may have gone elsewhere for fun but he'd done his 'duty' by her. And that was just it. He'd always made it feel like a duty. Like it was all about producing an heir and never about desire. Never about lust. Fire. *This!*

And Cassie *was* on fire. Her entire body combusting with an explosive passion that she couldn't contain. She'd known her feelings for Hugo were growing out of her control but this...this raging heat in her bloodstream, this tension coiling through her body, this liquid heat pooling in her abdomen... She was kind of...scared.

'Hugo,' she panted, clawing at his chest through his T-shirt as she tore her mouth from his so that she could stare up at him, wide-eyed and dazed.

'Yes?'

'This is...'

'Crazy. Insane. Ill-advised.'

She gave a choked laugh. 'Yes!'

'You want me to stop, because I will.'

'No! Hell no.'

'Dieu Merci!'

She tugged him back to her kiss, marvelling at the way their mouths fit so perfectly together. The way his tongue teased and tangled with her own. Georges had never kissed her like this. With such passion, such intensity. Like he wanted all of her and more.

He walked her back into some hard surface, and she felt it rock. Heard something fragile rattle and he flicked a hand out to catch whatever it was without breaking tempo or the exploration of his kiss.

'Though we should take this to the bedroom before something hits the deck that shouldn't...'

She nodded and twisted in his arms, leading him down the corridor and into her room without pausing to turn on the lights. She was in too much of a hurry. Too scared that to pause would snuff out whatever this was building between them because *this* was what she had read about in books.

This was what she had seen on the TV.

This was what she had started to think was the stuff of make-believe...but was it possible that it was real after all?

Real and she could have it. With Hugo.

He spun her into his arms and she tore his T-shirt over his head before his mouth claimed hers once more. To be able to touch the body she had seen that first night, the broad shoulders, the chiselled pecs, the hard ridge of every ab...

She sighed into his mouth and he nipped her lip. 'Did you just sigh at me?'

'Maybe.'

'Sighing after sex is okay, but before?'

'I'm sorry, but your body is wholly satisfying.'

'I'll show you satisfying.'

And with that, he threw her back on the bed and stalked towards her.

'Wait!' She thrust out a hand and he paused, his cocked brow just visible in the light being cast from the outer hall.

'I'm all—' she wriggled against the sheets '—sweaty.'

'Believe me, you're going to be more sweaty by the time I'm finished with you, *mon petit chaton*.'

She wanted to laugh. She wanted to cry. She wanted to thank the heavens for bringing her this man, because Georges would *never* have stood for 'sweaty her'. He'd have marched her to the shower, but Hugo, he was her *real* prince.

'In that case...' She relaxed, ran her teeth over her bottom lip as she thought of all that lay ahead. 'Come get me.'

Come get me? Have you heard yourself? And what about after, when he has your heart too? Because there can be no coming back from this!

The bed shifted with Hugo's weight and then he was beside her, his eyes level with hers, his hand in her hair and all her worries evaporated in the heat of his kiss.

Because everything felt right. So right and perfect.

Because Hugo made her *feel* just right and perfect just the way she was.

CHAPTER TEN

IF THE WEEKS prior to Hugo's leaving for New York had been incredible, the week following his return could be deemed nothing short of revelatory. And Cassie wasn't just referring to the orgasms, of which there had been many.

All to varying degrees of exemplariness.

Which was a word, right? Because it was Hugo all over when it came to being a lover. Attentive, thorough, going above and beyond.

Now she understood what a true climax was and there was only one problem with that discovery—it made them quite addictive. It made the *whole* act quite addictive.

And she was starting to feel like the harlot the Duponts would love to paint her as.

But it didn't count if you craved them all with the same man over and over, did it?

Though she digressed, because what she was really talking about was the *L* word itself and all the wondrous feelings that came with it.

There was no proving the opposite any more.

She was wholeheartedly and unequivocally in love with Hugo, and it was joyous.

She had gone her whole life without love, and finally she knew what it felt like to truly love another, and she was starting to hope that he felt the same. Because how could it be like this and not be reciprocated? How could *he* be like this and not feel it too?

'What's that grin about?'

He offered her a spoonful of Pierre's ice cream as he asked, the black and white movie they were watching playing over his features as they lay in her bed late one night…

It turned out Pierre's ice cream wasn't just perfect for a sunny Parisian autumnal day but the perfect post-make-out dish too.

'I was just thinking that you've turned me into a bit of a harlot.'

He chuckled. 'I think that technically a harlot has sex with multiple people for money, whereas you only do it with one man for Pierre's ice cream.'

'I was thinking that too.'

'So, you admit it, you do only have me for the ice cream?'

'Guilty as charged.'

'Why you…' In seconds he had the bowl shoved aside and he was upon her, tickling her ribs until she was laughing uncontrollably.

'Hugo, stop! Stop!'

'Not until you—'

And then he froze. Her body fenced in by his thighs as he rose above her, ears attuned to the outside world. 'Do you hear that?'

'What?'

And then she heard it. The rumble of people in the outer hall.

His phone started to ring and he sprang off the bed, reaching for it as he tugged on his lounge pants. Her mouth dry despite the recent ice cream, she eyed him, naked from the waist up. Would she ever be immune to him? She hoped not.

'Oui?' He blurted into his phone and his frown sharpened. *'Quoi?'*

His eyes launched to hers and she tensed—was he grey or was it the movie?

Please let it be the movie.

Are you okay? she mouthed, pushing herself to sitting.

The smallest shake of his head.

'Je viens.' He hung up the phone. 'I have to go.'

'Now?'

It was like *déjà vu*. Two weeks ago, the same thing had happened. The same wall had gone up. Work again? Or something else? But it was late, a Sunday too.

Though his companies were global, operating 24-7. She got that, but still.

'My parents are here.'

'Your *parents*?' She launched out of the bed, swept a hand over her wild hair. 'Oh, my God!'

'Exactly.'

She covered her mouth and stared at him. His parents. They were *here*? Across the hall? Right *now*? The parents of the man that she…that she *loved*. That was huge. A big deal. She swallowed.

She wanted to meet them. But not in her—not in her *underwear*. She'd dress first. But how did she broach that without broaching the real question of what they were. Him and her. For real. Not pretend. Because one couldn't meet the parents without first knowing how they would be introduced.

Because yes, they'd spent a week wrapped up in one another. To the outside world, nothing had changed, but behind closed doors *everything* had changed.

The problem was, neither of them had spoken of it. There'd been no heart-to-heart. Because she hadn't wanted to rock the boat. Too scared that she would push him away. Ruin whatever this was between them when it was too new, too fragile.

'Do they know about us?' she asked instead.

'I told my father we had an arrangement.'

'Oh.' Her heart gave a little shiver. That was news to her. And an arrangement wasn't a lie. It had been…in the beginning. 'When?'

He raked a hand over his hair, blew out a breath. 'A fortnight or so ago. The news got through to him so he called me, and I explained we were doing it for show.'

'You didn't say.'

'I didn't think I needed to. I wasn't expecting them to just turn up like this.'

'What are you going to tell them now?'

'Damned if I know, but I best go.'

She winced as her nails bit into her palms and he started for the door. 'Wait!'

He paused, angling his head just enough to eye her.

'Can I—? Do you want me to come too?'

'I don't think that's a good idea.'

'What about tomorrow?' She tried for a smile, though inside she could feel herself wilting. 'Perhaps we could take them for breakfast together somewhere?'

She could see the muscle working in his jaw—he didn't like the idea. Not one bit.

'Maybe. Let me just get the lay of the land first, yeah? See what's going on.'

She fought to keep her smile in place. 'Sure.'

He went to move off again.

'Hugo?'

He stopped.

'Aren't you forgetting something?'

She picked his T-shirt up off the floor, where she'd carelessly tossed it only an hour ago, when life had felt so very different, so very perfect. How was that possible? She wanted to bury her face in it and breathe in his scent. Relive that moment and the man he'd been then, to suppress the tears that wanted to fall now. Instead, she lifted her chin and handed it over.

'Thanks.'

And for a world-stilling moment she feared he would leave without a kiss goodbye. And when he bowed his head and swept his lips against her cheek for the briefest most heart-stealing kiss, she almost wished he had.

'*Bonne nuit*, Cassie.'

'Goodnight, Hugo.'

She gripped her middle, holding herself back when she wanted to race after him and confess all. Knowing that now wasn't the time. He needed to see his parents. He needed to deal with that challenge alone. Then they could face the next one together—their future and what it looked like.

Because she knew what she wanted.

The question was, did Hugo want it too?

* * *

'Maman. Papa. What are you doing here?'

'Hugo! Is that any way to greet your parents?' His mother hurried up to him, cheeks glowing from her time in the sun, but it was her eyes that truly sparkled. She looked joyous as they exchanged air kisses before she cupped his cheeks to take a closer look at his face. Her intense scrutiny heightened his nerves. 'How could you not tell me?'

'Tell you what?'

She smiled wide, patted his chest as she swirled away and took the drink his father now held out for her. In the time it had taken for Hugo to cross the hall and enter his home, his father had been let in by his team and made himself at home in the bar because, of course, he had. *What's yours is mine and mine is mine*, would be his father's motto forever.

'What's going on?'

'What do you think is going on, son? Your mother has discovered the news and was too excited to stay in paradise. She *had* to come and see it for herself.' His father raised his own glass in false cheer. 'Did you not want to bring the Princess with you?'

If looks could kill...

'Don't look so cross with your father, Hugo. It was my idea we turn up unannounced. I wanted to surprise you.'

He dragged his gaze back to his mother. 'Surprise me, why?'

Now she looked sheepish. 'I know you had us on that blissful retreat all these weeks, so I understand that you may not have wanted to break the rules to share your news, but something of this magnitude, darling. Don't you think you could have at least let a note slip in, given us just a little hint at your happiness.'

'My happiness?'

His eyes flitted to his father. Had he not told his mother the truth? Was that a sparkle in his father's eye, and to what end? Was he playing some kind of game with him?

'Father hasn't told you?'

'Told me what?'

'I figured this was your mess, son. You could be the one to explain it.'

'Mess? What do you mean? Will you two stop behaving like children and just explain.'

Hugo strode up to the bar and poured himself the same drink—like father like son. Only they weren't. They were chalk and cheese. And that was part of the problem. Why he was such a disappointment. Hugo wore his heart on his sleeve far too much for dear old dad. And he wasn't about to do it now.

'We're not in a relationship. Dad should have told you.'

Yet you were making love with her not an hour ago.

'I've been helping her out of a bad situation with her ex.'

And helping her into a new one with you.

'It's all an act for the cameras.'

An act that's been getting ever more real behind closed doors.

He threw back the drink with a wince.

'And you knew this and you didn't tell me, Antoni!' His mother rounded on his father.

'Don't blame me, Mary. I was on the retreat with you, remember.'

'But you knew all along!'

'I didn't know before he embarked on this whole debacle. If I had, I would have had something to say about it.'

His mother sank onto the edge of the sofa as she seemed to fizzle out before Hugo's eyes, and he scratched at his chest, the same sensation happening within him. And he felt his father's gaze on him, observing it all.

'Can you give us a second, Mary?'

His father's tone brooked no argument, and that's when Hugo knew, the real reason they were here was yet to come. His mother may think they were here because she wanted to be. Because she wanted to have it out with her son, the relationship she believed he'd been keeping a secret from her and to meet the woman she'd hoped had brought him happiness. But his father...

Slowly she got to her feet.

'The guest room is made up, Maman. You'll have all you need in there. I'll come and see you shortly.'

She looked so deflated, and he wanted to take it all back. The secret and the lies. He wanted to promise her the world with Cassie at the very top. Because hell, in a perfect world where he could have everything he wanted he would have that. Of course he would.

But a perfect world did not exist. Not for people like him. He'd believed in it once, and look where it had got him.

'We need to talk,' his father said as soon as his mother was out of earshot.

'Yeah, I got that.'

'It's about Sara.'

'I got that too.'

'I don't think you do, son.'

His knuckles flashed white around the glass, his eyes barely lifting from the drink as his father handed him his phone with a draft press article already active. There was the woman from his past, only she was very much in the present. She looked the same. Her warm caramel eyes, rich dark hair, alluring smile...

And there was his every flaw printed in black and white. Everything he had done wrong. His mistakes laid bare. The bodyguard who'd put his heart before his head and almost got her killed. Crossed a line when on duty. An absolute embarrassment. Brought shame on the company, on his family, and on hers.

'You need to bury this before it buries you and brings shame on her.'

He swallowed. Nodded.

And then he saw the profile shot of the reporter who had written the article. Frozen human snowman himself. How he must have loved getting his hands on this story. He shoved the phone back at his father. It didn't matter who had found the story, or how old a tale it was, it would be today's news tomorrow.

'Has Mum seen this?'

'Not yet. A friend gave me an advance read, but it'll be everywhere come tomorrow. Sara's family won't be happy.'

'It reads like it *came* from her family. A way to get their own back now that it won't affect them.'

'Perhaps.'

'I'll deal with it.'

'I'm sure you will. And what about the Princess?'

'Her name's Cassie.'

'Princess Cassandra. Cassie. They are one and the same.'

'They're really not.'

He could sense the curiosity in his father's gaze and avoided his eye. 'She goes by Cassie. And I'll talk to her.'

'I meant, what about this relationship you have going on? How long do you plan on keeping this up now this is soon to be out there? If it really is as fake as you say it is...'

He gripped the back of his neck with a curse. What a mess! What an absolute mess!

So tell him it's not. Tell him things are different now. That it's real. You can't, can you? Because the idea terrifies you.

He'd been so happy in their bubble of the past week.

Refusing to put a label on what they were now.

Refusing to think on what came next.

'She hardly needs this kind of a scandal following her about, Hugo.'

'Are you referring to me as some kind of an albatross around her neck, Father?'

'If the shoe fits. People like the Princess—*like* Cassie.' He changed it up with the look Hugo sent him, his brown eyes softening with what could even be interpreted as compassion. 'Like Sara, they come from another walk of life, son, and the sooner she goes back to it the sooner you can go back to yours. Before you get embroiled in her further... I've seen the way you look at her.'

'You haven't been here to see us together.'

'The photos are telling enough.'

'You don't know what you're—'

His father cut him off with the arch of a brow, and Hugo's chest tightened around the rest of his denial, the rest of his lie, because ultimately, his father was right. Cassie did come from another walk of life, just as Sara had. And she would return to that life and she would launch her career in fashion. She would forget about him and she wouldn't just survive, she would shine.

And if he thought life without Sara had hurt, life without Cassie…?

'Can we not do this now, please?'

'All those years I tried to make you more like me, harder, emotionally closed off,' his father said over him, 'but you had too much of your mother in you. When Sara came along, I knew she was trouble from day one. I saw what was happening and let it run its course, hoping it would teach you a lesson and I almost lost you in the process. This time I won't be so stupid. Don't be so foolish, son. Women like them, they're trouble. Why can't you find someone steady, someone home worthy, someone like—'

'Someone like me?'

'Mary!'

They both turned to find his mother stood in the hallway looking about ready to scream blue murder. 'So that is how you see me, Antoni?'

Oh, Dieu, here goes…

In a moment of madness, he thought about returning to Cassie. To escape the fight and find solace with her. But in mere hours the press would be pounding the streets outside, and his age-old wound would be tomorrow's tittle-tattle.

How did he even begin to bury it?

He didn't know, but he had to try.

Cassie barely slept a wink.

Funny how one could sleep alone for months, but a week with another and your body suddenly depended on that person to be there.

When her phone rang at the crack of dawn, she was grateful for the interruption. Grateful all the more to hear Louis's excited chatter on the other end offering to pay her for the designs she had finally sent over. A collaboration to get the name Cassie Couture out into the world—yes, please.

It was what she needed. What she'd wanted for so long. Only it landed…flat.

'You are happy—*oui*?'

'*Oui*, Louis. *Oui*.'

'You do not sound it? What is wrong, Cassie? I can… maybe offer you some more money. Is it not enough? Let me see. What about—'

'No, Louis. It's fine. Honest. More than fine. I promise.'

'Then what is it? Is it that Hugo? I bet it is! He is a big man. A beast! I am coming home tomorrow. I will sort him out!'

She gave a hitched laugh. 'No—No, Hugo is fine. We are fine.'

'I don't believe you. Don't lie to me.'

'Louis, behave. All is good. I will see you tomorrow.'

'*Oui, bien.* And then I will see you for myself and we will celebrate. Champagne! *Ciao*, darling.'

'*Ciao.*'

She hung up, a sad smile on her lips. She didn't even have the energy for a morning run. Instead, she got dressed and took her coffee out onto the balcony, watched the sun rise and Paris wake up. Surprised when the doorbell rang not long after.

Her heart did a little jig. It was too early for House-keeping and her heart did what it always did now—it sprang to Hugo.

She peered through the peephole to find an older woman on the other side. Dark hair to her shoulders, same heart-shaped brow, same blue eyes—Hugo's mother!

She eased open the door, trying to second-guess if this was a good sign or a bad sign. Could Hugo have sent her? And if he had, that would most definitely be good, wouldn't it?

'*Bonjour*, I hope you don't mind me calling by.' Her French accent was thick, her eyes and smile both warm and welcoming. 'But since my son was so rude as to keep you a secret for over a month, I thought I would introduce myself. I'm Hugo's mother.' She held out her hand, which Cassie took, and she gently covered Cassie's with her other. 'Mary Chevalier.'

'It's a pleasure to meet you, Mrs Chevalier. I'm Cassie.'

'So I hear.' Her smile widened as she released her. 'And you can call me Mary. Can I tempt you to break-fast, Cassie?'

'Erm…sure.' She stepped back. 'Would you like to come in?'

'I thought we might go out.'

'Out?' Cassie gulped. 'Just me and you?'

'Oui.'

'Does Hugo know?' She looked across the hall at his very closed door and Mary nipped her lip, leaning in conspiratorially.

'I won't tell if you won't.'

Cassie gave a nervous laugh. She couldn't help it. Now she understood where Hugo got his playful spirit from.

And what could it hurt, really? Though what did his mother know, exactly? Had Hugo told her the truth about them…were they fake…were they real…?

The problem was, not even Cassie knew the answer to that. Not from the all-important man himself.

But this was a chance to get to know more about Hugo. Hugo from before she knew him. Hugo from his mum's perspective. And if she knew more, maybe she could find a way to make this into more for him too.

'Let me get my purse…'

Hugo woke to laughter.

The kind of laughter that had no place in his penthouse. Two women. His mother and—*Cassie?*

He shot out of bed, following the ruckus into the kitchen, and there they were. The two thick as thieves, wearing aprons and smiles and an abundance of good cheer.

'What in the love of—?'

'Ah, Hugo!' His mother swept towards him and

clamped her flour-covered hands on his cheeks as she kissed him. '*Bonjour!* Cassie and I are making your favourite!'

'My *what*?'

'Madeleines, of course!'

'Madeleines?' he repeated.

'Yes, French madeleines.' His father put down the newspaper he was reading at the table before the window and eyed him over his glasses. 'It's good of you to join us.'

Hugo ran his hands over his hair. Had he walked into some strange parallel universe, because this could not be his life today?

And then he heard it, the frenzy outside. The press. It was like the day after the night before. Or rather, the day after the flower photo had broken. Only now it wasn't him with flowers on her doorstep that had sparked the uprising, it was his decade-old failing. Almost getting a woman killed. So much for spending half the night awake, calling in favours and doing what he could to smother it.

But this laughter, this chaos in his kitchen, it was all about distracting him from it. Pretending it wasn't happening. It had to be.

And Cassie was here. Smothering herself in his shame when she should be distancing herself, getting as far away from him as she could.

He shook his head. The pounding within not thanking him for the gesture.

'Maman. Papa. Can you give us a moment, *please*?'

'I think it better you give *us* a moment, because we

don't want to let the little madeleines burn.' His mother gave him a wink. A wink!

And he reached for Cassie's hand, pulling her from the room without looking at her because if he looked at her, all cute and homely in her apron, with flour on her cheeks, in her hair—*gah!*

He was going to surrender on the spot.

Too much emotion trying to overrun his good sense, and then where would he be?

Out of control of his life and lost to it. Just like he'd been all those years ago. His life in pieces with no way of knowing how to pull it back together again.

'You shouldn't be here.' He closed his bedroom door and stalked to the window, looked down over the Champs-élysées and the hovering journalists demanding their ounce of blood, *his* blood this time, and yanked the shutters closed.

'Why?'

'You must have seen the reports?'

'You mean the stuff about Sara?'

She said it like it was nothing. How could she say it like it was *nothing*? 'Yes!'

She walked towards him and he backed away. 'It's okay, Hugo. It'll all blow over soon enough. It'll be yesterday's news. They'll print something else and the world will forget and—'

'But *I* won't. I won't forget what I did.' He pounded his chest with his fist, spat the words out. '*I* won't forget how it felt.'

She covered his palm with her hand, and he flinched away as though burnt. 'Don't. Don't touch me.'

'But Hugo, you—'

'*Please*, Cassie!' Because she was killing him. *It* was killing him. This feeling. Crushing him inside. Suffocating him. The same feeling as back then, only it cut so much deeper now. 'You need to stay away from me. You deserve someone who won't bring this to your door. *You* deserve more. *You* deserve better.'

'Don't do that. Don't stick me on some pedestal like my parents did, telling me who I should or shouldn't be seen with. Who is considered good enough for me. *I* choose those things. And I choose you.'

He shook his head so viciously he thought he might be sick. Or was that just the rolling in his gut.

'I don't care what the press says any more, Hugo. I don't care what the world says. The only person I care about is you.'

He pressed his palms to his temples, pushing out her words. Because she couldn't mean them. She only thought she did because she had spent her whole life being treated so badly. So starved of love and affection that to have known it through him these past few weeks, she now felt him worthy of it in return. But he *wasn't* worthy of it. And she would see that once she got out in the world and experienced it properly. Once he freed her of the hold he had inadvertently cast over her.

'I can't do this any longer, Cassie.'

'Do what?'

He threw a hand towards the kitchen—at the baking and his mother's presence, all mixed up in Cassie's. All homely and sweet and nice. 'Live this lie.'

'Which lie? The fake relationship to the press or the real one we have...'

He shook his head, trying to cut her off, and she gave a shaky laugh and wrapped her arms around her middle.

'Because I know you told your parents it was fake too. But your mother took me for breakfast this morning, and she made it pretty clear that she thinks it's quite real and—'

'No, Cassie!'

Hugo stared back at her, the tortured look in his blue eyes crushing her with his words.

'No, Cassie?' she repeated softly. 'What do you mean, "no"?'

Though she knew, could already feel the chasm so vast between them.

'So, it's over,' she said, when he failed to speak. 'Whatever this was, it's over. You and me. This?'

Still nothing. Barely a flicker of his dark lashes over eyes that still raged a storm.

'Fine.' She lifted her chin, stood tall as if she owned her feelings and wanted him to know them too. That way there could be no confusion between fact and fiction when she was gone. 'But since we're done with the lies, Hugo, here's my truth—I love you.'

He blanched, and she wanted to choke on her own heart.

'Yes, I know you don't want to hear it, but tough. I do. You have given me so much. You have shown me how to live and to love and for that I will always be grateful to you.'

He'd gone so very pale, his eyes so very vacant. She pleaded with him to say something, anything, but... nothing.

'As for going forward, I'm moving out. Louis is coming back tomorrow, so you won't need to see me every day either. You can count your blessings there too.'

Still, nothing.

'Goodbye, Hugo.'

And she walked before her legs refused to function and she crumbled at his feet. Because she refused to let him see how broken she truly was.

She would be okay. She had her future. She had Cassie Couture. She had her whole life ahead of her. Her dreams were coming true.

Even if Hugo wasn't to be a part of them any more, it was better to have loved and lost than never to have loved at all.

And she truly believed that, having known it now, pain and all.

CHAPTER ELEVEN

Three days later

'IF YOU HADN'T made him feel so worthless growing up, maybe he'd feel worthy of her now.'

'And if you hadn't made him feel so soft, maybe he would have been man enough to fight for her.'

Hugo gawped at his parents, who had made themselves right at home on his sofa.

'Will you two just stop, please. This isn't helping.'

'Well, if you'd been honest with me about how you felt, son.'

'You didn't give him the chance to be honest, Antoni. You were too busy throwing Sara back at him!'

'*I* messed this up, Maman. Me! Nobody else!'

Now his parents gawped at *him* and he dropped his gaze to the note in his hand, fighting the reflex that would have seen it crumpled and creased. Scarcely able to believe the words on the card that had accompanied the bouquet of classic cream hydrangeas now on his coffee table.

He would think it some twisted joke of the paparazzi if he didn't know Cassie's elegant scrawl as well as his own handwriting, having pored over enough of her detailed fashion designs...

My darling Hugo,
I am sorry for what has come to pass.
   It was never my intention to hurt you, nor to fall in love with you.
   The press are my cross to bear, and what was printed in your name will pain me for ever. Because, as Wellington once said of Napoleon, you are worth forty thousand men—to my mind, you are worth all the men in the world. Because I have never met one such as you.
My heart is yours.
Always and for ever.
Cassie xxx

He strode up to the window, stared out over the streets of Paris, wondering which one was lucky enough to offer up a home to her now. Because to write the note by hand at the local florist he'd used himself all those weeks ago, meant she had to be in the city somewhere…only where?

He wanted to throw open the French windows and call her name from the rooftops, beg her to come home.

'This was my mistake and now I need to fix it,' he said, his breath misting up the chilled pane of glass. But how did he fix it when he didn't know where she was?

Louis was refusing to speak to him, so there wasn't a chance in hell he'd give away her location.

He pressed his fist against the window, gritted his teeth. How could he have been so stupid as to let her walk away? The one woman he had come to love with his all. The one woman who had chosen to love him with her all, and he had thrown it back in her face. Rejected it. All because he had deemed himself unworthy of it. How stupid could he be?

What he would give to be able to rewind to that night or that morning, he didn't care which, and make it right. Tell her the truth. Tell her that he loved her. That he'd always love her and only her.

'You know she has Lyon's security working for her.'

Hugo's ears pricked at his father's less than subtle comment. 'Lyon?'

'*Tak.* She asked me if I could recommend a close protection firm...after giving me what for.'

He turned his head. 'She gave you what for?'

'A bit like your mother's doing now. Some nonsense about not telling you I was proud of you enough. That if I'd loved you a bit more, then maybe you'd have accepted her love rather than thrown it back in her face.'

He huffed and his mother gasped. 'You didn't tell me that, Antoni.'

'Yes, well, it was hardly my finest moment to share.' His father cleared his throat and squeezed his mother's hand before getting to his feet and crossing the room. 'And it wasn't nonsense at all. She was right. And I'm sorry for that, son. Because I wish it wasn't the case. You're not me, and neither should I have tried to make you so. You always used this first.'

He touched his hand to Hugo's chest. The contact as surprising as the compassion in his father's brown gaze. So he hadn't imagined its presence the other day either but...his father, compassionate?

'Are you—are you *crying*, Father?'

'No. Absolutely not.'

'You could have fooled me.'

'But I am concerned about Cassie's well-being.'

'Why?' he blurted, all teasing forgotten as worry for her overtook all else. 'Why would you say that?'

'Because she's taken to running along the river at some ungodly hour in the morning like she's got some kind of death wish.'

Hugo's mouth quirked.

'I can't imagine why anyone in their right mind would do such a thing, but she's out there with a team every night like clockwork. Lyon is quite amused by it all and I told him in no uncertain terms he should quit laughing and talk some sense into her.'

'We used to go together.'

'You are joking.'

'No!' He grasped his father by his arms and planted a smacker on his cheek. 'Thank you, Papa!'

'What for?' he chortled.

'For giving me an idea.'

'You're not going to accost her at that time of night on the Seine? Surely?'

'It's our thing.'

His father eyed him dubiously. 'That's some *thing*.'

It really was, and it was all he needed...he hoped.

The witching hour wasn't the same without Hugo. It didn't stop Cassie trying to find its magic though. The peace, the rush, the joyous feeling between night and day when she could run and let go...or at least try and let go of the stress that plagued her through the day and wouldn't let her sleep at night.

That is, thoughts of Hugo and her love for him and the conversation that she knew could have gone better if she'd perhaps given him a little more time to adjust to his parents' homecoming. Hadn't ambushed him with his mother. Hadn't dumped the *L* word on him.

She toyed with going back. Every night she ran a loop that took her past the Avenue des Champs-élysées and every night she chickened out. Failing to find her peace, the rush, the magic, and her Hugo, all at the same time.

Because of course he didn't love her. How could he? She'd spent her life trying to earn the love of her parents, then the Prince. Why would Hugo be any different?

Because he is different, came the honest answer.

He was kind. He was good. He was honourable.

And she was glad she had met him, even if she had lost her heart to him and feared she would never feel quite whole again.

And she was glad she had sent him an apology too, because he hadn't deserved all that bad press over an isolated incident that had happened so long ago. Maybe if she'd read the articles, given them the time of day, she might have understood why they had cut so deep. But she hadn't wanted to. She hadn't wanted to justify a single word they had printed by dedicating a single second of screen time to them.

But she'd made herself read them in the aftermath. Having witnessed his torment, his self-loathing, his pain. She'd made herself read every word and had hated the journalist as much as she had hated herself for provoking him enough to go to the lengths it must have taken to uncover such a story. And she had hated the world for making it okay to print such words about the man she loved. Words that had cut open a wound that had barely healed, forcing her to leave him bleeding and in pain.

His reputation torn to shreds. His masculinity. His pride. His father's disappointment. His love lost. Not to mention the news spreading within his security company. How it must feel to know that he would have rookies reading the article, learning of his mistakes... All thanks to her.

'Ma'am, you need to slow down. There's someone up ahead.'

Jody, one of her close protection detail, came up alongside her and nodded to a guy as he rounded the exit of the Pont Neuf bridge. Cassie's heart fluttered in her chest. Recognising his broad frame before her eyes did.

'Hugo?'

'Ma'am?'

'It's Hugo!'

And she wasn't slowing down, she was speeding up. Racing towards him, because she knew, knew with every beat of her pulse that it was Hugo. Her Hugo. And there could be only one reason he would be here at this time of night...

'Ma'am!' Jody hurried after her, but Cassie was sprinting and so was Hugo.

'Cassie!'

'It's okay, Jody! It's Hugo! I know him! I know him!'

They came together in a collision of bodies, the air forced from her lungs as his arms closed around her and he hugged her to his chest. 'Cassie!'

He breathed her name into her hair, his voice as pained as the grip around her.

'What are you doing here, Hugo?'

'I had to see you.'

She prised herself back enough to look up at his face,

his eyes glittering in the lamplight. Lines of worry creased up his brow, bracketed his mouth—the man had aged a decade in a week and still looked like the sexiest man to walk the earth.

'Is everything okay?'

'*No*. Nothing is okay.'

'Let me guess, you're not sleeping very well again?'

'Hardly a wink.'

'So you've come to hijack my witching hour?'

'If you'll let me.'

'Is this to escape your parents?'

He choked on a laugh, his big strong hands lifting to cup her face as his eyes searched hers in wonder. 'No. For once it is not my parents. Though I'm having a tough time getting rid of them.'

'Then…'

'It is you, Cassie.' He took a ragged breath that vibrated through her too as he kept her ever close. 'It's this pain I now have inside of me because I was fool enough to let you walk away.'

'Then why did you? Why hurt us both so much?'

'Because I refused to accept your love. That for all you said you loved me, I refused to accept I could be worthy of it. But the truth is, I am too selfish to let you go, which probably means I'm even more unworthy of it.'

He gave another choked laugh, his fingers trembling against her face.

'What are you saying, Hugo?'

He lifted the rim of her cap to ease it off her head and the cool night air teased along her skin.

'I'm saying many things. I'm saying I let my fear of

getting hurt a second time around get in the way of us. I'm saying I refused to accept the truth of what was there all along. I'm saying my mother was right. I'm saying you were right. I'm saying this is real, Cassie. I am saying that I love you. With all my heart, I love you.'

She blinked up at him, her heart racing a million miles a second. 'You do?'

'I think I loved you the moment you came to my naked rescue. Loved you all the more when you stuck that ice cream cone on that jerk's nose. And I will continue loving you all the more if you can forgive me for being too foolish to accept it and hurting you in the process. I can't *bear* that I hurt you.'

'Oh, Hugo!' Tears filled her eyes, her throat, and she launched herself up, kissed him with all the love she felt inside. 'I'm sorry too. So very sorry. I never meant to hurt you. I never meant for all that stuff with Sara to get dredged up. I never—'

He kissed her deep, unrelenting, fierce. Lifting her off the ground as he pressed her body to his. 'You don't need to apologise,' he growled against her lips. 'That wasn't you. That was them. And I choose to no longer care too. My past is my past. It's a part of me and I can't change that.'

'And I'm not so sure you should… I kind of like the man you are.'

'You "kind of *like*" or do you still…?' He cocked one sexy brow and she chuckled.

'Oh, Hugo, are you fishing?'

'It's three in the morning, Cassie, give a man a break?'

She ducked his arms and backed into the middle of the bridge, her arms and smile wide as she twirled on the spot, glossy ponytail swinging out. *'écoute, Paris! J'aime Hugo Chevalier de tout mon cœur!'*

He chucked as she steadied herself to say, 'Was that loud enough for you?'

'You're going to get us arrested.' He chuckled as he walked up to her.

'Well, I mean it, Hugo. I love you with all of my heart.'

'And I love you, *mon petit chaton.*'

And then he tugged her to him and kissed her, and Cassie knew that this was it.

This was her love story. This was her man. It had taken thirty-three years and a wrong turn, but love and all its wondrous feelings was real. And it was worth waiting for.

EPILOGUE

September, two years later,
Paris Fashion Week

ROUNDING OFF FASHION'S 'Big Four', with the final week in Paris, was a dream come true for Cassie. Her label was out there amongst the world's biggest names in global fashion, and hearing the ripple of adulation and applause from the audience made up of fashion editors, writers, buyers, stylists, influencers, celebrities—*all* the people she needed to impress—was as joyous as exiting the Louvre on the arm of the man she loved. Her husband.

And she wasn't just exiting on the red carpet, she was walking on air because she had a piece of news to share with the man who had helped to make those dreams come true.

'Cassie! Hugo! Can we get a smile?'

He paused beside her, looking so very sexy in black tie. 'What do you say?'

She pulled her shimmering silver train to one side so that she could turn and smile up at him, remembering a time many moons ago. 'Do I have food on my face?'

He returned her smile, his eyes as wistful as hers

as he cupped her cheek and swiped his thumb along her lower lip. All the love in the world shining in his gaze and she couldn't wait to tell him. Was surprised he couldn't read her confession in her gaze.

'Do you think they'll get bored of that move?'

'Never. I told you, as much as they love to play the viper, they're just a bunch of old romantics who love a good love story.'

'Love story,' she said with him.

'Exactly.'

She kissed his thumb. 'I love you.'

'I love you too.'

The cameras went crazy—flashes going off, reporters cooing. Not that she was paying any attention to them—she was all about her man and the love overflowing within her.

'Shall we go home?'

'I thought you'd never ask.'

She led him to their awaiting car, pausing just long enough to say goodbye to all those that needed to be thanked. Good wishes exchanged. Promises to call. Meetings to be arranged passed to her very attentive PA.

He chuckled as soon as they were strapped into the rear seat of their limo, the privacy glass between them and the driver giving them the quiet they so desperately desired. 'Thought we'd never be free.'

She scooted into his side. 'But we're worth the wait, right?'

'We're always worth the wait, *mon petit chaton*.'

She smiled. 'When I said "we" I wasn't referring to you and me... I was referring to—' she took his hand

and pressed it against her tummy '—all of us. Another, even littler kitten.'

He tensed and his breath caught. 'Cassie! You're not. We're not.'

She nodded and peeped up at him. 'We're pregnant. I found out this morning, but with everything happening and we hadn't a moment to—'

He stole her explanation with his kiss, his elation in every impassioned sweep of his mouth against hers. When finally, he came up for air, his crystal-blue eyes glistened down at her.

'I never thought I could be happier than the day you told me you loved me. You've just proved me wrong.'

'In that case, our child proved us both wrong, because I feel the exact same way.'

'Just wait until my mother finds out.'

'Your mother? It's your father who keeps nagging about grandchildren.'

He gave a soft huff as he swept her hair back from her face and searched her gaze, his own filled with wonder. 'I can't believe he is the same man. Retirement has been the making of him.'

'Or maybe it's just softened him, giving him the chance to indulge that side of him that was always there.'

'And for that I'm glad.'

'Me too. You have a good relationship.'

'We do now. As do you.'

Her smile quivered about her lips. 'Thank heaven. I'm blessed to have that with both of your parents.'

'They feel lucky to have you too. A daughter they're very proud of.'

He'd guessed where her head was at. Thinking of

what she didn't have with her own blood, but she'd come to terms with that long ago, and she wasn't going to shed any more tears over them. She'd reached out once, with news of her engagement to Hugo, and they'd made their 'disappointment' clear. She wasn't a punchbag, willing to go back for more.

If they wanted to change their attitude and come to her, they knew where to find her. And they could bring their apology with them.

But she wouldn't hold her breath.

She didn't need them. She was happy with the people whose happiness truly mattered to her. With those she loved and who loved her in return. Who valued her happiness as she did theirs. Her family. Hugo, his parents, and their little baby Chevalier.

* * * * *

If you enjoyed this story,
check out these other great reads
from Rachael Stewart

Unexpected Family for the Rebel Tycoon
Reluctant Bride's Baby Bombshell
My Unexpected Christmas Wedding
Off-Limits Fling with the Heiress

All available now!

BOUND BY THE BOSS'S BABY

NINA SINGH

MILLS & BOON

For the many friends I consider to be my sisters.

CHAPTER ONE

ENRIQUE MARTINEZ RACKED his brain, trying to think of all his recent transgressions that he might have gotten away with. He'd clearly been mistaken about at least one. Because he was on the phone with the local police station at the moment. An Officer Clark was on the other end of the line, saying they had an important matter to discuss.

Enrique figured the matter couldn't be all that serious, whatever it was. Because they weren't at his door at the moment with an arrest warrant. Or some kind of search warrant, for that matter.

Unless that had more to do with who he was and where he came from. Even in this part of the world, his family name went far to afford him such considerations. Fair or not, just or not. Enrique didn't spend too much time analyzing the advantages his birthright afforded him. It was simply the way things were.

"Maybe we should discuss this face-to-face, Mr. Martinez," Officer Clark said into the phone.

Enrique sighed and pinched the bridge of his nose. He was a busy man; this officer had to know that. His schedule today was particularly chaotic.

"I'm afraid that would be quite difficult to do, Officer."

The other man chuckled lightly before responding. "Yeah, I get it. You must be a busy man," he said, echoing Enrique's exact thoughts. "Being a titan of industry and all."

Enrique pushed his executive chair back from the wide mahogany desk and lifted his feet to the surface, crossing his ankles. Leaning back with his head on the top of the chair, he did his best to summon some much-needed patience. This was obviously going to take a while. He really wished the man would just get to the point already.

"What's this about, Officer?" he asked.

He heard the other man clear his throat. "Well, it's a little awkward. Especially over the phone. But we think we might have something that belongs to you."

Huh. That was rather curious. For the life of him, Enrique couldn't surmise what item they might have of his that would have turned up at a Cape Cod police station.

Had one of his cars been stolen? Highly unlikely. Aside from his state-of-the-art security systems at every one of his residences, his security team on-site would have notified him immediately.

"I'm afraid I have no idea what you might mean."

"Someone dropped off a package at our door sometime in the predawn hours. They were wearing a hoodie and some type of surgical mask. We're still going over security footage, but an ID might be difficult."

"I see. What makes you think it's mine?"

"There was a note saying it needed to be delivered to you ASAP."

Okay.

The man went on. "Believe me, we debated even contacting you. It has to be some sort of scam. So we've already contacted the appropriate agencies."

Enrique swore under his breath. He was more confused now than he'd been at the start of the phone call. This whole conversation was making less and less sense with each consecutive word spoken.

But when the man finally got to the point, Enrique was certain he couldn't have heard him right.

Infant...

"I'm sorry. Did you just say that there was a baby left at your station?"

"That's right." The words were followed by a loud clearing of the officer's throat.

Enrique would have laughed if he wasn't so darn confused. "I'm sorry. But what does any of that have to do with me?"

"Well, you see, he was all bundled up and strapped into a basket. With a note attached to his little sweater."

"A note?"

The man cleared his throat again. Clearly a nervous habit. "The note claimed you're the father."

The words echoed in his head before Enrique could fully process them. *Baby. Basket. Father!*

Enrique rubbed his forehead. How was this phone call even happening?

"I know it sounds ridiculous. And I probably shouldn't have bothered you with it, but I figured you should at least know."

That settled it. Someone was almost certainly playing a joke on him. When he figured out who it was, there'd be hell to pay. He didn't have time for such foolishness. But most of the people in his life knew that very well. He couldn't imagine who in his circle might have believed for even a moment that such a prank might be a good idea.

"You're right, Officer," he finally replied when he could get his mouth moving again. "That is ridiculous."

Wasn't it?

A long pause followed from the other end of the line. Enrique wasn't typically at a loss for words. For the first time in his life, Enrique Leon Martinez was completely stumped as to what to say.

The police officer finally broke the silence. "What would you like us to do, sir?"

What did he want them to do? He honestly didn't know. The chance that this infant was actually his had to be slim. But he couldn't claim that it was zero. He frequented the Cape often on business. Even had a residence here.

The last time he was here…

Enrique swore. It had been a little less than a year ago. When he'd purchased the latest resort. He was here now to see about its renovations and rebranding. He'd celebrated his latest acquisition with a fine brandy and gourmet dinner.

And he'd left with the pretty brunette who'd bused his table in between courses. Damn.

Enrique made his mouth work somehow. "About how old does the child appear to be?"

"Well, I have four of my own. If I had to guess, I'd say he's about three months give or take."

Huh. Three months. That would seem to fit the timeline.

Enrique had an urge to ask the man what the child looked like. Or to send a picture. Then he realized how ridiculous a notion that was. There really were only two options here. He could bid this man goodbye and tell him none of this was really any of his business. That it was all clearly some colossal error.

Or he could see for himself personally about this child who was supposedly his.

The officer helped him make the decision a moment later. "The address we have on file for you happens to be on the way to the medical center where he's supposed to be taken for evaluation. It isn't standard procedure at all, but I can stop by on the way," he said. "You know, if you'd like to see him."

Fallon Duvall was trying desperately to stay asleep and ignore the alert sound coming from her phone and echoing off the walls of her tiny room.

What time was it anyway? And who was calling her? No one made phone calls anymore. Served her right for taking her phone off silent in the first place. She'd only done it in case one of the parents she'd been scheduled to meet that evening during parent-teacher interviews might have a need to reach her. She'd forgotten to switch it back.

Her mind still in a fog, she realized that the phone had been ringing for quite a while already. Between her exhaustion and how she'd trained herself to sleep through most noise, Fallon had been able to ignore it. Living right outside the Greater Boston area in a building overlooking the main expressway into the city had necessitated teaching herself how to sleep through almost any sounds. Almost.

Thankfully, the phone went silent. Fallon didn't even have the energy to reach over and fix the setting. She'd spent the day scrubbing and tidying her classroom. Then made sure to give each parent her undivided attention during their one on ones. She was utterly exhausted. Whatever the call was about, it could wait until later this morning.

A mere three seconds passed before her cell rang again.

Okay. Someone was clearly desperate to reach her. Fallon mentally wiped the cobwebs of sleep from her drowsy mind. Reaching for her phone, she switched the bedside lamp on at the same time. And then cursed herself for even thinking about ignoring the call.

The caller was the one person in the world she actually cared to hear from. Sasha.

Fallon nearly dropped the device in her haste to finally answer. "Sasha, hi."

"Hi, sis," came the breathy reply after a lengthy pause.

"Is everything all right?"

"Yeah, yeah. Of course," Sasha said, a little too quickly, and not terribly convincing.

"I haven't heard from you in a while."

"I know, sis. Just wanted to hear your voice, that's all."

A pang of guilt stabbed through Fallon's chest. She'd been so busy these past couple of years, and particularly over the last few months. Sasha had never been the best communicator, but she'd gone particularly silent recently. And Fallon had been too preoccupied with her own life to do anything about it. Finishing up her studies, then becoming certified as a public school teacher, followed by a stressful job search had taken all her time and mental energy. When she'd finally landed her job, she'd been much too busy, between teaching during the day and making up lesson plans in the evenings. Her summers weren't any better with all the waitressing she did just to make ends meet. But none of that was any kind of excuse. None of those accomplishments would even be possible if it wasn't for the woman on the other end of the line. The foster sister who'd taken Fallon under her wing when she'd needed someone the most. Fallon should have never allowed the silence between them to go on as long as it had. Sasha had been struggling for years to get her life in order. The impetus would have been on Fallon to maintain communication.

"It's nice to hear your voice too," Fallon said, lying back flat on her pillow. "Are you sure everything's all right?"

Again, the pause before Sasha's answer had alarm bells ringing in her head.

"Yeah," Sasha answered finally, drawing the word out into three syllables. "I just need to go away for a while. And I wanted to hear your voice before I did," she repeated.

"Go away?"

"Uh-huh. I'm not sure exactly where yet. But I wanted to tell you before leaving that I'm really proud of you."

The guilt in her chest grew by several factors.

Sasha continued. "I'm guessing you're a teacher by now, just like you always planned."

Fallon rubbed a palm down her face. "Uh, yeah. I teach kindergarten in South Boston."

"That's good, sis. Really good. Little kids are cute. They should all be well taken care of."

Okay. Even for Sasha, this conversation was starting to sound a bit too pensive. She was clearly in the depths of some kind of deep melancholy.

"Agreed," Fallon said. It was all she could come up with.

"Remember in that one foster home they sent us to, the mom had just recently had a baby. That kid was real cute."

Not like Fallon could forget. The woman had foisted her kid onto her and Sasha for hours on end. While she went on doing heaven knew what. "He was."

"Remember how she made us look after her baby for hours while she was out and about?"

"I do."

"I was terrible as a caregiver though." Fallon remembered that as well. At one point, Sasha had put the baby's diaper on backward. Then there was the day she had almost dipped his pacifier in a candy syrup and Fallon had luckily seen, or the time she'd turned her back and walked away from the changing table and the baby had almost rolled off before Fallon had rushed over just in the nick of time to catch him.

"I haven't thought about that house in years," Fallon said, though that wasn't quite accurate. She'd made an effort to try and push those days far back to the recesses of her mind. The only good thing about that period in her life had been the increasingly strong bond with the foster sister who'd taken her under her wing and protected her from bullies and leery fellow fosters alike.

The real question now was, why was Sasha bringing all this up?

"I have some news too," Sasha said, rather dramatically.

"Oh?"

Another long empty pause followed. The only sound coming through the tiny speaker was Sasha's quick breathing.

Fallon waited with all the patience she could muster. When Sasha finally spoke, she could hardly believe her ears. "Yeah, so I've had a baby myself, sis."

Fallon bolted upright and bounced off the mattress. She was fully awake now. Had she heard her right?

Sasha confirmed with her next words. "Nearly three months ago."

"Oh, my…"

"His name is Lucas."

"Sasha. What the—" Fallon had no idea what to say. "Are you all right?"

"Yeah, I'm fine. Took a while but I'm all healed up now. I've been staying at a shelter and the ladies there are very caring and helpful."

"And the baby? How is he?"

"I'm guessing he's fine."

The earlier alarm bells in Fallon's head turned to blaring loud sirens. "You're guessing? What does that mean?"

Sasha's large gulp of air could be heard over the small speaker. "See, I just couldn't handle it anymore. The work, the crying in the middle of the night, having another mouth to feed. It was all too much."

Fallon's throat went dry. "What did you do?"

"I left him."

Panic surged through her core. The Sasha she knew would never be careless or cruel. But had she changed so drastically? "What do you mean you left him? Where?"

"Relax, sis. I left him nice and wrapped up in blankets and a carrier outside the Falmouth Police station." Fallon released a deep sigh of relief. The police were sure to have made certain the baby was safe.

"I attached a note instructing them to contact his father," Sasha added.

"Who might that be?"

Sasha actually chuckled. "You might not believe me when I tell you. I can hardly believe it myself. God, it was a fun night."

"Just tell me," Fallon urged, mentally praying to all the deities that it wasn't one of the street criminals Sasha so often befriended.

The name Sasha uttered sounded vaguely familiar. Not a household name, as such, but definitely one she'd heard before.

A quick internet search on the man told her enough to have Fallon reeling in shock. What had Sasha gone and done?

If someone had told him this morning that there would be a police officer standing on his door stoop holding a carrier with a baby, Enrique might have laughed aloud. Added that said baby might actually be his own son made the scenario beyond surreal.

Yet here he was, inviting a uniformed policeman into his foyer and leading him to the sitting room.

"I'm afraid I can't linger here too long," the other man said once he'd stepped inside the room and Enrique had shut the door behind him. He didn't need his staff to see his unusual guest and begin a wave of questions and gossip. "Standard protocol is to take the baby straight to the medical center to be screened and evaluated."

"I appreciate you bending the rules. Not that I'm not thankful, but might I ask why you did so in this case?"

"Well, I hope you take this next comment in the manner it's intended. And that I'm not being terribly forward. But we did some online searches after reading the note. There's quite a few photographs of you on the internet."

"And?"

"And if you don't mind my saying, there appears to be a strong resemblance."

Something fluttered in Enrique's chest. "I see."

The other man's statement landed like a load of bricks over his head. Suddenly, the import of this moment became all too real, no longer a hypothetical.

He'd always prided himself on being fully prepared to tackle any circumstance. To be always ready to deal with any unknown or unexpected curve that might be thrown his way. It was how he'd taken a measly sum of pity money granted to him by his father when he'd turned eighteen and turned it into a vast hospitality empire. But in this moment, Enrique felt at a complete loss. Wholly uncertain as to what to say or how to feel.

Then again, how could he possibly have been prepared

for any of this? He hadn't so much as seen it coming. What in the world would he do if this child indeed was his? How would he even begin the journey of fatherhood? It wasn't as if he had any kind of example to follow. His own father had never been actually present in his life. Enrique wouldn't be able to pick him out of a lineup.

Strong resemblance.

It was time to see for himself. "Do you mind?" he asked, stepping forward and reaching for the carrier.

A wealth of emotion flooded his core the second he peered inside at the tiny bundle wrapped in blankets and wearing a knitted hat. Enrique had zero experience with babies, had no idea what a three-month-old might look like. Were they all this impossibly small?

Then the tiny face scrunched up and made a small whimper of a sound before opening his eyes.

Enrique's whole world shifted. He straightened, trying to get a hold of himself. "If it's all right, Officer, I'd like to accompany you to the medical evaluation."

One month later

She'd never been very good at deception. But here she was, about to try and deceive one of the most successful and shrewd men on the planet.

Fallon Duvall inhaled a deep breath and summoned all of her resolve. She could do this. She'd come this far.

She had to believe fate was on her side. Why else would she have overheard the conversation between those two nannies at school drop-off that day? Fallon had hardly believed her ears when she'd heard Enrique's name dropped excitedly and with no small amount of awe. He was apparently on the search for a nanny to care for his son. *Sa-*

sha's son. The idea had come to her then and there, and despite how outrageous and far-fetched it sounded to her own ears, Fallon knew she had to try.

After all, Sasha was nowhere to be found and maddeningly silent with no answer to her calls or emails. Fallon had to do something.

She'd enlisted with the nanny service that same afternoon, specifying that she was only interested in one particular opening.

The brief telephone interview with them had gone spectacularly well. Thank the stars above for that, because she didn't know what she'd have done if she couldn't get through that stage. Now, it was time to impress the man's staff.

"You can do this," she repeated, out loud this time. She had no choice but to try.

The door opened before she could so much as knock. A short, rotund woman with a friendly smile wearing a white service uniform greeted her.

"Ms. Duvall?"

Fallon nodded. "Yes, I'm here to interview for the nanny position."

The woman motioned her inside. "Come in, please. We've been expecting you."

Her tone implied that Fallon's arrival wasn't a moment too soon. The woman sounded as if she might be at the end of her rope.

Fallon heard her mumble something under her breath. "Let's hope this time's the charm."

Her heels clicked on the fancy marble tile as she followed the other woman into the grand foyer. Fallon took a moment to observe her surroundings. And what grand surroundings they were. She felt as if she might have stepped into a renowned European museum. Not that she'd know from any kind of personal experience. Traveling to such places had been a dream of hers since she was a child. But she didn't have the resources.

Maybe one day.

Fallon sighed deeply and pushed the thoughts aside. This was so not the time for self-pity. She was here for one purpose only. And there was no plan B. For Sasha's sake, she had to make this work. As well as for the sake of the child she already considered her nephew.

A chill ran over her skin. The house was so very cold, she felt as if she'd stepped into a walk-in freezer like those in the many restaurants she'd worked in as a teen and while putting herself through school. This mansion felt about as welcoming as those freezers too. And just as frigid.

The other woman hadn't so much as looked back over her shoulder as Fallon continued to follow her path through the foyer. A shrill sound suddenly pierced the air. Echoes of it bounced off the walls. The scream of an infant. Fallon's chest tightened. That had to be Sasha's baby. And he clearly wasn't happy.

"I'm Martha Ritter. There are monitors throughout the house," the woman in front of her explained, still without even glancing at her.

She continued. "Both auditory and video."

That explained why she could hear the baby's cries echoing off the walls. Echoes the other woman didn't seem too thrilled with.

Fallon's heart lurched in her chest. If the rest of the staff were anything like this woman, no doubt the baby could sense their resentment. Even small infants could sense when they weren't wanted. And the child screaming at the top of his lungs right now had been born unwanted. Even by his own mother.

Still, Fallon found she could forgive Sasha yet another fault. Her foster sister hadn't had the easiest life. Sasha had probably been confused and scared after having a baby by herself. At least she hadn't abandoned it completely. At least she'd left him in the care of his father.

Who happened to be one of the world's richest and most successful men.

"You'll speak to the head of staff," the other woman was saying as they made their way up a winding spiral staircase. "He'll be interviewing you first."

Another wail pierced the air before the woman got the last word out. Fallon could see her hand tightening on the banister. She whispered something under her breath that sounded less than pleasant.

Fallon didn't think, made a decision before taking the next step. She halted where she was. "If I could," she began.

Martha stopped three steps ahead of her. She turned around to face Fallon, a look of clear frustration on her face at the realization that Fallon had ceased following.

"What is it?" the other woman demanded, her tone rather icy.

"Perhaps I could see the child first?"

Martha's eyes narrowed on her face. Fallon's heart hammered hard in her chest. Great. Now she'd done it. She'd barely stepped into the house and she was about to be thrown out. But she hadn't been able to bear listening to the anguished cries of the baby any longer. He needed soothing. And clearly no one was there to give him any sort of comfort.

"You'd be there to supervise, of course." Fallon pressed

her case. "Perhaps I might be able to see what's distressing the little guy so."

Martha's eyes narrowed even further. "I don't recall that any of the literature mentioned the baby was a little boy."

Fallon cursed herself silently for the blunder. Frustrated or not, Martha Ritter was one astute woman.

"Just a lucky guess."

At the next shriek, Martha's features wilted. She shrugged her shoulders with tight impatience.

"Very well. I'm sure Mr. Watson's busy enough as it is. A few more minutes won't hurt."

Fallon had to restrain herself from blowing out a breath in relief.

"This way then," Martha threw over her shoulder and resumed her ascent up the stairs.

Fallon took a moment to gather herself together and scrambled after the woman who hadn't bothered waiting for her to catch up.

A strange tightening squeezed her chest. She was about to meet Sasha's sweet little boy. A boy she already loved and cared deeply for despite never having laid eyes on him.

"So, then, Señor Martinez, shall we move forward with the change in supply order?"

Enrique squeezed his eyes shut and tried to gather his thoughts. For the life of him, he wasn't sure how to answer. What exactly were the details of this order? It had been explained to him countless times. But his mind felt like mush from lack of sleep and sheer exhaustion.

As much as he had come to adore his newborn son, the child was clearly having trouble adjusting to his new environment. And nothing Enrique did seemed to be helping.

"I'll have to get back to you with the answer," he said

into the phone, knowing yet another delay was costing him precious time and money.

The man on the other end of the phone call remained silent, but his exasperation came through loud and clear.

As did the sudden shift in the air. Enrique's ears perked up at the change in the sounds ringing through his ears. Or lack thereof to state it more accurately. For the first time in what seemed like an eternity, the air was filled with blessed silence.

"I have to go," he said into the phone then clicked off the call, no doubt further frustrating his purchasing agent back in Mexico.

But Enrique couldn't focus on any kind of deal right now. The crying had stopped for more than mere seconds at a time.

What was this magic? Some kind of miracle, no doubt. Whatever it was, he had to figure it out and make sure it never stopped.

Tossing aside the spreadsheets he'd been studying, he strode to the door and out of his study. The golden silence was still there when he reached the nursery. Entering the door, he scanned the room for his son to find him cradled in the arms of a woman he didn't recognize. She certainly wasn't anyone on his regular staff. But she was holding Lucas with an air of what could only be described as familiarity. As if she'd somehow known him since birth.

Ms. Ritter straightened as soon as she saw him while the other woman remained oblivious to his presence. She appeared to be fully focused on the baby she held in her arms.

Enrique motioned toward Ms. Ritter to prevent her from announcing his arrival. In awe, he simply stared at the unexpected miracle he beheld. The woman who held his child cooed softly against Lucas's ear while rubbing his back and rocking him up and down. All the while, she paced slowly along the far wall.

"What's all this fuss about?" she asked softly against the baby's cheek before humming a lullaby of some sort.

Eventually, Lucas began to respond to her gentle voice. Enrique watched in stunned silence as his son began gurgling and cooing happily in answer to her voice.

How hard had he himself tried to elicit such a reaction from his child? To no avail. Enrique had lost count of the number of sleepless nights he'd spent on the rocker or pacing the nursery as he cradled his son. The sheer exhaustion was beginning to catch up to him. Business deals were hanging in the balance waiting for his response. He simply didn't have the time.

Had he ever even heard Lucas's voice except in the form of a screaming wail? Not that he could recall. Enrique could only continue to stare in stunned silence at the scene.

He took a moment to take a good look at her. He'd been right about the miracle. The woman could only be described as angelic. Thick, long curls cascaded down her back, her hair a shade of auburn he'd be hard-pressed to describe. She couldn't have been more than five foot six at most, yet her posture and standing gave an air of height to her. Her eyes were currently so focused on his son that they were slightly scrunched.

Suddenly, without warning, her head snapped up. Those golden hazel eyes zoomed square on his face like a laser beam. A flash of emotion shot behind her pupils that he could only describe as animosity before it was gone just as quickly. Only to be replaced by a questioning stare in his direction. Surely he had to be imagining any kind of negativity in her gaze. The woman didn't even know him, for heaven's sake. Definitely just his imagination. Or perhaps she'd simply been startled. He had been caught staring at her without saying a word, after all. He strode toward where she stood still cradling Lucas close against her bosom.

"I apologize for not announcing myself," he said when he reached their side. "But I didn't want to intrude on the effect you seem to be having on my son."

The baby's eyes were still focused squarely on the woman's face. As if in a trance. Lucas continued to gurgle away.

Angel or witch?

Enrique gave his head a brisk shake to brush off the nonsensical thought. Extending his hand, he waited for her to take it. She merely stared at it before simply offering a small nod of acknowledgment.

It was clearly all he was going to get.

Right. She would have to put the baby down to shake his offered palm. What a silly thing to do. What was wrong with him? With no small amount of awkwardness, he slowly pulled his arm back and jammed his hand into his pocket.

Ms. Ritter appeared at his side. "Sorry if we've disturbed you, Señor Martinez. We were just about to conduct the latest nanny interview. Miss Duvall wanted to meet the child first. I didn't see the harm—"

Enrique waved off the rest of his employee's words with his free hand. "That's fine, Ms. Ritter. I haven't been disturbed."

His employee's shoulders sagged in relief. "We'll just get on with the interview then."

Enrique surprised himself by stopping her again. "Actually, Ms. Ritter. You may go."

The woman blinked up at him. "Go? I don't understand,

sir. The young lady has an appointment scheduled with Mr. Watson."

"Tell him there's been a change of plans."

"There has?"

He nodded. "I've decided I'll conduct the interview myself," he blurted out without any real forethought.

Both women grew wide-eyed in surprise. Well, he'd surprised himself. Of all the items on his to-do list today, interviewing a prospective candidate for the role of nanny wasn't on the list. What would he even ask her? How many diapers she'd changed in her lifetime? Was that even relevant here?

He did know one thing. He wanted to get to know this woman who had such a miraculous effect on his son mere seconds after having laid eyes on Lucas. A nagging voice in the back of his mind taunted that it wasn't the only reason. He shoved it aside before it could grow any louder.

Ms. Ritter looked ready to argue, then must have thought better of it. "I'll leave you to it, then," she said, before giving the nanny a tight smile and turning on her heel to leave the room.

Huh. He'd referred to her as the nanny in his mind. That settled it then. Enrique realized he'd already made his decision. Unless there was some kind of red flag that popped up on her background check that gave him a glaring and obvious reason not to hire this woman, she was clearly well suited for the job.

And he hadn't even asked her a single question yet.

Well, there was one question he could start with. How exactly had she managed to quiet Lucas the way she had?

CHAPTER TWO

MISTAKE. NOW SHE'D gone and done it. What had she been thinking asking to see the baby first? The impulsive request had only served to draw the attention of the big man himself. Now here he was, staring her down. Demanding he interview her himself.

Stupid. *Stupid.*

She was supposed to stay under the radar, and certainly out of his periphery. Not having one on one's with him for heaven's sake. Fallon gathered a deep breath and willed her pounding heart to still. She needed to land this job. Needed to make sure she was an integral part of Lucas's life, at least until she got assurance that he was being well taken care of.

The moment she'd learned about Sasha's precious boy, she'd vowed that cycle would end with the two of them. Billionaire tycoon or not, she needed to know that Enrique Martinez would be a worthy man where it counted most—as a parent. Fallon had no illusions that he'd be any kind of hands-on parent. Men like him typically left the nitty-gritty day-to-day details of such mundane tasks as parenting to those in their employ, didn't they?

"Can I get you a coffee, Miss Duvall?" His question pulled her out of her thoughts. "I can ring for an espresso or a latte."

Fallon shook her head, the last thing she needed around

this man was any kind of stimulant. His bearing was stimulating enough. The way his employee had scrambled out of the room as soon as he'd dismissed the woman told her at least one person in his employ appeared to be intimidated by him.

Fallon shook her head. "No, I'm fine, thank you."

He nodded, then motioned toward the rocking bassinet in the corner of the room. "Might we risk putting the baby down for a moment while we speak?"

Fallon nodded in agreement and made her way to the bassinet. As gently as she could, she settled little Lucas on the plush, soft pillowy mattress of the small basket. She took a moment to study the piece of furniture. Certainly she was no expert when it came to craftsmanship. Nevertheless it was clear the bassinet was a handcrafted work of art. The mattress and blankets inside were soft as a cloud. At least she could be assured that Lucas's material needs were being met and exceeded.

Fallon stroked a gentle finger down his pudgy soft cheek, then turned around to face his father. She found Enrique standing at a coffee bar, pouring hot coffee out of a shiny silver carafe.

The man was striking.

Dressed in an immaculately tailored steel-gray suit with a magenta tie that brought out the dark highlights of his hair, his charcoal-black eyes must have melted the hearts of females all over the planet. Enrique Martinez was movie star gorgeous. Sasha probably fell hard as soon as she set eyes on the man. But how could she have not seen right away just how far out their league this man was? Though who could blame her? He was tall, imposing, successful. He'd probably flirted with her until all her defenses crumbled. Not that Sasha was exactly known for her restraint or self-discipline.

All the more reason Fallon should have done more to protect the woman from herself as well as from men like Señor Martinez. But she'd been too focused on her own ambitions, her own life. Now, look where they were. In a state of chaos. With an innocent little baby caught in the middle of it all.

Enrique held up a ceramic mug. "Are you sure you don't want a cup as well?" he asked.

Fallon merely shook her head.

He gestured to the sofa between them. "Then please, have a seat."

Slowly, Fallon walked across the room and did as he requested. Enrique didn't follow suit. Instead, he leaned back against the coffee bar behind him, studying her. Fallon immediately felt at a disadvantage. As if the man's natural height wasn't enough to have her feeling inferior, now he was practically towering above her from across the room.

"So," he began, "tell me, Miss Duvall. What brings you here this morning?"

Fallon swallowed. What was he getting at? He knew she was here to interview for the nanny spot. "Please, call me Fallon. And I'm here regarding the position of full-time nanny." *As you very well know*, she added under her breath.

Enrique set his cup down and crossed his arms in front of his chest. "Yes, but why?"

"Why?"

"Why do you want this position in particular?"

Fallon blinked. Could he somehow know her real reasons? How would that even be possible?

For one insane moment, she felt the urge to come clean. To just blurt it all out. To tell him the complete truth.

That child may as well be my nephew. His mother is practically my sister. We grew up together. I was supposed to take care of her, to keep track of her. I was supposed to make sure she didn't make the kind of mistake that has led me here today.

What might his reaction be if she simply told him all of that?

No. Bad idea. She had no faith that Enrique Martinez could be trusted to do the right thing with the truth. After all, there was a good chance he harbored resentment toward Sasha for abandoning her child. He might very well resent Fallon by extension if he found out who she really was. Worse, he might accuse her of being here with the intent to spy on him for Sasha.

She couldn't risk telling him the truth just yet.

Instead, she swallowed and took a deep breath. "I'm looking for a change from what I'm doing currently."

That was a lie. One that fell from her lips rather easily, so much so it was disconcerting. Fallon actually loved her job, and it was breaking her heart to have to give it up. Knowing that she wouldn't be returning to her darling students next fall brought a sting of tears to her eyes.

"And what is that exactly?"

"I teach at Latin Elementary in South Boston. Kindergarten. I've been there about two years. I have a bachelor's degree in early education and a graduate degree in child development. My thesis centered around early childhood development and—"

Enrique cut her off with a raise of his hand. "No need to get into all that," he said, surprising her. "I can do it with a simple look at your CV."

"Then what is it exactly that I can tell you, Señor Martinez?" she asked, addressing him the way Ms. Ritter had earlier, figuring that's what he must prefer.

"You've decided to leave your current job. Why is that?"

Fallon shrugged, hoping to sound convincing. "I realized I'd prefer a home setting. And to work with a child or children directly one on one. I believe I'd have more of an impact that way." That was certainly close enough to the truth.

He nodded once. "Well, you've certainly had an impact on my son already," Enrique said, tilting his head in the direction of the bassinet. "I can't recall the last time he's slept so soundly. Why do you think that is?"

Truth be told, Fallon couldn't really explain why she'd been able to soothe Lucas so swiftly and so effortlessly. The only explanation she could come up with was that the baby must have somehow sensed a kindred spirit. He'd instinctively known that Fallon already loved him and cherished him. Or maybe it was much more basic. Perhaps he'd recognized the scent of his mama? She and Sasha grew up sharing the same toiletries and soaps. The same toothpaste. The same lotions. Lucas might just be smelling his mother on Fallon's person. The thought both touched and saddened her.

Enrique cleared his throat across the room. She'd drifted off into her thoughts again and he'd noticed. Fallon gave her head a brisk shake to get her bearings. This was turning out to be much harder than she'd anticipated. But she hadn't counted on even laying eyes on the man himself let alone having him conduct the interview on his own, for heaven's sake.

He was staring at her expectedly. That's right. He'd asked her a question. What was it? Focus!

That was so hard to do with those intense, dark eyes staring down at her with such scrutiny. This was unlike any job interview Fallon had ever been through in the past.

Just as she was about to ask him to repeat his question, he spared her the need. "I see you find it a mystery too. Whatever the reason, my son seems to have taken to you. That's enough for me to have your application move forward. Contingent on a complete background check, of course."

Fallon felt a moment of panic. He was going to do a personal check on her? "I believe the agency has already done a thorough investigation."

He nodded once. "Be that as it may, I prefer to have my own security staff play a role as well. I'm sure you understand. You'll be in my household in charge of my only child. I can't have any questions about your character arise later on."

Fallon did her best to mask the apprehension churning in her gut. She had to relax. It was unlikely even his private security would be able to uncover the fact that she'd grown up with said son's mother.

"Is there a problem?" Enrique asked.

So the mask was less than convincing. She immediately shook her head. "No, no. Just seems like a redundant step, that's all."

"Maybe so. But I'm not a man to take anything for granted. And I always look to see what's below the surface."

Fallon swallowed the lump that formed in her throat at his words. Clearly, the man had trust issues. Someone had to have betrayed him gravely in the past. Well, she could relate.

"You're not a very trusting man, are you?" she blurted before she realized she'd even intended to speak the words out loud.

An expression of weariness washed over his face.

"I'm sorry, I shouldn't have—"

He held a hand up to stop her before she could continue with her apology for being so blunt. "You're correct, Miss Duvall. There are only two people on this planet I trust."

Seemed they might have something in common, after all. Fallon had learned herself at a young age not to easily give her trust away to just anyone. In fact, since the deaths of her parents, Sasha was the only one in her life who hadn't betrayed her in some way or another. "I can appreciate that, Señor Martinez," she answered with sincerity, then just to move on from the rather uncomfortable conversation added, "I look forward to the next steps."

He took another sip of his coffee, not tearing his eyes from her face. "As do I. If you'll just wait here, I'll have Ms. Ritter escort you back out and explain what those next steps will be."

"Then I won't need to meet with Mr. Watson? Or any of the other staff?"

"I don't see any reason to do so. Now that I've spoken to you myself."

Right. That made sense. And she had to get the silly security check out of her mind. Her background was squeaky clean. There was only one secret she didn't want Enrique Martinez uncovering, and it was unlikely to show up on any type of document or computer file.

But as ready as she was to leave this room and Enrique's intense gaze, Fallon's heart lurched in her chest. When would she see little Lucas again?

Try as she might, she couldn't help but turn in the baby's direction to take another look at him before leaving.

"Would you like to say 'goodbye'?" Enrique asked, apparently reading her all too well.

Fallon lied yet again. "Oh, no, that's okay. I wouldn't want to risk waking him."

Or risk appearing even more invested than she did already. Enrique made no move to leave. He continued watching her, his eyes clouded with curiosity. Or suspicion. Probably both.

Finally, he spoke. "Aren't you going to ask?"

Fallon blinked up at him in confusion. "Ask what?"

He put his cup down and wandered over to take the seat across the sofa she sat on. "About my wife."

His what?

Nothing she'd read about Enrique Martinez alluded to him being married. Unless it was a very well-kept secret.

"You're married?"

He slowly shook his head. "No. I am not."

Another flush of relief spread through her chest, though she'd be hard-pressed to explain exactly why.

"Then... I don't understand."

"I just find it curious. That you haven't asked about meeting Lucas's mother. Even though you inquired about other staff."

The man was too sharp by far. Such a simple thing to overlook. It hadn't even occurred to her to pretend to be curious about the child's mother. Because she already knew the truth about her.

Fallon tried hard not to visibly swallow. As nonchalantly as she could, she gave him a small smile, then shrugged slightly. "I just assumed it wasn't any of my business."

To her surprise, Enrique's lips grew into a wide grin and he winked at her. "Discretion is a quality I find important, Miss Duvall," he said. "I think you might fit in very well indeed."

To: sashabird2@ethermail.com
From: Nofall7811@ethermail.com
Subject: Where are you?

I have no idea if these emails are making their way to you, Sasha. But I will continue to send them until you respond. I know I don't have to repeat how worried I am about you, but I'll say it all the same.

Please, if you're receiving these, write back to tell me you're okay. If things work out as I've planned, I hope to have some news for you soon.

Love, your Fallon

P.S. I'm sorry I haven't been there for you.

Fallon closed the laptop lid and pushed away from the coffee table it sat on. The apology was redundant at this point. But she'd felt compelled to sign off with it on each email so far.

Emails that hadn't been returned in weeks now. Wherever Sasha was, she was either ignoring them or not receiving them. Fallon would guess on the former. Sasha had done this sort of thing before, ghosted her because she felt overwhelmed and at odds with life in general.

But never before had the stakes been quite so high.

Speaking of said stakes, why hadn't she heard anything regarding the nanny position? It had already been a week since she'd met with Enrique. Had she imagined his enthusiasm about hiring her? Had someone else come along afterward who'd impressed him more than she had?

Had she turned Enrique off with her bluntness when she'd questioned his trust issues?

That would be the end of the line then. She had no plan B. The best she could hope for if Enrique didn't hire her was to try and keep track of little Lucas from afar through website articles and social media. The thought sent a surge of sadness through her chest.

To think, just a few short weeks ago, she'd had no idea Lucas even existed. She would have been perfectly content sitting in her small, modest apartment with the whole summer ahead of her before the start of classes in September. She'd be wondering which of her creative projects to focus on during the day while earning some pocket cash waitressing in the evenings at the trendy brewery tavern across the river.

Maybe she might have even met someone during one of her shifts. Someone who might have taken her to dinner. Or offered to walk her home after she got off work. Someone who might ask to kiss her after a few dates. Someone with dark hair and dark eyes with tanned olive skin who wore tailored suits.

Fallon bolted upright. That wayward thought had no business skittering through her mind.

She really couldn't go there. Sasha had turned all her summer plans upside down. Now the only project Fallon had occupying her mind and efforts revolved around Sasha's baby. The last thing she needed was to entertain any kind of romantic fantasies about the boy's father.

Rubbing her palm across her forehead, she began to pace the room. Of course, all of that was moot if she didn't even land the job. She would have failed before even starting.

You're such a failure. Your name should be Failin', not Fallon.

Her second foster mother had taken immense pleasure in mocking her name for the entire year she'd been with that family. It wasn't long before the other members in the household had followed her lead. Fallon squeezed her eyes shut and shoved the memory from her mind. Though such memories were always just below the surface ready to surge above it at any moment.

The ring of her phone came as a blessed distraction from the hateful recollections of her earlier life. Fallon scrambled to get to the couch where she'd tossed it and answer before it switched to voicemail. The nanny job. Were they finally calling her about it? Would it possibly be Enrique himself on the line? Her heart thudded in her chest at the thought of hearing his voice when she answered. The screen displayed an unknown number, not one in her contacts app. This had to be it.

Fallon quickly clicked the answer button only to be met with disappointment a moment later. The call wasn't about the offer at all. And the caller was definitely not Enrique.

Instead, Mary Harlon's voice greeted her. The vice principal at her school, the woman she directly reported to. Or would have if she were to return. No wonder she didn't recognize the number. Mary must be calling from her personal phone.

"What's this I hear about you not returning?" the other woman asked without bothering with a hello.

Her boss had left for vacation a couple weeks early before Fallon had had a chance to speak to her directly. She was taking a risk, of course. Quitting her job before securing the nanny spot was probably unwise. But she didn't want to make Mary and the others scramble at the start of classes to find her replacement. This way they would have the summer to launch a search. She could always pick up extra shifts at the tavern.

"I thought you liked working at the school," Mary added before she'd had a chance to answer.

"I do, Mary. Truly."

"Then why?"

Fallon bit her lip. This lying thing wasn't getting any easier. "I'm just looking for something a little different this coming year."

"Like what?"

The woman could be persistent. Though Fallon figured it was only fair, she did owe Mary something of an explanation. Not that she could exactly tell her the truth. How in the world would she even begin to explain?

You see, Mary, I've recently found out there's a child out there I feel a personal responsibility for. And I can't bear the thought that he might be mistreated in any way. I'd like to find out myself for certain. Also, I'd really like to be a part of his life, at least during the early years. Because the thought of Sasha's child experiencing anything remotely like what his mother and I went through growing up is absolutely shattering.

No, she couldn't say any of that. But she could stick to the truth as much as possible.

"I just find myself needing to do this," she answered simply, then bid the other woman goodbye.

It didn't take long after she'd hung up for her phone to ring again. Fully expecting to have to restate her case to Mary yet again, she was surprised when a male voice sounded from the tiny speaker when she answered.

"Ms. Duvall. This is Lance Watson, Mr. Martinez's personal assistant. I'm calling to offer you the position of full-time caregiver to his young son. I've sent detailed documents to the email address you provided on your application."

Fallon fought the urge to cheer out loud. "Oh. Wow. Uh, thanks."

"You're welcome. Now, how soon can you start?"

CHAPTER THREE

ENRIQUE'S EYES GREW blurry as he studied the figures on his laptop screen. The baby had cried all night again, and no amount of soothing and rocking had served to calm him until the break of dawn this morning. Thankfully, little Lucas had finally fallen asleep. Leaving his sleep deprived father with a full schedule and loads of work that needed attention that he'd have to attend to now with barely a wink of sleep.

As Lucas's father, it vexed him that he couldn't figure out how to lull his own child to sleep. Shouldn't he have some kind of natural ability to soothe his own baby? Like Fallon Duvall had. He'd wanted to hire her then and there. But of course they'd had to wait for an extensive background check to be completed. Which luckily came back clean. Even with his connections and resources, it had still taken a week. He'd been surprised to hear that Fallon Duvall had grown up in foster care, bouncing from house to house after losing her parents to a terrible accident. Enrique couldn't imagine being uprooted in such a manner. His mother had essentially abandoned him and his brother, but they'd both always had a steady and loving home with his *abuela*. According to the records his security team had dug up on her, Fallon had never known such stability. Rather impressive then just how far she'd come in life despite such loss and lack of resources.

Enrique paused and rubbed a hand down his face. Honestly, he had no business thinking about the woman this much. She was a potential employee, nothing more. It mattered little how impressive she was. His only thoughts should revolve around how she might help him to concentrate on his massive to-do list if she was around to take care of Lucas.

First thing first. He was going to need a gallon of espresso just to get though the morning. How did new mothers do this day in and day out? Particularly ones without the benefit of nannies or close family members nearby to help?

Speaking of nannies, after his espresso, he'd stop by Watson's office to see how negotiations were going with Miss Fallon. The sooner the woman could start, the better for both him and little Lucas.

Much to his surprise, and he had to admit, to his delight, Watson wasn't alone when Enrique made his way to assistant's office twenty minutes later. Very good news. She'd already been hired. At least that part of the process had gone relatively quick, thank the saints above. Maybe he could finally get some work done without constant distractions and actually be able to sleep more than two or three hours a night.

Fallon Duvall sat across the desk, signing paperwork. Neither one noticed him hovering in the doorway. Enrique took the moment to study her profile. A delicate nose above lush, pinkish lips. Her skin slightly darker than olive. A few curls of thick auburn hair appeared to be escaping out of a tight top bun.

She wasn't classically beautiful but he had to admit that she was rather striking. And that figure…

Enrique gave himself a mental thwack. As if this was the time to be entertaining such inappropriate thoughts. The woman was his employee for heaven's sake. Hired to watch his son. He couldn't harbor thoughts of being attracted to her.

Without warning, her hand stilled and she turned her head to look at him over her shoulder. Clearly, she'd sensed his presence. Another point in her favor, she was obviously very aware of her surroundings. His own assistant hadn't even noticed him standing there. And Watson was facing the door.

Watson spoke first. "Enrique. I didn't realize you were there." He gestured to where Fallon sat across the desk as Enrique made his way into the room. "Happy to say that Ms. Duvall has accepted the position. She's ready to start right away."

Fallon turned back around without acknowledging his presence. Why that vexed him, Enrique couldn't begin to explain. The only thing that mattered was what Watson had just confirmed. She'd accepted the job and was ready to start. Enrique resisted the urge to throw a celebratory fist punch in the air.

"Welcome to the staff," he said. She had no idea just how much he meant that.

"Thank you," she replied. This time she swiveled around in her chair to face him fully. The smile on her face was guarded, hesitant. Was it just her personality to be so reserved? Or was there something about him specifically that had her appearing so apprehensive?

No matter. She wasn't there to look after him. Though the thought had a certain appeal.

Dios! He really shouldn't be going there. At all.

"We're looking forward to having you to help care for little Lucas, Miss Duvall."

"As am I. But please call me Fallon."

He nodded. "And you must call me Enrique."

"Enrique might finally get a full night's sleep now that you're here," Watson added.

Fallon's eyebrows lifted just enough. "You mean you've been staying up with him yourself?" Surprise laced her voice and words.

"Yes. Of course. He is my son."

"Huh," was all she said in response.

"You sound surprised."

An almost imperceptible shrug of her shoulder. "I guess I am."

Well, she was candid, at least.

She continued. "It's just that, even without the full-time nanny position filled, I imagine you have the staff to take care of such matters."

Enrique walked farther into the room, sat one hip on the desk across from her. "That's true. But as I said, I am the boy's father. I'd like him to begin to recognize me as a source of security and comfort. I know he and I have some time to make up for."

Something shifted behind her eyes at his words. "That's...um...very commendable."

He wasn't sure if that was supposed to be a compliment or not, so he didn't bother to try and thank her for it. Commendable. If she had any idea about how he'd grown up, or any inkling about the man Enrique's own father had been, she'd know just how important it was for Enrique to bond with his child.

But of course she couldn't know. Not many people did, in fact. His father wasn't a topic Enrique liked to talk about. Or a topic he even wanted to revisit in his own head. One day he might have to explore the way finding out about Lucas had brought all the haunting memories of his own childhood rearing to the surface.

But there was no time for that now.

Sasha—
Great news! I managed to get the job. I can keep an eye on Lucas now. They offered me an exorbitant amount of money too. Several times over my current salary at the school.

But of course, this isn't about money. It's about making sure your little boy is safe and cared for. And I have to say, he does appear to be very important to his father. The man was dead on his feet that first morning because he'd stayed up all night with his son. Imagine that. The staff he employs—yet he wanted to stay with his baby himself.

Still, until I know for certain that all is well, I plan on staying close by him. You should see him now, Sasha. He's a bit fussy at times, but such a little sweetheart when he calms and grips my finger or lays his head on my chest. I know you want that too. Don't you?

Please write back and let me know you're okay. I'm so very worried.

Fallon sighed, rereading the message she'd sent weeks ago now that hadn't received a response. Just like all the others. She'd keep trying, though with each passing day she was losing more and more hope that Sasha was ever going to get back to her.

She hadn't been exaggerating in her email about the

hefty salary. She'd make sure to set aside a good portion of the money in a separate account for Sasha to have whenever she resurfaced. That was only fair.

If she resurfaced.

Lucas slept soundly in his crib in the corner. She'd already tidied his room of the various toys and books they'd spent the afternoon playing with. His afternoon naps were pretty unpredictable. He could be down for over an hour or barely fifteen minutes. She might not have much time to take a quick break and grab a bite of lunch.

Slipping the baby monitor in her pocket, she quietly opened the door to step into the hallway. Only, she somehow ran into a solid wall instead. A tall, muscled, hard wall that smelled of sandalwood and mint.

It took all her might not to shriek and risk waking the baby. Clasping a hand to her chest against her thumping heart, she looked up to find Enrique watching her with an amused smile.

"Apologies. I didn't mean to startle you."

She gave her head a brisk shake. Even without the element of surprise the man was remarkably startling. Today he wore a casual cream V-neck sweater that contrasted strikingly with his dark features. He'd rolled his sleeves up to the elbows, and it was hard not to stare at the muscled contours of his arms. A pair of tailored black slacks fit him all too well.

"I should have been paying better attention."

He merely stared at her so she felt compelled to break the silence. "Lucas is finally sleeping. I figured this might be a good time to head downstairs for a quick bite before he wakes up."

He nodded once. "Perfect. I'll join you."

Fallon swallowed. She'd hardly seen the man since starting a month ago. Which was a relief as he made her jumpy and anxious for reasons she wanted to kick herself for. "You will?"

"Yes. Lunch is prepared and awaiting me in the dining room. We can eat together."

Right. As if she'd be able to swallow a bite with Enrique sitting at the same table. "I don't want to infringe on your lunch," she protested. "I was just going to make myself a quick sandwich in the kitchen."

He gave a dismissive shake of his head. "You're not infringing. And I'm sure chef's prepared plenty of food. Besides, there's something we need to discuss." He stepped aside and gestured for her to continue.

How in the world could she argue with any of that?

So much for a relaxing breather while Lucas napped. Fallon summoned a calming breath and made her way to the spiral staircase all too aware of the man trailing behind her. What did he have to speak to her about? He couldn't have found out the connection between her and Lucas's mother, could he? The thought of that possibility sent a rush of panic through her chest. She'd never be able to explain herself or justify her motivations in the face of questioning.

But that couldn't be it. For one thing, Enrique appeared much too calm. Surely if he'd found out the truth, he wouldn't be so even-tempered at the moment. He'd probably be demanding answers of her while launching another search with the nanny agency.

By the time they made it to the dining hall on the first floor, she'd managed to get her pulse somewhat under control. Whatever Enrique wanted to discuss, it couldn't have anything to do with her true connection to Lucas. When they reached the table, he stepped behind her to pull her chair out, then took the chair opposite her.

Fallon had to make an effort not to gawk at the surroundings. She hadn't been in this particular room before. It was beyond extravagantly decorated. The table was long and wide, polished to a high shine. She counted twenty-two chairs. Heavy draperies hung over floor-to-ceiling glass windows. A plush Oriental rug covered the floor.

Did the man always dine so formally? Even for a simple midday meal with his nanny?

A middle-aged gentleman in a crisp white shirt and necktie appeared within seconds of them taking their seats. This had to be what dining in a fancy, expensive restaurant must feel like. Except they were the only two people in the room and the man seated across from her happened to own the place. The man addressed Enrique in Spanish. At Enrique's response, he turned to greet her with a friendly smile. "Welcome, miss. Lunch will be served right away."

Less than a minute after he'd walked away, he returned carrying two steaming bowls. The aroma had Fallon's mouth watering. Another employee immediately followed with a tray of assorted rolls and crackers. She willed her stomach not to growl in anticipation when the bowl was placed in front of her. A rich, savory broth with loads of spinach and other colorful vegetables.

"Please, begin." Enrique gestured to the food in front of her.

Fallon draped the cloth napkin on her lap and picked up her spoon. "You said you needed to discuss something with me?"

Enrique picked a plump roll off the tray and nodded. "Yes. I'm afraid our schedule must change. I've had some rather unexpected glitches in a business project that will need my immediate attention."

That's all this was, then? A simple matter of scheduling? Perhaps he was about to travel on business for several days. What a relief that would be. To not be nervous about running into Enrique as she got to know her Sasha's son better.

Fallon released a sigh of relief and dipped her spoon into the steaming hot soup. Only to have his next words stop her midsip.

"We'll be flying into Mexico next week."

Why in the world had she just gone as white as the tablecloth and porcelain dishware? Her pallor was the least of it. Fallon sputtered on the sip of soup she'd just taken, followed by a couple of coughs.

Enrique quickly pushed her glass of water closer within her reach. "Is something wrong? Is the soup not to your liking?"

She actually grunted in answer.

"Is it too hot?"

Fallon shook her head. "Believe me. It's not the soup."

"Then what is it?"

She gingerly took a small sip of water and wiped her mouth with her napkin. Enrique found himself momentarily distracted by the luscious curve of her lips, the way they turned more red as she wiped them with the silk napkin. Kissable lips. Lips that had a man wondering what they might taste like.

And that was enough of that. He still had to figure out why she'd come near to choking on a spoonful of soup she'd barely tasted. Unless...

"You are upset about having to leave the States?"

She hesitated before answering. Her pause was answer enough. Of course, she must have someone she was loath to leave behind. Enrique was pretty certain she wasn't married. A boyfriend or lover then. The thought sent a tightening sensation in his chest that he didn't want to examine.

Her answer was a tight shuttering of her eyes. Enrique knew his next question was borderline over personal. He asked it anyway. "Is there someone here who will be sad to see you go?"

She shook her head. "No. That's not it. I don't really have any family. And I'm not seeing anyone."

The admission sent a lightning bolt of pleasure through his core. Not that he had any right to feel it. "Then I don't understand."

"I guess I'm just a bit surprised."

"But you knew the requirements of the job upon application included a willingness and ability to travel. Why is it a problem?"

She shook her head. "It's not. Really. I just wasn't expecting it to have come up so soon. I've barely been working for you for a month."

"I can have one my personal assistants help you get your affairs in order before you leave."

"That won't be necessary."

"If it's a matter of a passport, we can have it expedited and delivered within a day or so."

"I actually will need to do that."

"Very well." He fished his phone out of his pocket and sent the necessary message to get the process started. "You'll be sent instructions on applying for an expedited one within the hour."

"Thank you."

He studied her. She looked anything but thankful. And she'd clearly lost her appetite. "You're welcome. Yet you remain appearing as if someone has asked you to slay a dragon. Why?"

She ducked her head ever so slightly before answering him. "I've never actually traveled outside the United States before." She looked pained to have had to admit the fact. No excitement about the prospect of heading somewhere new. On the contrary, she looked terrified about the concept.

"Then maybe you can consider it a bit of an adventure." He really didn't want to have to look for a replacement nanny. Plus he'd gotten somewhat used to having Fallon Duvall around. As had his son. No, whatever this issue was on her part, it would have to be addressed and fixed.

For both their sakes.

"Yes, I'll try and do that."

She hardly sounded or looked convincing. Actually, she still looked terrified. He knew some of the more recent news reports from his home country could be a little disconcerting. But that could be said about almost any country. "We'll be traveling to a luxe resort visited by celebrities and other VIPs. You have nothing to be afraid of. As soon as we land in Cancun International Airport, we'll have a car waiting to take us to Tulum."

"I'm sure I'll be fine once we land."

Enrique leaned back in his chair as understanding dawned. "You're nervous about flying."

She ducked her head, averted her gaze. So that was clearly a yes.

"Then, if you don't mind my asking, why did you apply for and accept a job that specifically stated would involve travel?"

She shrugged. "I guess I hadn't really considered it until the very real possibility came up just now."

He reached for his phone again. "That's simple enough to fix," he said, calling up the contact of his personal physician at Boston Medical. "I'll have you see my doctor—he can give you something to calm your nerves before we board."

Something in her expression had him halting before making the call. "You don't like that idea."

She shook her head. "I try to stay away from any kind of mood-altering medications. I never have taken them. And I never will."

Well, that was a rather comforting statement coming from the woman in charge of caring for his son. But her voice was heavy as she said the words. There was a story there. Maybe one day she would confide in him and tell him what it was.

He knew from the background check that she'd lost her parents at a young age. Could her fear of flying have something to do with that loss?

She threw her hands up, palms facing him. "Please don't give it another thought. I'll get over my phobia before we have to begin the trip. I love being Lucas's nanny. Even in this short period of time, I've grown tremendously fond of him. I'll do whatever it takes to get past my fear. I don't want you to even consider finding a replacement for me."

Well, that was good to hear. Neither did he. Still, he had to do something to help her.

CHAPTER FOUR

IT WAS THE second time in less than forty-eight hours that she nearly ran into Enrique's chest as she was exiting Lucas's room.

"We have to stop meeting like this," he said with a smile and a wink as she did her best to recover her bearings. Why did the man have to smell so good all the time? Why didn't she ever run into him when he was sweaty after a workout or dripping wet from a shower?

Mistake to think that way. Those two images hardly helped her racing heart about having him so near. Why was he again anyway? The last time he'd come to see her, he'd dropped the bombshell on her about leaving for Mexico in a few short days. Was he here to remind her about it? Not that she could have forgotten. She could barely get it out of her head that she'd be thousands of feet up in the air. Just whizzing through the sky in a steel contraption.

"What can I do for you, Enrique?"

"Is the baby sleeping?"

She nodded. "Though, as usual, I have no idea how long he'll be down." She held up the baby monitor in her hand. "It's why I carry this."

He reached for the device and took it from her. "We'll just give this to Ms. Ritter. You'll be coming with me."

She would? "What about Lucas?"

"Martha and Watson can handle him for a bit. We'll only be gone a couple of hours."

He gestured for her to follow him. "Where are we going?" Fallon asked, reluctantly trailing after him.

"You'll see. It's something of a surprise."

Oh, boy. She didn't really like surprises. She hadn't had too many fun ones in her lifetime. Then again, she'd never met a man like Enrique Martinez before.

With no small amount of trepidation, she followed him down the stairs and out the door where a sleek, black sports car sat purring in the circular brick driveway. A young man in a gray sports coat approached them. "I pulled the one you wanted out of the garage, sir."

"Thanks, Mario," Enrique said, passing the baby monitor to him. "Do me a favor and hand this to Ms. Ritter."

"Sure thing," the other man said, giving them both a brief salute before making his way into the house.

Enrique led her to the passenger side of the vehicle and helped her inside.

"Can you give me a clue about our destination, at least?" Fallon asked, her curiosity fully piqued. The warm leathery seats felt like butter against her skin as she pulled the seat belt across her torso and buckled it in place. This piece of art in the form of a car was a far cry from her small hatchback hybrid. It was probably worth more than the entire dealership she'd purchased her own car from.

"I'm afraid not," Enrique answered, retrieving a pair of aviator sunglasses from the console and slipping them on. His sleeves were rolled up again, his collared shirt slightly unbuttoned at the neck.

Dear god above. He looked like something out of a men's magazine spread.

She didn't know what kind of car they were in, just that

it was an Italian model and clearly very expensive. Enrique handled it beautifully. Soon, Fallon felt herself relax enough to stop fretting about Lucas waking up without her there and allowed herself to take in some of the beautiful Cape scenery.

If she were the daydreaming sort, she might even indulge in a little pretending. She could make believe that she was out for a joyride with a date as they toured this scenic part of Massachusetts. Maybe they were on their way to the beach to spend some time in the sun. Or perhaps they'd board a boat and spend the day sailing around the harbor together. In the evening they could share a glass of wine while they watched the sunset.

It was silly, of course. But a girl could dream. She'd allow herself this small indulgence.

Until they reached the rotary break in the roadway. Then her instincts kicked in. Fallon knew enough of the Cape that she knew this road led to the Hyannis airport. Already she could see the small prop planes overhead as they descended toward the runway barely a few miles away.

Why in the world would he be taking her to the small island airport? If Enrique thought watching a few small planes land and takeoff would help her, she wasn't sure how she felt about that. Nor did she think it might help her dilemma much.

Then another disquieting thought struck and had her pulse skyrocketing. "Uh, you're not going to make me get on one of those things, are you?"

He took a hand off the steering wheel to clasp it to his chest in dramatic fashion. "You wound me. Do you think I would do that to you knowing your apprehensions about flying? Without so much as a warning?"

She would certainly hope not. Fallon felt her shoulders sag in relief. "Phew. For a second there I thought we might be headed to the airport."

"Not exactly."

What kind of answer was that? They were either on their way to the airport or they weren't.

"Trust me," Enrique simply said.

Surprisingly, she did.

Was it foolish of her to trust him? She barely knew the man. Looked like she would find out soon enough. For each passing mile took them closer to the regional airport that mostly serviced small prop planes and other private aircraft.

Another one flew overhead and over the tall steel fence surrounding the runways.

She really didn't want to quit her job, but if Enrique was about to insist she board one of those bucket of bolts, she seriously had to reconsider her recent life choices.

Fallon sighed and leaned back against the seat, closing her eyes. The truth was, she'd do anything for little Lucas. Even get on one of those flying canisters if she had to.

The car seemed to be turning. When she opened her eyes, she saw they'd turned onto a small dirt road just before the gated entrance of the airport. So they hadn't actually turned toward the runways. Probably too early to breathe a sigh of relief though. She wasn't going to do that until they were far enough away that no more planes were flying overhead. Soon, they approached a long hangar-type building with no windows, just a tall steel door in the center of the side wall.

"Is there a plane in there?" she asked, a heaviness settling into her stomach.

Enrique flashed her a smile. "Probably, but that doesn't concern us."

Okay. So far so good, she supposed.

Enrique was at her side and opening her door an instant later. Stepping out of the car, she adjusted her eyes, squinting against the bright sunlight.

"Although," he began, shutting the car door behind her, "if you were to change your mind, it does seem to be a beautiful day to take a quick spin in the air above the Cape."

She immediately shook her head. "The chances of me changing my mind are slim to none. Closer to none."

The steel door opened as they approached, and a man around Enrique's age strode over to them wearing scrubbed jeans and a pea green military-style puffed jacket. His smile was both familiar and friendly. The two men executed one of those combo handshake slash shoulder claps as they greeted each other.

When they were done, Enrique gestured to where she stood. "Fallon, I'd like you to meet Manuel Esposo. He's an expert pilot who has flown everything from cargo planes to commercial jumbo jets. Trained via the United States Navy. Semiretired. Does some teaching but still spends most of his time in the sky. Manuel, this is Fallon Duvall. She takes care of my son."

Two things struck Fallon as Enrique spoke. One, he hadn't referred to her as any kind of help or nanny. She couldn't help but feel touched by that.

Second, now she understood what they were doing here. Enrique had brought her for some sort of encouraging pep talk from an experienced pilot. Go figure. Who knew if it would even work or not. But a tingling sensation crawled up her spine at the thought that he'd made an attempt at finding a solution for her rather than telling her to just get over her fear. Or, heaven forbid, telling her she was relieved of her duties and that he'd just find someone else. Instead, Enrique had gone out of his way to have her talk to an expert who probably experienced daily what she was so apprehensive about trying even once.

That theory flew out the window when Manuel spoke. "Nice to meet you, Fallon. So, tell me, are you ready to learn how to fly a plane?"

Turned out, Manuel hadn't been referring to an actual plane. Thank heavens. Much to Fallon's relief, he'd led the two of them to a darkened room in the back of the hangar. Against the wall was a bevy of instruments, panels and screens. And two tall leather chairs.

"It's a flight simulator," Enrique announced.

A very convincing one at that. If Fallon had awakened in here facing this wall, she wouldn't guess that she was in an isolated room within a hangar and not the cockpit of an actual aircraft.

Enrique continued. "This is how Manuel starts teaching his students."

"That's right," the other man added. "They spend hours and hours in here before even stepping foot in an actual plane."

Enrique thrust his hands into his pockets. "I figured if you saw how the controls worked, how experienced pilots handled them, it might make you feel better about flying in a few days."

So it wasn't just a pep talk he'd brought her here for. It was to be much more hands-on apparently.

Fallon wasn't sure exactly what to say, or even what to think. No one had ever tried this hard to make her feel comfortable before. She knew Enrique's primary motivation was driven by his son. Fallon wasn't naive enough to think this gesture might have something to do with her personally. Still, Enrique could have very easily left her to her own devices to figure out her hang-ups about flying to Mexico.

"Have a seat." Manuel gestured to the seat on the left and waited until she sat down before adding, "You too, copilot."

Enrique sat down next to her.

With a flick of a switch on one of the panels, the green screen in front of them came on and Fallon's breath hitched at the result. The screen turned into a landscape that looked so real, Fallon might have sworn he'd lifted a blind to reveal a large window. Or that some magic had opened a portal into the outside. But it was completely virtual. The most realistic looking runway with greenery along the path and city buildings in the distance. A glance in Enrique's direction told her he was equally impressed. He was smiling from ear to ear.

That was something. At least he was enjoying this. He had to be a busy man. Not only had he planned all this, he'd taken time out of his day to be here.

"First thing first," Manuel began. "Before anyone touches any of the buttons, experienced pilots always take a moment to study the environment in front of them. Check out all angles around the aircraft. Make a note of anything that might seem out of place, any kind of obstruction or hazard. Your eyes and ears are your most relevant instruments, above all these knobs and buttons."

With that, he handed them each an earpiece. "This is what you'll use to communicate with your crew and with ground air traffic control."

For the next hour and a half, Manuel meticulously went over the functions of the various knobs and buttons. He demonstrated the best way to adjust the steering apparatus and explained the communications and safety devices in detail.

By the time they left and made their way back outside, Fallon's trepidation about flying had lowered by several degrees.

"Wow," was all she could think of to say.

"Wow good?"

She nodded. "Definitely 'wow good.'"

She couldn't even begin to figure out how she might thank him for being so thoughtful. And to think, she'd been afraid at one point that he might insist she get on a small propellor aircraft, that it might have been some sort of test to see if she was scared enough to back out of the actual trip.

It was as if Enrique read her thoughts. "Did you think, even for a moment, that I might make you do something against your will?"

The answer to that question surprised her. Deep down, she really hadn't believed that he might. Or she wouldn't have even stepped out of the car when they'd first arrived. Sometime within the last few weeks, since she'd started working for him, Fallon had realized she could indeed trust him.

She'd learned to trust her instincts over the years, in both good situations and bad. So far, all her instincts told her Enrique was a man of character. One who not only loved his son, despite the way he'd discovered the child's existence, but a man who'd gone out of his way to make his newly hired nanny feel comfortable.

Definitely not what she'd been expecting when she'd first walked through his door.

"To be honest, I wasn't sure what to think."

"And what about now?" he asked. "Did Manuel's lesson help to ease your anxiety at all?"

She couldn't help the smile that formed on her lips. "You know what? I think it did. Some of the mystery and uncertainty has been alleviated. And the way he explained how everything is controlled and monitored was more helpful than I might have guessed."

Enrique let out a whoop and said something in Spanish that definitely sounded congratulatory. He reached for her then and for an insane moment, Fallon thought he might embrace her. But he lifted his hand in the air instead, palm open. She high-fived him with an unwelcome sense of disappointment. Of course her employer wasn't going to hug her, for god's sake. There was no reason for her to want him to.

"This calls for a celebration," he announced. "It's Friday afternoon. There's a beachside clambake on Sterling beach. I say we celebrate with steamed clams, some lobster and corn on the cob."

As wonderful as that all sounded, she was beginning to think about Lucas and how he might have reacted upon awakening and not having her there to greet him.

He held a hand up before she could mention her concern. "I know what you're going to say. And he's fine. I've been checking throughout the afternoon. Ms. Ritter says he was a bit fussy when he first woke but calmed right down after she handed him the little bunny you always use when you play with him.

"I'm famished and this will be our last chance for a good beachside meal around a bonfire for at least the next few months. You don't want to deny me one last clambake, do you?"

Fallon couldn't come up with any argument to counter that. Especially since he'd assured her that Lucas was fine. In fact, she felt rather guilty that it hadn't occurred to her to check on him during the ninety minutes they were in the simulation. She'd just been so preoccupied. But Enrique had thought to do so.

"Come on," he said now, nudging her to answer yes. He dramatically cupped his hand to his ear. "Do you hear that?"

"I don't hear anything but the airplanes above."

"Well, then, their noise is covering up the sound of my grumbling stomach."

Fallon had to laugh at his exaggerated pained expression. She didn't have it in her to argue. Besides, she felt a bit hungry herself. She couldn't recall the last time she'd had lobster. And she'd certainly never had it at a beachside clambake. And wasn't it good for Lucas to spend some time bonding with other people in the household?

"What do you say?" Enrique pressed her.

She didn't have the heart to say no. And she didn't want to.

CHAPTER FIVE

THAT WENT A lot better than he'd hoped it might.

Enrique removed his shoes and socks and tossed them in the trunk of the car. Hard to believe he'd found parking along the quaint town street during one of the most popular times of the week to be here. He motioned for Fallon to do the same, but for some reason, she just stood there staring at him. Did she not like being barefoot?

"Is something wrong?" he asked.

She inhaled and released a quick sigh before answering. "No. Nothing's wrong. You're just not what I expected."

What a curious thing to say. "How do you mean?"

"You don't really fit the picture I might have had in my head."

Huh. Did that mean she'd been thinking about him? Exactly when?

"Go on," he prodded, interested to learn more about what specifically she meant about him that didn't fit the mold she'd somehow preconceived.

"It's hard to explain, really. But then again, I don't have much experience with men like you."

"Men like me?"

"You know, megamillionaires who take time out of their day to put their newly hired nanny at ease about a trip. Who drives what has to be a million-dollar car and parks it on a busy town street to attend a clambake. A serious businessman with a mountain of responsibilities who stays up all night with his son himself despite having plenty of staff."

The fact that she'd made note of all those things about him sent a hit of dopamine through his system.

She continued. "You take off what I'm guessing has to be an expensive pair of Italian leather shoes and cuff tailored pants so that you can walk on a sandy beach. It's quite remarkable really. You're definitely not what you appear to be on the surface."

Did that mean she found *him* remarkable?

If she only knew how humble his early life had been, how hard he'd had to work to get to where he was today.

She'd underestimated the extent of his wealth and the price of the car. Not that he was about to point those things out. As far as the rest went, he wasn't quite sure whether he should be thanking her for all she'd just said. How did one respond to such a thing?

It wasn't often a woman, or anyone else for that matter, rendered him uncertain about what to say.

"I know what you're going to say," Fallon said.

Well, that was good. Because he really had no idea. "What's that?"

"That I'm old enough to know not to judge a book by its cover."

Enrique chuckled. "I wasn't sure what to say, honestly. But most of that sounded complimentary. So, thanks? I guess."

She sent him a smile that caused a flipping sensation in the middle of his chest. "You're welcome."

To curtail the onset of an awkward silence, Enrique figured he should move things along. "You know what else I might have said? That we should go get some lunch finally."

She nodded once. "Right. Your grumbling stomach and all."

"Yes, and all this fresh sea air is only making me hungrier. Let's go."

The line for food was several feet deep when they made their way onto the beach. "Mind securing us a picnic table while I wait in line?" Enrique asked.

"Sure thing."

She had a way of walking that Enrique couldn't help but appreciate. A slight sway of her hips that brought attention to the contours of her waist and bottom. And what a delectable bottom it was.

Enrique squeezed his eyes shut and pushed the thought out of his head. He really couldn't be appreciating his nanny's body parts. Wholly inappropriate. He wasn't some hormonal teenager who couldn't control his thoughts. He had to do better.

Tearing his gaze away, he turned back to face forward to realize the line had moved on and he hadn't even noticed. The couple behind him gave an impatient huff and he strode along to close the gap. He'd actually been gawking at his son's nanny long enough that he hadn't noticed the line moving. How mortifying.

When it was finally his turn, he ordered two steaming buckets of clams and lobster with all the trimmings. He added a big basket of greasy fries and two bottles of water. Fallon waved him over from one of the tables when they handed him the food on a tray almost the size of a card table.

Between the deep sand and the size of the tray, it took a good half minute to get to where she sat.

"I'm sorry. I didn't realize we'd have company," she said when he finally reached her and sat across from her on the bench seat of the picnic table. "We're clearly meeting several other couples as all this food can't possibly be for just the two of us."

Couple. Enrique knew her statement was innocuous and she certainly wasn't implying anything. But to anyone else here on the beach with them, they must have indeed looked like some kind of couple out on an afternoon date. The idea held more appeal than he wanted it to.

"Are you kidding?" he asked, starting in on the clams first. "I believe I mentioned I was starving. I'll eat any part of your share you leave behind."

Now he was speaking as if they were a couple, offering to polish off her share if she didn't eat it all.

Fallon didn't seem to notice. "Something tells me you might have to do that. There's no way I can finish all this." She gingerly took the lobster out of the basket and set it on the paper plate in front of her. "It's been a while since I've had one of these."

"Would you like me to crack open the claw for you?" Another thing part of a couple would say. Why couldn't he revert to being the formal-sounding boss he was, already?

"I think I have it," she responded, then promptly dropped the lobster. "Ow, it's really hot."

She stuck the pad of her thumb in her mouth and gave it a small suck. A kaleidoscope of wholly inappropriate images traveled through his mind's eye. Enrique completely lost focus on anything around him except what Fallon was doing with her injured thumb.

Just. Stop.

Without asking for permission again, he reached for her lobster and made quick work of removing the claw, then breaking it open with the silver seafood cracker. He did the same with the other claw before handing her back her dish.

"Thanks."

"Sure thing," he answered, anything to get her to stop sucking on her thumb in front of him and giving him all sorts of untoward ideas. Though watching her take a bite of buttery lobster meat before slowly chewing wasn't all that much better. He really had to get a grip. What a cliché he was turning into. Having the hots for his son's nanny.

Well, he didn't have the hots for her. He was overwhelmed after finding himself in a whole other reality with a son he'd only recently found out about. No wonder his brain was looking for a distraction. This just happened to be a very inappropriate one.

Well, he couldn't very well sit here and watch her eat. He had to redirect his attention somehow.

He was scrambling for a way to make conversation and get his mind off her lips when she beat him to it.

"So, we'll be heading to Mexico soon."

There was still a hint of trepidation in her voice at the prospect, but he also sensed maybe a smidge of excitement in her tone as well.

Enrique took a swig of his water before answering. "That's right. And I might have fibbed a little earlier when I was trying to convince you to come to lunch."

Both perfectly arched eyebrows rose with curiosity. "You did?"

He nodded. "Yep, had to. A starving man makes desperate decisions. It wasn't a very big fib though."

Fallon reached for her own bottle and twisted off the cap and took a small sip. Her eyes remained focused on him. "What did you lie about?"

He wagged his finger at her. "Fib. That's different than a lie. Lies are less forgivable than harmless fibs."

Something shifted behind her eyes, and she quickly averted her gaze back to her food. "I suppose that's true."

"It is. And I fibbed about not being able to eat beachside anymore once we get there. We'll be staying at my private villa on the resort. There are nightly fiesta meals for the guests right by the water."

"That sounds lovely."

Was he imagining a hitch in her voice? Perhaps her anxieties about flying were arising again. His gut told him that wasn't the case. Something about this conversation had suddenly made her uneasy.

He was less curious than he was disappointed. He wanted to return to the easy camaraderie they'd been enjoying just moments ago.

"Tell me about the resort," she said, wiping her mouth with the paper napkin after taking another bite of lobster.

That he could do easily and with a great deal of enjoyment. The Martinez Tulum resort had been his very first major business venture after scraping by for years and investing what he'd earned.

"It's in Tulum. In a prime location on the coast. The first resort I built and started. Nothing but a couple of cottages at first. Now I can brag that it can host two hundred families and is one of the most successful vacation spots this side of the world."

Her eyes had grown wide. "I had no idea. How many do you own?"

He popped a greasy french fry into his mouth. Why did such tasty, fat-laden food have to be so bad for one's health?

"There are a dozen Martinez resorts scattered across the world, including the one just opened on the Cape."

"That's why you were in Massachusetts about a y—" She cut off whatever it was she was about to say and cleared her throat. "That's why you've been in this part of the United States, I mean."

"Correct. I was here to broker the deal with the investors. Now that we've broken ground in Falmouth and construction has begun, I can refocus my attentions on the expansion on the flagship property in Tulum."

"Is the expansion not going well?"

He shook his head. "I'm afraid not. Everything from bad weather to labor disputes with the construction workers to corrupt suppliers. I had hoped to stay here a while longer while building on the Cape is set to begin. But I'm afraid I can't afford to ignore Tulum any longer."

"That's why we're rushing there so suddenly."

It occurred to him just how unfair he'd been. He'd simply announced that they'd be leaving without explaining any of his reasons. No wonder Fallon had been hesitant and uncertain.

"I'm sorry for not having laid all this out much sooner. You should have known the reasons earlier."

"You don't have to apologize to me, Enrique. Trust me on that."

It was a rather odd thing to say. And Fallon had barely made eye contact in the last several moments. Maybe it was time to address the proverbial elephant in the room. "As you can imagine, such moves were logistically much easier before I discovered that I was a father."

Another fact of his life she deserved to know about as Lucas's primary caregiver.

"You sound as if it came as a shock."

"It did. See, I had a very uncharacteristic one-night stand during my initial trip out here. Not something I'd ever done before or since. One of my investors is Greek. He had a particularly potent brand of ouzo that he poured generously and often. I'm embarrassed to say that I didn't handle my consumption as well as the other men. And I came across an attractive woman who made it clear that she was interested in a very quick, no-strings-attached encounter. I never heard from her again after that night."

"Enrique, you don't need to explain any of it to me."

Maybe he did and maybe he didn't. But the more he talked to her about it all, the lighter he was beginning to feel.

Sasha

I wish I could explain to you the character of the man you share a child with. You would be so pleased. I have to admit to being quite frustrated that you'd just abandoned your baby with instructions to have him delivered to his father. It could have gone so horribly wrong. That's why I had to do everything I could think of to make sure.

Only, it didn't go badly. He's a caring father and a thoughtful man. If you only knew. I'm having a lot of conflicting emotions about my duplicity. My sense of guilt at not being truthful is growing by the day. Maybe I should just tell him the truth. But how would I even begin?

How I wish you would tell me what you think!

But enough about all that. You wouldn't believe what's happened. I'll be heading to Mexico in two days to care for Lucas there for the next several weeks. Definitely an unexpected turn. I'm both nervous and excited.

But I'll keep trying to contact you. As always, with the fervent hope that you will respond.

Fallon's hope of having that happen anytime soon was growing dimmer and dimmer. In the meantime, her life was on a fast track she could have never seen coming.

If someone had told her a few short weeks ago that she'd be traveling via private jet to Tulum, Mexico, in the employ of one of the wealthiest men in this hemisphere, Fallon would have laughed until her belly ached.

The fact that said man was the father of Sasha's baby only added another layer of surrealism to the whole scenario.

Another thing she found hard to believe—her anxiety about flying was almost near zero once the jet had taken off. Enrique's plan to have her learn about piloting a plane had most certainly helped. Plus she hadn't really had much time to focus on her own comfort as Lucas had become quite irritable and cried nonstop for the first hour or so. Poor thing seemed to be trying to tug at his ears, no doubt bothered by the changes in air pressure. It took a great deal of effort to coax him into taking his pacifier, which seemed to help. By the time Fallon had settled him and gotten him to sleep, they were well on their way.

Also, it didn't hurt that they were on board what could aptly be described as a flying hotel suite, complete with a wet bar, two queen-size beds on either side of the cabin and a full-size shower Enrique had had told her she was more than welcome to use during the fifteen-hour flight. A crib for Lucas had been set up beside the bed she'd be using.

He was working at a large wooden table when she drew the curtain around Lucas's bed and entered the main cabin. His laptop and a slew of paperwork consumed his attention.

Or so she thought.

"You should have something to eat while he's down finally," he told her, without looking up from his screen. "I can have Sandy prepare you a sandwich. Or she makes a mouthwatering pasta verde."

A small tingle traveled up her spine. She hadn't announced herself or made so much as a sound. Enrique seemed to be in tune to her entrances and very aware of her in general. A notion that both excited her and made her nervous.

"Maybe I'll have a bite later. I'm not very hungry right now."

"Then why don't you go lie down and get some rest."

"Thanks. I don't really feel like resting, either."

He looked up at her then. "Is something wrong? You seemed comfortable on the plane."

She shook her head. "It's not that. Between Manuel's lesson that day and the luxury of this plane, I feel perfectly at ease in the air."

"Then what seems to be bothering you?"

If he only knew. There was no way to explain. Their conversation on the beach last week, about how he'd discovered he was a father, the way he'd felt the need to explain to her how it came about, the guilt felt like an anvil on her shoulder, growing heavier and heavier.

"I guess I'm just a bit in awe, that's all." That was true enough.

"In awe?"

She motioned around her. "This is all quite something. I mean, I've seen pictures of private jets in magazines and online and such. But I couldn't have imagined the true splendor of such an aircraft. I feel like I'm in an entirely different world than what I'm used to."

The corners of his mouth lifted ever so slightly and he leaned forward, his eyes sparkling with what appeared to be amusement. As if she might have told a funny joke or punch line.

"What if I told you that it's all relatively new to me as well?"

For one thing, she would have a hard time believing it. Enrique seemed to fully fit his environment. She'd done enough background research to know he wasn't born into such wealth. But he'd clearly grown acclimated to it. "How do you mean?"

He shrugged, pushing the laptop away and leaning back against his chair. "I barely had enough to eat when I was a child. I never had any contact with the man who fathered me. My single mother worked a few odd jobs here and there until she gave up altogether, foisted me onto my grandmother and went back to my father."

How unexpected. Maybe the two of them had more in common than she might have thought.

He continued. "Didn't hear her from aside from a phone call around Christmas. Not even my birthday. As if she only thought to call because the holiday itself reminded her of my existence."

Fallon remained silent, a man like Enrique wouldn't appreciate even a hint of anything resembling pity. "Then she showed up a few years later to hand another child over to her mother and leave once more. Luis, my younger brother."

Luis. Fallon had wondered how Sasha had decided on the name Lucas for her baby. Enrique must have mentioned his younger brother and she'd chosen something similar.

"You and your brother are close?"

"He's a major pain in my backside." Despite the harsh words, there was clear affection in his tone. "He's six years younger than me, and we're as different as the stars and the ocean. You'll meet him when we get there. As well as my *abuela*."

His grandmother. His voice had grown even more tender as he'd said the last word. She knew it was none of her concern but her curiosity got the best of her. "And what of your mom?"

He shrugged again. "You're more likely to see a Mayan goddess. She gets a hefty amount of funds deposited into her account regularly and occasionally sends a postcard. Neither Luis nor I have so much as heard her voice for over three years now."

Fallon couldn't help but feel moved for him. And for the little boy he'd been. She'd lost her own parents to tragedy and the loss had both shattered her and upended her life. To be deserted by the people who were supposed to love you more than anyone else was such a betrayal. At least Lucas was too young to be aware that his mother had left him. Plus he had the benefit of one parent to love him and make sure he was cared for. It was no wonder Enrique was such a devoted father already despite the circumstances. He wanted more parental love in his child's life than he'd been given.

Many men might have taken the exact opposite approach. To want as little to do with their unintended offspring as possible. But not Enrique.

CHAPTER SIX

WHY IN THE world was he getting into all this? And why now, with this particular woman? Enrique couldn't remember the last time he'd discussed his mother with anyone. Let alone someone who worked for him. The simple answer was that he was drawn to Fallon in a way he couldn't explain. And in a way he hadn't experienced with anyone else.

"Is there anyone else I should be prepared to meet once we arrive?"

"Such as?"

Her cheeks reddened to a soft pink and he instantly realized what she was asking. She wanted to know if he was involved with anyone romantically. A shiver of pleasure ran up his spine that she was interested in such a detail. It had to be more than curiosity.

Her face was tight when she spoke again. "I mean, I would imagine a man such as yourself doesn't often lack for female companionship."

She would be surprised. "As a matter of fact, I haven't had time for much of a social life these past few years." Hence, part of the reason for such an indiscretion back in Massachusetts over a year ago. Not that it was any kind of excuse. "The encounter with Lucas's mother was the last time."

Heavens. Her cheeks were growing redder by the second.

"It's really none of my business. I just wondered if Lucas would have to adjust to someone else in the household who wasn't a relation."

Of course. She was only asking out of concern for Lucas. Which confirmed that she was a good nanny who cared about his son. So why did he feel a frisson of disappointment in his chest that her questioning hadn't been for a more personal reason? "No. There is no such concern," he admitted.

So now she knew about the lack of a partner in his life. And she also knew how he'd grown up. About being abandoned by both his mother and father. He supposed that was fair. After all, he'd done an extensive background check on her.

"You grew up in foster care."

She swallowed before speaking. "That's right. I lost my parents in a boating accident on the Charles. I've always been hesitant to board any kind of boat since. I hadn't realized the fear extended to aircraft until..." She trailed off.

"I'm so sorry, Fallon," Enrique said, imaging the hurt and lost little girl she must have been and vowing to never ask her to board any kind of maritime craft unless she was absolutely ready and willing.

Her eyes glistened slightly. "Thank you. After they were gone, there was no one else. My grandparents had all passed when I was a toddler." Her eyes gained a faraway look and she turned her head to the side. "I had to go into the system."

"You have an aunt. Your mother's sister. She's married to a very successful investment banker. Were you not able to go live with them?"

She chuckled in a way that held no mirth. "I wasn't invited. They wanted nothing to do with a child who wasn't theirs."

Enrique knew he couldn't hide his distaste. How utterly inexcusable for a couple with such wealth. "Despite their resources?"

Another small laugh. "If I had to guess, I'd say it was because of their money. They didn't want an outsider sharing any of theirs."

"You are her niece. A blood relative."

She did a small eye roll. "That didn't seem to mean much to them. I don't think my mother and my aunt were close. She didn't even bother to come to the funeral service, just sent a large bouquet of flowers."

Enrique felt an overwhelming sense of revulsion for a woman he'd never met. Fallon's wealthy relatives had everything at their disposal to bring her into a loving home. Instead, they'd turned their backs on her and let her go into the system.

"That is unforgivable of them. As much as a pain as my brother can be, I can't imagine turning my back on him under any circumstances. Or any child he may eventually have."

She tilted her head, studying him. "That's very admirable. Not everyone is as honorable as you clearly are, Enrique. As I personally know from experience."

Honorable. Admirable. The way she described him sent vibes of pleasure deep within him. He wanted her to see him in the best possible light. For some reason, it was important to him that she do so. "I'm sorry you were put through that. You deserved better." He meant every word.

"I have to admit, the sting of rejection after such a tragic loss was a bit hard to take. Not to mention…"

"Tell me," he prodded.

"I shouldn't be unloading on you in such a manner. You hired me for a job, not to use you as a sympathetic ear."

"And yet I have two I'd like to lend to you right now."

She clasped her hands in her lap. "It's just...not every family I was placed with was exactly pleasant."

An icy sensation speared his chest. "Do you mean to tell me you were abused?"

"Never physically. Though the danger of it happening was certainly there."

How many moments had she lived through where she felt the eyes of her foster father inappropriately ogling her. Or the threatening taunts of the school bullies who mistook her quietness as weakness to be exploited.

She added, "I learned ways to protect myself, to stay out of the way. Taught by a foster sister much more savvy than I was."

Enrique sucked in a breath with relief. "Thank heavens for that foster sister. I'm glad you had at least one person on your side."

If he ever came across this sister, Enrique would make sure to find a way to thank the woman.

She was floating on clouds. The sky was crystal blue. She felt peaceful and calm. But what was that noise? Fallon could hear a sound. A sound she should pay attention to. But she felt so relaxed. So at peace. Couldn't she just ignore the sound a little while longer?

Fallon's eyes flew open as her fogged mind realized she'd fallen asleep on the reclining leather bucket seat chair in the cabin. The lights of the aircraft were dimmed, and someone had settled a thick, plush throw over her. The noise she was hearing was the baby. With a silent curse at herself, she flung the blanket off and jumped up.

How long had Lucas been fussing? "I'm coming, dear one," she said, rushing to the crib. Only the baby wasn't in it. In fact, he didn't appear to be crying anymore. A deep voice reached her from behind.

"We have it covered here—you can go back to sleep."

She turned to find Enrique standing a few feet away, Lucas cradled in his arms, the baby's cheek against his chest. His bare chest.

The sight had her breath hitching. Enrique had changed into gray sweatpants and not bothered with anything on top. It was so very hard not to gawk at the chiseled muscles along his torso, chest and arms. Dear heavens, please let it be too dark for him to notice just how much gawking she was doing. But she'd been taken by surprise.

What would his skin feel like if she were to touch it?

Hard and smooth, no doubt. And darned if her mind didn't perfectly conjure up exactly how that would feel against her own. Her fingers tingled and she crossed her arms tightly across her chest. Somehow, finally, she averted her gaze.

Then the horror of what had just happened hit her. She'd slept through the baby awakening. Enrique had had to come himself to soothe him.

"I'm so sorry," she began, moving to take Lucas. "I don't know how I fell asleep so soundly. You can go back to bed."

But Enrique stepped aside, shifted the baby higher against him. "He's fine. We both are. I've got a bottle warming up to give him."

"You shouldn't have had to do that! That's my job."

"Your job does not require you to be beyond human. You clearly needed the rest. You should be the one to go back to sleep."

Right. As if she could drift off again now, between the chagrin of having slept through the baby's crying and the picture of Enrique standing in front of her without a shirt on. In fact, she was going to have trouble getting that picture out of her head for the foreseeable future.

"I'll just go get his bottle, and then I'll take him."

"No, you won't, Fallon," he said in a firm tone that left no room for argument. "I'm going to get his bottle and stay with him while he drinks it and eventually falls asleep. You are going back to bed."

She opened her mouth to counter, but his expression left no ambiguity. "I guess if you insist."

He nodded once. "I do. Go get some rest. We have up to a two-hour drive ahead of us when we land. And then it will be one thing after another." He rested his chin on top of his son's head. "Besides, us boys are spending some quality time together."

That settled it. Far be it from her to further interrupt a tender moment. She began to turn around but indulged in one last look at the two of them. Lucas was nestled tight against his father, his palms resting on Enrique's chest by his rosy cheeks. Enrique was swaying gently back and forth. The two of them made such a touching picture, something shifted in the vicinity of her heart.

If she thought the man was attractive dressed in a business suit and holding a laptop, the way he looked with his son cradled against him had her heart hammering against her ribs. A heaviness settled deep within her core.

This was bad. She was falling deep. Between her love and affection for Lucas and her growing attraction to Enrique, she wasn't sure what she'd managed to get herself into. Or how in the world she would get out again when the time came. And it would come. This wasn't going to last forever. Someday, maybe sooner than she could guess, Enrique would meet someone who would happily play stepmother to his son. Where would that leave her? As much as she loved Lucas, would her heart be able to handle seeing Enrique belong to another woman day in and day out? Would she feel out of place and in the way?

Would the future wife see her that way? Worse, might Enrique also come to see her like that?

She'd do anything for little Lucas. Would love to watch him grow up. But she would be sticking by him for her own selfish reasons.

That she wouldn't be able to live with.

Then there was the fact that she'd installed herself in their lives under dishonest pretenses. How would she ever be able to explain that if it came to light before she figured out a way to tell Enrique?

Settling back in the chair, she pulled the throw over her face in case Enrique walked out and saw how miserable she was. It had to be written clearly on her face. As it was, she was barely keeping the stinging in her eyes from turning into falling tears.

Enrique had told her to go back to sleep. But there was no chance of that happening now.

Her heart felt too heavy to allow it.

When she saw Enrique again in the morning, the sweatpants had been replaced by pressed black slacks and he had a shirt on. A deep, rich blue shirt that brought out the dark depths of his eyes. Dear lord, there she went again. She'd sworn last night that she'd fight her ever growing attraction to him as hard as she could. So far, that pledge wasn't exactly going so great.

So try harder.

It didn't help that he was smiling at her with that charming smile of his, having freshly showered and dressed while she was still in her crumpled clothes that she'd fallen asleep in.

"Lucas is still asleep. You have time for a shower and some coffee before we land," he told her. "In any order you wish."

That was a tough choice. She was in desperate need of both. She mentally flipped a coin and pointed to the steaming hot carafe sitting on the tray in front of him next to a large round plate laden with various pastries.

"I'll start with the coffee, thanks."

He poured her a generous cup and handed it to her. "So how much time do we have exactly?"

He glanced at his watch. "Approximately twenty-five minutes. Give or take."

They dropped wheels on the runway at Cancun International Airport exactly twenty-seven minutes later. A car and driver awaited them on the busy roadway outside.

Enrique addressed the driver in Spanish and helped Fallon inside the back seat where a baby's car seat was already tightly secured. Fallon settled the baby, then buckled herself in next to him. For his part, Lucas appeared to be fully aware that something different than his regular routine was happening. He seemed to be studying his surroundings and trying to figure it all out.

Fallon could relate to the little fella. This was all quite new to her too. She'd never been on a plane before and she'd just taken a shower on one, for Pete's sake.

"What's so funny?" Enrique asked.

She hadn't even realized she'd actually chuckled out loud. "Nothing. I just wish there was a way that we could explain to Lucas what's happening. I wonder if he's confused about where we are."

Enrique's features tightened. "Yes, he's had quite a bit of disruption in his young life already so far. I'm going to do everything I can to ensure that he experiences a routine now, for as long as possible."

He really was a devoted father. Considering how little time he'd had to get used to the title and the responsibility, Enrique was wholly embracing his role. Look at the way he'd stayed with the baby last night when Lucas had awakened.

"What?" he asked. "Why are you looking at me like that?"

Oh, lord. How was she looking at him exactly? Was her attraction and admiration written clearly on her face? She really had to snap out of it. She had to stop focusing on all the good traits the man had and remind herself he was simply her employer. One she was keeping a rather heavy secret from.

"I guess I'm just nervous about being here. It's all so new. And about meeting your grandmother and brother."

He flashed her another heart-tripping smile. "That's the last thing you need to be nervous about. Abuela will love you. And Luis will try to charm you with such sweetness, your teeth might actually begin forming cavities."

"He sounds like quite a character," she laughed.

"He is. Believe me." Again, his tone held pure affection for his sibling. Luis was lucky to have Enrique as a big brother. And Lucas was lucky to have him as a father.

Just stop.

There she went again. Focusing solely on the man's virtues. The problem was, she had yet to see anything but admirable qualities in the man. There had to be at least a few flaws, didn't there? But damned if she'd seen any yet. Maybe she just had to look harder.

He leaned over suddenly, reaching over the baby and pointing to the scenery outside. "The ruins lay over that way. Tulum was one of the last cities built by the Mayans. You can see part of the wall that surrounded the city borders. So much history and culture here. The city is an intriguing blend of Mexico and Caribbean influences. But to me, it's just home."

"It's lovely so far," she said, taking in the view outside her window. A crystal blue sea could be seen in the distance. Lush greenery surrounded the road. The water appeared calm and smooth. Very different than the choppy waves of the Cape Cod beaches she was more familiar with.

"I think you'll like it," he declared, returning to his side of the car. But the scent of his now familiar aftershave still tickled her nose.

To distract herself, she dug one of Lucas's toys out of the diaper bag and dangled it in front of him. The baby gave her a wide-eyed look before trying to grasp the plastic toy key ring that also served as a teether.

"You won't have to keep him distracted too much longer," Enrique told her.

They then passed much of the rest of the journey in a tense silence until Enrique said, "We're approaching the resort. The villa is just a couple minutes after that. Abuela is already waiting with bated breath to dote on her great-grandson. And she's looking forward to meeting you."

That gave her pause. "She is?"

"Of course. I've told her all about you. And what a godsend you were when Lucas and I most needed help."

His words sent a bolt of pleasure through her center.

That was something, wasn't it? She may be here under less than truthful circumstances, but she was needed. Lucas appeared to be thriving now, his fussiness vastly reduced. Overall, he was a happy baby who appeared to perk up when he saw her or Enrique.

She liked to think she'd played a part in that improvement.

Still, the feeling of guilt gnawing at her was only continuing to grow.

CHAPTER SEVEN

"WE'RE HERE," Enrique announced after about ninety minutes in the car. Lucas had drifted off to sleep, lulled by the ride.

The car turned onto a winding paved road that led them to a large, wrought-iron double gate. Fallon watched as a uniformed man stood up in a narrow booth behind the gate stand and gave them a small wave. Slowly, the two panels opened and the driver proceeded forward.

She wasn't sure what she'd been expecting but, just from what she could see from the car, the poshness of Enrique's flagship resort was breathtaking. Luxurious cabanas, marble bridges connecting blue water pools, dining areas and trendy-looking shops—all set against the backdrop of a sandy beach and sparkling ocean. The resort was like its own little town within a city. A paradise of a town at that.

And it was clearly a popular destination. People clad in everything from swimsuits to casual shorts to formal attire milled about. A group of about half a dozen children were kicking around a soccer ball on a patch of green grass.

"Wow." It was the best her brain could come up with.

"What do you think so far?" Enrique asked.

"I think this is as close to paradise on earth as is possible."

Enrique returned her words with that dazzling smile

of his. "Perfect. That's exactly the mood we're trying to accomplish."

"It's clearly working. The resort seems very popular, packed with visitors."

"It is. We have trouble keeping up with the booking requests. Hence my need to fly down here so suddenly. I'm trying to expand the accommodations with a new high-rise hotel as well as individual cabana cabins. But as I mentioned before, the expansion has not gone smoothly."

"I'm sorry about that."

He shrugged. "The nature of the business. But first thing first. Let's get to the villa and introduce this little one to his *gran abuela*."

That's right. Enrique didn't just live in a house next to his private resort, he owned a villa. How could she have forgotten? She really had somehow entered an entirely different universe than the one she knew.

The shops, cabanas and swimming pools soon gave way to a singular, narrow road. They traveled up a hill until the car finally came to a stop in front of a sprawling structure straight out of a storybook. The red brick hacienda-style building might have featured in one of the telenovelas Fallon occasionally came across while surfing channels, complete with a circular fountain in front and bendy palm trees along either side.

"Home sweet home," Enrique said, once the car had come to a complete stop. He unclicked the belt on Lucas's car seat and gently lifted his son out. What he called his home would be considered a palace by most of the world's population. Including her.

Did Sasha have any idea what her son was born into? What would her reaction be once she found out? There was no way to know anything about Sasha as long as she kept ghosting her. Fallon badly wanted to tell her about her son, about all of this. But her emails still went unanswered, no doubt going out into the nothingness of the cyber universe without Sasha so much as receiving them. Wherever she was.

"You seem to be a million miles away," Enrique said, pulling her out of her thoughts.

"Just taking it all in," she answered, resisting the urge to pull her smartphone out and check for any messages that might have come in. Not that she had any real hope there would be any.

"I'll give you a grand tour once we get this little one settled. After he meets his great-*abuela* and his *tio*."

"That would be lovely."

What would be really lovely was if the woman who'd actually given birth to Lucas was here to see this, to truly comprehend who her son was and the family he'd been born into.

But that would have meant Fallon herself would not be here. She might not have even met Enrique let alone started working for him.

And maybe that's how things should be.

You don't belong here. You don't belong with us. I'm sorry, that's just how things are.

Wow. Her aunt's voice hadn't surfaced in her mind for a good while now. Yet here it was again. Reminding her of all the ways she was out of place once more.

"Are you okay? You seem to have gone rather pale."

Fallon forced a relaxed smile on her lips. "I'm fine. Just a little jet-lagged, I think."

"Then I think I know how you should spend your afternoon once we've seen my grandmother and this little guy goes to sleep."

"How's that?"

"There is a world class spa at the resort. With master masseuses and skincare experts. I think you need a spa day."

That sounded like a luxurious indulgence she'd normally never be able to afford. She was more tempted than she wanted to admit. "That sounds like it would take longer than a five-and-a-half-month-old's afternoon nap. What about Lucas?"

"Between my grandmother and me, I think we can handle him. Besides, something tells me Abuela isn't going to want to part with him until they're both good and tired. He might actually sleep well into the night. They both might, for that matter."

There was that smile again. And the charming sparkle in his eyes. His aftershave subtly filled the car interior, invoking yearnings within her she had no business feeling.

"In fact, I insist you take me up on the spa day offer." He pulled out his phone and fired off a message before she could guess what he was doing. "I've notified them that they should expect you and to schedule you for the full treatment."

She didn't deserve this. Didn't deserve his kindness or his thoughtfulness. Once he learned the truth about who she was and why she was here, would he gift her with that dashing smile ever again?

The answer wasn't hard to guess.

"Ay, mi bambino!"

His grandmother's booming voice greeted them as soon as they exited the car. Enrique was relieved to see she was as sprightly as ever, despite her advancing age. Each time he went overseas, his concern for her grew that he might be away if she happened to need him. The woman had not only raised her own child, but she'd reared her daughter's two unwanted sons as well. She deserved to live out her later years in comfort and peace. And Enrique would do everything in his power to ensure she did just that.

His businesses took him away from home so often, he couldn't help but feel guilty about leaving her behind. Granted, there was a full regular staff of fifteen here at the hacienda as well as seasonal employees who returned yearly. A few whose job was to ensure Abuela was safe and taken care of. But he was blood. At least Luis was often home.

Of course, today there was a particular reason for the bounce in her step. She was about to meet her first great-grandchild. She barely acknowledged him and made a beeline straight for the baby he held in his arms. Cradling his small head in her wrinkled hands, she whispered to Lucas in Spanish. The baby was smart enough to recognize a loving soul and offered a toothless smile at her. Enrique could practically sense his grandmother's heart melting in her chest.

"May I take him?" she asked, her hands outstretched.

Remarkably, Lucas answered for him. He shifted himself toward Abuela as if he wanted to go to her. Beyond pleased, Enrique handed him over. The last time he'd seen his son react that way had been with Fallon that first day.

Fallon stood off to the side, watching the three of them. Her stance gave every indication that she was unsure what to do. For such a smart, accomplished woman, she could act quite uncertain at times.

Enrique waited a few moments while Abuela snuggled with her great-grandchild. Then he took Fallon by the shoulders and pulled her forward with him.

"Abuela, this is Fallon Duvall. She's the one who came to our rescue when we needed someone to help care for Lucas."

Fallon hesitantly stepped forward, her hand extended. Abuela ignored it, instead shifting the baby and using her free arm to pull Fallon into a three person embrace. *"Gracias, gracias. Tu eres una angel."*

Fallon recovered quickly from the clearly unexpected embrace. Then she surprised him by answering his grandmother in Spanish. *"De nada. Es un placer."*

Huh. He'd had no idea she was even trying to learn any Spanish. She gave him a small shrug when he shot an inquisitive glance in her direction.

"You are trying to learn Spanish?" Abuela asked her.

"Yes, I'd like to very much. I'm afraid I'm not very far with it yet," she added.

She hadn't shared that with him. The discovery sent a jolt of pleasure through his chest. She was already so ingrained in his life, the fact that she was trying to learn his mother tongue touched him deep within.

He studied her now, as she spoke to his grandmother while they both doted on his son. They were discussing the benefits of raising a child bilingual if possible. How it enriched their communication skills and opened up a world of opportunities.

Whatever had caused her shyness and hesitation earlier, Fallon had clearly gotten over it. Enrique was happy to see she'd relaxed. But Abuela had that effect on most people with her natural warmth and graciousness.

He didn't often bring women to the hacienda. And Fallon certainly wasn't any kind of date. For an insane moment, Enrique couldn't help where his mind wandered. Couldn't help wishing that things might have been different between them. It was pure fantasy, but how much more fitting it would be if Fallon was Lucas's mother. If they were embarking on parenting together.

If maybe they would be up to exploring what else might develop between them.

She looked right here, in his home. Like she belonged.

Like she belonged by his side. As more than just an employee.

What would be so wrong with that? Sure, it was risky. But so was any kind of personal involvement with another person. Would it be so wrong to try and get to know her?

Maybe it was wishful thinking. Maybe he was growing tired of not being in a meaningful relationship at his age. He was a father now. He had more than his own future to think about.

Lucas deserved to be brought up in a stable home with two loving parents. And by some inexplicable stroke of luck, Fallon seemed to love the baby deeply.

"Luis is away for several days on a university outing," his grandmother said, pulling him out of the rather surprising and probably ridiculous thoughts skittering through his head. The notion of he and Fallon becoming more personal was just that; ridiculous. Wasn't it?

She turned to Fallon. "He's a postgraduate student at Universidad de Cancun. Studying archaeology. They're always on some expedition or other," she explained in perfect English with a slight charming accent.

She turned to Enrique. "Speaking of which, his department is holding another one of their extravagant parties in two weeks to raise money. Of course, he expects you to be in attendance."

Enrique chuckled. "No doubt he also expects a generous donation and has probably already committed to one in my name."

"I'm almost positive he has. But he was absolutely insistent that you attend when he heard you'd be back in Mexico."

He nodded once. "I'll clear my calendar." Enrique worked to keep the begrudging groan out of his voice. He despised attending such events in general. At Luis's department galas, he often stood around munching on dry food and making small talk with people whose names he couldn't remember. While Luis spent the evening with friends, Enrique pretty much spent the evening by himself surrounded by strangers.

He glanced over to where Fallon stood. Maybe this time he didn't have to.

She'd forgotten what it was like to enter into a loving home. What it was like to be a part of a family unit where you felt you belonged, knowing the people within those walls loved you and always would. She'd only met Enrique's grandmother seconds ago, but she knew instantly and without a doubt that that's how Enrique had grown up in the care of this woman.

Perhaps she herself would never have that again.

But it warmed her soul to know that Lucas would grow up that way, just as his father had. No matter what Sasha ultimately ended up deciding about her part in Lucas's life, the boy would always have what Fallon was witnessing right now.

"What a lovely child," the older woman was saying now, dropping a light peck on Lucas's cheek. "You have done such a good job taking care of him, Señorita Duvall."

"I had a little something to do with it too, Abuela," Enrique said.

"Hmm," was his grandmother's only response.

Fallon chuckled at the exchange. "Please call me Fallon."

"Very well, then you must call me Rosa. Agreed?"

Fallon had the strong sense that she might agree with anything this woman said. She had such warmth and such an inviting spirit. It was easy to see where Enrique got his charm from. "Agreed, Rosa."

"*Bueno.* Now, you two must be so tired after such a long journey. Let's go inside and get some refreshments. I've had some chalupa prepared and a corn salad. Also, some refreshing *ponche.* Enrique's favorite." She bounced Lucas on her hip. "And maybe this little one can have a siesta, *si*?"

She and Enrique followed Rosa inside, and Fallon did another double take once they entered the foyer. There was almost as much greenery inside the house as there was out. A red tiled floor and stucco walls topped by a high arched ceiling overhead. Across the doorway, a V-shaped stairway led to opposite sides of the house. Despite the grandeur and highly polished floor, the house lent an air of welcome and warmth.

"Let's eat on the terrace, shall we?" Rosa suggested. "It's such a beautiful day."

"I'm afraid I can't join you," Enrique announced, with a tight expression at his phone. "Word is out that I've arrived and I've already been called to a scheduled meeting with our workmen and suppliers."

Rosa reached over and patted his cheek with affection. "You work so hard. At least take a chalupa to go. We can wrap one up for you."

"Wouldn't turn that down, Abuela."

"I can do it, Señora Rosa." A petite brunette with blond streaks wearing a white uniform darted from around the corner as they entered the patio. The young woman's eyes were planted squarely on Enrique, loaded with adulation. She may as well have worn a neon sign on her chest that declared she had a major crush on him.

Fallon sighed at her eagerness to tend to him. She could certainly relate. She and this young employee had a lot in common. After all, that's pretty much what she was also—an employee who had the hots for her boss.

"*Gracias*, Maria," Rosa said.

Fallon thrust her hand out in Maria's direction to introduce herself. "Hi, I'm Fallon. I'll be working here too. I'm the baby's nanny."

Maria shook her hand with a smile, then got to work wrapping food for Enrique to take. Much to the young woman's clear disappointment, Enrique was still rather distracted by his phone and only offered a quick thanks before bidding them all goodbye then leaving.

Rosa had a cushy playpen set up for the baby with a slew of plush toys. She set him down gently and cradled a fluffy faux fur toy monkey against his side.

Fallon waited for Rosa to sit before taking a chair across from her at the wooden table. The other woman had referred to this as a patio, but the word didn't do the area justice. It was more a courtyard that overlooked a lush, green garden dotted with colorful plants and flowers and palm trees surrounding it all. Fallon could hear and smell the fresh air of the ocean in the distance.

"This is so beautiful out here."

Rosa began pouring from a frosty glass pitcher into two tall glasses. A bright red beverage with chunks of fruit and a cinnamon stick floating on top. It tasted like ambrosia when she took a sip.

Rosa gestured toward the garden. "It's how I spend most of my time now, tending to these flowers and plants. A fitting hobby for an old woman without the energy for much else."

Rosa appeared plenty energetic from what Fallon could see. And the beauty of this garden was more than the result of just a hobby. "I imagine it's a lot of work."

"Enrique does hire landscapers to help me, I must confess. The rest is a labor of love on my part."

"It's lovely," Fallon said, taking another sip of her drink.

"It occupies my time," she said, then glanced in the direction of the crib. "And now I have this precious *bambino* to occupy it as well."

"He is indeed precious," Fallon agreed.

"He looks so much like Enrique as a little boy."

A gentle warmth spread through Fallon as she thought of a younger Enrique, playing with the types of toys his son held.

Rosa's affectionate smile turned downward. "I do often wonder about the mother though. Enrique says he hasn't heard from her and wants to respect her obvious wish to remain anonymous. I do hope she's all right and safe wherever she is."

There it was. An opening. A segue of sorts. A confession suddenly materialized on the tip of her tongue. She could take this opportunity right here and right now to admit who she was and exactly who Lucas was to her. Rosa seemed so kind and genuine. Surely she'd be the understanding type, wouldn't she? Maybe Fallon should finally take the opportunity to get the truth off her chest and soften the blow from Enrique discovering it later.

No. Of course she couldn't do such a thing. How horribly unfair it would be of her to burden Rosa in that way. Fallon's cheeks reddened with shame that she'd even considered it for a moment.

Suddenly, the tasty food and fruity punch no longer held much appeal. She'd lost her appetite.

"I hope she's okay, too," she said through a dry mouth. Rosa had no idea just how much she meant it.

CHAPTER EIGHT

THE BLASTED MEETING had gone much longer than he might have guessed. Enrique rubbed a palm down his face and strode through the patio and into the hacienda, making a mental note to go over the details he might have missed when his mind had wandered. As it often had. It didn't help that he was so distracted throughout that several points had to be repeated to him. His mind had kept wandering to Lucas and the way he was settling into his new surroundings. Luckily, the others in attendance had attributed his uncharacteristic attention deficit to jet lag.

Right, a voice in his head mocked. Lucas hadn't been the reason he'd been distracted. No, it had been the auburn-haired, doe-eyed nanny who was taking care of him who'd kept steering his focus away from business.

Enrique knew Lucas was being well taken care of. But how was she settling in? She seemed to be getting along very well with Abuela when he'd left earlier. He wasn't surprised. Fallon was charming and warm, characteristics his grandmother would have picked up on immediately. She often complained about the perils of getting older, but the woman was as sharp as she'd ever been.

He found Abuela exactly where'd he'd expected to find her. Puttering around in her garden.

"You're back, *hijo*," she said when she saw him.

"Finally." He glanced around. She was alone.

"Your son is down for his afternoon nap," she informed him.

"Great. That's great." He wanted to ask where Fallon was but didn't want to appear too anxious.

"I take everyone has been settling in okay, then?"

His grandmother tilted her head and gave him a knowing smile. He had no intention of asking exactly what she might think she knew. "Yes, they have."

He simply nodded.

"There's something I need to ask Fallon about."

Was it his imagination or did Abuela's eyes just brighten with merriment? "She is upstairs. I showed her to her suite after she fed the baby and he fell asleep."

"Great," he repeated like a stuttering fool. Why was she studying him like that? "Thank you for doing that. I guess I'll go find her, then see about settling in myself."

Another wide, knowing smile. "You do that, *hijo*."

Sometimes, he had to wonder if his grandmother was too sharp for his own good. He turned to leave then pivoted back around. She was still studying him, the smile still firmly in place.

"I promised her some time at the resort spa. I just want to see that she intends to take me up on it. She's been working really hard since coming on as Lucas's nanny," he said, not sure why he was trying to explain any of it. Of course, there was something else he wanted to ask Fallon about, but his grandmother didn't need to know that. In case she said no.

That thought had his chest tightening.

"Then you should absolutely see that she does," Abuela said.

"Right. I will."

When he made it upstairs, he checked in on Lucas in the nursery first. His son was sound asleep, clutching what appeared to be a fluffy dragon about the same size as he was.

Fallon's suite was the one adjacent. He knocked on her door and waited. No answer. Maybe she'd indulged in a nap herself. She could probably use it.

A wave of disappointment washed over him. He'd been looking forward to seeing her. To ask how she was adjusting to her new home. That was all. What kind of employer would he be if he didn't check on her the first afternoon?

He was about to give up and turn away when her door swung open. She clasped a hand to her chest at the sight of him. "Oh! I thought I heard a knock. I was listening to some instructional videos and wasn't sure."

"Instructional videos?"

She nodded. "Yes, about bringing children up in bilingual households. The best ways to go about it."

So even during her downtime she was still technically working. He wagged a finger at her. "You should be resting. You've had a lot thrown at you in the past week."

She gave a small shrug. "I want to be sure I know what I'm doing when it comes to Lucas. I'm learning a lot already." She paused to take a breath. "What can I do for you, Enrique?"

Now that was a loaded question. She'd changed into a pair of red shorts and sleeveless collared shirt a shade darker. Her feet were bare, revealing brightly painted toes. He was finding it difficult not to stare at those shapely legs so he kept his gaze firmly on her face.

"First of all, I'm here to make sure you take me up on the spa package. The technicians are waiting for you."

"Oh, I see." She glanced back over her shoulder in the

direction of the desk and the laptop sitting on it. Her expression clearly said she was torn.

"Lucas is sound asleep. I just checked on him. And if that changes, my grandmother has the baby monitor in her skirt pocket."

Fallon bit her bottom lip. "The massage cot is being heated to the ideal temperature as we speak," he said, a little verbal nudge.

A sigh escaped her lips. "A heated massage does sound rather lovely."

He stepped aside, motioned with his hand. "Then let's get going. I'll show you where the salon is. And you can see part of the resort as we walk."

He could sense her weakening resolve but still held his breath until she finally let out a breath and nodded. "Okay. You're on. Let me just get my shoes."

He'd managed not to gawk at her bare legs but couldn't help himself from admiring her shapely behind once her back was turned. Barefoot, she walked with the slightest sway to her hips.

Enrique cursed under his breath. He had to keep his thoughts about her platonic and tame if he was going to ask her what he wanted to as they walked to the spa. He couldn't be thinking about the shape of her bottom, or her golden tanned legs, or her pretty pink toes…

Ay, Dio. Enrique rubbed a palm down his face in frustration. Telling himself not to think about those things only had him doing just that.

They made small talk as they walked along the property to reach the resort border. Enrique pointed out the new double pool with the connecting bridge and told her how he was modeling the Cape Cod property along the same lines as this one. And then he could think of nothing else to say. Except to do what he planned and ask her about attending the university gala ball with him.

For the life of him, he couldn't seem to just come out and say it. Beyond frustrating. He'd asked countless women out before. There was one big difference here, though; he didn't have the same confidence that Fallon would actually accept.

It hit him all at once.

Que sorpresa. He was actually nervous! To ask a woman out on a date. And it wouldn't even be a real date! Her accompanying him was simply a matter of practicality. He just had to explain that to her and that would be that.

"Is there something on your mind, Enrique?" Fallon asked. Clearly the silence had gone on long enough that she'd noticed it.

He stopped strolling to face her. "In fact there is. I want to run something by you."

She lifted an eyebrow. "Oh? What is it?"

"You were there when Rosa mentioned that Luis attended the University of Cancun."

She nodded. "Yes. He's studying archaeology. This must be a particularly rich part of the world for that field."

"Right," he answered, hoping he didn't sound dismissive. But now that he'd begun, he wanted to plow forward and just get this over with. "You also heard that his department throws a fundraiser every year. A fancy ball where they serve dry appetizers and convince past benefactors to write bigger checks than they did last year. There's also music, speeches. All quite dull." Probably shouldn't have said that. He was about to try and convince her to go, after all. Hardly a good way to sell it.

"Sounds fancy," she said, a smile lifting the corners of

her mouth. "I can't wait to hear all about. I haven't been to many such parties. The ones I attend run more along the lines of pizza and cake."

"That's just it."

"What is?"

"You."

She gave her head a shake in confusion. Man, he was really making a mess of this. Why was he acting like some awkward teenager about to ask out his school crush?

"Me? What does any of that have to do with me?" Fallon asked.

"I'd like you to come with me." There, he'd said it. Or he'd blurted it out, would probably be more accurate. Judging from Fallon's expression, maybe that hadn't been the best approach.

She tilted her head, her eyebrows drawn together in confusion. "Me?" she repeated. "Why me?"

Enrique rubbed his fingertips along his forehead. He really was botching this. First of all, he probably should have asked her back at the hacienda rather than in front of a loud, crowded pool.

"These events are rather tedious. And I often find myself alone fending off unwanted conversations about the next big business deal I should be looking into." Or fending off the advances of the women in attendance when they thought their significant others weren't paying attention.

"But I don't understand. Why are you asking me? Instead of going through what I'm sure is an extensive contact list of women."

He wasn't sure what might have given her the impression that he kept such a list. He decided to let it go.

"This would simply be a platonic event. Just to have

a companion by my side to make it a bit more bearable. That's all."

Her lips tightened before she spoke. "Surely there must be other women who would jump at the chance to attend a fancy gala with you, Enrique. If a simple companion is all you're after."

Did that mean she wouldn't be one of such women?

He pinched the bridge of his nose, trying to come up with a way to answer that wasn't going to sound arrogant or muleheaded. "In the past, when I've asked acquaintances to events like these, there's been some misunderstandings." He cringed as he recalled the up-and-coming telenovela star who posted pictures of them all over her social media accounts throughout the entire night. The posts released a flood of gossip about "their budding relationship."

"Oh," Fallon said on a small chuckle. "I get it. It's simply easier to ask me then. No expectations or ambiguity."

He nodded with relief. She was indeed getting it then. "Exactly. Just an evening out so that I'm not bored to tears and/or swatting away unwanted conversations."

"I just don't think I'll fit in. What if I say or do something wrong? I don't want to embarrass you in any way."

"I have zero concerns that might happen."

She shook her head. "That makes one of us. I don't tend to mingle much with the type of people who donate to universities."

"I'll be there with you."

Her head tilted as she studied him. "What does that mean?"

"It means you'll fit in because you'll be my plus-one."

She crossed her arms in front of her chest, tapped her

toe. Enrique wasn't quite sure what to make of the action. "What about Lucas?"

Of course, he should have led with that particular concern. "This will be fairly late at night. I can't imagine he'd still be awake. If so, Abuela is there, and Maria is scheduled to work Saturday evenings."

She looked off to the side.

He pressed. "Who knows, you might even enjoy yourself."

She looked quite skeptical on that score.

"Yours are the tensest shoulders I have ever worked on."

The accented feminine voice lamenting about her muscles belonged to the masseuse currently kneading her skin like a mound of dough. Ilga, who was here on a work visa from Sweden. Somehow, she was strong yet gentle at the same time.

"Sorry, I've just come off a rather vexing conversation."

Given just how luxuriously she was being pampered, Fallon was having an incredibly hard time relaxing. Enrique wanted her to attend some fancy party with him.

"Ack!" Ilga hmphed above her. "You've somehow gone even tighter just now."

Fallon closed her eyes and inhaled deeply the lavender infused air. Ilga squeezed some more heated lotion on her back and she tried to loosen the muscles she rubbed. Easier said than done. It would be a much easier task if she could just get Enrique's voice out of her head.

Of all the ways she'd been asked out by men in the past, she could hardly think of a time when she'd felt less flattered. But that was just it. He wasn't actually asking her out. He just wanted someone to be there with him. A body. Nothing more.

And why in the world did she find that disappointing in any way? On the surface, everything he'd said was logical and sensible. He didn't want to attend the party alone. And he didn't want to ask a woman who might entertain any romantic thoughts about his invite. Clearly, he expected her to do no such thing.

So why was she doing just that? Why was she imagining how it might have felt to have him really ask her out? If he'd wanted to walk into that ballroom with Fallon on his arm simply because she was the only one he wanted to be there with.

"Do you want to talk about this conversation that has you tense as a brick wall?" Ilga asked, sounding exasperated.

"I don't think that will help, honestly."

"Then you should try and forget about it. At least for now."

Ha! As if she could do that. She still owed Enrique an answer, telling him she'd think about it. As if she'd be able to think about anything else.

"Maybe we'll try some music," Ilga said, walking to the other side of the room. A moment later, a slow, soft melody began to play. Fallon took another deep breath and tried to focus on the soothing song.

"That's a little better," Ilga said, resuming her kneading of Fallon's shoulders. "Let's try to keep it this way, can we?"

"I'll try."

"I have to admit," Ilga said, "I find myself very curious about what has you so…out of sorts during what should be a relaxing massage."

Fallon puffed out a breath of air. "I just have a decision to make and I'm having difficulty deciding."

"I see. The best approach would be to weigh the benefits and cons, then. Look at the question from all angles. Yes?"

Right. She could do that. Were all massage therapists this wise?

On the one hand, it was only one evening. He really wasn't asking for all that much. But there were so many other hands, so to speak. For one, she really was concerned about how she might come across to such a group of people. Unlike Enrique who seemed to think she'd fit in fine, she wasn't nearly as secure. What if she said or did something inappropriate? Like use the wrong fork?

What if someone asked her about her background or family?

People at this kind of event could never understand how awkward and uncomfortable it felt to talk about having grown up in foster care. They couldn't relate to wearing secondhand clothes or going days eating nothing but crackers because there never seemed to be enough food to go around.

The dry appetizers Enrique complained about being served would have probably felt like a feast for her and her foster siblings all those years ago.

Then there were the practical issues. She was absolutely certain she didn't have anything remotely appropriate in her closet for such an event. What would she even wear?

She must have mumbled the question out loud because Ilga actually answered her. "I think, with your coloring, you should wear something red. Burgundy or a rich wine color."

Huh. That was actually helpful.

"There's three specialty boutiques on the resort," Ilga added.

Too bad there wasn't a thrift store. Because she definitely couldn't afford any kind of boutique. Let alone a specialty one on a world class resort.

"Thanks, Ilga," she said.

Another errant thought hit her. What if there was dancing at this party? She had no idea how to dance. Unless it was in a downtown Boston club. She didn't know any kind of a waltz or a foxtrot or…she couldn't even name any other dances. There was no way she was going to dance.

"Are you sure?" Ilga asked. "Dancing is fun," she declared, digging her elbow under Fallon's shoulder blade.

She must have been more relaxed than she realized, considering how she kept speaking her thoughts out loud.

"Sure, if you know how," she said through a labored breath, given the sharp elbow digging into her back.

"I bet you could learn."

Fallon was really starting to like Ilga. And not just because the woman seemed to have magic hands. Her muscles really were beginning to feel rubbery and loose in a very pleasant way. She'd had no idea just how tense and stiff her whole body had become caring for a baby every day.

She didn't plan on admitting it to him, but Enrique had been right. The spa visit was doing her a world of good. Once again, just like back on the Cape with the aerial simulation visit, he'd been considerate enough to arrange something special for her.

She could at least seriously consider granting his ask about attending the fundraiser.

CHAPTER NINE

FALLON HAD TO be back by now.

Enrique knew he shouldn't go seek her out. But trying to get any work done was proving futile. He wanted to hear how her spa treatments went. Also, what she thought about what she'd seen of the resort so far.

And he wanted to know if she'd given any more consideration to attending Luis's fundraiser with him.

Funny, really, he couldn't ever recall being this distracted before. Working was typically his refuge. Hours would often go by without him even noticing the passage of time when he was at his desk. He might have blamed fatherhood. But knew that wasn't an excuse.

He just couldn't seem to get Fallon out of his mind.

Another glance at the laptop screen in front of him told him it was no use. He stood up and closed the cover in frustration. He just couldn't bring himself to stare at the spreadsheet any longer.

He needed a stroll.

And if he happened to come upon a pretty nanny along his wandering, well then so be it.

He walked out of his study and strolled along the hall. Both Fallon's suite and the nursery doors were wide open with no one inside. Enrique made his way down the stairs and to the kitchen first. Empty. Grabbing an apple from the large fruit bowl in the center of the table, he tossed it in the air before taking a bite. He'd try the sitting area next.

He could hear Abuela's voice as he got closer, followed by several other gushing and cooing female voices. Sounded like his grandmother had some friends over and was showing off the baby. He pivoted away before they were aware he was nearby and could try and snag him for what could be an hour of dull conversation.

Fresh air. That's what he needed. The sun was just about ready to set, his favorite time of day. He'd grown tired of the apple by the time he made it to the patio door and tossed in a nearby bin before he strode outside to the patio.

And there she was.

Fallon sat reclined on a cushioned wicker chair in the corner, facing the house with her back to the garden, a paperback propped open in her hands. The title told him it was a book on infant development.

She looked up when she saw him, and the smile she sent him had a fluttering sensation gliding within his chest.

He walked over to the matching seat next to her, and she closed the book and set it down on the glass table between the chairs. "I see you found your way back okay."

"Yes, the walk back to the hacienda from the resort was almost as therapeutic as the spa treatments."

Good to hear. She'd enjoyed the massage and other services he'd had set up for her. Enrique studied her from the side. Her skin had taken on a golden glow; her cheeks were slightly red. He imagined that's how she might look after an amorous night spent with a man.

Do not go there.

He shoved the thought away before it could take further root in his mind. Dangerous territory. The images alone might have him tempted to take her by the hand and ask her to follow him upstairs.

"So you enjoyed the massage and the rest then?"

She nodded emphatically. "Ilga was lovely. A real magician with her hands."

He could make some magic happen with his hands too if she was so inclined.

Just stop!

"A girl could get used to such treatments," she said.

"Then plan on having them regularly." She was clearly much more relaxed. A regular massage was the least she deserved given how hard she worked.

"Oh, no," she immediately replied. "I couldn't do that."

"Why not? You can consider it part of your benefit package as an employee." Enrique had to pause on the last word. Calling her that no longer felt right. She was so much more now. Exactly what, he couldn't quite define just yet. "As you can see, Abuela is happy to spend time with the baby if you want to head to the spa for a few hours each week."

"The baby is with your grandmother now," Fallon said, effectively changing the subject. Why was the woman so hesitant to indulge herself? It was as if she wanted to deny herself any pleasure. "She has some friends over and wanted them to meet Lucas," she added.

"I heard. We'll have to bathe him a bit longer this evening."

She tilted her head in question. "Why is that?"

"My son is going to smell like four different varieties of women's perfume by the time the visit is over."

She chuckled. "He's also going to be rather exhausted. They're taking turns holding him and playing with him."

"I'm guessing the ladies are going to be rather tired as

well. There was quite a commotion of laughter and cooing when I walked by."

Fallon laughed again. "Maybe they'll all need naps after."

He returned her laughter. "They just might."

"I don't know how to dance," she blurted out suddenly. Enrique felt completely thrown off by the rather random change in conversation. Had he heard her right?

"I beg your pardon?"

Fallon leaned her head against the back of the chair, blew out a deep breath as she stared at the sky.

"If I go to this fundraiser with you, if there's any kind of formal dancing involved, I'm afraid I don't know how."

Enrique couldn't help the laughter that rumbled from his chest. The woman really was something else, unlike anyone he'd ever met. She was actually nervous about how she might dance at a benefit gala.

"You're laughing, but it's the truth."

Enrique turned in his seat to look at her. She was biting her bottom lip, her fingers tight around the binding of the book she held.

"Well, there is typically an orchestra and a dance floor, but you absolutely need not dance if you do not want to."

Her shoulders actually sagged in relief. "Phew. That's good. Really good."

Enrique resisted the urge to do a fist bump in the air. She hadn't exactly come out and said yes to accompanying him to the fundraiser.

But it certainly seemed implied.

Well, that was at least one less thing to stress about. If she were to accept Enrique's invite, at least he knew not to expect her on the dance floor.

"I think you'd be good at it, though," Enrique said.

Leaning back in his chair with his ankle propped on the opposite knee, he looked relaxed and fully at ease. He'd undone the top three buttons of his shirt, revealing a triangle of hard chest muscle. The man was such a specimen of good looks and allure. To think, she'd be spending the evening with him as his date.

Well, not really. He'd made sure to tell her it wasn't to be a real date at all. He'd made that abundantly clear.

And when exactly had she actually decided?

"If you gave it a try," he added.

What was he referring to? It was so hard to focus with him sitting across from her with his shirt partially undone, smelling the way he did, looking at her so intensely.

"Good at what?" she asked.

His lips twitched with mirth. "Dancing, of course. The topic at hand."

Right! How could she be so out of it? "Maybe. I'm not sure a fundraiser would be the best time to find out."

"Let's find out now, then," he said. To her consternation, he then stood and extended his arm out to her.

He couldn't be serious. "What, here?"

He nodded once. "Why not?" He pulled his phone out of his pocket and clicked on the screen. Soon the notes of classical music sounded from the small speaker.

Fallon hesitated, staring at him.

He wagged the fingers of his outstretched hand in an inviting gesture and flashed her a mischievous smile. "Come on, just give it a try. What do you have to lose?"

What a loaded question. She couldn't remember the last time she'd danced with a man. Or when she'd been held by one for that matter.

"You're overthinking this," he told her with a tilt of his head.

He was right. He was only asking to show her how to dance. A completely innocent gesture. At the least, it would give her a chance to prove that any such effort would be futile.

Fallon took his outstretched hand and stood. "All right. But I have to emphasize that I'm clumsy and have two left feet."

He merely chuckled at that.

"Now," he began, "I'll lead so all you really have to do is follow me. Just in the opposite direction."

"Got it," she answered, stepping into his embrace. His free arm went around her waist and her breath hitched in her throat. Would that distinctive scent of his ever cease to make her dizzy?

Enrique took two steps forward and then a few backward. Fallon did her best to follow without stepping over his toes. But it was so hard to focus on what her feet were doing with Enrique up against her length. The warmth of his body sent waves of heat along her skin, his breath hot on her cheek, the scent of him filling her senses.

She didn't dare risk a glance up at him. No doubt he'd be able to read her tumultuous emotions all over her face.

"You're doing great," he assured her.

"If you say so," she managed to answer through lips that had suddenly gone dry.

He continued to lead her, staying in step with the music coming from his phone while Fallon continued to stare steadfastly at her own feet, willing the song to end already.

Enrique had been so very wrong earlier. She hadn't been overthinking this at all. If anything, she should have thought long enough to realize what a bad idea it was. Did she honestly think she wouldn't be affected after stepping into his arms and having him hold her?

She missed a step and managed to recover with Enrique's gentle nudge against the small of her back. One... two...three...

Had he chosen the extended version of the melody? This was turning into an exercise in sweet torture.

It was only a matter of time before she stumbled again. Fallon's mind barely registered that her toe had caught on one of the brick tiles of the patio floor when she went tumbling forward, straight into Enrique's chest. Her urgency to pull away only made things worse, and she further lost her balance.

A pair of strong arms instantly gripped her like a vise around her center, managing to keep her upright. The problem was, Enrique was the only thing keeping her up.

Fallon knew she should try to pull away again, but couldn't seem to do it. She felt so right to be in his arms, with his warmth surrounding her as he held her tight.

He'd kept her from falling. But she was falling in another, much more dangerous way.

She was only stumbling because she was clearly so tense. Why? She couldn't be that concerned about her dancing skills.

"I'm so sorry," she said abjectly against his chest. "I tried to tell you I'm rather clumsy with two left feet."

He'd never noticed any hint of clumsiness in her. Well, not until now. So why had she made such an admission so emphatically? Someone must have done a number on her somewhere in her past. Given her the impression that she was a klutz. A wave of anger washed over him. That anyone would have put her down so carelessly, hampered her self-confidence.

"Nonsense," he replied. "You just need to relax. Think

of how you felt after the massage earlier. How loose your muscles were. Try and regain that sensation. You'll be less prone to missteps the more at ease you are."

"I'll try," she answered, hesitant and uncertain. He began the count again.

They managed a few more strides than the last time when she took a step that was too big and her foot landed on his and he had to catch her again. Her cheek collided with his chest, her head under his chin.

Enrique wasn't even sure what happened next. One moment she started looking up at him with yet another apology on her lips, the next their mouths were less than a centimeter apart. The rush of desire hit him like a punch in the gut. The scent of her under his nose, the heat lighting up her eyes, her breathless pants. He could take no more. It was all too tempting. He had to taste her.

"Fallon?" Her name left his lips on a whisper.

"Yes," was her soft reply.

And then he gave in. With an urgency that shocked him, he pressed his lips against hers, relishing the feel of her mouth on his. The gentlest of a nudge and then she was opening to him, welcoming his kiss to deepen. He didn't hesitate to take her up on the invitation. The taste of her was like an ambrosia he'd never get enough of. The feel of her against his length sent pulse waves of desire throughout his core and moved lower.

Nothing else existed in the moment but his desire for her. And her reaction told him her longing for him was just as strong.

He'd known, hadn't he? On some level he'd always anticipated this exact scenario would happen. Deep in his gut he'd acknowledged that at some point they'd be in this very position. With Fallon in his arms and his lips against hers. Maybe he'd known it the very first day he'd laid eyes on her.

So one would think he'd be better prepared for the reactions coursing through his body. He had half a mind to lift her up and carry her upstairs to his suite of rooms. The way she was kissing him back right now, he knew without a doubt that Fallon would be willing. They could worry about the consequences later.

His assumption was confirmed when she ran her hands up along his arms to his shoulders and moaned against his mouth. Enrique lost the ability to breathe at her roaming touch. Instinctively, he pulled her tighter against him, showing her the vast strength of his desire.

At this rate, if he wanted to act on his desires, they might not even make it upstairs. Her hand moved along his shoulders until she reached the nape of his neck and she thrust her hands through his curls.

That was it. He had to know. He had to ask her if she was ready to find a more private spot to take things further. To finally give in to what they both so clearly wanted.

He was about to do just that when a commotion of voices echoed from down the hallway. His mind barely registered enough to identify the sound.

Abuela. Along with the friends she had visiting. They were making their way to the patio and drawing perilously close to walking in on him and Fallon. And what a scene they would encounter if that happened.

With a reluctance that was almost painful, Enrique made himself pull away from Fallon with a gentle nudge so that they might both take a step back. The confusion and desire behind her eyes and the way she rubbed her lips nearly had him reaching for her again, damn the consequences if they were to be seen.

"Oh…my…" she whispered before her eyes grew wide as she noticed the approaching intruders as well. Her cheeks, already blushed pink, turned crimson. Clasping her hand to her mouth, she whirled to face away from him.

Abuela and her friends entered the patio a moment later. The babyish sound of his son's cooing could be heard among the noise. He and Fallon had been mere seconds away from being discovered in each other's embrace.

How careless. How utterly impulsive of him. Fallon was new here in his home. She'd only just met his grandmother. She certainly didn't know Abuela's friends. She didn't need the kind of talk that would be triggered if she were to be caught being thoroughly and passionately kissed by her boss. The fuel that would throw on the all too ready gossip mill was immeasurable.

And what was he thinking anyway? He couldn't be giving in to his whims like some hormonal teenager, no matter how strong they were. Fallon was here as a professional to care for his son. He couldn't do anything to jeopardize the stability and affection she provided as Lucas's nanny. He couldn't risk losing her. Neither could Lucas.

As much as he wanted her, and as much as Fallon seemed to reciprocate that desire, he had to keep his hands to himself.

Fallon still had her back turned to him as the ladies strode over to where they stood. When she finally turned, she stepped right past him and over to where Abuela stood with Lucas in her arms. The baby immediately began squirming and leaning toward Fallon when he saw her, a toothless smile on his face.

His choices were clear. His wants and desires would have to take a back seat to his son's well-being.

CHAPTER TEN

"SO, WHEN I move forward, you would move back," Fallon said to the baby as she gently twirled slowly in a circle, holding Lucas against her chest. "Well, you would if your legs reached the ground, that is."

Lucas's response was to stick his tongue out and gurgle. As far as partners to practice dancing with over the last few days, she figured she could do worse. Though, Lucas was no match for his father.

Enrique. Fallon's lips tingled as they did every time she thought of him since. She'd had to keep averting her eyes from the spot where he'd held her and kissed her whenever she'd made her way out to the garden with Lucas. As if any amount of avoidance was going to get that kiss out of her head anytime soon.

Still, the fresh air and sunshine and being surrounded by lush greenery served to help to clear her head and unjumble her thoughts. The kiss was a momentary lapse in judgment. It could never happen again. She would make sure of it.

It should have never happened in the first place. Fallon should have never succumbed to her desire and returned his kiss the way she had. As for Enrique, she was aware that he regretted losing control as he had. It had been written all over his face when his *abuela* had come upon them with her friends, and she'd hardly seen him since.

Heat rushed to her face as she thought about how close they'd come to being discovered in such a state. Fallon would have been horrified. So the small twinge of hurt in her chest at the way Enrique had swiftly broken their kiss and nudged her away was absolutely ridiculous. If anything, she should be thankful for his quick reflexes when she herself hadn't even heard the others approaching.

He was her employer. She had no business being attracted to him. This wasn't some type of Valentine's romantic movie of the week. Or her own version of *The Sound of Music*.

Giving her head a brisk shake to push away the images, she continued moving through the garden, holding Lucas and mimicking the dance steps Enrique had shown her.

She'd racked her brain each night, trying to figure out if she should find some way to back out of going to the fundraiser with him. The evening was sure to be tense, with the specter of their kiss hanging awkwardly between them. But she'd already committed to being Enrique's "date." It would be untoward of her to back out now.

"I think I can guess which one of you is leading." The masculine voice came from behind her and startled Fallon out of her thoughts. She panicked for an instant before realizing that, although similar, the voice didn't belong to Enrique.

She turned to find a lean, dark-haired young man striding toward her, a wide and charming smile on his face. He had the same sharp, dark features Enrique did. But his were less angular somehow, with a softness to his mouth and eyes that Enrique lacked. Still, the family resemblance was as clear as the morning sky.

"You must be Fallon," he said when he reached her side, his smile growing wider.

She nodded. "And you must be Luis."

"Sí, es mi," he said, his gaze falling to Lucas. "And this must be my handsome nephew," he added, running an affectionate finger along the baby's cheek. Lucas's response was a messy sneeze in his uncle's face.

Luis chuckled as he wiped his cheek with the back of his hand. "Is that any way to greet your uncle upon our first meeting?" He gave the baby a gentle tickle on his tummy. Lucas let out a giggle and pumped his legs.

"May I?" Luis asked, and held his hands out toward the baby.

Fallon handed him over and watched as the baby placed his little hands on his uncle's cheek and continued giggling at him. Warmth spread over her chest at the sight. Yet another image to show just how loved Lucas would be throughout his life. Another blood relative who would care about him and look out for him. She couldn't have asked for more for the baby.

"You're starting him with the dance lessons early, huh?" Luis asked, his affection for the nephew he'd just met clear in his eyes.

She ducked her head in embarrassment. What a sight she must have made, dancing around Rosa's garden to imaginary music with her charge. At least it hadn't been Enrique who'd walked in on it. "That was more for my benefit. In case there's any dancing that I can't avoid at your university's event next Saturday."

"Ah, yes. I'd heard you were the saint kind enough to accompany my brother this year. Maybe he'll be less surly this time having you with him." He bowed, ever so slightly, lowering the baby before straightening again. "My deepest, sincerest thanks."

Well, that settled it then, didn't it? If she backed out of attending now, she'd be disappointing not just one but two Martinez men.

"Uh, you're welcome? I guess?"

"I'm hoping he won't behave the way he normally does when he's there if you're with him."

"And how is that?" Fallon asked.

"The man checks his watch about a hundred times during the evening, looking miserable and completely put-upon. Which, of course, in reality he is."

"I heard that." The three words came from a booming masculine voice sounding from the direction of the patio. This time, there was no mistaking the source. Enrique.

Fallon's heart did a giant leap in her chest as he approached the three of them.

Luis didn't bother to turn Enrique's way when he answered. "You heard the truth, *mi hermano.*" He shot Fallon a playful wink before finally turning to his brother.

"I see you met your nephew," Enrique announced when he reached their side. "And Fallon." He gave her the slightest nod in acknowledgment, without a hint of anything out of the ordinary. As if his lips hadn't been plastered against hers only a few days ago.

"Sí," Luis answered. "And I was just about to remark to Fallon how lucky this little man is."

Enrique reached for his son and cupped his palm around his small head. "Yeah? How's that?"

"Well, he doesn't appear to look like you very much. Thank heavens."

"You need to work on your insults, little brother. That was a rather lame one."

The teasing banter brought a smile to Fallon's lips, despite the rapid pounding of her heart at seeing Enrique.

Enrique hadn't missed the flirtatious wink his brother had sent Fallon upon his approach. Not that surprising. It was second nature for Luis to flirt. His brother had never been one to hold back the charm. Particularly when it came to an attractive woman like Fallon. So why was it bothering Enrique more than usual. Why did he have the sudden urge to wrestle his brother to the ground and give him a good throttle the way he had wanted to when they were kids?

It also wasn't surprising that Luis had been slighting him to Fallon when he'd walked out to the garden. Enrique didn't often miss an opportunity to taunt his brother. Luis gave as good as he received. But did he have to make Enrique sound like such a curmudgeon too? He didn't behave that badly at those blasted fundraisers, did he?

When had Luis returned home anyway?

Enrique had spent most of the morning trying to figure out what exactly he would say to Fallon so that they could get past that ill-conceived kiss. He couldn't just keep avoiding her. When he'd finally summoned to courage to seek her out and do so, Luis was there with her, thwarting his plans.

Not that he'd had the slightest idea exactly what he would say to her. Maybe Luis had done him a favor. His appearing back home at this particular moment might prove to be a welcome distraction. Then he and Fallon wouldn't even have to discuss what had happened between them. They could both simply let it go as…well, as one of those things. The less made of it, the better.

Plus he had to acknowledge, it was good to see his sibling again after so many weeks in the States. They spoke on the phone whenever they had the chance to. But long-distance conversations didn't prevent Enrique from missing his only sibling. Not that he would ever admit any of that to Luis.

Fallon hadn't said a word since he'd arrived.

He glanced at her now. She seemed to be directing her smiles to him and Luis in turn. Though she wasn't quite meeting his eyes. Luis seemed oblivious to any tension that may be in the air. So clearly they were both hiding it well. As well they should. They were both mature adults who'd just gotten carried away.

"So, what does this little man have planned for today?" Enrique asked by way of conversation.

Fallon pointed to Luis and the baby. "Well, I figure I'll let these two get acquainted for a bit. They seem to really be enjoying each other's company."

Luis gave his nephew a bounce resulting in a squeal of delight. "I'd like that," he said. "Lucas seems to be a cool little dude. I wouldn't mind spending some time with him. But only until he looks like he might begin to cry," he said in a solemn tone, his features growing serious.

Fallon gave him a mock salute. "Understood. I will stay close by to intervene ASAP at the first sign of fussiness."

"On whose part?" Enrique asked dryly. "From Luis or the baby?"

"Either or," came Fallon's quick reply.

"Very funny, bro," Luis said with a grin. "I think I'll go hang with my nephew one on one for a while," Luis said before reaching for Fallon's hand with his free one then bringing it to his lips for a small kiss. "Pleasure to make your acquaintance," he said, fluttering his eyes in such a dramatic way, it had to be intentionally comical. "I look forward to seeing you in a fancy ball gown. I'm sure you will wear it well," he added before walking to the patio and settling into the wooden swing with the baby. He bounced Lucas on his knee while swinging him back and forth.

Enrique felt his midsection tighten. It was one thing to flirt but kissing Fallon's hand followed by the comment about what she might wear was a bit much. He would have to speak to him about conducting himself better around his son's nanny.

The hypocrisy of that thought wasn't lost on him.

"Why do I get the feeling Luis is going to be the type of uncle who spoils his nephew rotten every chance he gets?" Fallon asked, her gaze fixated on where Luis and the baby sat.

"Leaving us to deal with the aftereffects."

Fallon's smile faltered slightly. The "us" hung heavily in the air. "You've read my brother well," Enrique added, to move the conversation forward past the awkwardness.

Easier said than done. Fallon still hadn't quite met his eyes.

"Uh, speaking of the dress," she began after several heavy moments of silence. Her voice sounded tight, troubled. "I'm not quite sure exactly how I'm supposed to be attired at this thing. And I fear I haven't packed anything that may be appropriate."

Enrique wanted to kick himself. He'd been totally remiss about making sure she felt ready for the fundraiser.

"Think nothing more of it," he told her. "I will have a stylist from our premier boutique bring over an array of choices. You may pick whichever one you like."

Her hands and lips grew tighter. "I don't think I can afford that, Enrique. As well as you pay me, I still have school loans I'm responsible for and other debts that take a good chunk of my earnings each month."

The woman was quite remarkable. She actually thought he would make her pay for a dress she needed for an event she was only attending as a favor to him.

He knew better than to try to persuade her to accept the dress as a gift from him. He may have only met her recently, but he knew Fallon well enough that she would steadfastly refuse any such giveaway.

"The merchandise in all the resort shops are my assets. Consider it a loan that you will be returning."

She looked ready to argue but Enrique held up a hand to stop her. "I insist."

He didn't give her a chance to say any more, knowing she was sure to try and turn down his offer.

He had no intention of letting her.

Dearest Sasha
It's been several weeks now. I'm worried about you still.

Fallon's fingers stalled over the keyboard, unsure what to say next. Or even if what she'd already written was worth sending. What was the use, really? The emails were clearly not being read. For all she knew, Sasha was holed up in some shelter or some kind of medical center without access to any kind of technology.

Or she was in an even worse predicament. That thought had tears stinging her eyes and she shut the laptop cover without trying to write any more.

As difficult as it was, she had to remain positive. Sasha was a fighter who knew how to take care of herself. Her friend had to be fine. She had a little boy to see again someday.

A faint knock sounded on her door, pulling her out of her erratic thoughts. Fallon rose from the desk and took a deep breath before getting up to answer it. A petite blonde woman stood on the other side. Her hair was done up in a complicated bun at the top of her head, and she wore a simple beige wraparound dress that showcased her hourglass figure.

Such a simple outfit. But this woman looked like the most stylish person Fallon had ever laid eyes on.

"I'm Tiffany," she announced, reaching out a slender glossy manicured hand. "I'm the new stylist from the Debutante Boutique. We have an appointment?"

Well, that made sense. If anyone fit the image of a fashionable stylist, it was this woman. Though she'd be equally fitting on a walkway modeling haute couture.

"Yes, please come in," Fallon said, opening the door wider and stepping to the side.

Tiffany wasn't alone. Two men also entered the room, each pulling two long clothing racks behind them. Yet a third wheeled in a large wooden chest. Depositing it all in the center of the room, they gave both ladies a friendly nod before leaving.

Tiffany pulled the chest over and opened it, turning it into accordion-style shelves with shoes and accessories. Fallon's room had become a fashionable women's store in the blink of an eye.

"Where would you like to start?" Tiffany asked.

Fallon had no idea. Most of her clothes were purchased from local thrift stores, and she'd certainly never had the need to buy anything more than slacks and tops for work, with the occasional overcoat for the harsh New England winters. She owned all of three dresses for the occasional school function.

"You have a lovely neckline," Tiffany declared, stepping closer. "May I?" she asked.

May she what? Fallon didn't know but nodded anyway. The woman cupped her chin and lifted her head, studying her.

"I'm thinking a low plunging high waisted number. In red. Yes, I think that's your color."

Huh. That's what Ilga the massage therapist had said too. Fallon had no idea she'd even had a color.

Tiffany pulled a bright crimson red dress off one of the racks. "Let's start with this one." She laid the garment on the bed and made a motion with her hands in Fallon's direction, signaling her to disrobe.

Growing up in various foster homes, this wouldn't be the first time she'd been in the company of another female in only her bra and panties. She'd had to share a room with at least one other girl at all times. Making fast work of changing, she turned to look in the mirror. And her breath caught in her throat. She hardly recognized herself. Even without her hair and makeup done and nothing but sandals on her feet, the dress made her feel like Cinderella.

"*Oui*, it is quite breathtaking," Tiffany said. "I believe your husband will thinks so too."

Fallon clasped a hand to her mouth. "Oh! He's not— I mean, I'm not—" She took a deep breath before continuing. "I'm just the nanny," she explained. "I need a dress for something of a work function."

"Dresses like these? For a work function, huh?"

"Yes, I'll just be there to fill a seat, really."

Tiffany shrugged one elegant shoulder. "So terribly sorry, then," she said, though she hardly looked bothered. Fallon got the impression that not much bothered this woman. She exuded self-confidence in waves. Fallon couldn't help but feel envious. She couldn't recall a time she'd ever been that sure of herself.

"I just started at the boutique. I'm new in Tulum," Tiffany informed her. "Still getting to know everyone."

"Me too." Sadly, that was probably the only thing she had in common with this stylish, secure woman who, judging by her accent, must have spent some time in Paris. Someone like Tiffany was much more likely to be married to a man like Enrique.

She may feel like Cinderella at the moment, but the notion that Enrique might be her husband was indeed a genuine fairy tale.

He felt like a teenager on the day of the prom. Enrique glanced at his watch again, barely listening to his project manager on the other end of the line. He'd actually been counting the hours all day. How ironic; he usually dreaded this event. But now he was incredulously waiting with bated breath for it to start.

But his anticipation had nothing to do with the fundraiser itself. It had everything to do with Fallon.

And wasn't that a sorry state of affairs?

He seemed to feel more and more drawn to her with each passing day. He could no longer deny it. Did he even want to?

Two hours later, he was showered and shaved. When the time finally came to get Fallon and be on their way, he practically bounded up the stairs to knock on her door.

The world stopped short once she opened it. His mouth went dry at the sight of her. She was a vision out of a storybook or some kind of movie. Enrique liked to think of himself as a worldly man. He'd had his share of romantic encounters and might have even considered himself falling for a woman once or twice. It took a lot to take Enrique's breath away. But the Fallon before him indeed left him breathless.

"Ay, mi Dio..." The words escaped his lips before he could help himself.

Fallon's eyes grew wide and she rubbed a hand down her midsection. "Is that good? Will this work? I can quickly change, if not."

She had no idea just how well it was all working. Her hair fell in luxurious waves over her shoulders. The dress fit her like a glove, hugging her curves in all the right places. And the color. He wondered if there was any way to mandate that she wear that shade of fiery red at all times.

"It's good," he answered when he finally found his voice, thinking what an understatement that was.

CHAPTER ELEVEN

ALL THE NOTABLES were here.

Enrique scanned the ballroom to find the usual impressive crowd. Some of the continent's most influential and successful entrepreneurs and businesspeople. A few politicians. Fallon stood rod stiff next to him, her grip on his forearm vise tight. He wished he could get her to relax. Though part of him understood. She was in a new environment for her. Both foreign and unfamiliar. It wasn't all that long ago that he himself would have felt out of place at such a soiree. Not long enough that he'd completely forgotten.

Fallon was breathtaking. And those around them were starting to notice. More than a few heads turned in their direction as they walked in. Appreciative male glances landed on Fallon and lingered before catching Enrique's glare.

Not that he could really blame the gentlemen, as well as several ladies, who seemed to be staring. Fallon was the most striking woman here. Though perhaps he was a bit biased about his date.

He'd had to fight the urge during the drive over to redirect the chauffeur. The temptation to instruct the man to drive right past the venue and instead take them somewhere private where they could enjoy a real dinner and each other's company was nearly overwhelming. Then they would have been able to see where the evening might lead, and damn the consequences.

Common sense had prevailed and he'd resisted. But it had been close.

He stole a glance at her now as they moved farther into the ballroom. Despite the fact that she was clearly nervous, she appeared to be glowing. The auburn streaks in her hair shone under the yellow-hued mini chandeliers hanging from the ceiling. She wore nothing but simple gold earrings in the way of jewelry, yet her neck bare was magnificently showcased over the low neckline of her dress. A slit in her skirt showed off just enough shapely leg to have his pulse humming with each step she took.

He wouldn't be surprised if by the end of the evening, he'd have to beat the men off her. Starting with his own brother, who was making a beeline for them. Luis's gaze was fixated squarely on Fallon, with barely a glance in Enrique's direction.

"Oh, my," his brother said, reaching for Fallon's free hand. *"Muy, muy, bonita,"* he added, dropping a small kiss on Fallon's knuckles, just as he had the other day when he'd first met her in the garden.

"Lovely to see you again, Luis," she said with a dazzling smile in his brother's direction before addressing both of them. "Do you both mind if I go freshen up quickly?"

"Of course," they said in unison.

"Your nanny seems to be attracting all sorts of attention this evening," Luis said, watching Fallon's back as she walked away.

"So it appears."

"And what about you?" his brother asked knowingly.

"What about me?"

"I'm guessing you're pretty distracted by her as well. She's a knockout, you have to admit. Maybe you should tell her so."

Enrique swiped a flute of champagne off the tray of a passing waiter and took a small sip. "I've made sure to mention how nice she looks."

Luis grunted a laugh. "Nice. Is that what you said to her? That she looked nice?"

Little did Luis know. He'd barely found any words to say to her at all, as gobsmacked as he'd been at the first sight of her this evening.

"Well, if you won't tell her how much more than *nice* she looks, maybe I will."

Enrique knew his brother was simply indulging in his favorite pastime of taunting him. And he knew he shouldn't take the bait. He made himself silently count to ten before answering.

Luis let out a burst of laughter.

"What's so funny?" Enrique demanded, draining the last of his champagne.

"You're practically snarling at me, bro. Simply because I mentioned wanting to compliment your date. That's what's so funny."

This night was going to be a memory she would cherish forever. Fallon knew that as soon as Enrique had arrived to fetch her at her door. Her pulse jumped under skin, her senses on overload. She just needed a moment to compose herself.

It hadn't helped that dozens of sets of eyes had landed on them as soon as she and Enrique had entered the ballroom. Nor had the close proximity to Enrique in the limousine on the way over. In a well-fitting tux with his hair combed back, the man looked like walking temptation.

After splashing some cold water on her face, making sure not to mess her makeup, she made her way back to the ballroom. Enrique and Luis were in the same spot she'd left them.

Fallon paused at the image the two of them presented. The Martinez brothers seemed to command the room, though she would bet neither of them knew it.

By far the most handsome men in here, with Enrique a distant first. Luis was drop-dead good-looking, no denying it. But his was a boyish, mischievous handsome, while Enrique's features were striking in a much more mature way. She supposed enough women found Luis more attractive, the young boyish type.

Not so herself.

No, she much preferred the quiet maturity behind Enrique's allure. The man was successful, considerate, and he'd taken to fatherhood like a charm.

Someone accidentally brushed past her, bringing her back to the moment. What was she doing? How long had she just been standing here gawking at the two of them? At Enrique in particular. It would be horrifying if he were to look up and catch her staring at him like a besotted schoolgirl. Gathering herself, she made her way back to his side. Just as another woman approached the two men from the opposite direction.

Fallon watched as without any hesitation or preamble, the woman leaned into Enrique and gave him a kiss square on the mouth then patted his cheek, her moves full of familiarity and affection.

The next moment, she was tugging Enrique onto the dance floor. He didn't hesitate to follow her.

* * *

Luis gave Fallon an exaggerated bow as she approached. It took some effort but she managed to pull her gaze from Enrique and the mystery woman long enough to return his smile.

He extended his hand out to her, palm up. "May I have the pleasure of this dance?"

Surprisingly, the rush of apprehension she'd been expecting at having been asked to dance didn't appear. Rather, it was replaced with a crushing dose of disappointment that Luis was the one asking her.

"I don't think you know what you're getting yourself into. It's probably not a good idea. You risk crushed toes and banged shins." She glanced in Enrique's direction once more. Unlike his dance partner, with her smooth and graceful movements, Fallon was likely to appear stiff and she was certain to miss at least one or two steps.

Luis gave a solemn shake of his head. "Tsk, tsk. That's nonsense. I've seen you practicing in the garden, remember?"

"Hardly the same thing."

"Close enough." He waved his fingers at her. "Come on, one song."

Despite her misgivings, she took the hand he offered and followed him onto the dance floor.

"Something tells me you don't get told no very often, do you?"

"Ah, but it pays to be persistent."

"So it seems."

They moved in silence for several beats. So far, so good. She was managing to keep up with him and no stumbles. Yet.

"I know you're dying to know, so go ahead and ask me already."

"Ask you what?"

"Who Enrique is dancing with."

Was it that obvious? She'd been trying so hard not to look over at them. Clearly, she'd failed.

Luis didn't wait for her to respond. "Esmerelda Pina. Highly popular influencer with over three million followers."

Great. An accomplished, beautiful woman, leagues above her. Not that she was competing with anyone.

"I'll tell you a secret," Luis began, then leaned closer to whisper in her ear. "Enrique's not terribly fond of her."

The rush of pleasure at those words was actually a tad embarrassing. "Oh?"

"He's probably cursing silently and willing the song to end already. I'm sure he didn't want to embarrass her by turning down the dance, though he wanted to."

"Why's that?"

"Every move Esmerelda makes is so she can post it on her social media pages. Enrique's not a big fan."

"Huh."

"The last time he went out with her, he found himself plastered all over her feed."

Did that mean that if Esmerelda promised not to display him on her pages anymore, he might ask her out again? Was she doing so even now? Apologizing and swearing it wouldn't happen again? After all, she hadn't hesitated to approach him mere minutes after their arrival.

"So, you don't have to worry about her," Luis added.

Fallon felt a rush of heat to her face at his assumption. "I'm not. At all," she said, stuttering. "It's really none of my business, is it?"

Luis narrowed his eyes on her. "I don't know. Is it?"

"No," she said with an emphatic shake of her head. "Absolutely not. And for all you know, Enrique's forgiven her and they're rekindling their relationship."

He threw back his head and laughed before answering. "Highly unlikely."

"You don't know that for sure," Fallon argued.

"Ah, but I do. My brother finds it hard to trust others—and he is certainly not the forgiving type."

That statement ran a shiver down her spine. Chances were high she was going to need Enrique's forgiveness herself in the near future. Once he found out the truth. Luis's statement did not bode well for how that might go.

Fallon was desperate to change the subject. "So this is all to raise funds for your department, then?"

Luis flashed her an amused smile that said he knew exactly what she was doing. *"Sí,"* he answered, indicating he would play along. "Those archaeological digs get pricey between the equipment and all it takes to make sure the discoveries are handled well and preserved."

"It sounds fascinating."

"It is. Tulum is an ancient city with vast numbers of undiscovered sites still. And what had been uncovered is majestic. The city is rich with ancient history."

"I hope to see more of it."

"You have to see the ruins first. They're breathtaking. In fact, I'll take you myself. We'll strap the baby in his stroller and head out late tomorrow morning."

"My very own archaeology expert as a tour guide. I'm beyond excited."

"Excited about what?" The question came from a deep baritone voice behind her. A voice she would now recognize anywhere. Enrique.

Without waiting for an answer, he addressed his brother

in Spanish. Fallon didn't need to be fluent to gather that he was asking to cut in.

"Of course," Luis answered, then gave her a friendly nod before stepping away.

Fallon's heart fluttered in her chest as she stepped into Enrique's arms. Her breath felt labored. Why did this man have such an effect on her? He was paying her to take care of his child. That's all there was between them. Why did her traitorous body forget there could never be anything more between them? For a moment she wanted to heed all those physical reactions. Pretend there was a chance for something more. What would it feel like if she really were here as his date? What if she were his wife? The thought had her mentally gasping. It was hard not to remember the last time they'd danced together and how it had ended in a deep, passionate kiss that had her knees buckling.

"Your breathing is heavy," Enrique commented, leading her on the dance floor. "You really must be excited about something."

Huh?

Enrique answered her unspoken question. "That's what you were saying to Luis when I walked over."

Right! The ruins. The distraction that was Enrique Martinez had zapped the conversation right out of her mind. "Oh, that. Your brother has kindly offered to take me and Lucas to the Tulum Ruins tomorrow and act as our expert tour guide. I'm quite looking forward to it."

Enrique's lips tightened. "He did, did he?"

"Yes, it was quite nice of him, offering to take time out of his day."

"Hmm. My brother is so very selfless," he said, his voice tight and strained.

Enrique's tone nowhere near matched his words.

* * *

"I think I could use some fresh air."

Fallon forced herself to step out of Enrique's arms as soon as the current song ended. Otherwise, it was just too tempting to linger in his embrace, to ease into the next song and the next and let him continue holding her, as she'd been doing for the last hour or more.

She didn't think her senses would be able to take it. She needed to keep her wits about her if she was to have any hope of getting through the rest of the evening without her heart turning into a mush of goo in her chest.

"As you wish."

She knew she didn't imagine his hesitation in releasing his grip before he led her off the dance floor and toward the back of the ballroom. They reached a set of double doors that led to the rear of the building.

Enrique held the door open for her and she stepped outside to a sprawling garden with a tall fountain a few feet away. The full moon above cast a silver glow across the surface of the gushing water. The breeze tickled her cheeks. Fallon felt as if she might have stepped into a scene from a storybook. Complete with a dashing, handsome hero beside her.

A chill ran over her skin.

Enrique shrugged out of his jacket and draped it over her shoulders apparently misinterpreting her reaction to him as her being cold. The scent of him off the jacket immediately engulfed her senses, further magnifying the effect he was having on her. Heaven help her, he was now rolling up his sleeves to reveal tanned, muscular arms. The man was much too handsome in a tux as it was. Partially out of one, he was downright scorching.

"Warm enough?" he asked.

If he only knew. She was a river of molten lava inside. "Yes. Thanks," she answered abruptly.

Maybe it hadn't been such a good idea to want to come outside, after all. At least inside they'd had the buffer of other people. Out here they were completely alone. Together.

"So, this takes place every year?" she asked, grasping for a subject of conversation. Any subject would do to try and take her mind off her out-of-control attraction to him.

"Unfortunately," Enrique answered. "Although it's much more bearable this time."

They'd reached the fountain. Enrique planted one foot on the rim and leaned his forearm over his knee.

"Luis is lucky to have you," Fallon said, determined to keep the focus of the conversation on relatively benign matters.

A smile of affection spread over his features. "I make sure to tell him that as often as I can."

Fallon chuckled. "It's the truth. Not every big brother would go out of his way to show such unwavering support. I mean, you could easily write a check and essentially be done with the fundraiser. Yet, you attend the gala every year."

And she was guessing Enrique was the one paying for Luis's education.

Enrique released a long sigh, the smile faltering ever so slightly. "I'm the closest thing to a father he's ever had. I figure at least one of us should have a father figure in their lives."

The man was too good to be true. Did he have any flaws whatsoever? Luis had told her in the ballroom that it was hard for Enrique to put his trust in people easily. But that could hardly be considered a flaw. Especially considering the current circumstances. It galled her that she might turn out to be one of the people who proved him right to be so mistrustful of others.

"Our own father never wanted anything to do with either me or Luis."

Fallon wrapped the jacket tighter around herself, her heart tugging at the bitterness and hurt in his voice. "He was married into a very powerful and wealthy family in South America. After my mother dumped me on Abuela, she was his mistress for years until he decided he needed a younger model. She was eventually tossed aside just like the two of us were."

"Do you think she regrets her choices?"

He scoffed out loud. "No. The exact opposite in fact. She views that relationship as the highlight of her life. It afforded her exactly the kind of lifestyle she wanted. And the small trust fund she convinced her lover to set up for me, her oldest son, enabled me to make other profitable investments and eventually led to my line of luxurious resorts. All of which allows her to maintain said lifestyle. I think she believes she was quite shrewd actually."

Tension seemed to be rising off him in waves. It was beyond apparent that this wasn't a topic he spoke of often. Yet, here he was, opening up to her so completely. The ever-present guilt sitting like a boulder in her rib cage grew heavier. What a coward she was. How could she not have found a way to come clean already?

"I hope you realize what an extraordinary man you are, Enrique. The way you've built so much from so little, the way you take care of your little brother and your grandmother, it's all so impressive. Not to mention, how much of a devoted and loving father you are to Lucas."

Fallon wanted to clamp her hand to her mouth. She hadn't meant to say any of that out loud. She'd just bared her feelings about him, which hovered much too close to the surface.

Even in the dark she could see the full impact of her words. Enrique's eyes narrowed on her, a muscle twitched along his jaw. "Careful there, sweetheart. I might begin to think you find me appealing or something."

He leaned closer, trailed a finger along her cheek. "Do you?"

Her mind seemed to shut down, and she moved closer too. There was only a hair's breadth between them now. The next moment, she felt his lips on hers. There was no telling even which one of them had moved first. The kiss was the barest brushing of his lips against hers, gentle as a light feather. Yet she felt the effect in every cell in her body.

"Fallon." He whispered her name against her mouth. It was a question. Heaven help her, she knew exactly what he was asking, wanted desperately to say yes.

"There you two are," came a masculine voice from the direction of the building. Luis.

Though it felt like ripping a scab off a wound, Fallon made herself pull away. Luis was far enough away and the evening dark enough that she didn't think he could have seen much except for their silhouettes.

Thanks heavens.

She'd barely recovered her breath by the time he reached their side.

"I'm going to head out with my friends now," Luis informed them. "Just came to say good night."

Fallon couldn't decide if she was grateful or not for his appearance.

She was wreaking havoc on his senses.

Enrique escorted Fallon out of the ballroom to the limousine waiting outside the venue. A surprising whisper of sadness echoed through his head that the night was over. What a turn of the screw that was. If someone had told him at the last gala he'd attended that he'd be disappointed to see the evening end, he would have laughed until he was out of breath.

But the truth was that he wanted this night to continue. He wanted to watch Fallon sipping champagne through those luscious ruby-red lips of hers, holding the narrow crystal flute in her elegant fingers. He wanted to feel her against him in his arms as they moved on the dance floor.

The dress she had on complimented her perfectly. Whoever the boutique had sent had done a commendable job of dressing her. The rich red color brought out the golden specks of her mesmerizing eyes. The material hugged all her curves in the most enticing ways. The neckline just low enough to have his imagination running wild.

The driver saw them approach and immediately opened the door. Enrique helped her into the car then sat in the seat opposite. What he wanted to do was sit next to her, hug her shoulders and pull her up against him. He wanted to take up where they'd left off before Luis had so maddeningly interrupted.

Heaven help him, then he wanted to kiss her again. Like he had back by the fountain this evening and that day in the garden the other week. He'd lost control with her twice already. He couldn't seem to get enough of her.

Fallon released a melodic chuckle, luckily pulling him away from his wayward thoughts. But what sweet, enticing thoughts they were.

"I'm so relieved that went well," she said in a breathless tone. "I didn't even make a fool of myself on the dance floor."

She really was rather self-deprecating. For the life of him, he couldn't understand why. How did she not realize how magnificent she was?

"On the contrary, you moved beautifully. You had nothing to worry about," he assured her.

Her lashes fluttered downward. "Well, to tell you the truth, I've been practicing a bit. With a very motivating partner."

Enrique felt his fists tighten. Who would have been practicing with her? The only logical conclusion was his brother. He wasn't foolish enough to suspect there was anything between Luis and Fallon, but it still riled his blood pressure that his brother had been spending time with her, twirling her in his arms.

"He's a little on the young side and I have to be the one to lead," she added.

Who in the world…?

"And he almost always falls asleep immediately after," she added.

What she was getting at finally registered and Enrique had to chuckle. "I hope my son was the perfect gentleman during your practice sessions."

"Of course he was. A total angel, as always."

How imbecilic of him. Was he that far gone on her that he was so ready to bristle with jealousy at the thought of another man—his younger brother—dancing with her? Clearly so. The ramifications of that acknowledgment were almost too much to weigh right now.

They arrived at the hacienda twenty minutes later. Enrique spent most of that time debating how and if he should find a way to invite her to spend more of the night with him. He shouldn't even be entertaining the idea, let alone acting on it in any way. After tonight, they would have to go back to their initial working relationship. He was nothing more than her employer. Starting any kind of relationship with his son's nanny was asking the universe for trouble. He couldn't forget the truth of that.

Easier said than done.

Not to mention, he hadn't missed how often Fallon had yawned during the ride back home, her eyes slowly drifting closed until she realized it and blinked them open again. The woman was clearly tired, no doubt a combination of excitement and the hour growing late.

She turned to him after her helped her out of the car. "Thank you, Enrique. I genuinely enjoyed myself this evening. I honestly wasn't expecting that."

Ouch. Enrique decided to let that comment go for the sake of his masculine ego. "I'm the one who should be thanking you. You did me quite the favor this evening."

She immediately shook her head. "No, that's not how it felt at all."

Enrique paused on the veranda, knowing he shouldn't ask what he was about to ask. He should just walk her to her room and bid her good-night. But here he was, stalling. Fishing for some kind of acknowledgment that she'd enjoyed the evening because he'd been with her. "Oh? What did it feel like?"

She ducked her head. "Well, for one thing, once I finally managed to relax a bit, I actually started to have fun," she said.

"Surprisingly, I had fun too." *With you.*

She laughed. "Glad to hear it. We both expected the worst and look how it turned out."

It doesn't have to end. The words were on the tip of his tongue. He resisted uttering them out loud when all he wanted to do was lean over and whisper them softly in her ear.

Several moments of awkward silence hung in the air before Fallon finally broke it. "I think all the excitement has caught up with me. I should head on up to bed."

Invite me to come up there with you. Enrique willed her to say the words he so desperately wanted to hear.

Instead, she handed back his jacket, then cupped her palm over her mouth on another soft yawn.

If he didn't feel so pathetic, he might have actually laughed at himself. The woman could barely stay awake in his company. While here he was entertaining romantic thoughts about her he had no business thinking.

Pathetic indeed.

CHAPTER TWELVE

FALLON SHUT HER door behind her and leaned her back up against the cool wood, willing her racing pulse to slow.

Highly unlikely anytime soon.

Enrique had just walked her to her suite and bid her good-night. All the while, looking devilishly handsome. His sleeves rolled up to his elbows, the top buttons of his crisp white shirt undone. He looked like a man out of every red-blooded woman's fantasy.

A fantasy she had to get out of her head once and for all.

All that yawning had been more due to her nervousness, coupled with fighting the urges she'd had all night. Like the urge to lean tighter up against Enrique's length when they'd been dancing. Or the urge to trail her hand along his upper thighs during the ride back to the hacienda. What about the urge to ask him to kiss her again to see where it might lead?

He hadn't even asked her to share a nightcap with him.

And why would he?

Only one of them here had wholly inappropriate feelings they had to fight against. Sure, he'd gotten carried away back there by the fountain, they both had. But she couldn't look too deeply into the how and the why when it came to that kiss. The romantic setting, the fake date, the novelty of a gala ball—it had simply led to a tender moment, that was all.

It was just as well he hadn't asked to extend the evening. She would have had no excuse but to come clean about her identity after the evening they'd spent together. And she simply didn't feel prepared.

A voice in her head mocked her immediately. The truth was, she didn't want anything to mar this magical night in any way. Better to have it end than have it end badly.

Fallon kicked her stilettos off and slipped out of the dress, then hung it carefully on the suede covered hanger. The chances of her wearing such a fancy garment ever again were highly doubtful.

As was any chance of her attending another gala event on the arm of a successful, handsome, billionaire.

Womp-womp.

She was skating perilously close to self-pity here. She wouldn't allow it.

The evening had been one of the best times she'd spent. She should be happy it had ever happened. Not woeful that it had come to an end.

Her heart had other plans.

With a sigh, she made her way to the bathroom to wash her face and clean up, certain that a sleepless night awaited her.

Despite all the yawning, her adrenaline was too high. Her mind too focused on the man under the same roof. So close and yet so far out of her league.

Oh, and then there was that whole other complication about who exactly she was to his son.

Fallon sighed and stared at herself in the mirror, the realization washing over her. She had to tell him. The deception had gone on long enough.

Somehow, someway, she had to sit Enrique down and explain exactly who she was.

And if he sent her packing?

It was chance she had to take. And hope he understood and considered her motivations and how much she loved little Lucas.

She would just have to convince him to let her stay.

But first she had to get through tonight and try and get some rest. Or she'd be useless tomorrow to Lucas.

As far as Luis's invitation to see the ruins, as much as she wanted to, it would have to wait. She simply couldn't imagine summoning that much energy. Not to mention, how preoccupied she'd be with the nerve-racking task that awaited her.

Or the uncertainly about the aftermath of her confession. A sob tore out of her throat at the thought that this time tomorrow, she might well be on her way back to the States and never see little Lucas again.

Nor his father, the man she was so headily falling for.

By the time the morning sun rose in the distant horizon, Fallon was convinced she'd barely managed to sleep more than a few extended winks.

Coffee. She desperately needed coffee. The soft sounds of Lucas gurgling echoed from the monitor telling her the coffee would have to wait. Dressing quickly, she made her way to the nursery.

Lucas lay on his back in his crib, wide-eyed with his fist partially in his mouth. "Hey there, little man." Fallon lowered the side panel of the bed and reached for him. "I missed you last night. Did you behave for your great-*abuela*?"

Fallon lifted him into her arms and gave him a gentle hug. He'd grown so big since that first day she'd interviewed for the position as his nanny. And her heart had grown with more love for him. Enrique wouldn't be cruel enough to overlook that love once he found out the truth, would he?

She shuddered to even think about it.

"I'll bet you were a really good boy last night, huh?" she asked, lifting him up off the changing table once he'd been cleaned up.

"Abuela says as much," came an answer behind her. Her heart did a somersault in her chest, the voice unmistakably Enrique's.

Even if he hadn't spoken, the now familiar, masculine scent of him reached her nose the moment he entered the room and had her pulse racing.

"She says he was an absolute angel all night," he added.

"I'm glad to hear it but not surprised," she managed to say, doing her best to focus on the conversation and not the way Enrique's mere presence affected her.

"So different than the first few weeks after he arrived at my door," he said, before his gaze found her. "I have you to thank for that."

How she wished he hadn't said such a thing given what she would be divulging to him soon.

He was at her side a moment later, and Fallon had to remind herself to breathe. The effect this man had on her was turning her to mush inside.

And she had no idea what to do about it.

He stepped closer and cupped his hand around Lucas's cheek. Fallon had to resist the urge to lean closer into him against his chest and inhale deeply of that tempting, alluring scent of his.

"So, a big outing planned for today for this little fella. He's sure to nap well himself after all the fresh air and excitement." He reached out and took his son into his arms. "He can stay with me while you go get ready."

Right. The ruins.

She was about to tell him about her plans to ask Luis for a rain check when his next words stopped her.

"Oh, and you won't be going with Luis, after all."

That gave her pause. What had changed since last night? He answered her next question before she could ask it. "I'll be accompanying you myself."

She certainly hadn't seen that coming.

Fallon was totally unprepared for Enrique's announcement that he'd be taking them out today instead of Luis. In her surprise at the unexpected announcement, she'd totally forgotten about wanting to postpone the outing.

Right, a little voice inside her mind mocked. *As if that's the reason.*

She sighed as she gathered Lucas's bag with the essentials he would need for a day away. If she were to admit the truth to herself, she would have to acknowledge that she'd changed her mind about not going. And that change of heart had everything to do with Enrique.

As much as she enjoyed Luis's company, spending the day with Enrique held an entirely different appeal. Her heart had done a little leap of excitement when he'd told her the change in plans.

Oh, man, she had it bad, didn't she?

What if he wanted to kiss her again? Heaven help her, Fallon didn't think she could resist him a third time.

The car was waiting for them when she went back downstairs with the bag and her own items. Enrique had instructed her to bring a bathing suit for both herself and the baby. Just in case it was needed.

So they might be spending some time at the beach. The thought of seeing Enrique bare chested again gave her heart a thud. She would have to make sure not to ogle the man. Her imagination was already running wild with all sorts of images.

She took care of feeding the baby during the ride. So that by the time they arrived at the ruins, he was fed, dry and seemed content. He didn't even make a fuss when Enrique strapped him into the stroller like he usually did when placed in it.

"Welcome to one of the most visited sites in Tulum," Enrique announced, pushing Lucas toward the structures. Fallon's mouth fell open in awe. She could clearly see in her mind's eye the grandeur this place must have held all those centuries ago despite their crumbling status now.

"This is amazing."

"I figured I can show you around them just as well as Luis. And you won't have to put up his nerdy overexplanations. Besides, I think I should be with my son the first time he lays eyes on such a historical sight in his ancestral home."

So the swapping places with his brother had nothing to do with her at all. How silly of her to have entertained such a notion for even a brief moment.

He let go of the stroller to point into the distance. "The Mayans built this before the thirteenth century. A self-contained city bordered on one side by the sea and a wall for protection on the other."

"I've never seen anything like it."

Enrique's smile at that response had her skin tingling. He seemed pleased at her reaction. But how could anyone not be awed by this place?

"That building over there is the Temple of the Frescoes.

They used it to track the movement of the sun. Tracking the sky like that was way ahead of the time for that era."

A sudden movement near her foot stopped her midstep. She looked down to find what could only be described as a shrunken dragon, mere inches from her foot. Black with sharp spines running down its back and along its tail, the creature looked like something out of a nightmare.

Fallon couldn't help the shriek that tore from her throat. Nor could she help the way she pushed the stroller away from it. All the while she hurled herself at Enrique, then jumped at him so that he had no choice but to catch her.

"What is that monster?"

Enrique's response was a hearty chuckle. "What's so funny?" she demanded to know, calculating if she'd pushed Lucas far enough away from whatever it was.

"Relax," he told her through a grin. "It's just a basilisk lizard."

"A what?"

"A type of iguana. They make their home here among the ruins. It's here to say hello."

"Well, I don't want to make its acquaintance, thank you very much."

"Aw, that's too bad. They're so used to the tourists they actually greet them. Look, it's bobbing its head at us."

"I half expected it to start breathing fire."

Enrique laughed again, his chest vibrating against her. That bewitching scent of his surrounding her, his closeness sending pulsing waves over her skin. She almost forgot about the lizard, which had by now skittered away. Then common sense finally kicked in. She had to get down.

With no small amount of reluctance, Fallon lowered her feet back to the ground and stepped away.

"Sorry about that then."

His eyes darkened and his lids lowered, the smile faded from his mouth as his expression grew serious. "No need to apologize."

Several beats passed in silence. What exactly was happening between them at this moment?

She didn't get a chance to examine it any further as Lucas let out an impatient cry. He'd been dormant too long.

Fallon gave herself a quick moment for her heart rate to settle. She couldn't even be sure what had spiked it more, the lizard or the way Enrique had caught her in his arms. Or the way he was looking at her now.

"What's that other tower," she finally managed to ask after several beats, to try and refocus. It worked. The ad hoc history lesson fascinated her more than she would have guessed.

"That's the Temple of the Descending God. It's got some impressive carvings. The devout often used it as a place for confessionals. Let's go take a look."

Confessionals. Fallon paused. It was as if Enrique had given her a perfect segue. Once they got to the tower, she could take the opportunity to announce that she had something to confess herself. An ancient tower for confessions was an apt place for such a revelation, was it not? Her heart started pounding in her chest. She had to take the opportunity to finally come clean.

They hadn't gotten far when an older couple approached them, smiles wide. They'd clearly witnessed her little jump scare at the lizard and seemed amused.

"Hola," they said in unison. "Buenas tardes."

Fallon and Enrique both returned the greeting.

Their eyes focused on Lucas in his stroller.

Fallon could make out just enough of the Spanish to get the gist. *Hermoso bebe... Que angel...encandora familia.*

Fallon felt a tug at the last word. That one was easy to guess. Family.

The couple could be forgiven for their mistaken assumption. To any observer, they must look the perfect image of a happy couple out with their new baby. They had no idea what a fantasy it all was. On her side anyway. With a lengthy sigh, she waited for Enrique to correct them.

But his reply surprised her. *"Gracias,"* was all he said.

The interaction was enough to dissolve her earlier resolve. She couldn't do it here. Not in front of all these strangers at such a sacred place.

Yet another excuse, whispered a nagging voice in her head.

She ignored it.

Enrique figured he'd done a pretty good job introducing Fallon to Tulum's history. Sure, Luis would have had much more detailed information at the top of his head, given his field of study. But Fallon could hear about all that at some future time. He'd gone to bed last night with his decision made. As a native son, Enrique knew enough about his ancestral lands to make today an informative visit for her. Besides, he wasn't going to sit around in his study all day staring at a spreadsheet or a computer screen while the three of them were out playing tourist.

Now, on the beach as he waited for Fallon to change into her bathing suit in the nearby cabana, he knew the decision had been the right one. Though he hadn't appreciated the knowing look on his brother's face when he'd informed Luis of the change.

He couldn't remember the last time he'd skipped out on a day of work to hang out at the Tulum Ruins and then the beach. Nor could he remember the last time he'd enjoyed himself quite so thoroughly.

Lucas seemed to be enjoying himself too. The baby was clear-eyed and alert, and appeared to be studying his new surroundings with a look of fascination on his cherubic face.

How new and full of wonder the world must seem to the little guy. Enrique was looking forward to watching his son discover his world as he grew up, though he had no illusions about all the hard work and challenges that would come with being a single father.

Only, he didn't feel quite so alone on his fatherhood journey. He had Fallon to partner with him in raising his son.

The realization had come to him gradually but it was clear. She was so much more than a nanny.

That was why he hadn't bothered to correct the older couple at the ruins earlier when they'd assumed her to be his wife and Lucas's mother. They were already something of a family. She was a large part of their lives now.

And if things between the two of them continued to develop, who knew where it might lead? For as much as he'd fought it in the beginning, there was no longer any denying that there was a pull between them that could no longer be ignored.

And he no longer wanted to ignore it, in fact.

The jolt of desire he felt when she reappeared after changing confirmed his thoughts. Her suit was modest by any means. A tankini that covered her midriff with matching boy shorts. But the way the fabric clung to her enticing curves and the way the shorts accentuated her shapely legs made it hard not to stare.

He wasn't sure how he'd cope if she asked him to rub sunscreen lotion on her back.

Not that he'd imagined doing that very thing upon seeing her.

She lowered herself onto the beach blanket next to him, rubbing Lucas's cheek. "So, is it safe here?"

"Safe?"

"No lizards lurking about, I hope?"

The comical shudder that shook her shoulders as she said the last word made him laugh.

"It's not impossible but highly unlikely. They prefer the shaded stones at the ruins."

"Glad to hear it."

Although, if the appearance of a basilisk had her jumping into his arms again, he wouldn't exactly complain about it. It had taken all of his will not to lean down and drop a gentle kiss along her lips as she clung to him. Dancing with her last night and feeling her against him again today, he was starting to get used to touching Fallon and holding her. She felt right in his arms.

He couldn't recall having that thought about any other woman.

He wanted to touch her now. To run his fingers along those shapely curves then trail them higher up her body. Then...

Enrique gave himself a mental shake, grateful for the loose fit of the swim shorts he'd changed into earlier. He had to cool down here.

He reached for the baby. "What do you say we introduce this little guy to the ocean?"

Fallon jumped up with an excited clap. "Yes! I can't wait to see his reaction."

He was pretty excited about his son's first ocean swim himself.

When they reached the edge of the water, Fallon waded in without hesitation. Enrique followed, then gingerly set his son's feet in. Lucas gave a gasp, then looked up at his father in question.

"He doesn't look as if he's too sure about this," Fallon said above their heads.

"No, he certainly doesn't."

Just when he thought he might have to pull the baby out and try again some other time, Lucas gave a kick of his little legs. Then he did it again.

Fallon squealed with delight. "He likes it!" She dropped to her knees next to them. Lucas was kicking with both feet now, splashing the water and clearly enjoying himself.

Fallon gave him a little tickle on his tummy. What happened next had Enrique's heart flooding with emotion.

His son gave his first proper belly laugh.

Fallon cupped a hand to her mouth, her eyes wide. She'd made note of it too.

One of many of his son's firsts Enrique had no doubt they'd witness together.

"I'm starving," Enrique announced about three hours later as the day slowly drew to a close. The sun had just begun its descent, washing the sky in bright color with streaks of lavender and bright orange over the water. If she ever took up painting, this would be the view Fallon would strive to capture on canvas.

"If we rush back, I can help Abuela prepare dinner," she said. "I think this little one will be out cold by the time we make it to the front veranda."

It struck her then what she'd just said. She'd actually

referred to Rosa as Abuela, a note of familiarity she had no claim to. If Enrique noticed, he didn't acknowledge it.

"Abuela isn't home," Enrique responded, gathering the baby's things. "It's her monthly game of conquian. We'll be lucky to see her before midnight. Those ladies take their card games seriously."

"I suppose I can throw something together. Though obviously it won't stand up to Rosa's usual fare." She'd made sure to use the elder's real name this time.

Enrique stood, hoisting Lucas up with him in his arms. "I have another idea. There's an outdoor cantina about a quarter mile down the beach. It's always booked weeks in advance."

"Do we have reservations?" If they did, why hadn't he thought to mention it?

"No," Enrique answered. "But I think they'll fit us in."

"Because you're the owner of the town's most renowned resort?"

He smiled at her. "Something like that."

About fifteen minutes later, they were walking up a wooden pathway to a straw-roofed open-air eatery. The place looked packed, every table full. The bar area appeared to be standing room only.

Regardless of Enrique's prominence in town, Fallon didn't see how they could possibly find a spot. Before they'd made it to the entrance, a middle-aged woman wearing a smock and a tight bun appeared out of nowhere and made a beeline for Enrique. Fallon watched as she patted his cheek and then clasped her hands to her chest as her gaze fell on the drowsy baby in his arms.

"Ay, hermoso bebe," she said, followed by rapid Spanish Fallon had no hope of interpreting. Luckily, she switched to English right after. "What took you so long to get here,

hijo?" she asked Enrique. "We've been dying to finally meet this little one."

"Lo siento," Enrique answered, handing the baby to her outstretched arms. "We are here now, Tia."

"Blessedly so."

Enrique turned to Fallon. "Fallon, this is Anna. I call her Tia Anna. She owns and runs this place with her husband, Tio Ramon. And the two of them gave me my first job busing tables when I desperately needed one."

Well, the connection explained why he'd been so confident about getting a table at such a popular spot.

"So nice to meet you," Anna said, giving Fallon a one-armed hug while she cradled the baby with the other, her voice full of warmth and joy.

Fallon's heart flooded with happiness at the affectionate way the older woman held Luis against her bosom and nuzzled his chubby cheek. Yet another person who seemed to adore him.

"Come, come," Anna said, motioning them forward. "I'll take you to the table in the back."

They followed her past the crowded bar and through the dining area until they reached a sliding screen door. Anna opened it and ushered them through to a patio outside with a long wooden table. Tea lights were strung from wooden poles and trees. Bouncy salsa music sounded from floor speakers on opposite sides.

"Siéntate," Anna instructed, motioning to the chairs. Enrique pulled one out for her and waited for her to sit before taking his seat outside.

Lucas was staring in awe at the tiny light bulbs scattered around the patio.

Before Fallon had even had a chance to settle into her seat, a trio of people arrived through the screen door, each carrying a tray of food. Two others arrived on their heels, one holding a pitcher full of golden icy liquid, the other two long-stemmed bowl glasses.

How had Anna summoned them so fast and when exactly had she even done it?

Fallon felt like a VIP being catered to with designated staff. Which she supposed was exactly what Enrique was.

The food smelled mouthwateringly good. Fajitas sizzling in cast iron pans, a variety of tacos, a large plate of cheesy tortillas and thick rolled chimichangas. Her stomach began to grumble.

"Comer," Anna said, bouncing the baby on her hip and motioning to the food.

Just as Fallon was about to ask where she could heat up little Lucas's baby food, Anna added, "I'm going to go puree some vegetables and fruit for this little one."

That was so much better than the prepared packaged food she would have had to give him. And rather selfishly, Fallon figured it would also give her a chance to dig into this amazing spread.

"Your *tia* was so nice to have all this ready for us," Fallon said, unable to decide where to start. "I'm glad I got a chance to meet her."

Enrique reached for a tortilla and popped it in his mouth. "You haven't seen anything yet," he told her, his voice dripping with amusement.

"What do you mean?"

"You're about to meet a slew of other people. This meal could take a while."

Before she could ask him to clarify, two tall men strode through the doors greeting Enrique with smiles and claps on the back. One wore a chef's apron and the other had a bar towel draped over his shoulder.

Enrique introduced them as two servers who'd started working here around the same time he had. Following on their heels was an older gentleman about Anna's age. Fallon guessed that would be Tio Ramon. She was right. She'd barely gotten a chance to be introduced to him when two teenagers dashed in and each gave Enrique a hug. Anna came back still carrying the baby, with a middle-aged woman behind her pushing a high chair for Lucas. She sat him down and began feeding him.

Fallon's head was spinning. This was more than a meal at a family-owned restaurant. It was more like a celebratory party. Before she even knew what was happening, there were close to a dozen others around the table, laughing and joking and clearly enjoying each other's company. And they seemed to be taking turns doting on Lucas who was having a grand time and basking in all the attention.

It was chaos. In the best possible way. And so different than any meal Fallon had ever been a part of before. The bond this group of people had with each other was palpable.

More than once, Enrique flashed her a dazzling smile from across the table. At one point, he actually winked at her and she felt pleasure flush through her core. As much as she was enjoying herself, a trickle of apprehension nestled at the base of her spine. What she wouldn't give to enjoy a meal like this again sometime soon, to be part of this group of people and be included in such gatherings as a matter of course.

Could this possibly be the kind of future she might be able to look forward to? Could there be more days and evenings like this in her future?

The answer depended on how understanding Enrique would be when she finally told him the truth.

CHAPTER THIRTEEN

SEVERAL DAYS AFTER visiting the ruins and the beach followed by the boisterous dinner, Fallon still couldn't stop thinking how magical that day had been. This morning was no different. To her delight, Enrique had offered to show her more of the city this weekend. Just the two of them. Rosa confirmed she'd watch the baby so that they could stay out later and see more of the nightlife.

She'd hardly slept the night before in her anticipation and excitement. To spend all that time alone with Enrique.

Maybe he'd even kiss her again.

A nagging voice surfaced in her mind that this was her chance. The outing today would finally give her the perfect opportunity to tell Enrique the truth about who she was to Lucas and his mother.

No more excuses; she had to get it done. Enrique would understand her motivations, he had to. She would find a way to make him.

Her excitement faded at the thought of finally making her confession.

She had to do it today. Somehow. Some way. She couldn't let another day go by with her secret between them. How angry could he possibly get? After all the time they'd spent together since she'd been hired, and the way their relationship had grown, surely he'd understand that she'd only had the best intentions. That she'd only been looking out for Lucas in her own way.

First thing first, she had to make her way downstairs and get some coffee if she had any hope of functioning this morning given how elusive sleep had been last night.

Luckily, the baby monitor remained silent as she slipped it into her robe pocket. Hopefully Lucas would even stay asleep long enough to let her enjoy the cup with some amount of leisure.

She found a pot already brewing when she made it to the kitchen. Luis was already at the counter taking a large mug out of the cabinet.

"One for me too, *por favor*," she said, grateful when he nodded then began pouring coffee for both of them. He turned to her with a smile, offering the precious, very much needed brew in his hand then pulling out a chair for her.

"I'm not sure how long I can sit." She extracted the monitor out of her pocket and set it on the table between them.

Luis sat down across from her. "I'm sure my nephew will be cooperative enough to let you have your hit of caffeine before you're summoned."

"Let's hope so," she answered, taking a long sip of the rich, hot coffee and savoring every drop.

"I hear your day visiting the ruins went well," he said.

"You were so right, Luis. The ruins were magnificent. Thank you so much for offering to take me, even though it didn't work out that way."

Luis's eyebrows lifted about an inch as he took a sip of his coffee. He looked like a toddler who'd swiped a cookie from the cookie jar and had gotten away with it.

"What is it?"

"Why, I have no idea what you mean." The fluttering of his eyes said otherwise.

"I think you do. Now, fess up," she urged, amusement and curiosity twisting in her stomach.

"Let's just say I know my brother well."

The implication wasn't lost on her. Of course. She should have guessed all along. "You knew he'd want to come with Lucas and me instead, didn't you?"

Luis responded with a mischievous smile and a sly wink.

Before Fallon could process his motives let alone come up with anything else to say, Lucas's long wail sounded from the monitor. He didn't sound happy.

"I should get up there," she said, standing up. "I think the poor little fellow might be on the verge of teething. He's been quite ornery in the mornings recently."

"Yet another way he takes after his father," Luis quipped. "And Enrique doesn't even have an excuse like teething."

Fallon couldn't help but chuckle as she made her way upstairs, gripping the hot mug firmly in both hands and drinking as much of it as she could before she'd have to set it down and tend to the baby. All the while contemplating the ramifications of Luis's setup.

Well, she'd just have to focus on it later. Lucas needed her. He looked miserable when she went to his crib and lifted him. After giving him a quick change and retrieving his bottle from the warmer, she sat down with him in her lap and began to rock while feeding him.

He definitely wasn't as enthusiastic about feeding as usual. Poor thing was clearly uncomfortable. To comfort him, she began humming a familiar melody that absentmindedly came to her head before she recognized it.

"You know, this was your mother's favorite song," she told the baby, talking more to herself. Not like Lucas understood a word she was saying. "She used to sing it all the time. I told her often that I was tired of hearing it. But I wasn't serious. She actually had a good voice and could carry a tune. I just said that to tease her because she knew it wasn't true."

She rubbed her cheek against the top of the baby's head. "I really miss her, did I ever tell you that?" she went on. "Still no replies to any of the emails I've been sending her. She'd be so emotional to see what a sweet and adorable child her baby is. If she would only return my messages. I'd be so happy to finally be able to talk to her about you."

Fallon couldn't explain the sense of unease that settled over her in that moment. It was more than her usual concern for Sasha. An alert had set off in her mind and her gut subconsciously.

The heavy footfalls on the stairs in the next instant surged the unease into alarm. Enrique swung open the door a moment later, his eyes wide and accusing. His fist in a tight grip on whatever he was holding.

She didn't need to identify the object he held to guess what it was. His expression said it all. The baby monitor. In her tiredness and haste to get to Lucas, she'd left it behind on the table.

Enrique had heard her every word.

"Who are you?"

Enrique searched Fallon's face for an answer, any answer that might make some kind of sense. Because she clearly wasn't who she'd said she was. And he'd been a fool to take her at face value.

She stood, still cradling the baby against her chest. "I can explain."

He strode into the room, holding up the incriminating

monitor in case she had any doubts about all that he'd just heard and how he'd heard it. A maddening mixture of disappointment, hurt and anger was whirling like a storm in his center. "Please start."

Fallon swallowed, her face pale. She looked panicked. Just how bad were her answers going to be? "How much of what you've told me is a lie?"

She visibly cringed, her face tightening. "Not a lie. Not exactly."

Semantics? She was talking semantics with him at a moment like this?

"Then what?" he demanded.

"More of an omission. I'm exactly who I said I was. Just like your background check proved."

"You know what I'm asking. Who are you really? To Lucas? To his mother?"

"You know I grew up in the fos—" Before she could get the words out, Lucas started wailing in her arms. The poor little guy no doubt could sense the tension in the air.

He had to calm down. Enrique took a deep breath, released it slowly. It didn't do much to scale down his red ire. "I'm sending Abuela up to take the baby. Meet me in my study downstairs as soon as she gets here." It wasn't a request.

When he tracked his grandmother down in the garden, Abuela looked startled at his expression and curious about his request to have her rush upstairs. Luckily, she was astute enough not to ask any questions and simply nodded in agreement.

Good thing. How in the world would he begin to explain any of this? He couldn't wait to hear Fallon's explanation himself.

All this time, she'd been lying to him. She'd tried to

call it something else. But Enrique wasn't buying it. A lie by omission was still deceit. And he intended to get to the bottom of why she would have done such a thing.

She didn't bother knocking when she appeared in his doorway moments after he'd gotten to the study.

Still pale, her hands tight against her sides, she appeared to be shaking. For one insane moment, Enrique longed to go to her. To tell her not to fret. He wanted to ease the anguish visibly rushing over her. Apologize for not approaching her better earlier. Then his common sense prevailed. If there were any apologies owed right now, he wasn't the one in debt. She also owed him an explanation still.

"Tell me," he said simply.

He didn't bother to take a seat. Nor did he offer her one.

She took a hesitant step farther into the room. "You know I grew up in foster care."

"Yes. My security firm did a thorough background check that verified your history. What does this have to do with my son and his mother?"

She squeezed her eyes shut. "Sasha and I were foster sisters for about five years before we aged out around the same time. She was the closest thing I've ever had to family after I lost my parents."

Enrique stood silent, absorbing the information. He nodded for her to continue.

"She took care of me. Made sure I was safe. From the over friendly father in the home we were assigned to. And from the bullying antics of other siblings or classmates who saw my shyness as a weakness. She often did so at great cost to herself."

He still wasn't hearing the piece of the puzzle that he needed to understand.

"Once we left the home, our lives took very different

paths. I knew she was hanging with the wrong kind of people. She was in trouble with the law often. I only heard from her sporadically. Usually via email. She'd sign on in a café or the library."

Enrique knew something about Sasha's troubles with the law. Fallon wasn't the only one he'd done an investigation into, but not much else had turned up.

She continued. "Over three months ago now, I got a phone call from her after not hearing from her for several months. She told me that she'd given birth due to a night of 'fun,' as she called it."

It was Enrique's turn to cringe. The uncharacteristic loosening of his restraint after too much ouzo had had such dramatic consequences. But he wouldn't regret the ensuing result—his son.

"She told me that she couldn't take care of the baby," Fallon said. "She told me she intended to make sure the infant, who'd she'd named Lucas, would make his way safely to his father. You."

Well, that certainly gave him a hearty dose of information. But nothing she'd said so far explained why she was here in his home under false pretenses. "Why did you do it? Why did you deceive me and my family?"

She physically winced as if he'd struck her. When she spoke, her words were closer to a sob than conversation. "I owed Sasha. And I was concerned for her child. I wanted to make sure he was being taken care of and not neglected. The way I'd seen happen all too often."

And the way she'd experienced for herself, no doubt. Which was legitimate, he wouldn't deny. But it didn't give her license to lie to him nor was it an excuse for what she'd done.

"I began to look into you and who you really were. I

was just trying to get some more information. But then I heard that you wanted to hire a nanny…" She trailed off.

"And you had the inspired idea to apply yourself."

She nodded. "It didn't seem like a good idea to tell you my connection to your baby when I first interviewed. And then there just didn't seem to be an ideal time to finally come clean."

She took another step in his direction. "You have to believe that I wanted to, that I eventually would have."

But she hadn't. Instead, she'd let him get to know her better, to begin growing fonder and fonder of having her around.

To slowly start to fall in lo—

Enrique stopped the train of thought in its tracks and bit out a vicious curse.

Served him right. For the first time in his life, he'd let his guard down. Had taken a chance on someone who clearly didn't warrant such trust. What a fool he'd been.

Turning his back to her, he willed the burning fury in his core to cool. Something told him that wasn't going to happen anytime soon.

A boulder sat in the pit of her chest, crushing her from the inside. As bad as she'd imagined this moment might have been, this was so much worse than she ever would have believed. Enrique's face was tight with fury; his expression held nothing but hostility. For her.

She couldn't blame him. She had no one to blame but herself.

"Why?" he demanded, cramming his hand through his hair. "Why wouldn't you just tell me the truth from the very beginning?"

Fallon stepped forward, then immediately regretted it

when Enrique flashed her a fiery glare. "I wanted to. There were so many times it was on the tip of my tongue."

He actually scoffed. "But you just couldn't bring yourself to do it."

"I was trying and failing to come up with a way to explain it." Fallon heard the pleading in her tone, had no way to stop it. Wasn't sure she even wanted to. "I didn't know how to make someone like you understand."

"Someone like me? What's that supposed to mean?"

Fallon squeezed her eyes shut, grasping for the right words. "I know how much you've had to overcome in your life. How you were betrayed by those who should have loved you."

His darkening glare immediately told her she was on the wrong track, but there was no going back now. "But you still had Rosa. And Luis. Not to mention all those people at the cantina who clearly love you."

"What does that have to do with any of this?"

"I've never had anyone but Sasha ever since my parents died. She took me under her wing when I needed someone the most. I owed it her to make sure her son was okay."

"So you decided to lie. And to spy on me for her, is that it?"

"No!" Fallon longed to reach for him, to somehow make him see. But she was making a mess of this. It was just so hard to find the right words. "That's not what I was doing."

Enrique looked beyond skeptical.

"You have no idea how lucky you are to have your family." Tears stung her eyes, the words scratched her throat as she said them. "Like I said, I've only ever had Sasha. And now she's gone too. I haven't heard from her in months. Was it so wrong of me to want to take care of her baby?"

But Enrique either didn't hear her or he didn't care

to answer. Several moments passed in agonizing silence. Nothing but anger and accusation between them. "Please go back upstairs," he finally said, his voice full of steel and ice. "See if Abuela needs help with the baby."

Fallon began to argue then deflated like a pinned balloon. The stiffness in his shoulders made it clear there was no use.

Enrique's stance was beyond clear. As far as he was concerned, there was nothing more to say for either of them.

CHAPTER FOURTEEN

HE WAS AVOIDING HER.

A full three days had gone by since Enrique had confronted her after her horrid fiasco with the baby monitor. He was gone in the morning when she awoke, and arrived late at night after everyone had retired for the night.

It served to add another layer of guilt to her already crushing load. Because of her, Enrique was spending less time at home and hence less time with his son. No one to blame for it but herself.

For all she knew, he was spending some of that time away in search of her replacement. He might be calling agencies and having his staff screening potential candidates and was getting ready to show her the door.

Which meant she would have to leave the hacienda and leave Lucas. She might never see him again if she was fired.

Nor would she see Enrique.

It didn't bear thinking about, as it was crushing her heart. Fallon released the sob she couldn't hold at bay and turned over onto her back in bed. The clock read eleven thirty. She had no hope of falling asleep anytime soon.

Was he back home yet?

Was he really planning on firing her and shipping her back to the States? Had he ever felt a smidgeon of affection for her? Because she could no longer deny that she'd fallen head over heels for him. The look of betrayal on his face had nearly shattered her. That's when she'd known just how far she'd fallen in love with him. Because his disappointment in her had devastated her.

Would he ever be able to forgive her?

So many questions scrambled around in her brain. Suddenly, it was all too much. She had to know, had to search for some answers.

Tossing the covers aside, she rose out of bed and strode to the door. If Enrique was home, she was going to find him and ask him once and for all what her fate was to be. Rushing out of the room before she lost her nerve, she didn't bother with a robe or slippers.

She almost lost her nerve midway down the staircase.

The house was eerily quiet when she made it downstairs. The kitchen and hallway dark. The only light she could see was the dim one spilling in from the outside window.

The veranda.

With a deep breath and a silent prayer, she made her way to the front door and stepped outside.

Enrique didn't seem surprised to see her.

Reclined in the wicker chair, he gave her a perfunctory look, as if he'd been expecting her.

Fallon's heart lurched in her chest at the sight of him. The top three buttons of his shirt were undone revealing a triangle of olive skin, his sleeves rolled to his elbows. One ankle resting on his opposite knee.

A surge of longing so strong rushed over her it nearly had her knees buckling.

How could she have not acknowledged sooner that she'd fallen in love with the man? The way her entire body reacted at the mere sight of him left zero doubt of it. She just hadn't been ready to face the inconvenient truth.

And now she may never get a chance to.

"Is there something I can do for you?" he asked, his voice so devoid of any emotion, her eyes stung.

"I just wanted to see if you were home."

"I am. As you can very well see."

Every instinct told her to turn tail and run. He was clearly still angry with her. Somehow, she held her ground, kept her gaze steadily on his. Several awkward beats of silence pulsed between them rubbing her nerves raw.

Surprisingly, he gave in first. "How is my son?"

A slow breath of relief left her lungs. At least he hadn't sent her away. Yet.

She took a cautionary step closer. "Good. I believe he's about to pop a tooth through any minute now."

One eyebrow rose at her announcement. "Oh?"

She nodded. "Won't be long now. He's practically worn out his favorite teething ring."

"Hmm," was his only response.

"Will you be sending me away then?" she blurted out, the question rushing out of her before she'd even known she'd intended to say the words. "I wouldn't blame you if that's what you intend. But I implore you to reconsider."

His eyes narrowed on her before he turned away and stared into the dark, starry sky. "So you'd like another chance, is that it?"

"Yes," she answered plainly. "I would. My intention was never to mislead. I thought I was looking out for a child I care for and trying to be a good friend to someone who means a great deal to me. In the process, I deceived you and your brother and grandmother. I will always regret that decision."

There, she'd finally said it all. Finally got off her chest all that she hadn't been able to put into words that day in his study when she'd been too stunned to string any kind of sensible sentence together.

The ball was fully in Enrique's court now.

He took an agonizingly long time to answer, still hadn't bothered to look back at her, his gaze focused on the stars in the distant sky.

Finally, when she thought she couldn't stand the silence any longer, he rose out of the chair and turned to face her.

"You should know I've begun the search for another nanny," he said, without any preamble or emotion. So matter-of-fact, each word landing with an icy spike into the pit of her stomach.

So she had the answer to her question then, didn't she?

How ironic that she felt the loss so deeply. Of something she'd never even actually had. But she did feel it. She felt hollow and raw. And she felt the loss each day of what might have been developing between her and Enrique.

It was painfully clear he had no intention of even entertaining the possibility of forgiving her. Not ever.

She thought back to the night of the fundraiser when Luis had told her that Enrique wasn't the forgiving type. She should have paid more attention.

The warm and genuine man who'd taken her to a flight simulator to ease her fears, the one who had insisted she needed a day at the spa and had set it up for her was no more. That Enrique was gone.

How unfortunate for her that she'd fallen head over heels in love with that Enrique. This new one she didn't recognize. Which was just as well. Because he wanted nothing to do with her.

He was polite if not curt when they happened to run into each at the hacienda. But he was completely cool and distant with her at all times. His attitude was no less than what she deserved, so she would take it without complaint.

Still, the change in his demeanor toward her was chipping away at her heart, bit by bit.

As much as she tried not to let his coldness affect her mood, it was hard not to give in to melancholy at times. The weather these past few days certainly hadn't helped. It had rained and been overcast in Tulum for close to a full week.

So this morning when she'd seen the sun finally peek out from behind a thick, fluffy cloud, she hadn't hesitated to pack the baby up and make their way outside. She was convinced Lucas felt as stifled by being indoors as she did. The resort sported a top-line playground for the little ones who visited. The baby was too young to enjoy much more than the toddler swings. So off they went right after his midday lunch.

She used the time walking from the hacienda to the resort grounds to clear her head. In hindsight, she would have done it all so differently. First of all, she would have been up-front that first day about who she was and why she wanted to be hired to watch Lucas. But that cliché about hindsight existed for a reason, it being clear in the rearview and all that.

The playground was relatively empty when they arrived. The guests no doubt waiting for things to dry out before venturing out to play. She for one couldn't wait. Using one of Lucas's diapers to dry off one of the toddler swings, she strapped him in and began gently rocking him back and forth. His little burble of giggles told her he was enjoying himself.

From what she could ascertain, Enrique hadn't shared what had transpired that afternoon with Rosa or Luis. She didn't even know what to feel about that fact. Maybe they ought to know who she was too. Would they think less of her for not telling them sooner? The way Enrique clearly did?

Maybe Enrique was being gracious enough to leave the decision to her. Or perhaps it was a test of her character, one she was failing badly just as she had from the beginning.

You'll always be a failure. You can't do anything right.

Fallon shook the harsh memories away and gave Lucas another gentle nudge in the swing, her thoughts a mishmash of questions scrambling around in her brain.

It didn't take long before he started to loll his head and his eyelids grew droopy. He needed to be put down for his nap. It was time to go back.

Fallon did her best to focus on the baby and the routine she'd established to get through the day. She'd spent a lot of her life alone. She was used to loneliness. But this time, the sensation cut deeper. She'd come so close to having so much fulfillment in her life. And her own stupidity and cowardice had been the reason it had all been snatched away.

What she wouldn't give to talk to someone right now. To talk to Sasha in particular. Her foster sister had always known what to say. But Sasha was being as silent as ever. There was no way to know if Fallon's emails were even being read.

Fallon had to accept reality. She was on her own. Sasha wasn't going to ever answer her messages—Fallon could only hope she was okay. Enrique barely tolerated her presence, and that was only because he was avoiding her at all times.

Fallon had no one.

They made it back to the nursery just in time to get Lucas changed and fed before his eyes fluttered closed and she laid him down in the crib.

One thing was certain, she couldn't go on this way. Even the baby could sense that she was off. He was fussier than usual. Less willing to take his naps and quicker to cry at the slightest discomfort.

She couldn't risk having her mood affect Lucas in any way. It appeared she had a decision to make.

Enrique had told her he had already begun his search for her replacement. With his resources, the process was certain not to take long. Between Enrique, his brother and grandmother, Lucas was sure to be well taken care of until another nanny was hired. Just the other day, she'd seen a woman she recognized from the resort's childcare program enter Enrique's study. It didn't take a sleuth to surmise her reason for meeting with him.

The writing was on the wall. Fallon's days at the hacienda were clearly numbered anyway.

Her choice was clear, wasn't it? She would spare Enrique the effort of sending her away.

It was the very least she could do.

CHAPTER FIFTEEN

"Ms. Duvall? Is that right?"

Fallon gave her head a brisk shake and pulled her focus back to the whiteboard. The figures were a blur, and she couldn't tell what Missy had written down as the final answer to the calculus problem they'd been working on.

No wonder. She'd been on the verge of crying again.

Blinking away the moisture, she brought her attention back to the present, to the small study room in the Boston Public Library where she was spending her days tutoring high school students until her shift at the riverside tavern began in the early evening.

As nice as the metro Boston library was, it was a far cry from the paradise she'd left two weeks ago.

"Yes, Missy, that looks right," she said when she could clearly see the figures. "Good work."

She glanced at the simple office clock hanging on the wall. "That should do it for the day."

The teen didn't need to be told twice. She immediately started packing up her things and bounded out the room.

Her tutoring students were much older than the kindergarteners she'd been teaching before. But until she found another teaching job, she had to make do with whatever helped to pay her bills.

Again, a far cry from just a few short weeks ago when

she'd been living in a grand mansion and being paid handsomely to take care of a child she loved.

Thoughts of Lucas brought the all too familiar burn of tears back to her eyes.

How she missed him. She missed his little palms against her cheek, the way he smelled after his baths, his toothless smile. Had that one tooth finally made its way out?

Lucas wasn't the only one she badly missed.

Fallon squeezed her eyes shut to push away the wayward thoughts that did nothing but make her want to weep. Tulum was behind her now. She had to accept it and move on.

Packing up, she hurried out of the room and made her way to the first floor to catch a ride share. There wasn't much time for her to get home and grab a bite of a snack bar, then change. Her shift at the tavern started in under an hour.

Fallon released a deep breath as she ran to the sidewalk. How her life had changed. At least she had a routine. In the mornings she worked on applying for teaching jobs, did her tutoring in the afternoons, then served tables until last call at night. Then the pattern repeated the next day. And the next day. And the next day.

So different from Tulum. She'd looked forward to waking up in the mornings. Now, she had nothing to look forward to. Her only hope to keep from weeping all day was to stay busy.

But the pang of longing caught up to her every once in a while. When she least expected it, it would all come rushing back. The way Enrique smiled at her, the charming winks he would occasionally send her way, making her heart melt. The scent of him.

Just stop.

The memories did nothing but tug at her heart. There was no point in rehashing them. Enrique probably hadn't given her another thought after she'd left Mexico. He hadn't so much as contacted her to make sure she'd arrived back in Boston all right, or to give her any kind of update on Lucas.

A myriad of emotions roiled in her center as she located her waiting ride and climbed in. Everything from sadness and despair to anger. She'd messed up. Of course she had. She should have never kept her secret for so long. But Enrique hadn't even considered her motives. Hadn't bothered to listen when she'd tried to explain. He'd simply wiped his hands of her. She shouldn't have expected anything more.

You'd think she would have learned her lesson as a teen when she'd expected her one remaining family member to take her in and instead her aunt had happily sent her away into the foster system.

Her aunt had wiped her hands of her too. Fallon had thought that particular rejection would be the worst one she'd ever have to face. Little had she known.

"Are you all right, miss?" the driver asked, extending a box of tissues over the seat to her.

Damn it. She hadn't even realized she'd actually sobbed out loud. She had to get ahold of herself. She had to forget she'd ever come across Enrique Martinez.

By the time she made it to her shift an hour later, she'd almost convinced herself that was possible.

Enrique knew his brother was back home the moment he arrived. Commotion and noise seemed to follow Luis, and it was no different today. Good. Enrique could use the break. He'd been poring over supply sheets and construction plans all day. He wanted the distraction of hearing about the excavation in Peru his brother was returning from.

Luis didn't bother to knock when he showed up in his

office moments after Enrique had heard him enter the hacienda and greet Abuela.

"I'm ho-ome," Luis declared, striding inside the room and plopping down into the chair across from Enrique's desk. "Did you miss me?"

Enrique couldn't help the smile that tugged at his lips. The truth was, he had missed his little brother. The last two weeks at the hacienda had been dark and depressing. The halls had felt empty. The rooms and gardens too quiet.

Maybe having his brother back would finally alleviate some of the bleakness.

Right. As if that was possible.

The truth was, the emptiness Enrique felt in his hollow core had nothing to do with Luis and everything to do with Fallon.

"How's my little nephew?" Luis wanted to know. "I missed him more than I would have guessed. Is he up in the nursery or does Fallon have him out in the gardens?"

So Abuela hadn't told him yet. Made sense. She finally figured, correctly, that it was Enrique's responsibility to break the news to Luis about Fallon.

This wasn't going to be easy. He just had to rip the proverbial bandage off and let Luis know what had gone down during his absence.

"He's in the nursery. But he's not with Fallon."

"Oh, does she have the day off? I hope she's out shopping at the resort. Maybe I'll try to catch her later. I wouldn't mind running into that new stylist from Paris."

Enrique dropped the pen he'd been jotting notes with and leaned back in his chair. "Fallon's not on the resort. In fact, she's not here in Tulum. She's gone."

Luis lifted one eyebrow. "Gone? What do you mean gone?"

"Would you prefer I say it in Spanish? She isn't at the hacienda. She's left Mexico."

"But why? She loved that *bambino*. Why would she leave him?"

"She's no longer in my employ as a nanny." There, it was out. He'd said it. Now, he just had to explain it. Somehow.

Luis narrowed his eyes on him. "What did you do, *hermano*?"

Enrique pinched the bridge of his nose and tried to ignore the irritation his brother was calling to the surface. Little did Luis know, he was already perilously close to losing all sense of balance here.

"I didn't do anything. Fallon Duvall was not who she presented herself to be. She lied to me."

"What in the world are you talking about? What did she lie about?"

The question somehow opened the proverbial floodgates. Before Enrique knew he'd intended to do so, he found himself spilling the whole story. Every detail, some he hadn't even realized he'd been thinking of, poured out of him like water through a sieve. He actually had to catch his breath when he was done.

Luis sat staring at him, open-mouthed.

"It's shocking. I know," Enrique said. Luis merely shook his head slowly from side to side. Once, then again. "What's shocking is that you let her go."

Whoa. Not the reaction Enrique was expecting. Why wasn't Luis outraged? He'd been duped. They all had.

"Por que?"

"You let that woman walk out of your life when she was the sole reason that I'd ever seen you happy, actually happy. And her only crime was to personally ensure your son was being well taken care of. That's all she cared about. And you punished her for it."

Well, when he put it that way.

But... Fallon's deception couldn't be ignored. "Don't you get it?" he demanded, pushing back the chair and standing. "She lied to me."

Luis tilted his head, crossed his arms in front of his chest. "Oh, I get it. Loud and clear."

"Huh?"

"I don't think I've ever seen you scared before, bro. No wonder I didn't recognize it. But she did it. She scared you."

Enrique scoffed but the effect fell flatter than he'd intended. "Scared of what? Do tell."

"Scared that you'd fallen for her," he declared, shaking his head again. His expression could only be described as one of pity. "So you saw an excuse to send her away and you took it. You took the easy way out."

Enrique did his best not to react to that statement. "That's not what happened. She lied to me," he repeated, sounding like a petulant child even to his own ears. "After leading me to trust her."

Luis narrowed his eyes on him. "Really? Are we really going to go there? Any fool could see it, the way you looked at each other when you thought no one was watching. And it frightened you."

Huh. Had he been that obvious?

"Yes, it was that obvious," Luis said, somehow reading his unspoken question. "And it spooked you in case she rejected you like our dear parents did. So you let her walk away."

What in the devil was he talking about? Luis didn't know the details. He had no idea what had happened between him and Fallon. Sure, he'd thought he might be developing feelings for her, but that had taken a major hit when he'd overheard her on the monitor. Unless...

Had he used the incident as an excuse to push her away? Could his pesky, annoying brother possibly be right that he'd done so out of some kind of fear of ultimately being rejected himself?

"Do you know exactly where she is?" Luis wanted to know.

Enrique nodded, his heart pounding. "She's back in Boston. I'm assuming she went back to her apartment. The same address listed in her employment papers from the agency."

Luis clapped, frustration etched in his features. "You're a fool if you don't go get her right now. You and I both know it."

"There's a gentleman who insisted on being seated in your section."

Fallon had barely managed to get her apron on after clocking in for her shift when the bartender let her know. "He was adamant. You want me to tell him to scram?" he asked.

She could guess who it was. Mr. Ramos. He came in every Friday around the same time. She'd happened to wait on him once, and they'd gotten to talking about her time in Tulum. He was from Cozumel and had recently lost his wife. The man just wanted an ear to listen. He was lonely.

Fallon could certainly relate. "No, it's okay. I'll wait on him."

She didn't even need to check his order; he asked for the same thing every time. A bottle of beer, which he called *cerveza*, and a plate of the tower-high nachos. He always got the key lime pie for dessert. Fallon went to put the order in and then walked over to the booth to say hello.

Then stopped cold in her tracks. The man sitting there was most definitely not Señor Ramos.

She made herself blink to ensure she was seeing straight. Once, then again. Yet the image didn't change.

"Enrique?"

"Hi, Fallon."

She had to be imagining this. Maybe she'd fallen asleep after her tutoring session and she wasn't even here at the tavern. She was still back at library study room, pressing snooze on her phone alarm and falling back asleep on the table.

"Is that really you?"

He stood, did a slow turn. *"Sí, es mi."*

Certainly sounded like him. And the accent seemed authentic. She pinched herself on the arm just to be sure.

Heaven help her, she felt the pinch. It *was* him. He was really here.

"What are you doing here?" A curl of hope sprung in her chest before she squashed it down. She couldn't make any assumptions. There had to be a logical explanation why he was here that had nothing to do with her. He was angry with her. He hadn't so much as sent her a text since she'd left.

He was in Boston on business. That had to be it. It was the only explanation that made sense. A flush of disappointment washed through her. She tried to paste a casual smile on her face.

"Uh, it's nice to see you. Is… Lucas with you?"

He shook his head. "No, but he's one of the reasons I'm here."

Alarm bells rang in her head. Why had Enrique felt the need to travel all the way to the States on Lucas's behalf?

"Is he all right?" she asked, feeling the color drain from her face.

Enrique held up his hand, palm up. "Yes, he's totally fine. It's just his last nanny didn't work out. I'm looking to make other arrangements for him."

Huh. So that was it then. He was here to visit the agency he'd used before. How silly of her that for even one moment she'd thought he might be here for her.

"I see. I hope the search goes well. How is he? He must be getting so big. Do you have any pictures?"

She didn't want to sound too anxious, but she couldn't help herself. She'd missed the baby terribly. And having Enrique here was wreaking havoc on her senses. It was hard to think straight.

"I can do better than show you a picture. Come back with me to see him."

She recalled hearing he had a town house in Boston. Excitement speared through her chest. To be able to see Lucas again, to hold him in her arms!

How kind of Enrique to do this, given how irate he must still be with her. She whipped her apron off. "I'll see if someone can cover for me for a couple of hours."

He tilted his head. "A couple of hours? It's going to take longer than that."

What did that mean? Was Lucas at the Cape instead? Crushing disappointment shot through her. There was no way she'd be able to get coverage for that long. She couldn't just take off for several hours, she needed this job.

But if Lucas was at the Cape? Why was Enrique here?

"Where is he?" she asked.

"At home. In Mexico."

Was he being cruel? Had he come here just to punish her? Maybe she'd underestimated just how cross he was with her.

He reached for her then, trailed a finger along her cheek. "Come with me to see him," he repeated. "He misses you. I miss you."

But that would mean…

She couldn't dare hope, could she?

"Enrique. I think you have to be really clear now about exactly what you're doing here."

"Fair enough," he said, dipping his hand into his pocket. "I'm here for you, sweetheart. Because nothing has been the same since you left. The hacienda feels empty. My life without you feels empty." When he pulled his hand out, he held a small box in his palm.

Fallon's breath caught when he flipped it open. Inside sat a sparkling solitaire cut diamond set on a thin gold band. "It was Abuela's," Enrique said. "She insisted I give it to you when I told her I was going to propose."

A loud ringing sound echoed through Fallon's ears. Her knees nearly gave out. "Propose?"

"Sí," he said, taking her by the hand and pulling her toward him. "Marry me, Fallon. You're the best wife I know I don't deserve and the best mother my son could hope to have. You've been the only mother he's ever known, and I was selfish to forget that for even a moment because of my pride. I've been a stubborn fool who didn't know how to accept happiness when it found me. Please forgive all that and do me the honor of saying yes."

It took several moments for Fallon's mouth to work in tandem with her mind. When she finally found her voice, the whole tavern heard, if not the entire street.

"Yes, my love! A million times yes!"

EPILOGUE

One year later

Dear Fallon

I know this message has been a long time coming. Please forgive me for how long it's taken. Know that I've read every single word of every note you've ever sent me.

My dear sister, please understand that I kept quiet because I wasn't sure what to say. I was lost and confused and didn't know where the next roof over my head might be. But I've come a long way since then.

Somehow I ended up at a counseling center on a ranch in Western Colorado. And now I can't imagine being anywhere else. I don't know if it's the air or the vastness of the land or the clear skies. My head feels clear for the first time in as long as I can remember. I look forward to waking up in the morning. That's never happened before. I even help the counselors with other patients now. I've found my calling, sis. For the first time ever. And unfortunately that calling doesn't seem to include motherhood.

You've always been the more nurturing one. I don't have what it takes to be a good mom to little Lucas.

You do.

Thank you for taking care of him for me. I can rest easy knowing he's in your very good hands. I'm not sure when I'll write again, sis. The past seems so distant behind me now and I'd like to keep it that way. All of it.
Love always
Sasha

FALLON READ THE email and then read it again, tears filling her eyes and streaming down her face. Sasha was alive. And she was fine. She was more than fine. Even through the electronic screen, Fallon could sense a peace from her sister she'd never witnessed in her before. As much as she missed her, Fallon could understand why Sasha had felt the need to go quiet all this time. And her need to keep her distance going forward.

All that mattered was that Sasha was in a better place now. And that Lucas was thriving with two parents and an extended family who loved and cherished him. A family that was about to grow by one.

Her dear, dear sister was responsible for so much good that had happened in Fallon's life. Fallon would always be there for her when and if Sasha ever wanted her.

"Almost ready, *carina*?" Enrique's voice sounded behind her. Fallon wiped the tear away from her cheek and clicked off the message before turning to her husband.

"*Sí*, I'm ready," she answered.

A mischievous smile spread over his lips before he managed to hide it. He still thought she didn't know. The ruse was that he was taking her to a late lunch at the seaside tavern they'd visited that day after they'd visited the ruins. But she'd figured it out. Various clues dropped here and there along with Luis's inability to keep any kind of secret and she'd put two and two together. They weren't heading to a simple meal.

She would make sure to act surprised when she walked into the baby shower they'd all planned for her.

Just a small fib.

* * * * *

*If you enjoyed this story,
check out these other great reads
from Nina Singh*

Their Accidental Marriage Deal
Part of His Royal World
The Prince's Safari Temptation
Two Weeks to Tempt the Tycoon

All available now!

COMING SOON!

We really hope you enjoyed reading this book.
If you're looking for more romance
be sure to head to the shops when
new books are available on

Thursday 24th October

To see which titles are coming soon, please visit
millsandboon.co.uk/nextmonth

MILLS & BOON

MILLS & BOON ®

Coming next month

THE BILLIONAIRE'S FESTIVE REUNION
Cara Colter

"FAITH CAMERON?"

It had been so long since anyone had called her that, that Faith felt faintly puzzled. Or maybe it was shock.

Who was she, again?

"Saint-John," she said, correcting her rescuer.

Her voice felt like it was far, far away, detached from her, coming from outside of herself. She was so cold. She had never been this cold in her entire life. She wondered, foggily, if maybe it went deeper than being cold.

Maybe she was dead.

There had been a moment out there in that icy water when she had resigned herself to fate. *This is it*. She had fully expected to die out there, the price to be paid for that foolish decision to go after the dog.

Not that it had felt like a decision.

She'd felt compelled, and had been out on the ice in an instant. It was as if her brain had turned off, and instinct had kicked in.

She mulled over the possibility that she might be dead. She had read stories—scoffed at the time—of people who had died and been unaware of it.

Maybe all the rest of it—that man coming on his belly across the ice—had been a fabrication of hope.

And Faith, of all people, should know the dangers that lay in hoping.

So, possibly, she was dead. Somehow, it seemed totally

unfair, that on death she would be greeted not by the husband she had spent thirty years with, Felix Saint-John, but by her first love.

Continue reading
THE BILLIONAIRE'S FESTIVE REUNION
Cara Colter

Available next month
millsandboon.co.uk

FOUR BRAND NEW STORIES FROM
MILLS & BOON MODERN

The same great stories you love,
a stylish new look!

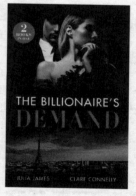

OUT NOW

MILLS & BOON

LET'S TALK

Romance

For exclusive extracts, competitions
and special offers, find us online:

- **f** MillsandBoon
- **X** @MillsandBoon
- **⊙** @MillsandBoonUK
- **♪** @MillsandBoonUK

Get in touch on 01413 063 232

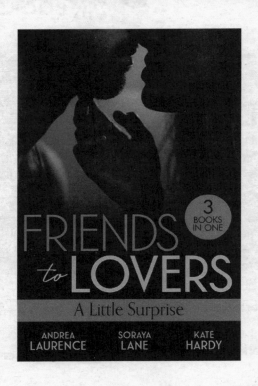